MERCURY

THE BATTLECRY SERIES - BOOK THREE

EMERALD DODGE

Mercury by Emerald Dodge

www.emeralddodge.com

Cover by Mario Lampic.

EMERALD'S MAILING LIST

To receive the latest freebies, sneak peeks, news, and more, visit this sign-up form to receive Emerald's mailing list.

Emerald's mailing list registration form can also be accessed at www.emeralddodge.com.

ALSO BY EMERALD DODGE

The Battlecry Series

Ignite (Prequel Novelette)

Battlecry

Sentinel

Mercury

Enclave Boxed Sets

Of Beasts and Beauties

The Oceanus Series

Sea of Lost Souls

House of the Setting Sun (coming soon)

Valley of the Shadow (coming soon)

Crown of Sorrows (Prequel Novelette)

Other Works

Novenas for Mothers

Novenas for Students

Novenas for Singles

This book is dedicated to Sarah Gonzales, of course. Whether I need a laugh, a cry, sage advice, or just an ear, you've always been there. The days are long, but twenty years have flown by.
Here's to many more.

ITEM ONE

Excerpt of letter sent from Ernest Bell to his father Josiah, dated 1874.

...I have received word that our Energizing Solution is immensely popular with the immigrant populations in the cities, especially those that work from dawn to dusk in the factories. In his last letter Thomas told of selling several cases to a redskin from Arizona and that he secured a contract with the Jew-men in Los Angeles, but I did warn him that we don't want our products associated with those populations. Profits are also rising in the South with sharecroppers and freedmen.

I have seen children born from mothers who drank it while with child and marvel at their height, which can be a whole half foot above their peers...

1

Jillian was being tortured to death. I wouldn't be able to save her in time.

I didn't know it for sure, couldn't prove it, couldn't do anything but face the reality that I'd undoubtedly been outsmarted by my older brother, Beau. He'd probably purposely left Graham to die on the floor of the kitchen, knowing full well Ember's telepathy would pick up the final memories of Jillian's abduction.

Why else go to the trouble of burning Jillian before taking her unless he wanted me to see the burn and hear her scream?

"Because he's a psychopath," Ember growled from the passenger seat. "Stop thinking like that."

My telepathic teammate popped her last remaining anti-nausea pill into her mouth and took a swig of water. I wasn't sure whether this latest wave was from the bug she'd contracted or the images she'd seen in my head.

"Sorry," I muttered.

I relaxed my white-knuckled grip on the steering wheel and tried to still the cyclone raging in my mind. I'd spent nearly every minute of the last eight hours mulling over my team's predicament. The surge of confidence I'd felt upon leaving our headquarters to begin the rescue mission had quickly dampened as I pondered what lay ahead of us.

When we arrived in Baltimore, we'd have to locate the Baltimore superhero team. If they didn't attack me on sight for the crime of being Benjamin Trent, ex-supervillain and one-time almost-murderer of one of their members, we still had to convince them that a team of trained assassins, called a strike team, was zeroing in on them.

After we fought the strike team and managed to survive, we would still have to travel south to Annapolis and... what? Storm my old house and rescue Jillian?

I was certain she was being held in my childhood home, with its convenient basement dungeon in which countless people had been "interrogated," but I of all people knew how difficult that task would be. Perhaps Beau truly didn't know that I knew he had my wife, but he wasn't stupid. He would expect some kind of reprisal. We *were* superheroes.

And if we somehow managed to succeed at rescuing Jillian, the Baltimore and Saint Catherine teams would then attempt to find the wretched chemical potion that had started all the trouble in the first place. The bottle of JM-104 was the holy grail of all supervillains, and its location was the information my brother—and mother—wanted so badly from Jillian. She didn't know where it was, yet she'd have to maintain under torture that she did, but wouldn't tell.

After that, we'd destroy it, possibly fight some supervillains, and then we'd all go home.

I had to consciously relax my fingers again. Even the "easy-sounding" order of events sounded impossible.

I took a steadying breath and glanced in the rear-view mirror, in which I could see the grim faces of my other two teammates.

Marco was staring out the window, lost in thought. He'd only spoken during the trip to ask me random questions about how I controlled the vehicle, which I assumed was to keep his mind off our dark mission.

Reid had finally fallen asleep while we drove through Waldorf, Maryland, apparently exhausted after asking me question after question about Beau, his cronies the Rowe twins, and any known supervillains in the Baltimore area.

We passed a sign for Baltimore. We'd be there in less than twenty minutes.

I swallowed the bile that continually rose in my throat, then forced myself to mentally divide up the tasks ahead of us. The image of Jillian, sick and powerless, in my brother's inhuman, metal hands was a thought-stopping horror—I could not allow myself to dwell on it if I wanted to find her in time. I had to focus on the immediate.

Right now, that was locating and alerting the Baltimore team.

"Marco, wake up Reid," I said. "He'll need to be ready when we enter the city."

Already the thick forest that lined our approach into Baltimore had thinned and widened, with high cement walls soon replacing the woods. Graffiti marred much of them, and all were crumbling and faded. Within minutes, our ancient truck sped over a wide bridge, and we were in Maryland's largest city.

I'd committed many crimes here. Yet, as the morning sun shone weakly through thick snow clouds, I failed to recognize the sights around me. On our right stood two stadiums, but bookish me had always preferred more scholastic pursuits. A sign on our left pointed the way to the Inner Harbor and the aquarium, but I'd never seen or been to either of them. My jobs had been confined to grimy industrial areas, not the bright world of downtown.

"Turn right here," Ember ordered. She was staring at her tablet, which displayed a website about the Baltimore team. "Then another right in three blocks. Their house is at the end of the road."

I turned the truck down the residential streets. The homes were no longer tidy townhouses and brownstones, but tired old family homes with sagging porches, bars on the windows, and no front yards. It didn't surprise me that Baltimore's team lived in such a neighborhood; from what I'd heard, my team had lived in an even crummier house before I met them.

I parked the truck in front of the squat little house and opened the door. A blast of biting wind raised the hairs on my neck, reminding me that we'd driven into the path of an oncoming snow-storm. Indeed, flat dark gray clouds were gathering overhead, warning of imminent precipitation.

I gritted my teeth. *Just what we need.*

Ember hopped out and narrowed her eyes at the front door. "Someone's home, but I can't tell who. They're sleeping, but not dreaming. It's only one person."

"Well, we know it's not Peter," Marco said. "So whoever it is, they're friendly. Let's go."

Peter, whom I'd long known as Imperator, had been killed by his team only hours before. My team had spent a while during the car ride theorizing the circumstances of his death. All of them agreed that Peter's death had probably been less murder, more self-defense. Apparently, Peter, who'd been able to manufacture and manipulate fire, had been overly fond of burning his teammates for the most minor infractions.

As I'd listened to their reports, I'd idly wondered if the heroine I'd shot, Artemis, had been so punished for nearly dying.

God, I hoped the person in the house wasn't Artemis.

I knocked on the door. When nobody answered, I moved to peer through the window to the left, but Reid pushed past me.

"There's no time for that now," he said, raising his hand. His eyes were white.

A small boulder burst out of the earth behind us and soared over our shoulders and through the door, splintering it with a loud crash.

Reid gestured to the large hole.

"You know," Marco said conversationally, "If someone did that to our door, I'd kill first and ask questions second."

We all paused, waiting for the onslaught of superpowered fury. None came.

I wordlessly clambered through the hole, my eyes darting around the drafty foyer. The living room to the right contained many ancient chairs and couches, but no Baltimore team-member. The kitchen was similarly deserted, though several cracked and chipped mugs were littered around the counters. A plain teapot sat on the stove. Someone had been here recently.

"Upstairs," Ember whispered, gazing up the narrow wooden stairwell. "They're not asleep anymore, but—"

We all froze and stared at the top of the stairs.

A massive Bengal tiger slunk down the steps towards us, silent as death. Dried flecks of blood covered its muzzle, and its green-gold eyes glimmered despite the low light in the house.

The cat, which had to be at least six feet long and five hundred pounds, never took its eyes off my face. I couldn't recall any of the Baltimore teammates being *tigers*, but this one knew me.

I took a cautious step back.

"Everyone," Ember breathed, her voice placating, "This is Abby, but she calls herself Tiger when she's in this form." Tiger jerked her head towards Ember, pausing with her foreleg in the air. Her eyes narrowed infinitesimally. "Yes," Ember said quietly. "I'm a telepath. I'm from the Saint Catherine team. That man there is Reuben's brother Reid. We're your friends."

The large green-gold eyes jerked back to me.

"He's good now," Ember said. "He's a hero. He won't hurt you or Artemis, I promise."

There was a bizarre sucking sound, and the tiger appeared to dissolve inward. In its place, a small young woman with sallow skin, stringy, waist-length mouse brown hair, and large blue eyes was clambering to her feet. Behind the curtain of her hair, I could see smears of blood around her mouth. She wore the Baltimore uniform with which I was familiar, but the black thermal top and khaki pants hung loosely on her emaciated frame. I was torn between wondering where her clothes went when she transformed and how the blood had gotten onto her face.

Abby steadied herself and squared her shoulders. She walked right up to me, and for a brief second she stared into my eyes without blinking.

She punched my throat.

ITEM TWO

English translation of an excerpt of a letter sent from Maria Sangia-como, resident of New York City, to her sister Ludovica Vallalunga, resident of Catanzaro, Italy, dated March 1885.

> *...I have passed along your greetings to Marco, and will continue to pray for the safe delivery of your child and that Our Lord spares you the agonies of childbed that I suffered, which has caused me to not bear but the one child...Cristiana has grown out of her school dress though the year has not yet passed...She is a tall girl, near to my shoulder though she be just eight years old.*
>
> *Her disposition is womanly and graceful, and she is a charming child...but I confess that her abilities frighten me, and am only comforted by seeing her receive the Eucharist without the devil being thrown from her...I want her to seek a convent in Italy, but Marco has already written his brother to arrange a marriage with his nephew, that piggy little boy I wrote of in my last letter, Patrizio.*

2

I fell to my knees, coughing and sputtering. She put her hands on her hips. "Trent shoot Artemis. Trent go cliff jump."

"Nice to meet you, too," I said, wheezing a little. I wasn't angry, though. In fact, I was a little surprised that she'd chosen so mild an attack.

"Hey, you can talk," Reid said, pleasantly surprised. "We were told that Peter had burned the words right out of you."

Abby smiled slyly in my direction. "Peter taste good."

There was a long silence. "Um, so, Abby killed Peter," Ember said, wincing. "I think we need to go sit down and hash out what happened."

Abby didn't move. Instead, she looked me squarely in the eye. "Peter hurt Gabriela," she said calmly. "Artemis go Bird go Metal fight Peter. Peter hurt Artemis. Tiger hurt Peter." Her wolfish grin made a shiver shoot down my spine. She inclined her head towards me with a devilish squint. "Peter taste good."

I recognized the threat.

"You keep saying that," Marco said, his voice oddly high. "You didn't actually *eat* him, though, right?"

Abby smiled wider. "Hunt. *Kill.*"

"Okay, we get it," Reid said, his face white. "Listen, Abby, where's your team? The elders have sent a strike team to eliminate you all because you killed Peter. They won't care about the circumstances. We need to warn the others and come up with a plan."

Abby blinked several times, then looked at Ember.

Ember gasped. "Peter attacked Gabriela. Topher grabbed her and ran off, leaving Berenice and Lark to fight Peter. He burned Lark bad and was going to kill Berenice when Abby showed up." She grabbed Abby's hand. "But where did they go, Abby? Think."

It was still odd for me to think of the Baltimore team as having actual, real names. To me, Lark, Topher, and Berenice had always been the masked and dangerous Valkyrie, Argentine, and Artemis. My enemies. However, if I wanted them to think of me as an ally, I had to meet them in the middle and give them the humanity of names.

Abby shook her head. "Artemis tell Abby go home."

I massaged the bridge of my nose as I reviewed the information. Abby had killed Peter in defense of her friends, if not self-defense, then ran off at Berenice's behest. If Berenice and Lark were injured, they'd have to either go to a clinic or the Super hospital in Virginia. However, the Super hospital was an hour and half away by car, which I was certain Berenice didn't have.

A small part of me longed to leave the Baltimore team to their fate and go after Jillian.

As her name passed through my mind, a fleeting image of our hands bound together by medical gauze—our wedding ceremony— caused my chest to throb painfully. *Focus. You need to focus.*

"Who's the leader now?" I asked, my voice slightly choked. "We need to talk to them."

Abby's large eyes filled with sorrow. "Reuben."

Reid put a hand to his chest. "Where is he?" The last time Reid had seen his older brother, Reuben had been recuperating from a flogging. I'd heal him as soon as I could, provided Reuben trusted me enough to let me get that close.

Abby pointed to the hole in the front door. "Gabriela."

"Then let's go," I barked, moving to climb through the hole again. "We'll find him, figure out a plan, then—"

A firm hand on my shoulder made me stop and spin around. Reid let go of me and shook his head. *Oh, yeah.* He was the leader, not me. I crossed my arms. "Sorry. What's your call?"

Reid glanced at Ember. "Take Marco and Abby to Gabriela's and guard them until we return. Ben and I are going after Berenice and Lark. They're injured, so I doubt they've gone too far from the fight scene. Abby, where was the showdown?"

Abby looked again at Ember. Ember nodded. "Johns Hopkins," she said. "By the dorms." Ember and Abby then shared a strange look. Abby shook her head a little, then Ember's eyes widened. "Who was that?" she demanded.

Abby lowered her head. "Berenice normal friend."

"Huh," Ember said. "I didn't expect that. Do you know where she is?"

"For the love of *God*, just tell us what she's saying," Marco growled. "This just in, Em, but we all hate it when you do this."

Ember shot Marco an evil glare, then turned back to Abby. "After Abby killed Peter, a civilian ran up to Berenice and insisted that Berenice and Lark go to the hospital. Berenice knew the woman well. They were arguing over going to the hospital when Abby left. The woman called Berenice by her name," she said thoughtfully. "Interesting. Berenice called her 'Jen.' They must be friends."

"Benjamin and I are going to find this Jen person," Reid said. "Ember, go with Marco—"

"And sit around uselessly while you guys search for a single person in one of the biggest cities in the country," Ember finished, disgust in every word. "How about the medic hangs out with the guy who was whipped, and you take the telepath with you to find Jen?"

Oh, God. My gaze darted around the room, settling anywhere that wasn't on the couple who'd just broken up. I didn't let myself simmer on the fact that Ember had chosen now to do this. If I did, the urge to grab her shoulders and shake her might become overwhelming.

Reid let out a long breath. "You still have the stomach flu, and

Berenice and Lark were injured. Benjamin can heal them, and then we will all rendezvous with you."

Ember crossed her arms. "You're loving this, aren't you?"

Reid threw his hands up in angry exasperation. "I can't say I'm loving anything about this moment, but I'll bite. What is it now?"

Ember scowled. "You love that you can make me go sit in the house where I'm safe, even if it makes more sense for me to go out with you."

Instead of an angry retort, Reid's face smoothed over, though there were new spots of pink in his cheeks. He turned to Marco. "If we're not back by nightfall, defer to Reuben."

Ember's scowl deepened. "North Broadway and Jefferson."

"What?" Reid asked.

"The intersection, moron! Where the fight was!"

I opened the front door and shoved Reid through it before he could shout back, as was his habit these days. We hurried back into the truck. Snow had started to fall, blanketing everything in a thin white layer.

While I started the engine and put the truck into drive, he rested his head against the window. "Where did I go wrong?" he murmured.

"No idea," I said, never taking my eyes off the road. I wasn't accustomed to driving in snow. Now I had to contend with inclement weather on top of the hot steaming turd that was our situation. "Can we get back to the mission, please?"

He rubbed his eyelids. "She was right. Damn it, I can't even argue with her like a normal guy because she can just read my mind. She was always complaining about how she never had combat training and felt unsafe all the time, so I figured she'd like to be in the house instead of out on the street. But even that didn't make her happy."

"You know what would make me happy?" I muttered. "You shutting up about this."

"Do you think she's just doing this to be petty?" he mused.

I slammed on the brakes, causing the truck to slide a few feet. Though a car behind us honked for several seconds, I whipped around and laid on Reid an expression of pure rage. My chest rose and fell raggedly. "I have watched my brother burn people's feet with a blow torch," I hissed. "I've watched my mother put needles under a grandmother's fingernails. I've watched Alysia break bones with a smile on her face. I've heard men and women scream for hours on end in the night as Will and Beau *played* with them for the sheer freaking fun of it."

I put my face closer to his and lowered my voice. "And I have spent every minute of the last nine hours determinedly not letting myself believe that they will do every single one of those things to my wife. Now," I spat, "Get over your issues. You can complain about your ex-girlfriend after Jillian is safe." My voice shook on the last few words.

Reid had covered his mouth with his hand. He lowered it and looked down. "I'm sorry. You're right. Let's just focus on Jill right now."

I shoved the gear stick into drive again, then pealed out into the intersection.

We drove in heavy silence until we reached the cross streets Ember had seen in Abby's mind. Johns Hopkins University Hospital stood to our right, imposing and stately. To our left, a small barren area of dead grass and trash cans contained a few straggling students.

A telephone pole bore a large handmade sign announcing an anti-camp protest that had taken place on campus earlier that day. I was grateful that we'd missed the protest. I'd always been led to believe that Baltimoreans loved their team, but who knew how idealistic college students felt? As the Sentinels had showed us, it was easy to conflate the camps and the people who represented them. We were safer going unnoticed.

I parked the truck in a spot by the sidewalk. "Your call, leader," I said, struggling to keep resentment out of my tone.

Reid swallowed hard. "Word will have gotten around about the fight." He pointed to a campus police officer sitting in a nearby cruiser. "I'll go speak to him. Ask those students what they know. Maybe someone will have heard a rumor about two injured superheroes."

So much for going unnoticed. I hopped out of the truck and immediately made my way towards two huddled students I'd seen minutes before. They were bundled tightly in winter gear, sipping steaming drinks from paper cups and chatting amicably. As I approached, I saw that they were garbed in US Army uniforms and GI fleeces—cadets, most likely. Even in my agitated state of fear, I felt a stab of envy. I'd almost been a ROTC cadet once.

They smiled in surprise and interest as I approached.

"Are you a superhero?" one of them asked as he eyed my uniform. He was tall and blond, like myself. For some reason, I thought I saw a bit of envy is *his* eyes.

Another cadet, a young woman with Jillian's dark hair and fair skin, stuck out her hand. "I've seen you online," she said genially. "I'm Cadet Prose. This is Cadet Irvin. How can we help you, sir?"

My face heated up. "There was an incident near here yesterday," I said, injecting as much authority as I could into my words. It worked; they straightened, their faces instantly professional. "My team is here to find out what happened. We need to speak to the Baltimore team immediately. Do you know where they might be? They're not home."

Cadet Prose's forehead wrinkled. "There was a campus email alert about that. They mentioned at the protest that Artemis was taken to the hospital. Not that I was at the protest," she said quickly. "I was just walking by to class and heard it. We're not allowed to go to rallies and protests in uniform, no matter how we feel about injustice."

I hid my smile. There was something very Jillian-like about Cadet Prose.

Cadet Irvin opened his mouth to speak, then craned his head to peer around me. "Um, someone's watching you."

I turned to see whom he was referring to. Across the street, a young woman stood by the truck, her eyes all but boring holes into me. She was petite and possibly Asian, though I couldn't be sure at the distance. Like all the students walking past her, she was clad in drab winter gear. A rainbow-print scarf provided the only color in her wardrobe.

What stuck out most was the expression pasted on her face. It was more than dislike—it was hate. As far as I knew, the only people in Baltimore who hated me were the Baltimore team. This woman wasn't one of them. That pointed to one conclusion: she was on the strike team.

I was about to tell the cadets to run when Cadet Prose raised her hand and waved energetically. "Oh, that's just Jen. Jen! Come here!"

Jen...

"Oh, crap," I murmured. Jen, Berenice's mysterious friend, apparently knew about my past with Berenice. I turned to the cadets. "Thank you for speaking with me. I need to speak to Jen alone."

They took the hint and hurried away. Jen stormed across the road, shaking with obvious fury. "Are you here to kill Berenice?" she demanded. Though she wasn't taller than five foot four, she seemed larger than life. "Because you can think again. She's so well-protected that—"

"I'm not here to kill Berenice," I said quickly. "I'm here to help her and the whole team. Are you the friend who tried to convince her to go to the hospital?"

She drew herself up, her face red. "Nice try," she growled. "I know who you really are, Mr. *Trent*. She told me everything. You tried to kill her."

"And now I'm trying to save her. But there are people in the city who *do* want to kill her, and I need to warn her team. Are you going to help me or not?"

Uncertainty passed over her features. "She did... mention...that someone might come for them because of what Tiger did. How do I know you're not that person?"

"You know what? I don't have time for this," I said, waving her off.

I stalked away toward the truck. I didn't need to prove, again, that I wasn't a psychopath. What was I supposed to say to Jen anyway? I stopped on the sidewalk and turned my head back and forth. Would I have better luck trying the front entrance or the ER?

Reid wasn't in sight anymore, so I began to walk purposely towards the front entrance.

"Mercury, wait!" Jen called from behind me. I ignored her, continuing to walk up the front steps. "Wait!" She ran up beside me, huffing and puffing little breaths of condensation. "Dammit, I'm not going to let you hurt her again!"

"I'm not going to hurt Berenice!" I shouted. Several people turned to stare at us. I lowered my voice. "For Heaven's sake, I'm here to help her."

"Mercury? Are you Mercury?" a pleasant female voice floated from behind me.

Groaning internally, I turned to see who'd spoken. A pretty young woman approached me. She was tall and sturdy, with incredibly long, straight black hair that fell to her waist. My distinct initial impression was that she was Native American, though her eyes were the exact gray shade of Reid's.

"Can I help you?" I asked dully.

"You're the medic for the Saint Catherine team, aren't you?" she said, a hint of shyness playing around her eyes. "I saw your picture online. I... I was wondering if you could heal the cut on my face." She moved her bangs aside, revealing a bandage on her forehead.

"Yes, fine," I said, moving to pull off my right glove.

She held out her ungloved hand.

For a quick second, the world seemed to stop as I took in several details at once: the woman's shy gaze becoming alert and fixed, her muscular build, and her ungloved hand. Why wasn't she wearing gloves? It was below freezing out. And something else... something else was wrong.

There was no healing energy spiraling in my stomach. My inborn sixth sense always sensed a nearby injury, even when my eyes couldn't see it. If she had a cut on her forehead, my power would've sensed it.

I withdrew my hand. "I'm so sorry, ma'am, but my power isn't working right now. As a medic, I advise you to keep your cut clean and dry." She took a step forward, her hair rippling in the light breeze. It was so long—as long as camp women kept their hair. "I need to go now," I said. Every instinct in my body screamed at me to run.

"Emily?" Reid called from behind me. "Emily Begay?"

Emily's eyes widened. I looked over my shoulder to see Reid walking up the steps, bewilderment clear on his face. I turned around and saw Emily's furious expression. Cold understanding hit me like a train: if he knew her, then she was from the camps. And that meant—

I dodged Emily's knife just in time. The blade, which she'd pulled out of god-knows-where, sliced the air by my ear. Before I could recover, she slapped me across the face, stunning me momentarily. She grabbed Jen and held the knife against the small woman's throat.

"Don't take another step," she hissed. Jen froze, probably too scared to even whimper. The few civilians lingering out in the cold shrieked and ran inside.

I held my hands up. "We're not moving," I said hastily. "Just let her go. This is between superheroes. She has nothing to do with this."

My words were calm, but my mind was reeling. What kind of superhero used civilians as shields? If Emily was on the strike team, what could we expect from the team at large?

"Emily, it doesn't have to come to violence," Reid said softly. "I'm your friend. Let the civilian go. We can work this out. I'm the same guy you've always known. I'm your *friend*."

For one second, I thought I saw Emily deliberate. Then she plunged her knife into Jen's neck.

"NO!" I lunged forward to grab Jen, but Emily kicked Jen's limp body down the stairs, then threw her knife—or was it another knife?—into Reid's neck. He collapsed where he stood, his head hitting the cement step with a terrible crack. Blood began to pulse from his skull and drip down the steps. Emily fled down the stairs and down the sidewalk.

I was at Jen's side immediately, my hand on her face. While the electric healing energy flowed from my body into hers, I twisted around and touched Reid's face. The knife popped out of his neck and to the ground with a clatter. Both sat up and coughed uncontrollably for several seconds.

Though I was just as concerned for Reid as I was for Jen, I clasped

Jen's thin hands in my own. "Are you okay?" I asked. I knew she was, but the question made people feel better.

"Who *was* that?" Jen choked, stroking her throat repeatedly.

The motion made me aware of how warm my own neck was. And now that I was thinking about how I felt, I became aware of a fast-growing headache in my temples. I unzipped the collar of my thermal fleece a little to let in some cold air, but it didn't help.

"*That* was Emily Begay," Reid said with a groan. He rubbed his neck, then picked up the bloody knife and scowled at it. "My deceased fiancée's older sister, and one of my many relatives. I remember her being sent away for service, though I didn't know she was on a strike team. Now that I think about it, her power would be useful for assassinations."

"What does she do?" I asked, kneeling to help Reid to his feet, though I wanted to sit down next to him. I felt weird, like my head was filled with water.

"She makes you sick," Reid said. He helped Jen to her feet. "When we were kids, if you pissed her off she'd make us throw up or have diarrhea or something. Since you're not throwing up or soiling your-selves, I guess you got off scot-free. Sort of," he added quickly, patting Jen's shoulder. "I'm sorry you got mixed up in this, miss."

Reid's voice sounded odd, simultaneously near and far. I lowered myself down to the cement step and put my hands on my knees. Dammit, why was it so hot suddenly? I dropped my head back to stare up at the snow clouds. Fat, fluffy flakes fell on my nose and cheeks, offering blessed cool relief from the heat under my clothes.

Jen and Reid were talking. Jen pointed to the hospital and I thought I saw her mouth form the word "Berenice."

The cement step was cold. It was cold because of the snow. If I just laid in the snow a little... bit...

"Benjamin!"

The world dissolved into a mural of heat and color.

ITEM THREE

Wedding Announcement in the *New York Times*, Saturday, June 5, 1897

The wedding of Miss Cristiana Sangiacomo, daughter of Mr. And Mrs. Marco Sangiacomo, to Mr. Patrizio Sangiacomo will take place next Saturday afternoon at four o'clock at St. Peter's Catholic Church, Barclay Church and Church Street. A reception will follow the ceremony at the home of the bride's parents. Mr. and Mrs. Sangiacomo will reside in Richmond, VA.

3

The world moved in lurches and lulls.

One moment I was on the blessedly cold ground, the next, I was in someone's arms and inside a mesmerizingly white building. My surroundings were confusing and indistinct, filled with faces that melted into necks and white coats. Every so often, pink and blue shapes would appear and make noise, but I could not understand them. Red was a constant, always nearby.

And the heat—it could not be ignored.

Static and snow, like an untuned television screen, pulled my vision away occasionally. Darkness would overtake me for a while, and then I'd be assaulted by colors and noises again. I had no sense of time or place, just of simple stimuli, such as my hand in someone else's. A kind voice I thought I recognized spoke to me often, but the words were lost to me. A different voice, higher, occasionally spoke.

I closed my eyes.

Beeping in the distance called me to itself. I focused on the noise. It matched my heart.

"Hey, how are you feeling?"

I opened my eyes.

Reid sat in the dingy vinyl chair next to my hospital bed. He leaned forward with his elbows on his knees, watching me with exhausted wariness. My head ached as though I'd been hit with a heavy object, but the heat was gone. I moved my head to the side and immediately groaned. "What happened?"

"105.7," he said simply. "That's how high your fever spiked before they could get it under control. The doctor said if it had risen by another degree or so, you would've died, or at least had irreversible brain damage. You had at least one seizure." He glanced at the wall clock. "The fight with Emily was four hours ago." He handed me a cool wash cloth. "For your face."

I gently dabbed my face with the cloth, immediately sighing at the pleasure. The momentary relief allowed me to take in my circumstances for the first time since waking up. I was in a mint green hospital gown, hooked up to an IV drip through the back of my hand. My right index finger was inside an oximeter, itself connected to another machine which provided the beeping in the background.

My uniform was folded neatly on another chair, sitting on top of my bulletproof vest. The small hospital room was unusually cool for a building in winter; I assumed this was because I'd been struck with such a high fever.

The light in the room was odd. It was early afternoon, and the sunlight should've streamed in brightly between the cracks in the clacking blinds that moved back and forth in the breeze from the air conditioner. Instead, watery paleness barely illuminated the small room, recalling the infirmary in which I'd worked in Liberty.

Reid sat back in his chair, his face receding into the slatted shadows cast by the blinds. "I'm sorry," he said, so softly I wasn't sure if I heard him for a moment.

"For what?" I began to extract myself from my treatments.

I took off the oximeter, then gingerly slid the needle out of the back of my hand. The machine flat-lined, no doubt remotely announcing my death to the nurses' station down the hall. I hastily swung my bare legs over the edge of the bed and began to pull my pants on, relieved that the nurses hadn't removed my underwear, at least.

Reid didn't react for a second. "I don't know," he whispered. "I couldn't have guessed that Emily would be here. I didn't know she could inflict fevers. All I've ever seen her do is cause vomiting and things like that. You saved Jen and me. But I just... I'm sorry."

I stopped in the middle of dressing, standing in just my khaki pants. Déjà vu washed over me. Only weeks before, Jillian had apologized to me for a mysterious something, and in the dark infirmary to boot. I'd been in the middle of washing blood off her face. She'd apologized in heart breaking tones, the weight of a thousand tragedies causing her shoulders to sag.

I didn't know it at the time, but she'd been coping with a sexual assault as well as her not-so-dead little brother's rejection, her team falling apart, and her horrible boyfriend's immaturity and lies. I'd told her to "let it go." She'd eventually taken my advice by letting *everything* go via a suicide attempt.

Now another beloved leader of mine was apologizing to me. I pulled my undershirt on, strapped on my vest, then yanked my gray medic's tunic over everything. Perhaps the fever had taken away my edge, because I didn't feel angry that he was still mired in his issues.

"Look, we've got a hell of a road ahead of us. I was kinda harsh back there in the truck when you were talking about Ember. I promise, we'll sit down and figure out what to do about your relationship as soon as we can."

I'd calmed down enough to admit that the implosion of a long-term relationship as intimate as theirs had been was just one of those things a guy couldn't ignore.

But Jillian's safety was paramount. I wasn't budging on this issue.

The door burst open and nurses flew in with a crash cart. There was an awkward moment in which everyone stared at each other, then the head nurse deflated. "You're not supposed to—"

"No," I said curtly. "I'm going."

Ignoring mutters about superheroes and medical law, I pulled

Reid out of his chair and we marched past the nurses into the hallway. My head thumped its protest, but with every passing minute, my body felt better. Fevers generally left a lingering weakness in the system, but Emily's attack hadn't been a natural fever. It followed that the fever would recede as quickly as it came on. Still, we'd lost precious time.

I turned to Reid, whose blank sadness emanated from him in waves. "Where's that woman? Jen, right?"

"With Berenice and Lark in the burns unit." He gestured to the elevator across the hall. "She's been ducking in and out of your room for hours."

I pressed the 'up' button next to the doors, and the elevator came a few seconds later. A sign next to the doors displayed the floor location of every unit, so after the occupants filed out, Reid and I stepped into the elevator and I pressed the button for the third floor, home of the burns unit.

Before the doors closed, I turned to Reid. "We'll find Jillian, and then we'll figure out you and Ember. It's not that I don't care—"

"No, I get it," Reid said. He looked away. "Jill first."

It was a testament to our friendship that I didn't feel awkward as I asked, "Is there anything else?"

His eyes met mine, and in them I saw what he simply could not hide: despair. "Jill left me with Will and Beau while you guys were cleaning up in the compound. They told me, in the most lurid way possible, everything they planned to do to Ember. And now they have Jill," he finished, his eyes going unfocused. "This mission isn't going to be a rescue, Ben."

I sucked in a breath. "Don't—"

"We're going to be recovering her remains. You need to face that reality." He spoke a little louder, though not unkindly.

"No," I growled. No, she was not dead. No, we were not—I was not —going to give up on her. No, I would not give in to pessimism. Jillian was my wife, and I'd see her again, alive and well.

"She has the flu."

"That doesn't mean she's going to die. She's a fighter."

"She doesn't have powers. She is physically weaker than Ember right now. Even if she were to somehow escape from your parents' house, she'd walk outside into a snowstorm. If the flu and injuries don't kill her, the cold will."

"She's not going to die!"

"Listen to me." He swallowed. "You've already witnessed what just one member of the strike team can do. We probably won't survive an encounter with all of them. But if we do, and we somehow manage to get to Annapolis, you need to prepare yourself for what we'll find."

"Shut up. Just shut up." My racing pulse thrummed against my temples, causing my abating headache to roar back into existence. Reid was just upset about Ember. That was all. This was a tantrum, a last attempt to drag me down with him into wretched misery over a doomed relationship.

The elevator dinged and the doors opened, sparing him a profanity-laden rant. Jen was standing in front of the doors, texting on her phone. She glanced up and jumped a little. "Oh! You're awake!"

"I'm here to heal Berenice and Lark," I said. "Where are they?"

"Follow me." She tapped her smart phone's screen, and I heard the whooshing sound of a sent text. "I've been texting Gabriela, by the way. Everyone's at her house. There've been no signs of the strike team, but they're staying away from the windows just in case. Reuben is very concerned about Berenice and Lark. Gabriela was burned in the attack, but it's all pretty superficial. Berenice and Lark, on the other hand..."

She trailed off and cleared her throat. "They're in here," she said as we reached an unassuming door on the left marked 365. She knocked in a little pattern.

"Come in," a weary voice called.

Jen faced me. "Stay here for a minute. I'm going to warn her that it's you." She opened the door a few inches and slipped inside. A few seconds later, she poked her head out. "You can come in."

This was the moment I'd long dreaded: the moment I'd have to face the woman I'd shot two years ago. She remembered me and had told her friend of my crime. What would happen once I crossed the threshold? Artemis... no, *Berenice* was possibly the strongest person on the planet. I was sure she'd imagined crushing various parts of my body in her hand many times since I'd attempted to murder her.

I walked into the dimly lit hospital room. Healing energy coursed through my nerves when I saw the two patients.

Berenice lay on the bed closest to the door, propped up at a sitting angle. Her face was red and peeling, while her hands were bandaged in thick white gauze. An IV dripped fluid into her veins through the back of her hand. Beautiful blonde hair cascaded down her shoulders, but the appealing image was marred by the ugly scowl on her face. Her green eyes squinted at me, though that could have been because they were burned.

Lark lay in the opposite bed. I'd been nearly defeated by the statuesque teleporter once; she wielded a staff that packed quite a wallop when slammed against the back of one's legs. My speed was an even match for her teleportation, and we'd been in a stalemate until she'd nearly shattered my shins and I'd fallen on all fours.

Her skin then had been a rich dark brown, but the little of it that was visible now was red and black. She lay still in her hospital bed, swathed in bandages and tubes. Of her facial features, only her nose and mouth showed. Her leader had done that to her.

The bruised and bloodied faces of my four closest friends flashed across my eyes.

"You," Berenice snarled.

Lark shifted uncomfortable and moaned.

Every possible response melted away as I walked to Lark's bedside and kneeled. I took her hand in mine and, with the energy that flowed from me to her, willed the sincerity of my condolences and regrets to go with it. Today was a new day. I was a new man. This would be the beginning of a new chapter for the Baltimore team and their relationship with Benjamin Trent.

Lark inhaled deeply. "Wha...?"

"Lark, my name is Benjamin," I said tenderly. "We've met before."

She pushed herself up on her elbows and pulled off her bandages, rubbing at her eyelids and wincing against the light from the windows. She finally focused on me. Recognition, surprise, confusion, and finally understanding played across her features.

She sat up fully and stretched. "So you really are one of us, huh?" Berenice snorted.

I patted Lark's hand. "Yes," I said. "And we've got a lot to talk about, but not much time." My eyes flickered toward Berenice, who was watching us without blinking. "I need to heal you, too."

"You stay the hell away from me," she said, her fists clenching the sheets. "I can walk just fine."

Before I could argue, Jen sat down on the edge of the bed and took Berenice's hand in hers. "You know that's not true," she said softly. "And he won't hurt you. He saved my life, and Reid's too. That woman very nearly killed me."

Berenice's eyes darted back and forth between Jen and me. "Don't take his side," she pleaded. "He—he—"

"I'm not taking anyone's side. Remember, he's why I'm here with you right now," Jen said, her voice even softer. "Instead of in a body bag. Emily stabbed me in the neck and threw me down a stairwell. If Benjamin hadn't saved me..."

Berenice rubbed at her eyes. "Don't talk about that. I've dealt with enough death in the past day to last a lifetime."

"You'll be hearing about a lot more death if you don't let Benjamin heal you so we can meet up with the others," Reid said flatly. "He won't hurt you. Even if he tried, there are two fully capable superheroes within arm's reach, remember?"

"Thanks, bro," I grumbled.

Berenice thrust her free hand towards me. "One second, that's it."

Suppressing a sigh, I tapped my finger to hers. It was enough. Immediately the red skin faded to her normal peachy tone, and the swelling around her eyes receded.

She smiled despite herself, and a moment later swung her long legs out of the bed. "Okay, Trent, you've got a cool power. I'll give you that. No wonder Jill wanted you so bad." She grabbed a hairband from her bedside table and casually swept her hair into a long pony-tail while she rooted around in the bedside drawer. "Jen, where's my uniform?"

"Here," Jen said, reaching underneath a nearby chair. Reid and I turned partially to give Berenice privacy.

"Speaking of Jill, where is she?" Lark asked from behind the privacy curtain she'd partially pulled around her bed as she dressed.

"Yeah, I need to thank her face-to-face for sending in Benjamin Trent to heal us without popping in herself," Berenice drawled.

I glared at Jen, then at Reid. *Why* hadn't they filled in Berenice about Jillian's whereabouts? Explaining it required thinking about it, which I'd done too much of already.

Reid cleared his throat. "Jillian was abducted by Beau Trent and two members of the Rowe family last night. We came here to help you fight the strike team that's after you, and then we will all go after Jillian."

For a few seconds, all I could hear was the rustles of Lark and Berenice dressing. I closed my eyes, waiting for the scathing response I knew was coming from Berenice, if not Lark. My wife had spoken only a little of her childhood bully, but already I'd picked up that there was no love lost between them, even as adults. Even if Berenice didn't wish torture and death on Jillian, she probably wouldn't want to stick her neck out for her.

A hand on my shoulder made me turn around. Berenice stood before me, fully dressed in her sharp black-and-tan uniform. I couldn't read her expression—she looked almost suspicious, as if she were, perhaps, trying to read mine. "Why did your brother grab Jill?" she asked evenly.

"He thinks Jillian knows where the rest of the JM-104 is," I said, taken aback by her demeanor. She hadn't tried to crush my shoulder.

She pursed her lips and frowned as she thought. "I have no idea why he'd think that. Jill was just as blindsided by that stuff as the rest of us, and I'm positive she would've mentioned knowing where the rest of it is." She straightened. "I've fought your brother. I know what he's like." She crossed her arms, assessing me. "Just how badly do you want Jill back? You're screwing, right? But do you actually love her?"

Lark gasped, while Jen's mouth fell open. "Berenice!"

I mirrored Berenice's stance, casually folding my arms in front of me. "What's it to you?"

Berenice shrugged. "I want to know how far you're willing to go for her. I'm not going to rush into Trentland at your side if you're going to wimp out when things get scary. I know how well you can run, kid. You're good at running away, if I recall our, oh, half a dozen fights correctly."

I kept my face blank, but my insides had twisted. Berenice really was the witness of my worst moments. She was being mean, but she was also being honest.

"We're married," I said quietly. "And it was your kind of wedding, with your kind of vows." My hand instinctively moved to my right pocket, which contained the necklace I'd bought for Jillian to commemorate our wedding. I'd rescue her if only to see her wearing it again.

Her jaw dropped. "Why on earth would *anybody* marry *you*? Did you force her? Get her pregnant?" All her sarcasm had turned into insultingly genuine concern.

Lark shook her head. "Berenice, can you not show your butt for five seconds, please?"

I narrowed my eyes. "I don't know why she married me. Why don't you tell me why anybody would be friends with *you*?" I pointed at Jen, who did a double take. "All I've heard about you is stories from Jillian. Take a second and digest what that means."

She tutted. "Well, that's skewed. I'm not..." She took a breath, clearly thinking. "Okay, I get your point. I was a jerk for years, but we made up. We're cool now. I'm not... I'm not like that anymore." She had the grace to look embarrassed. "I was never a murderer, though," she muttered.

I swallowed the lump in my throat. "I am sorry for trying to kill you. I have no excuse. I know you'll never forgive me, so I won't ask.

Maybe you'll take comfort in the fact that it's a memory that haunts me every day."

She stared at me for several seconds, a tiny wrinkle between her eyes. Finally, she raised an eyebrow. "Well, I guess that's one thing we have in common," she murmured. "I'll help you find Jill."

ITEM FOUR

Excerpt of a letter from Christina St. James to her mother, dated December 2, 1897

Dear Mama,

Thank you so much for the beautiful table linens you sent us last month. They arrived in time for Thanksgiving....Patrick is so at peace down here in Richmond, especially with his salary, though there is much anti-Italian rumbles, and we have changed our names. I am Christina St. James now and he, Patrick St. James. When the child comes we will call it by an Italian name at home and an English name in public...Patrick and I adore Edward and Edoardo for our son, but can't seem to agree on our daughter's name. I prefer Juliana, for Grandmama Giuliana, but Patrick insists on Antonella and Nella for his aunt. I so much want to please him, Mama, but I hate that name...

4

Snow had fallen continuously since I'd passed out on the steps of the hospital.

Almost a foot of snow carpeted Baltimore, making our journey to the truck—itself covered in thick white flakes—and the subsequent ride to Gabriela's house slow, arduous, and cantankerous. Snow had melted into my socks on the way to the truck, and twice Berenice and Lark got into a shouting match over the route while I ignored them. Both times Jen had to bellow above both of them that she knew the way.

The three women were squished into the back of the cab. Berenice had insisted that Jen accompany us to the Fischer house since she'd been pulled into our strike team drama. Lark stared out the window when she wasn't yelling at Berenice, searching for the strike team. Or maybe she was wishing she was anywhere but in that truck. I couldn't blame her.

We pulled up to Gabriela's modest, unremarkable townhouse after thirty of the longest minutes of my life. Snow was falling thicker than ever.

I slammed the driver's door and awkwardly marched towards the front door, noting that the front curtain had just moved. The front door swung open. Marco's tired, worn face greeted me. "Bro, a fever? She kicked your ass with a *fever*?"

"It could've been dysentery, so let's count our blessings," I muttered. "Get ready for the circus," I added, jabbing my thumb over my shoulder. I walked past Marco into the warm living room.

Reid came up next and spoke quietly with Marco. They disappeared upstairs.

Ember and Abby were sitting on a rag rug by a crackling fire in the fireplace. They smiled at me as I entered the room. A pretty woman in her mid-twenties was perched on the arm of a couch. I guessed she was Gabriela Fischer, Reid's sister-in-law.

I'd heard the sordid tale of how her husband, Reuben Fischer, had been punished for his unsanctioned marriage to a civilian. I'd fought Reuben—whom I'd thought of as Obsidian for years—several times. He was brave in battle, and it appeared that he was equally courageous in his personal life.

When my eyes had adjusted to the dim, I saw that she was bandaged and burned. I held out my hand. "I can heal you. I'm the Saint Catherine medic."

She took my hand and grinned, her expression softening me a bit. "And the former supervillain," she said with a roguish wink. "I bet you get all the girls with that line. Bad boy chic, you know."

My chest throbbed yet again, but I couldn't help a smile. I liked Gabriela already. "Yes. We'll talk later," I added in an undertone. I'd just looked up.

A hilariously tall man stood in the corner, sipping from a mug with a Catholic icon on it and watching me with unapologetic amusement. I knew from his height alone that he was Argentine, the guy who could turn into metal.

He looked me up and down and began to laugh silently, aiming a finger gun at me and pretending to shoot. I drew my eyebrows together, not sure what to think of this greeting, but he smiled at me and mouthed, "Relax."

Berenice stormed in, dragging her unique intense atmosphere with her. "Abby! Where's Abby?"

Abby jumped up and streaked towards Berenice, flying into her chest with a *whumph*. Berenice's moodiness melted away as she embraced her teammate, who nuzzled her shoulder. Jen watched from the side, clearly familiar with this behavior.

"I'm fine, I'm fine," Berenice said with a smile as she stroked Abby's messy hair. "That was one hell of a stunt you pulled, girl. Ripped his throat right out."

Abby pushed away from Berenice and grinned. "Tiger hunt kill Peter."

Berenice gasped. "You can talk now?"

Lark pushed past them. "Abby can talk, Trent's a hero, Jill's gone, the strike team is circling. Now that we've gotten all the surprises and talking points out of the way, let's get down to business. Where's Reuben?"

Gabriela stood up. "In bed. Benjamin, can you heal him?"

The room quieted.

"Yes," I said. "Let's get this out of the way. Marco gets my stuff if I die." I was only half-joking.

All eyes in the room followed me as Gabriela led me up the narrow wooden stairwell. At the top of the stairs, a door stood ajar, allowing me to hear low male voices from within. Reid and Marco were speaking to Reuben, whose deep voice carried Reid's north-western accent.

Gabriela opened the door wider. "Darling, Benjamin's here."

I ducked into the room and took in the sight of one of my most formidable past opponents.

Reuben Fischer sat propped up on pillows in the middle of his bed. Even in convalescence, he exuded authority. His light blond hair was combed neatly, and his gray eyes conveyed no pain, though I knew he felt it—his face, so like Reid's, had been disfigured by a branded D on his right cheek.

The burn was partially healed, but my power would erase it completely. He wore no shirt. Instead, his torso was wrapped in bandages because of his flogging injuries. Bloody, crusty bandages filled two small trashcans beneath the desk.

Reuben folded his hands in his lap as he assessed me. "Benjamin Phillip Trent," he said, completely calm.

"That's me." I didn't pause to wonder how he knew my full name. Superhero crap, no doubt.

"I carried Berenice home, that night you shot her. I tended to the broken ribs."

I stared at my boots. "I'm sorry."

He chuckled. I jerked my head up. "Word in the underground is that you've made some *new* friends since we last met. Friends your family doesn't approve of."

"You could say that."

A warm smile lightened his face. "And now you went and got married to the last person on earth you were supposed to fall in love with." He extended his hand to me. "I'll make you a deal. You help me protect my wife. I'll help you save yours." He shot a significant look at Reid. "Call me a romantic, but I believe in happy endings."

Reid glared at his brother. "You know better than any of us what Beau is—"

"Don't you dare take your failed relationship out on your teammates," Reuben said, his volume increasing. "You've always been maudlin, and we've always put up with you, but the day you let your bad mood dictate whether you think your teammate is alive is the day I'm ashamed to be your brother."

He pointed at me without breaking eye contact with Reid. "Did Jillian sit around dithering over his chances of being alive after the tribunal? No. Did she bang her head against the wall and complain that she didn't know where they were going? No. She laced up her boots *and found him!*"

I took an instinctive step back from Reuben, whose ferocity entirely overshadowed the fact that he was bedridden. Reid, however, wasn't chastened yet—perhaps he was used to such treatment from Reuben, who *did* have an air of "professional older brother."

Reid's mouth twisted as though he'd tasted something foul, and then he said, "I have never implied that I don't want to go after Jillian. I'm just being realistic about our chances. Her chances."

Reuben turned to face me and thrust his hand towards me. "Heal me so I can get out of this bed and kick my brother's ass."

"Reid, leave," I said, striding towards Reuben.

Reid shoved past me, not bothering to excuse his rudeness before exiting the room. I clasped Reuben's warm hand, once again relishing the relief of the turbulent healing energy that had been swirling in my stomach.

He sighed, then threw back the covers. "Good grief," he muttered as he stood up. He raised his long arms and stretched, rolling and cracking his neck as his brother often did.

I was secure enough in my masculinity to admire the sheer power exhibited in his muscular frame—but at the same time felt a stab of envy. Even after six months of near-daily training, I was still as lanky as ever. Yet Jillian, ever mindful of my insecurities, had run her hands over my biceps and abs on our wedding night and almost purred in pleasure...

The thought sideswiped me, causing me to stagger as fear and longing gripped my chest. Reuben finished buttoning his shirt and turned to me. "Get my idiotic brother's doom prophecies out of your head. He's depressed about Ember."

"You think?" I mumbled, sagging on the bed.

He rolled his eyes. "Be prepared for him to do something melo-dramatic. After Stephanie died he...well, no need to get into that. But he's acting out, and if someone doesn't slap some sense into him, he'll keep acting out until he does something genuinely regrettable. Like I said before, our father and brothers all put up with it, but I must draw the line at letting his moods get in the way of his leadership ability."

I hung my head. Now that I'd been forced to stop and think about Jillian's chances—about all that lay ahead of us—it seemed as though there was no "easy" option. There never had been. There'd been a cavalcade of impossibilities, improbabilities, suicide missions, and pipe dreams.

Reuben gripped my shoulders and gave me a rough shake. "Hey. Look at me."

I obeyed, weirdly comforted by his decisiveness. It reminded me of Jillian. "What?"

He stared down his nose at me. "Get up, get your team, and get ready for the mission briefing."

ITEM FIVE

Telegram sent via Western Union from John Kettlethorpe to his brother Calvin, dated July 10, 1899

MARTHA HAD BABY BOY STOP BOTH HEALTHY STOP NAME IS ALPHONSO LEWIS STOP HIS SISTER SAYS SHE CAN SEE THE BABY'S INNARDS STOP HIS BROTHER TOUCHED AL'S FOREHEAD AND SAW A GREAT WAR STOP GEORGE HAS NEVER BEEN WRONG STOP START STOCKPILING FOOD STOP ALSO SAW MAN ON FIRE STOP SO STOCKPILE FIRE BLANKETS MAYBE STOP

5

It was the strangest gathering of people in which I'd ever been included, and I'd sat down to dinner with terrorists.

Berenice, Lark, and Abby sat on the couch. Jen sat cross-legged at Berenice's feet, where she tickled Berenice's calves from time to time, eliciting a small smile from Berenice whenever she did so.

Lark's face was utterly impassive, except for whenever she squeezed her eyes shut as though she'd had a particularly unpleasant thought. Abby shot continual, furtive glances at Ember, who remained in her spot on the rug in front of the fire. Ember frequently smiled and nodded at the silent conversation.

Topher and Marco sat on the opposite side of the rug from Ember, an amusing contrast of short and tall. Gabriela sipped juice while sitting next to Reuben on a love seat. Reid glowered in a folding chair in the corner, though he occasionally turned his wrathful look on both Ember and Reuben. Neither of them paid him any attention.

I sat against an empty wall, unwilling to get involved with the many powder kegs.

Reuben cleared his throat. "This is the first mission of this kind I've ever briefed before. I want that to be clear. Does everyone here understand the risks of being here?"

Everyone murmured assent.

He continued, "Okay. Earlier today, a strike team member named Emily Begay attacked Benjamin in front of the hospital. My brother Raphael kindly informed the Saint Catherine team that his team, strike team four, was dispatched to eliminate the Baltimore team, and then the Saint Catherine team. So right there we have our first abnormality."

"What do you mean?" Marco asked.

"I strongly suspect Emily was at the hospital to kill Berenice and Lark," Reuben said. "Strike teams are extraordinarily singular, dispatched for one job at a time. Raphael said my team first, *then* your team. They had no way of knowing you'd be alerted and beat them to the city. So that begs the question of why Emily approached Benjamin and tried to kill him right then and there."

"She got sloppy," Topher said with a little shrug. "Or scared. Or maybe just overeager. She saw another target and decided to go for it."

"Hunt kill," Abby volunteered. Berenice nodded as if this were a profound statement.

"Um, excuse me," Jen said in a small voice while raising her hand. "If I may...?"

"Of course," Reuben said graciously.

Jen blushed vermillion as we all looked at her. "I don't know much about fighting or anything like that, but using a human shield is kind of desperate, right? She only did that when she saw Tank—I mean, Reid—coming up the steps."

"That's a very cogent point, so thank you for bringing it up. Jen's right. Strike teams aren't like us." He gestured in a circular motion to the gathered superheroes. "They're allowed to bend the rules a bit if they can argue that the collateral damage couldn't have been avoided. But grabbing Jen was stupid. It was open, it was flashy, and frankly, I wasn't even there and I know it was unnecessary. She panicked because she knew Reid and realized the mission was compromised."

"Do you think they retreated?" Topher asked in his grating New York accent.

"A strike team doesn't retreat," Berenice said, pulling a face. "They wait."

I hoped Berenice couldn't see my shudder.

"So what are they waiting for now?" Lark asked, her tone dark. It was the first time she'd spoken since we'd gathered. "Why haven't they brought down the wrath of the Titans on us?"

"Because Emily *compromised the mission*," Marco repeated, his tone equally grim. "Their mission was to whack all of you Baltimore upstarts. The Saint Catherine upstarts were never part of the picture. I bet right now their leader is pacing back and forth like Jill used to and…" He trailed off, his eyes glazing over for a minute. "They think Jill's with us."

"Who's their leader?" Reid demanded abruptly.

"Buck," Abby said. "Elder son make Abby dizzy."

Berenice gazed sidelong at Abby. "Ozark guy, eh?"

"And in English?" Reid asked.

Topher raised his hand. "I know what she means. I met Buck McClintock a few years ago when I visited Ozark camp at a courting swap. He's a few years older than you, Rube. He makes people confused and disoriented—dizzy, you might say. He needs eye contact, though, and I'm pretty sure it's only for a limited time. He's Elder McClintock's third or fourth son or something. His younger brother Jim is the leader of the Columbia team."

"May he get hit by a bus," Lark muttered.

I hid my smile. James McClintock had once called Marco "unnatural" for being biracial. Lark, who was also black, probably had her own stories to tell about the unsavory Columbia leader.

"Who else are we dealing with?" I asked. "We've got a walking biohazard and a guy who makes you drunk."

"Daisy Guarino," Berenice said. "Last time Buck visited my camp, I overheard him telling Jill about a new teammate of his named Daisy. I don't know what her power is, but she's supposed to be a knife nut. That's what he was saying to Jill, that Daisy was even better than Miss Stabby with bladed weapons. Jill just laughed."

Abby barked a laughed. "Miss Stabby," she said to herself. "Name funny."

"Jill has a cousin on a strike team," Ember said quietly. "His name is Kyle Johnson. We met his sister Christiana in Liberty. I don't know for sure, but they might have deployed strike team four to take Jillian's team out because of their familiarity. Kyle and Jill weren't close, so we can't guarantee that he'd recuse himself like Raphael did."

"I've never even heard of Kyle," I said. "What's his power?"

"He's like Topher, except he can turn to stone instead of metal," Ember said. "And he doesn't need to be touching stone to activate the change."

"So let me get this straight," Lark said. Curiously, anger sparked in her eyes, though I couldn't imagine why. I would've expected various types of trepidation, but not fury. "We're facing a guy who can confuse us, a chick who can stab our eyes out before doing who-knows-what, a guy who can turn to stone, and someone who can literally slap a fever into us." She slammed her fist onto the arm of the couch. "So what are they waiting for? *Why* haven't they attacked?"

All at once, I understood her mood—she *was* afraid, but the waiting had made her fear morph into anger. Lark wanted to get the fight over with.

Reuben answered. "Like Marco pointed out, Emily compromised their mission. They didn't expect the Saint Catherine team to be here. Plus," he said, pointing to the curtained window, through which we could all see thickly swirling snow, "There's a snowstorm. They're coming up with a contingency plan, and then waiting until the opportune moment."

"So we attack first," Reid said. "Break off into teams and hunt them down. Ember can search for—"

"There are more than half a million people in this city," Ember cut in, her voice harsh. "Do you know what that means, Reid? Do you understand the implication of telling me to listen in on that many minds? Can you conceive of what that's *like*?"

Her volume had steadily risen as she unleashed on Reid, who stared at her with a mix of worry and confusion.

Before he could respond, she kept going. "Instead of suggesting that I invade the privacy of every human being in a ten-mile radius, how about you just raise a platform and fly us to Annapolis? That wouldn't be hard, right? Who cares if your power requires immense strength and concentration? What does it matter if that task would be so taxing that you'd be useless for a day?"

Ember jumped up, her slim chest rising and falling sharply as she surveyed Reid in his little folding chair. The occupants of the warm room waited, held back by the palpable tension, for Ember to continue her tirade.

Instead, she fled upstairs. A door opened and slammed, and the faint sound of retching echoed down the stairwell. Reid paused as if he were about to speak, then silently folded up his chair, set it against the wall, and walked up the stairs.

Even Abby was visibly stunned by the scene we'd all just witnessed. She looked at Berenice for confirmation, who held up her hands in a clear "don't ask me" gesture.

Marco let out a long breath. "Anyway..."

"What are we going to do about Jen and Gabriela?" I asked as gently as I could. "I don't want to see another civilian hurt because of us. Before everyone, I want to make sure they're safe."

Berenice's expression, which had automatically hardened when I'd spoken, softened again. She turned to Gabriela. "Could you stay with Jen at your salon?"

"Or at my apartment?" Jen offered. "I have lots of food and blankets."

"That works," Reuben said. "Are you okay with that, honey? I don't have powers for another few months, but I can't leave my team."

His words were still in the air when Abby jumped to her feet, her fists balled. "Bad!"

We all leaned back slightly from her, as if she were emanating a physical force. Berenice stood up and tried to put her hand on Abby's shoulder, but Abby swatted her hand away.

Abby's face twisted into an enraged grimace. "Bad, bad, bad," she growled.

Reuben held his hand up to stay us, then slowly stood. "I don't understand," he said cautiously. "Please explain why you're angry at me."

Abby jabbed her finger at Gabriela. "Reuben stay Gabby. Reuben stay protect Gabby. Team fight good weeks no Reuben. Reuben stay *Gabby!*"

That was easy enough to interpret: Abby expected Reuben to stay with his wife. The Baltimore team had lurched on without Reuben for weeks after the tribunal.

Yet, I couldn't see the source of her sheer fury over Reuben's decision. He was pretty obviously the natural leader of the combined teams. I expected him to stay with us. Arranging safe harbor was necessary.

But Abby took a shaking step forward. "Reuben stay Gabby. If Reuben leave Gabby... Tiger scratch Reuben."

I didn't want to know what a tiger's "scratch" looked like. Still, Abby was an odd duck—tiger?—and I liked her already. She had a grasp of loyalty that any supervillain family would've been proud of.

Reuben sighed. "I have to stay here, Abby. This isn't an easy decision, but Jen will look after Gabriela. They're friends. I trust Jen, and I hope you do, too. There's no concrete reason for me to keep Gabriela and Jen here. And I really would appreciate it if you didn't maul me over it. Unless that's how you've decided to handle leadership decisions you disagree with?"

"Dear," Gabriela murmured. "Be nice."

Abby crossed her arms and frowned, though there was a hint of confusion in her eyes. Finally, she said, "Cub."

"I beg your pardon?" Reuben asked.

"Cub," Abby repeated, an unsaid "you drooling idiot" in her tone. "Reuben protect Gabby cub. Reuben *make* Gabby cub. Reuben stay Gabby. Team fight. No Reuben."

We all caught on simultaneously, five gasps breaking the tense silence. "No way," Berenice said, peering at Abby with her mouth open. "How do you know that?"

Abby tapped her nose.

Reuben spun around to look at Gabriela, whose stricken expression underlined her posture—she was holding her stomach in an unmistakable maternal gesture. "There's a baby?"

Gabriela nodded, tears brimming in her eyes. "I didn't want to tell you until this had all blown over. You didn't need another stress on top of everything."

Reuben collapsed into his seat. "This changes everything."

"No, it doesn't," Jen said. She eased herself to her feet and stepped into the middle of the room, between Abby and Reuben. "Abby, I may not be a superhero, but I've been responsible for Gabriela's safety for several weeks now. I'm aware of the risks, and I'm willing to fight to keep her safe. As soon as the snow clears, I'll take Gabriela to my parents' house down in La Plata. Reuben, you need to be with your team. As a *civilian*," she said with exasperated emphasis, "I would appreciate it if the most capable leader of my city's heroes were with his team if there's no good reason for him not to be. But really, the decision isn't ours," she said firmly. "Gab, what do you say?"

Gabriela wiped her eyes. "Jen's right. She's my friend and I feel safe with her. The strike team won't follow us. They don't care about us, they care about you guys. I want to be with you, but you being with me will endanger Jen and me. And the baby," she added. "If you want to keep me safe, please stay with your team."

Reuben's eyes darted back and forth between Jen and Gabriela as he processed what he was hearing. "I need to talk to Reid."

"I'll get him," I volunteered.

I was up the stairs and at the bathroom door in a second, the usual blur-and-stop a strange relief from the emotional turmoil downstairs. The bathroom was empty, so I raised my hand to knock on the bedroom door, which was cracked open an inch.

Ember's low voice made me hesitate.

"I said get out," she spat.

"Sweetie, please," Reid begged. "I didn't mean to say that I don't care about your well-being. I really thought a scan was easy for you. You've done similar things before, and—"

"Don't call me your sweetie," Ember shot back. "I ceased being your sweetie when you lost your mind in Liberty. You made a choice and this is the consequence."

"I said I was sorry!" Reid's voice quivered. "A million times! Just tell me what you want. I'll do anything."

"*I want you to get out.*" She enunciated every word, obviously speaking through gritted teeth.

I knocked on the door.

"Come in," Ember said.

I pushed open the door to find Ember standing with her arms crossed over her chest, her back to Reid. A reeking trashcan stood at her feet. Reid was so slumped that he resembled a question mark. He straightened a little as I walked into the room, but he never took his eyes off Ember's rigid back.

"Sorry to interrupt," I said, trying to keep my tone even. I closed the door behind me and put a hand on my hip. "I trust you weren't talking about anything other than mission-related subjects."

If Ember dipped into my mind, she would've received the same rant Reid had gotten earlier that day, as well as overheard my repeated reminder to myself that I would never hit a woman who hadn't tried to hurt me first.

Reid finally tore his gaze away from Ember to stare at me. "We're fine. It was just a bout of flu. Is there really nothing you can do about it?"

"No," I said flatly. "I can't heal sickness. Say whatever else you have to say and get back downstairs, *Uncle* Reid. Abby just announced that Gabriela's pregnant, and Reuben is just this side of a breakdown. We need all the help we can get."

"I knew she was pregnant," Ember said as she knotted the little plastic bag in the trashcan. "But she asked me not to tell. I didn't know Abby knew, though."

The yellow light from the desk lamp went out, plunging us into shadows. Elsewhere in the house every electrical machine failed at once," resulting in a single *whumph*. The only light present was the same low, watery light from the snowstorm that had illuminated my hospital room—except now, in midafternoon, the light was even dimmer.

Almost immediately I could feel the temperature in the room begin to fall. Without a heat source, the house's temperature would plummet.

"Hunted by a strike team in a blizzard," Reid said with a sigh.

"With a pregnant woman," I added.

They both shook their heads in exasperation.

"How about we go downstairs and figure out what happens next?" Reid said. He held the door for Ember, but she pointedly put her boot on the bed and began to retie it. Reid disappeared down the stairs with his head bowed.

As soon as he was gone, Ember said, "You got something to say?"

I took a deep breath. "Do you actually have a good reason for not wanting to scan, or are you just being recalcitrant to piss me off?"

Ember jerked her head up. "Piss *you* off?"

I narrowed my eyes. "You *have* scanned major portions of the city before, and I've never seen you so much as get a nosebleed from it. Hell, you volunteered to be on telepathy duty when we needed to find Lark and Berenice. So what is it? Is it really too big of a task or are you prolonging this mission just because you want to make my life hard?"

Forget Reid. My biggest concern was the vein in my forehead bursting.

Ember deflated. "Scanning isn't as easy as you'd think. A scan of that magnitude would physically drain me. When Patrick made me..." She closed her eyes for a second. "...search for Jill that day last summer, the effort of looking for her across the city weakened me so much that I couldn't fight back, though it's not like I had much of a chance in the first place. Reid knows that." She hugged herself protectively. "So I don't know where he gets off suggesting that I weaken myself right before a fight with a strike team."

I walked up to her, my ire cooling. I raised my hand to pat her shoulder, but she flinched away. I immediately regretted ever wanting to shake her or otherwise physically express my frustration.

Instead, I clasped my hands in front of me. "Do you remember why I didn't want to tell you the truth about my past? Last week, at the team meeting? Do you remember what I said?"

She looked up at me through her long eyelashes. "Yes," she whispered.

"The first time in my life, I have a sister who's my age, and whom I have a close relationship with. I love Eleanor, but we've always been distant. You're closer to me than I was ever was with her."

I dared to let my fingers graze her jaw, focusing on memories of us patrolling together, of conversations we'd had about her home in Oconee and her brother Brian, and of our weekly meeting in the sick bay when we reviewed her caloric intake and planned the next week's vegan-friendly menu.

I enjoyed my time with Ember, and I'd always hoped that she felt the same. "I'll sacrifice nearly anything to save Jillian, but not you. I've got your back."

Ember bowed her head. "I'm sorry for being difficult. I'll look for Buck." She inhaled heavily. "But please keep in mind that the more I'm in someone's head, the more they can sense me there."

"I understand."

Still hugging herself, she walked out of the room and down the stairs. I stood in the dark, cold bedroom for a long moment, until the weight of the moment pulled me down to my knees. I sank to the ground and stared through the delicate lace curtain into the white-out beyond the glass. I could see neither houses, nor sky, nor any living thing.

All I could see was the storm that raged.

ITEM SIX

Excerpt of letter sent from Christina St. James to her mother, dated March 2, 1903

> *...Nella pointed to the map of the city and declared the missing girl to be at <u>that</u> spot exactly. Patrick put on his hat and went to find her. Mother, she was just where Nella said she was. When questioned, she said she just "knew", and then pointed to where you and Papa live...We collected the reward money and will put it in an account so Edward can go to college, and his brothers if any come.*

6

There was nothing left to do but wait for the evening to unfold.

Not a minute after I'd returned from upstairs, Ember hushed us and said she was going to find the strike team. She ordered the rest of us to vacate the living room.

Watching from the kitchen, I saw her sit cross-legged on the living room floor in front of the fire and place her hands on her knees, as if she were meditating. She closed her eyes and breathed in deeply, then let out her breath in a long, slow exhale.

A tingle raced across my brain, but it was gone as quickly as it had come.

I leaned against the doorway, momentarily in awe of my teammate. All my friends possessed god-like powers, but if one quantified our powers by the ability to destroy and disrupt the machinations of our enemies... Ember Harris was the most powerful by an order of magnitude.

The temptation to fill my idle mind with worry and doubt always lurked. Lest I disrupt Ember's reconnaissance with obscene imaginations of Jillian's torture, I let myself consider the young woman sitting on the living room floor.

Jillian saw Ember in an almost worshipful light, even more so than the rest of her team. I knew my wife well enough to guess why. Ember was a few years older than Jillian, giving her a slightly more experienced air that Jillian respected. She was kind and thoughtful. She had courage of conviction, standing by her veganism even when none of her teammates did.

More obviously, she was beautiful, like the living embodiment of a Waterhouse painting. Jillian loved beauty in all its forms, whether it be in the plots of romance novels or the edge of a well-crafted knife. It followed that she'd be attracted to beautiful people, too.

But it was not Ember's physical attributes of which Jillian spoke most often. Instead, she praised Ember's amicability and social graces, her knack for knowing just what to say to comfort someone in need. Time and time again she'd moaned that she wasn't personable. I'd kissed Jillian after she said that and told her that she was exactly right just as she was. Just as the world needed many types of trees to make oxygen, so a team needed many types of personalities to operate.

I never voiced what I was thinking: Ember got along with everyone because she could hear what they wanted her to say. On some level, her personality was formed by the desires and expectations of others. *Cogitamus ergo ea est. We think therefore she is.*

So what, then, lived beneath the outer layer of telepathy and instant understanding of every social interaction? Who was Ember?

I wasn't sure, but I suspected that the real Ember had reared her head and roared in Liberty, when her telepathy had been blocked. She'd been forced to approach every situation at the level of the other person, ignorant of their thoughts and wishes.

True to form, Ember had made some friends, and quickly. But she'd also clung to her vows when nobody else had. She'd dug in her heels and called foul on the Sentinels. Most shocking of all, she'd dumped Reid for reasons none of us fully understood.

I turned to look at her ex-boyfriend, my team's acting leader. He was sitting at the table, watching Reuben and Gabriela as they held each other in the corner. Reuben smiled at Gabriela and rubbed her stomach. Gabriela kissed his jaw.

Reid folded his arms on the table and hid his face in them.

I turned back to Ember. Psychics and telepaths in the *Danger* television show always put their fingers on their temples when they used their powers, but her hands remained on her knees, relaxed and limp. She sat there for a minute more, silent and still—

She smiled and opened her eyes. "Got him."

She clambered to her feet and strode purposefully into the kitchen. "Reuben, we have to hurry. Buck knows we're here, and he knows there are two civilian women. I picked up that he's angry at Emily for dragging Jen into it, so he's waiting until the civilians are gone to minimize the risk of hurting them. However, I was only in his head for a few seconds to avoid detection. I know we're being watched, but I don't know how closely or by whom."

"What happens if the civilians don't leave?" Jen asked. "If we stay here, maybe..."

"They *will* raid," Berenice said, pinching the bridge of her nose. "They'll work as hard as they can to not hurt you guys, but their first mission is to kill us."

"What else did you pick up?" Reuben asked.

Ember sighed. "They're splitting up, probably for recon. I have a good idea where Buck is, at a parking garage nearby, but after that, it's only impressions. This house is their target, though, so we can safely assume that their positions are in a loose circle around it."

"And they'll start zeroing in eventually," I said. "I bet they're watching the roads."

"That's a good a guess as any," Reuben said. "And probably what I would do."

Marco stepped forward. "If they're split up, then they're the weakest they're ever going to be." He leveled a hard stare at Reuben. "We need to act."

I'd never heard Marco sound like that before. All traces of his usual boyish enthusiasm were gone, replaced by a stony determination to destroy anything and everything that stood in the way of his enacting justice for his murdered sisters, kidnapped cousin, and destroyed innocence. He had little left to lose, and the ability to vaporize human beings without batting an eye.

Honed self-preservation instincts whispered to me that he was the most dangerous person in that room.

Reuben squinted at the gathered people and clicked his tongue as he thought. "Reid, you'll be up against Kyle, obviously. I have no idea why they sent a guy who can turn into stone against a geomorph. Berenice, Marco, you'll go with him."

"Tiger fight Buck," Abby said calmly, her chin jutted forward. "Tiger kill Buck."

"How can you be sure?" Lark asked.

Abby smiled. "Buck make dizzy *Abby*," she said. "Tiger no dizzy. Tiger kill Buck."

Buck's powers didn't work on Abby in her tiger form. *Excellent.*

"You know this for sure?" Reuben asked. "From experience?"

Abby nodded. "Tiger Buck live Ozark. Tiger know Buck."

"Then that's settled," Reuben said. "Ember, since you alone can find Buck, you'll go with Abby. Taking out the leader is paramount."

My mind reeled: I'd promised Ember that I'd keep her safe, but this was rapidly flying out of my control. Could I somehow convince Reuben to keep her with me? Or maybe to just keep her out of the fight altogether until she was at full strength again?

I glanced at Ember and mentally pleaded with her to not hold this unkept promise against me.

She met my eyes and nodded once. *We're cool, Ben.*

For a half a second, I thought Ember looked scared—but then Reid, who'd been leaning against the wall, abruptly stood. "Whoa, whoa, whoa. Ember? I don't want her in the field like that. She's still weak. She can't fight. For all intents and purposes, she's a noncombatant right now." He frowned at Ember. "Hell, since you're weak from the scan, you're little more than a civilian in my eyes. You should go with Jen and Gabriela and wait for us to come get you."

Even in my earliest days on the team, I'd never been so condescending to a teammate.

Berenice's and Lark's jaws dropped. "She's not a civilian," Lark said. "Let's show some respect to the people who serve with us."

Ember blushed scarlet before she replied, "It's not about what you want. It's about what needs to be done. I can find Buck."

"At what cost?" Reid gasped.

"Possibly at cost of my life. That's a sacrifice I have always been willing to make. I'm not afraid." She narrowed her eyes. "Shocking as that may sound, since I'm little more than a civilian in your eyes."

"Well, as your leader, I forbid you to do that," Reid insisted.

Instead of lashing out, Ember laughed quietly. It was somehow scarier. "Try to stop me. I dare you."

Topher stepped up then, his height imposing on everything and causing the heat to fizzle. "Quick question," he said, a hint of impatience beneath his joviality. "How the hell did you guys kill Atropos and function as a team for as long as you did?"

Reid looked sheepish, but Ember glared at Topher. "Jill has a list of problems the length of my arm, but she knew—knows—how to cut the crap and get a mission going. She fought Patrick, she got us together and found a new home, and she got us through that whole Liberty situation. *She's* my leader, not Reid."

"And you know what your leader Jill would say?" Reid cut in. "She'd remind you that I'm the SIC, which means that *I'm* the leader right now!"

Marco grabbed a glass of water and hurled it at the wall. It shattered into tiny shards and sprayed water everywhere. "No, she'd say shut the hell up, you complete jackasses, and go save her! Now, *cut the crap* and get the mission going!"

His eyes glowed whitish yellow, with snaky tendrils of energy curling away from them. A hazy light appeared around the edges of his palms. "Defeating the strike team is nothing more than step one of saving Jill, and I swear to God, if you don't stop arguing over trivial bull like this, I'm going kill you both myself for hindering a rescue mission. I dare the *both* of you to put that to the test."

Ember and Reid wisely stepped back, their heads bowed.

Marco whirled around to face Reuben. "You're the more experienced leader. The way I see it, you're in charge. Assign the teams."

Reuben cleared his throat. "Ember, Abby, you go after Buck for the reasons I mentioned before. Berenice, Marco, and Reid will hunt down Kyle. Since he's the only other man on the team, it follows that he's the SIC, so he's second priority. If Reid fails to kill him, both Berenice and Marco have powers that can threaten stone. Lark and I are going after Emily."

"Why you two?" I interrupted. "You don't have your powers, and Emily is lethal."

"Emily knows you already, so there's no surprise there. While I don't have powers right now, I'm still an expert hand-to-hand fighter, which gives me the edge over a woman with average strength. Lark's teleportation will give her the element of surprise. I'm not saying it'll be easy, but we should be able to tackle Emily."

"That leaves me and Ben," Topher said. "Up against that Daisy chick."

"Right. Your power gives you a measure of protection against most physical attacks, especially knives," Reuben said. "If she's a psychic of some sort, then that's another issue, but there's just no way to know. I had to hedge my bets. You two will stay here, central to the fighting so Ben can better aid everyone else. Topher, your job is mainly to protect him."

Topher nodded, his eyes warm. "Can do."

"There's two more people," Jen said softly. "I don't think she and I will be of much help this time."

Reuben put his arm around Gabriela, then pressed his lips to the top of her head. "I need you to be brave again."

ITEM SEVEN

Partial text of a wanted poster printed by Pinkerton's National Detective Agency, distributed throughout the summer of 1905.

TIMOTHY THORNTON TRENT
WANTED FOR GRAND LARCENY
Age: 25 to 30
Height: 5 foot 8
Weight: 180 pounds
Build: Stout
Complexion: Fair

Timothy T. Trent was in the employ of Old Dominion Southern Railway Ltd. On the night of February 2, he left with $30,000, all of which was composed of $100 bills. The greater portion of the bills were new. Three witnesses report that Timothy T. Trent possesses a device or garment capable of producing "invisibility" which disallowed apprehension. Old Dominion Southern Railway Ltd. offers a suitable reward for the arrest of Timothy T. Trent and his delivery to a duly authorized officer of the Commonwealth of Virginia.

7

G abriela's ancient grandfather clock chimed an hour to midnight.

We huddled in the living room, the nervous energy making me shift from foot to foot for something to do.

Reuben pulled a thick winter hat over Gabriela's hair, securing it around her ears. "Keep moving," he said, holding up heavy-duty gloves. "And keep your extremities covered. If you feel dizzy from cold, get out of the wind until you're warmer, but don't linger outside. When you're at Jen's, drink warm beverages and get into dry clothes. The damp is the most dangerous, so—"

Gabriela placed a single finger on Reuben's lips. Reuben closed his eyes and cradled her hand to his cheek. He wore his broken heart on his sleeve.

I could not watch them without aching to take out Jillian's necklace and caress it, as if touching the silver heart was to hold her hand.

"I'll be fine," Gabriela whispered. She said something in Spanish, words that did not need translation. Reuben flung his arms around her and shook, though no tears fell. This was the second time he had to say goodbye to his wife like this, but unlike last time, both spouses were in danger.

Jen, already bundled for the freezing journey ahead of them, descended the stairs with Berenice behind her. They'd been up there for a few minutes, their indistinct voices coming down the stairwell every so often. I didn't ask why they wanted alone time; Berenice's bloodshot eyes said everything.

Jen shouldered a heavy backpack filled with supplies. "Gab, you ready?" She struggled with the heavy bag, and I had to stop myself from offering to take the load from her.

We were all certain that the strike team had no interest in two civilian women, but should they encounter a more mundane enemy...

"Wait," I said. There was at least one thing I could do. I unsheathed my extendable baton from its holster on my thigh and held it out to Jen. "Take this. I hope you never have to use it, but if you do, aim for the knees and throat. Face will do, too."

Jen grasped the metal rod and expertly whipped it a little, causing the telescopic baton to extend with a clean *snik* sound. She grinned. "This thing could really mess someone up. Thanks, Ben." She collapsed the baton and slipped it into her jacket pocket, then turned back to Gabriela. "Let's get going. It's only going to get colder."

Jen and Gabriela surveyed us all one last time, then Gabriela opened the front door. They stepped out onto the dark stoop. The door shut.

Just like that, they were gone. They were on their own as they walked four miles north through fresh three-foot snow drifts. The cloud cover was ubiquitous and the city's power was out, so no light reflected off the deep snow. The only illumination they had for their path was a small LED flashlight, and whatever ambient light remained.

Though the city's seedier inhabitants were just as snowed in as anyone else, if the two young women encountered trouble, we could not help them.

The decision to send Jen and Gabriela out alone, at eleven at night, into waist-high snow had been nobody's first choice, but Ember's report was damning. We were being monitored, a countdown clock ticking over our heads with an unknown amount of time left.

Reuben hated to risk Gabriela and Jen's safety by sending them out this night, but he would not risk the alternative. Nobody would. We didn't have any way to hear from them when they arrived at Jen's.

Faith was all we had now.

Reuben insisted on waiting half an hour after Jen and Gabriela's departure to send out our own little two- and three-man teams, so they'd be reasonably far from any violence. We stood around in the living room, awkward and tense, none daring to speak above a whisper.

Abby and Ember huddled in the corner, speaking telepathically, both of them occasionally nodding or shaking their heads. Berenice, Marco, and Reid stood tightly in the corner by the clock, their heads bowed together. Reuben and Topher occasionally peeked through the front window's curtain, exercising extreme care to not disturb the lace and reveal their position.

At one point, Reuben turned to Ember and said, "I want you to scan for Buck again, and then Jen and Gabriela." Had he not been a warrior, he probably would've been chewing on his lip.

"I told you," Ember said, her voice growing high, "I can't risk Buck knowing that we're looking for him. We both know that he's not moving, so why make me use more mental energy when I've got to go out into the snow and find the leader of a strike team in less than an hour?"

"But—"

"Reuben," I cut in. "Give her a break."

It said much that he simply turned back around and anxiously peeked through the curtain again.

Nobody wanted to talk to me, though I craved any distraction. I would've happily chatted about the bad old days with Berenice, but I could only stand in the middle of the room and feel the nausea roiling in my stomach. Hot nervousness clashed with the cool air in the house, making clammy sensations run up and down my skin.

Making matters worse was the fact that every time I looked at the clock, I was forced to remember that Jillian had been in captivity for nearly twenty-four hours. The drive from Saint Catherine to Annapolis was merely nine hours, so it was possible that she'd already endured nearly fifteen hours of interrogation. The worry mixed with the clamminess to form a creeping slime in my veins.

I sat on the bottom step of the stairwell and closed my eyes. Though I'd been in varying stages of unconsciousness in the hospital, I hadn't truly slept since the previous night. It seemed indecent to consider rest.

Jillian, at the very least, wasn't resting. Sleep deprivation was the first order of business for my family's guests. She'd have the bare minimum of sleep, food, and water. Usually our guests were also relieved of their clothes, though considering Jillian's sickness and the weather, it would be unwise of my mother to insist on doing so unless she wanted Jillian to expire far quicker than planned.

I hid my face in my hands. What was happening to her right now, at that very moment? Was she screaming? Sobbing? Begging for mercy?

A nasty thought occurred to me: there was a way I could possibly find out. All I needed was access to the deep web, where federal law protecting images of superheroes were an amusing technicality. My brain raced as I strained to remember websites my brother had set up to make a little extra cash on the side. Snuff videos, genuine torture porn, and worse were available in high definition for a price. And videos of a superhero—a famous one? That would fetch a premium.

A sudden warmth next to me alerted me to someone else's presence on the stairwell.

"Don't open your eyes," Marco said quietly. "Rest while you can."

"I can't sleep," I mumbled. As if I could sleep now, knowing that Beau had probably filmed Jillian being tortured. I'd never sleep again.

"Neither can I. What are you thinking about?"

"Jillian's so weak right now." My chest ached as I admitted it aloud. "She's sick, she doesn't have her powers..." Did she know she was being filmed? Was she trying to pass a message on to me?

Amazingly, Marco chuckled. I jerked my head up and stared at him, my macabre fantasies momentarily extinguished.

He inclined his head towards me. "I bet she's *so* pissed off about that. Like, she's probably cussing at Beau and answering his questions with 'your mom,' then making all sorts of stupid threats about what she'll do when her powers come back." He elbowed me. "Talk me through it. When her powers come back, what'll she do first?"

"Don't do this. Don't give me false hope."

"I think she'll go after Beau first," Marco said, his volume rising a tiny bit. "She'll throw, like, a chair through the door of her cell or whatever and jump on him, then beat him to death with her bare hands."

"The doors of the holding rooms are three inches of solid steel. They're electromagnetically locked," I said dully. "Berenice would struggle with them."

"Well, then, she'll wait until he opens the door. *Then* she'll pounce." He leaned back on his elbows, a little smile spreading across his lips. "And then she'll roundhouse kick that necromancing freak in the head. His sister will get a knife to the heart. That's when we'll all storm the house, by the way," he said, gazing sidelong at me. "I'll get into an epic fight to the death with your mom. There'll be music and lights and everything. Meanwhile, you'll heal Jill and then go make out somewhere, preferably far away from me. You even have my permission to have sex."

"Stop," I growled. "Her powers won't return for at least ten days. I don't know exactly how long they intend to keep her, but she doesn't have that long."

Marco pursed his lips. "You made me do this."

"Made you do what?"

He stood and pulled out his phone. "Dad always said that the fastest way to lose your woman is to let some other guy be her hero." He tapped out a number on his phone. "I wonder what Dean would do if he heard that big, bad Beau kidnapped Jill. I know she's married to you, but I bet she'd sleep with him just once. You know, as a thank you."

"Give me that!" I shouted, jumping up. I snatched the phone from his hands and threw it across the room, narrowly missing Lark's head. She swore and glared at me.

I whipped around and squinted at Marco, whose impassive face only served to make me more livid. "*I* am going to rescue Jillian, or I am going to die trying. Hell, I'll go right now and storm that stupid house myself if I must. Screw this strike team crap," I spat. "I'm tired of waiting for the hammer to fall."

Marco's smile turned into a sly grin. "You really thought I was going to call Dean, didn't you?"

"What do you..." I trailed off, aware for the first time that everyone was watching us. Surprise and amusement was evident on the many faces in the room, most of all Berenice's.

I could've slapped myself. Of course Marco wouldn't have called Dean. He probably didn't even know Dean's phone number. I wasn't even sure if the irksome Sentinel leader had a phone.

"You don't have to storm the house by yourself," Berenice said, obviously fighting the urge to laugh. "But I feel better about fighting the strike team with you now. In fact," she said, glancing at the clock, "It's time we get this mission going. Reid, Marco, let's go. Just as we planned."

The atmosphere had shifted, a new energy buzzing around the room. Marco raised an eyebrow at me, one side of his mouth quirked in an infuriatingly self-satisfied smirk. But my anger cooled as quickly as it came on. He'd intended to bring out the lion in me because that's what everyone—especially me—needed.

Marco was dangerous, and he was smart.

Reuben and Lark left first, following Ember's directions. Wrapped in a few winter items, they floundered out into the deep snow and began to call Jen and Gabriela's name, as if they were searching for them. Jen and Gabriela had already been briefed on the plan, so even if they were in earshot, they would not turn back. In reality, they were headed towards Emily's general location.

A few minutes later, Marco, Reid, and Berenice left the house with canvas bags in hand, to carry the firewood for which they were supposedly searching. Their path would take them west, near Kyle's last known location. They were loud and jocular, with no apparent interest in stealth. Before he left, Reid gave one last tormented look to Ember, but she turned her back to him without so much as a "see you later."

Ember and Abby slipped out next, the only two to display an interest in normal superhero activities. They would walk south, stopping occasionally to speak to citizens and offer moral support. Ember theorized that in such a situation, Buck would call for help to lure them in.

The "search and destroy" approach was flimsy, but what else could we do? As Marco had pointed out, the strike team was weakest when they were divided. It followed that they would attack when we were weakest, not pausing to consider that we'd divided into carefully designed teams. And no matter what, they hadn't planned for two superhero teams. If ever we would have salvation, it was in that fact.

Topher shut the door behind Ember and locked the deadbolt. Without speaking, we began to push furniture in front of the door and front window, even the upright piano. Whatever Daisy could do, it was enough to earn her a position on a hit squad. If she was going to kill us, she'd have to work for it.

When the last chair had been unceremoniously placed on the pile of furniture, Topher clapped me on the shoulder. "So, did you think that superhero life would be like this?"

Something about Topher's easygoing manner encouraged me to answer honestly. "No. I imagined a lot more thrilling rescues and a lot less hiding."

Topher laughed. "Sometimes I think hiding is all we do, honestly. We hide from the elders. We hide from our leaders. Heck, in cities like Baltimore we even hide from the criminals sometimes. Hide our faces, hide our feelings, hide our real life."

I slid down the wall until I was sitting. He copied me, sitting next to me and relaxing with a long breath.

"Now we wait," I said.

There was a long pause, and then Topher began to twiddle his thumbs. "So...I'm Christopher Cannostraci. I grew up in the Finger Lakes camp in New York. Lovely country up there."

I let my head fall to the side so he could see my sarcastic "really?" expression. "Now? You want to have a heart-to-heart *now*?"

He mirrored my posture. "You got anything better to do?"

"No."

"So, like I was saying, I'm from New York. I guess I pissed off Elder Wiśniewski or something, because I got sent to this armpit city a few years ago. I'm in the game because I have to be. Why the hell are you here?"

Once again, his casual bluntness was disarming. I tilted my head back and stared at the cracked ceiling. "If by 'here' you mean 'a superhero,' then I'm here because the night I shot Berenice, I looked at myself in the mirror and had one of those moments where I hated who I saw. I kind of had a breakdown. A few years later I almost let Jillian die after Beau sliced her neck open, and then I *really* had a breakdown. I ran to a lake and threw in my mask and the rest of my crime crap, and then starting raging against the heavens and all that."

He snorted. "Let me guess, 'I'm evil as hell and I'm not going to take it anymore?'"

There was a beat, and then we were both cracking up. "Yeah," I said between laughs. "Dude, that could be the title of my autobiography." I sighed, happy memories washing over me and easing the ever-present ache in my chest.

"Berenice has built up your relationship with Jill into some kind of crazy forbidden love saga," Topher said, tilting his head in curiosity. "Was it like that?"

"No. I mean, if someone wrote a book about us, the description on the back would probably tout it that way, but in reality we weren't together until I was a proper superhero. My love for her didn't sway me onto the side of the angels."

I ran a hand through my hair as I sifted through the myriad emotions and recollections of the previous summer. "Now that I think about it, my feelings for her weren't even why I joined the team. I just wanted to get away from my family. She was just a bonus." I blinked, taken aback by what I'd just admitted. "Wow. That's really unromantic, isn't it?"

"Meh, the truth's the truth. You didn't want to be a supervillain. I'm hardly one to judge." He jabbed his thumb into his chest. "I've never wanted to be a superhero. I don't want to be a criminal, but if I could walk out that door right-freaking-now, I would."

"What would you do?" I drew up my knees and wrapped my arms around them. I struggled to imagine being like Topher, on the cusp of a new life in which superheroes didn't have a cult over their heads. Why would he leave? What would he do with his incredible powers?

He shrugged. "I don't know what I'd do. Sometimes during patrolling I'd ditch my usual beat and just wander around the city, exploring everything. A few times I even snuck into big lecture halls at JHU and listened in. Maybe I'll explore the planet." He grinned at me, true happiness in his eyes. "I remember the first time I saw a globe. I had no idea the world was so big."

"You could be a travel blog writer. That would be a great angle: ex-superhero goes everywhere and writes about it. You'd have a million readers a day."

His face took on a dreamy, far-away expression. "You think?"

"Heck, yeah. Go to Antarctica first. Being made of metal would make the whole frozen wasteland aspect less burdensome."

He sniggered, then stood and stretched his long arms before helping me to my feet. "Let's do the rounds so we can tell the others we weren't sitting the whole time."

I dusted myself off. A new lightness spread through my body, burning away the fear and horror I'd carried in me for so many hours. I was with someone just like me—born into the wrong family —and we both had futures to fight for. I'd help Topher achieve his pure dream of world travel. He'd help me find my wife. Jillian and I would sit in bed together and read his blog, hand-in-hand.

I walked up the stairwell, my mind swimming with my thoughts. The assurance I'd felt while I packed for our journey nearly a day ago rushed back, like a flash flood in a desert valley. My hope-parched insides sucked in the confidence.

We were going to win.

Jillian was alive. I needed to get to her very soon, of course, but she was alive. Her captors *needed* her alive. I was a healer, and I could undo any injury they'd inflict. Jillian was a superhero, which meant she had a high pain threshold and a "screw you" attitude that would keep her going when others would've caved.

I'd save her, we'd all beat the bad guys, and then we'd go home and fight crime in the new world that Jillian had forged. Every night, we'd have lots of enthusiastic, fantastic sex. We even had Marco's permission to do so.

I turned the doorknob of a small room opposite the master bedroom. The door creaked open, revealing a small home office. The ghostly ambient light from the open window allowed me to see the furnishings. An ancient, scratched mahogany desk bore a laptop, a printer, and photographs of Gabriela's family. Novels and various religious volumes lined the cheap pressboard bookshelf in the corner. A floor lamp stood behind a squishy armchair.

The whole room's cozy civility clashed with the violence of the night. Remembering the rule about open windows, I crossed the small space and hastily jerked the curtain across the rod, plunging myself into almost total darkness. I was halfway to the door when I heard a noise that made me stop mid-step.

A woman had screamed in the distance.

I all but flew down the stairs. Topher was in the living room, inspecting the furniture we'd piled in front of the door. "Did you hear that?" I demanded.

He spun around. "Hear what?"

"That scream," I said, trying not to pant. "I couldn't tell if it was one of our women."

He glanced at the top of the front window, the only part visible behind the furniture. "I didn't hear anything. Let's keep our guard up, though. And I know you'll hate this, but we can't help civilians right now, and it was prob—"

"Stop talking," I whispered, holding a hand up. "Listen."

I focused on the sounds coming from beyond the walls. Shouting, definitely, though quite distant. Crackling, probably of flames. Rumbles of Reid's power.

"What am I supposed to be hearing?" Topher whispered, his face colored with confusion. "I can't hear anything."

"A battle," I whispered back.

The high, sharp sound of glass breaking made me spin around. "Upstairs! Someone's in the house!"

"What did you hear?" he gasped.

"Glass! She broke a window!"

Topher grabbed something from his pocket. In a fraction of a second, he'd become solid metal, his metallic skin glinting ominously in the low light. "Stay behind me." All vestiges of his optimistic former self gone. This wasn't Topher, this was Argentine. I fell in step behind him and grabbed a statue of the Madonna and Child from the mantle over the fireplace, raising it up like a club.

We silently ascended the staircase. When we were nearly at the top, the sound of a single footstep in the small office made me freeze. "She's in the office," I whispered. "The door on the right."

Topher sprinted the final few steps and burst through the door with a marvelous crash. I dashed in after him, statue raised to bash someone's brains out.

Nobody was in the office, though the door had been knocked off its hinges.

I lowered my statue. "I *know* I heard glass breaking and footsteps."

Topher pulled the curtain back. The glass was intact, as untouched as it had been minutes before. He looked over his shoulder at me, his metal face contorted in confusion. "You sure you heard glass breaking? Not wood splintering or something similar?"

"I swear it was glass," I said, holding up three fingers. "Scout's honor."

Topher shut the curtain abruptly, then hurried past me into the hall, turning back into flesh and blood as he did so. "Do you smell that?" He lifted his head like a dog trying to get a lock on a scent. "I can smell better in my normal form, by the way. All my senses are better like this."

I inhaled deeply and closed my eyes, straining to smell anything than the usual hardwood, dust, and vague "cold" smell of an unheated house. I couldn't smell anything, but I heard a new noise. It was faint, but constant. Was it water? No... not water. Something else... something...

Hissing.

"I know the smell. It smells like the stove at our house," he said slowly. "Like when it's turned on but there's no flame."

Hissing.

"It's gas!" I shouted. "Get out!"

We bounded down the stairwell and streaked to the furniture pile. The piano was shoved aside so hard that it fell over with a cacophonous bang. We tossed chairs and end tables across the room, then threw our weight into pushing the couch away from the door. My heart hammered to the tempo my thoughts. *We haven't blown up yet, we're still alive, we're still alive, we haven't blown up yet...*

I reached for the doorknob, then risked an extra second in the house to grab a winter hat from the coat rack by the door.

Topher unbolted the door and threw it open.

There was a brief pause while we braced ourselves against the subfreezing wind, and then two knives sliced through the air, sinking hilt-deep into Topher's eye and neck. He hit the ground with a bone-shuddering thud and didn't move.

I slammed the door shut with a kick and bolted the lock, then picked up Topher's limp hand. *I've healed two knife wounds already. They need to come up with something better.* Come on, man," I said between pants. "Let's go. This is it. Let's kick Daisy's ass."

A second passed, and then another.

And another.

There was no rush of healing energy. No sudden gasping for breath and a groan. His large hand lay still in mine.

Topher was already dead.

ITEM EIGHT

Text from poster advertising the annual county fair, Charles County, MD, dated circa 1906.

COME SEE THE BEAUTIFUL RUBBER WOMAN
SHE CAN FALL THIRTY FEET AND BOUNCE RIGHT BACK UP
BRICKS CAN'T HURT HER
STONES ARE AS NOTHING AT ALL
ADMISSION: ONLY 2 CENTS

8

I grabbed the two knives from their grisly sheaths in Topher's body and staggered backwards into the interior of the living room, away from the corpse and the door.

My boot caught the edge of an area rug and I crashed to the ground. I scrambled to my feet as my brain tried to supply the necessary steps I had to take to ensure my safety, but the panic made now my racing thoughts trip over each other. *Get away... bar the door... call for help... arm yourself...*

A deadly adversary was on the other side of the door. She'd already killed once, and her victim had been a highly competent superhero. I was nothing more than a rangy, unarmed medic with quick feet. What hope did I have? I'd given away my baton. My hand-to-hand skills were, as Marco was fond of pointing out, nonexistent.

The rushing sound in my ears began to drive out all thoughts. I couldn't feel my feet as I stumbled into the dark interior of the first floor, down a short hallway.

Away. I needed to get away. But where? Where could I go that would protect me from an assassin? I groped around, feeling for anything that could help me. All the while, my heart beat so hard that I was half-certain I was about to go into cardiac arrest.

My hand found a cold door knob. I turned it and rushed down the dark wooden stairwell beyond. The door slammed shut at the top of the stairs, casting perfect darkness over me. I tripped over a solid object, falling again onto the damp concrete floor.

After a few seconds of hyperventilating and wondering if I'd just broken my elbows, I calmed down enough to pull out my phone and turn on its flashlight. With my arm raised, I slowly stood up and squinted at my surroundings.

Gabriela's cramped, grimy basement was stuffed to the brim with odds and ends normally found in garages. A tiny lawnmower sat in the corner next to a gas can. Dusty wooden shelves above it bore supplies for her car, such as motor oil and rags. Another shelf carried extra cleaning supplies for the household, including glass cleaner, alcohol, baking soda, and lavender-scented cleaning solution. In the far corner sat stinking trash bags and a blue recycling bin filled with mostly wine bottles. A squat tabletop grill stood next to a small bag of charcoal briquettes, which had a lighter on top of it. In the wall above the grill, about chest level, was a metal plate with a handle. The final item confused me—was it an old decoration? A leftover piece of machinery?

I shook my head to clear my thoughts of ridiculous, pointless questions, then turned off my flashlight and took a deep breath. It was time to face reality like a man.

Chances were, I was going to die in this basement. That was an unavoidable fact. There was an implicit promise woven into the threads and fibers of my tunic: that I would be brave. I was a super-hero, if a pathetic one, and superheroes faced their opponents in battle. They did not run and hide in holes. They did not cower in fear. They held their chin up and looked their enemies in the eye before saying, "Come and get me."

"Come and get me," I whispered through stiff lips. I'd dropped one of the knives in my flight to the basement, but I gripped the remaining one so hard my fingers began to ache. Or was it because of the cold?

There was no light in the basement, so my eyes could not adjust.

All I could do was listen for footsteps above me and feel the various sensations around me. The basement smelled of mildew and dust, but not as much as I would've guessed. And it was freezing, unusually cold for a room that was technically insulated by the surrounding ground and foundation. It was as if someone had opened a window a few inches, but there was none.

I inhaled again. The prickly smell of ice and cold tickled my nostrils—the unmistakable mark of fresh winter air.

There was a connection to the outside somewhere in the basement.

Why hadn't I seen it? I turned on my flashlight and held it up as I slowly turned around in a circle, carefully surveying my surroundings. *Brick wall, brick wall, brick wall...* When my eyes fell on the metal plate in the wall, I froze.

It wasn't a plate. It was a coal chute.

Upstairs, the door crashed to the ground in the living room. Dust fell from the wooden rafters above me and landed on my head and shoulders.

I yanked the handle of the chute door and pulled with all my might. Rusty, ancient hinges creaked in protest as the door opened. A thin metal mesh grill blocked the entrance, but a few good hits with my phone popped it out of its place. I tossed it aside and gauged whether I could fit into the chute. It would be snug, but I'd be able to climb through. I could see the connection to the outside—the chute was only three feet long or so.

Floorboards creaked; Daisy was taking her first hesitant steps into the house. I stiffened, temporarily too tense to breathe—would she go into the basement?

The creaking moved overhead from near the front of the house to where I thought the main stairwell was, then grew fainter. She was walking upstairs.

I hoisted myself into the chute. My stiff fingers fumbled as I tried to remove the mesh grate on the other end, but it finally fell out. After tossing it aside, I awkwardly maneuvered my body into such a position that I could push on the outside chute door, all the while promising any god that would listen my soul and a great deal more if the second door opened just as easily as the first one.

I positioned my shoulder and elbow at the edge. With one burst of effort—

"Yes," I breathed. "Thank you, thank you, *thank* you."

The metal door pushed aside much of the virgin snow which, while heavy, had yet to become compacted and impassable. I opened the door just enough to squeeze my body through, then wiggled out into the snow. Never had lying in snow in the middle of the night felt so good.

I was in Gabriela's dark, postage stamp-sized backyard. Snow fell steadily, but the blizzard was over. In the bluish light I could see that it was fenced, with a gate leading to an alley between townhouse blocks. A cement birdbath a few feet away provided the only decoration. Two windows overlooked the space, a barred one upstairs one I thought might be in the master bedroom, and a small window on the kitchen door. Both were curtained.

For the first time in hours, I was somewhat calm. As I crouched in the corner of the yard, out of sight from either window, I reviewed my options.

The first was easy: run.

Before I could stand and make for the gate, Berenice's sneering summation of my tendency to retreat surfaced in my memories. *I know how well you can run.* No, I could not leave the house with Daisy still at large. I would not. I would make my team proud or die trying.

The second option was more complicated: stay and fight.

But how? What fight could I possibly put up against Daisy? I hadn't even physically seen her and I was already terrified of her. She was armed, she was clever, and I had a growing suspicion that she could make me hear and smell things that weren't there. How else could I explain why *only* I'd heard glass breaking upstairs, a battle, and hissing? Or why Topher had smelled gas, but I hadn't? I had no idea how her power worked, but I knew that I needed to stay away if I wanted to avoid more sensory manipulation.

I scanned the dim yard for anything that would help me decide what to do. When I saw nothing, I dashed to the gate and unlatched it, then shut the gate behind me before running down the alley and around the corner, squeezing through the narrow walkway between Gabriela's house and her neighbor's.

If I was going to sit on my hands, I'd sit on my hands in relative safety. From here, I could see the shadowy street, but nobody could see me.

I crouched at the entrance of the walkway, hidden behind over-grown bushes and several feet of snow. The sleepy quiet of the street confirmed to me that Daisy had somehow made me hear a battle that didn't exist. There was no glow in the sky indicating fire, no smell of smoke or shrill screams. It had been a ruse to lure us out. When that hadn't worked, she'd made us think there was a gas leak.

I grumbled under my breath, calling Daisy a slew of names Jillian probably didn't believe I knew. She thought I was ten times more of a gentleman than I actually was.

Jillian. Just thinking about her brought down a cavalcade of worry and pain. I leaned against the brown stone wall of Gabriela's house and sighed. I hadn't moved forward towards rescuing my wife, just sideways. Right now, "forward" could only be defined as stopping the strike team. But I could not stop Daisy. She'd find me eventually, no doubt tracking me through the basement and out the chute.

She would follow me. I couldn't stop that... but I *could* pick the place where she found me. I stood and ran down the walkway, turning back into the alley. If she was going to follow me, I'd ambush her. One good swipe with my knife and—

I tripped over a recycling bin that had been buried in snow, sprawling spectacularly in soft snow drifts. Cursing, I brushed myself off and glared at the offending bin. A wine bottle poked out of the snow, glinting slightly in the low light.

For one long moment I stared at the bottle, then slowly extended my hand and plucked it out of the snow. A dark idea began to form in my mind.

I closed my eyes and recalled a terrible night only weeks earlier, in Liberty. The Westerners had stormed the tiny settlement and destroyed most of the structures. They'd lit up the night with gunfire and...

"Molotov cocktails," I murmured, images of flaming accelerant and broken glass flicking up the edges of my imagination. Daisy could throw knives, but could she escape flame? I doubted it. Time and time again my team had struggled against fire, the great equalizer. Buck McClintock's team might've been the camps' answer to special ops, but they were as human as the rest of us.

And I knew exactly where to find the ingredients.

In a blur, I was at the entrance of the coal chute, my previous trail through the snow allowing me to run unimpeded this time. Mine were the only tracks. There was no point in worrying whether Daisy was in the basement— she either was and I'd be dead soon, or she wasn't and I'd walk away from this. I wrenched the door open and slid into the chute, landing with finesse on the other side. Daisy wasn't in the basement, so I hastily gathered what I needed.

I grabbed the two largest wine bottles from the bin and tossed them up the chute into the soft snow. Motor oil, rags, alcohol, cleaning solution, and the lighter followed. Finally, I wiggled my way into the backyard for the last time with the gas can in hand, then quietly shut the chute.

With new strength I dragged the cement birdbath in front of the door, ensuring that only someone of at least Jillian's strength could pass through it. When I was certain that I was unobserved, I went to work.

Gasoline was the main accelerant, naturally. Motor oil and cleaning solution would act as solvents that would help the fuel stick to whatever it landed on, like homemade napalm. I shoved the rags into the bottle of alcohol, then removed them when they were soaked. Each bottle got a rag. When I was done, I stood up with my twin creations in hand and approached the back door. If I was going to do this right, I'd have to do it fast.

I lit one of the bombs and hurled it through the small glass window on Gabriela's back door. Glass shattered, and then a tremendous, eerie *whoosh* filled my ears. Flickering yellow and red patterns eked out onto the snow through the broken window.

A breath, a blur—two seconds later, I stood on the stoop and threw the remaining bottle with all my might through the open front door. There was only one track of small footsteps leading from across the street to the door. She was still in the house.

The bottle exploded, casting its liquid inferno all over the pile of furniture, the hardwood floor, and Topher's corpse. My poetic side cheered when I realized that he would get his hero's funeral. That was very important to my new crowd.

Without checking to see if I was being followed, I wended my way through the snow until I was across the street. When I was safely behind a snow mound that was probably a car, I turned to watch my handiwork in action.

Thick, choking smoke poured out of the lower floor, entirely obscuring the living room. There was no way she could go through the front door. A quick survey of the windows made me sigh in relief. Anti-burglar bars covered literally every window on the house, and now that I thought about it, the large upstairs window in the back was also barred. While I looked on, a flashlight's beam lit up an upper window, which I guessed was the small home office.

The curtain was pulled aside, revealing my adversary for the first time.

From what I could see, Daisy was a petite woman with her hair pulled back into a bun. She was unmasked, though her facial features weren't clear at the distance.

She was speaking into a cell phone, though to whom, I couldn't guess. Her agitated, jerky movements as she tried to open the window communicated her panic, which must've only increased when she realized that the window wouldn't open. She disappeared, then reappeared at the adjacent window. The bathroom, probably.

When that window also failed to open—I blessed the unreliability of old window frames—she grabbed an item from inside the bathroom and shattered the glass. She knocked the largest shards aside and pushed on the cat-burglar bars.

I grinned. "Push harder!" I shouted. "Put your back into it!"

She aimed her flashlight at me.

I waved. "What are you waiting for?" I jumped up on the car and held up my arms. "Come and get me!"

She retreated into the interior again and didn't reappear.

A few neighboring doors opened and tired people in their pajamas poked their heads out. An elderly woman in a bathrobe hissed at me from the house behind me. "Boy, what the blazes are you yell—merciful God!" She disappeared into her house again and shouted for someone to call the fire department.

My grin widened. There would be no fire department to save Daisy Guarino tonight. More than three feet of snow covered the roads, and with each passing minute the fire I'd started grew hotter, brighter, and larger. It was only a matter of time before the internal structure collapsed, leaving nothing but a burnt-out shell.

People began to pour out of their houses around the time that smoke began to pour out of the lower windows so thickly that I couldn't see the upper ones anymore. I had to admit that the original architect, whoever he was, had built a sturdy house. Gabriela's century-old masterpiece had been constructed of solid wood and stone. Modern homes, with their pressboard and glue, would've been consumed already.

When the crowd around me had grown to a few dozen people, I jumped off the car and melted into the mass. One boy covered his nose and wailed about the "bad smell," unaware that he was inhaling the scent of burning flesh. Many people were watching in mute horror with their hands over their mouths. Some of them were filming the fire on their phones.

All of them shouted in alarm when the second floor finally collapsed onto the first.

I stepped away unnoticed from the wailing women and cursing men, walking calmly towards another walkway between two houses. When I was out of sight, I ran to the alley, then to Gabriela's gate, which I pushed open.

I couldn't help a fierce whoop of joy.

The birdbath was still in place in front of the chute. The tracks in the yard were the ones I'd left, and nothing more. Daisy was dead. I had finally moved forward.

I let myself fall backward into the snow carpeting the alley, where I resisted the urge to make a snow angel. I wasn't even cold anymore, not really. I was too psyched to feel something as mundane as cold. Instead, I felt only the delicious high of victory and... and...

I sat up, my high gone. I ran a hand through my hair as I processed what had just happened.

I'd just killed my first superhero. And it had been so *easy*.

I stood up and brushed the snow off, then began to walk down the alley towards the main road. Guilt settled in my chest, but I forcefully shoved it aside. I had a job to do.

Besides, the guilt wasn't *bad*, per se. I'd simply killed someone who was trying to kill me. I'd killed before in similar circumstances, not even a month earlier. I hadn't enjoyed shooting the Westerners, but their deaths did not haunt me. Very few people would argue that I hadn't been justified in killing Daisy. The guilt was a sign that I was cognizant of the seriousness of my actions.

I reached the mouth of the alley. I had a good idea where the others were, and now I wanted to help them. I turned left, calculating where Ember and Abby had gone.

As I walked, an amusing thought hit me: if the strike team were *technically* superheroes, did that make us all *technically* supervillains? What did it mean to be a supervillain? And if we were supervillains, did we have the same moral and ethical limitations when we fought our adversaries?

If they were going to hunt me like a monster, should I become one?

ITEM NINE

Letter from Christina St. James to her mother, dated September 15, 1910

Dear Mama,

In your last letter you asked that I update you on the children and their school progress. Eddy has started the sixth grade, though he is behind in his arithmetic because he would rather play baseball with the neighborhood boys than study. Juliana has moved to the fourth grade...Nella remains in the third because of her reading...she mixes up her letters and detests her studies. No amount of stern lectures or strapping seems to help, and I despair of her, since her teachers say she will probably be an imbecile all her life.

Joseph and Mark are studying at home until they can control their abilities. Amelia has not yet shown whether she has the family trait.

I have a tricky situation with my neighbor, Mrs. Esposito. She normally puts out her odious dog, Orso, when I visit, but was too ill to do so yesterday. Orso hates all living things and bit me, but instead of puncturing the skin, he merely gnawed on me until I slapped him and called him a beast. Mrs. Esposito has a telephone and dialed an ambulance because surely my hand was mangled!

I jested that Orso's bark is worse than his bite, then tried to explain my "parlor trick." Now she believes I have a fake hand because of a tragic childhood injury and has asked to meet my hand-maker so her cousin can get a decent fake leg.

Perhaps we should move.

Love,

Christina

9

E mber and Abby weren't hard to find. I followed the route we'd
all planned out earlier until I saw a woman and a tiger in the
distance, about a city block ahead of me. We were downtown, so a
few businesses still had lights, no doubt hooked up to generators
intended to keep refrigerators running, security systems in place, and
similar. The effect was a ghostly blue light everywhere.

I could've mentally hailed Ember, but I wanted to make sure she
was able to use her powers in the search for Buck every second
possible.

When I was in shouting distance, I cupped my hands around my
mouth. "Hey! You two!"

Ember and Abby turned to find who'd shouted. When she saw
me, Ember waved. Abby transformed into a human and waved both
of her skinny arms over her head.

Benjamin! Where's... oh.

Don't tell Abby. I'll tell her myself.

Oh, how horrible.

I jogged through the haphazard trail they'd left behind them, not
sure enough on my feet to try running at my full speed. When I

caught up with them, Ember patted my shoulder. "I'm glad you made it," she murmured.

Abby stood on her tiptoes and craned her neck, a curious little smile on her face, as if she were watching for a delivery she was expecting. After a second, she squinted down the street. "Where Metal?"

Ember looked away.

I held out my hand to Abby and she accepted the invitation, a wisp of concern in her large, blue eyes. "Where Metal, Trent?"

God, she sounded like a small child, all innocence and curiosity. No wonder her team had hated Peter so much for burning her. If she'd been my teammate, I would've ripped the guy's arms off.

I bit my lip. "Daisy tricked us into opening the door. She threw her knives and—"

"Trent heal," Abby interrupted in a steely voice. "Trent *heal* Metal."

"Metal was dead before he hit the floor," I said quietly. "I can only heal someone if they're still alive. It all happened too quickly for me to be of any use. I'm so sorry, Abby."

Abby shoved my hand down and backed away, trembling and shaking her head back and forth. "Metal walk talk joke," she said in a rush. She pressed her fists to her temples and squeezed her eyes shut. "Metal live. Daisy dead."

"Daisy is dead," I assured her, that lone fact providing slight warmth in my chest. "I set the house on fire and trapped her inside. She's dead, and Topher got his pyre."

Abby's response, a disgusted expression in my direction, didn't dampen my happiness over Daisy's death.

Ember stepped up and reached out for Abby. "Let's find Buck and finish this. We need your help."

Abby's anger evaporated, and she seemed to deflate. She batted a tear away, then leaned on Ember's shoulder. Ember stroked her hair as she said, "I know it hurts. I know. I know."

The intimate gesture made me uncomfortable, and I turned away slightly to give them privacy. My thoughts immediately turned to

Buck, wherever he was. Could he also throw knives with deadly accuracy? What about the other strike team members? And why were we still here on the sidewalk when we should be moving forward? Jill wasn't getting any freer. Ember needed to find the strike team and tell us what was going in.

Ember's wispy telepathic voice chided me. *Let her grieve now, for a minute, and then she'll be able to fight.*

Fiery, poisonous fury exploded. I spun around, my hands turned into white-knuckled fists. "We don't have a minute," I hissed. I could feel the blood in my ear tips.

Ember patted Abby and gently pushed her away. She crossed her arms. "I'm getting tired of your mood swings, Ben."

I nearly choked. "*My* mood swings? You're the one who can't decide whether she's psychotically angry at her ex-boyfriend or just *fine*, thank you very much," I said through gritted teeth, making sure to sound as mocking as possible.

Ember turned pink. "I admit that I haven't been the most mature, but I'm already sick of you hopping from happy to furious to nearly catatonic with worry. And—and—yeah, maybe I've got issues, too," she said loudly, stumbling over her words a little. Abby backed up from us, confused. "Every single person in this little drama of ours has problems. We're trying as best we can to work through them, but..." She trailed off, breathing hard and gesturing all around. "Did you forget that Marco's sisters were murdered less than two weeks ago? Or that the rest of us are still trying to come to terms with the whole Westerner... slavery... *thing*?"

I swallowed, uncomfortable with the veracity of what she was saying. It was true that I didn't think Reid and Ember's relationship problems were the most important items to discuss, but even I couldn't ignore that Marco was in unimaginable pain. I didn't know how to address the "Westerner slavery thing," since I'd never liked the elders, and finding out that they'd been involved with something as nefarious as human trafficking hadn't exactly shocked me.

Ember's face was slowly turning from red to white. "And you know what?" she continued, still louder. "Good for you for not being surprised that our elders were selling our brothers and sisters! Wow, Ben! You're so special! What would we do without you on our team?"

"Ember," I said as I held up my hands in surrender. "*This* can wait. Right now I need you to find the strike team. We're getting off track."

Her faced morphed into an inhuman mask of fury. "For the last time, I can't look for the strike team without them *knowing I'm there*!" Her scream made my ears hurt.

"Well, they know you're there *now*!" I shouted back. "Just look into their minds and see what you can get, because the whole damned Baltimore metro area knows you're there!"

"That'll put me in more danger!"

"Who cares? We're all in danger!"

Ember tackled me, sending me flying backwards into the snow with an icy thud. Her small, delicate fists didn't seem so small and delicate now that she was straddling my chest and pummeling my face and neck. Snow collapsed around my face, blinding me to her attack and cutting off most of my air. Her shrieks came through loud and clear, though.

"—betrayed by the people we trusted most, and now we're being hunted like *animals* for daring to tell people about it! Superheroism is crashing down around us and I don't know if my best friend is alive!"

"Ember—!"

"—*your mother* and *your brother* are going to break into my camp and kill *my* parents and *my* brother—"

"Please, stop—"

"—of course you didn't! It's just you, you, *you*!"

I kept trying to shove her off, but without being able to see or easily breathe, I couldn't coordinate my hands enough to get her off me. *Ember, please, stop, please, we can talk...*

Ember's presence, and her disgust, overwhelmed my mind as she grabbed my neck and pulled my head out of the snow. My vision cascaded into being, but I was no longer on a frozen Baltimore sidewalk.

I was no longer me.

Rough hands shove me to the hard floor, and Patrick's face hovers above mine. His hatred and loathing of Jillian, me, and life itself flow into my body. "Where is she?" he demands, his nails digging into my skin through my blouse.

If I answer, Jillian will die. This maniac will kill her without hesitation.

"No," I whimper. "I'm not telling you."

His fingers tighten around my collar and his intention overwhelms my mind. I have to betray my friend or I'll die. I will not survive his sick attack. Reid will come home and find my destroyed corpse on the floor.

"Ember, stop," I gasped. "Please, stop. I don't want to see—"

I jog to keep up with Jillian, who walks down the sidewalk like she owns it. She does own it. She owns the whole city, marching through the darkest parts without so much as a backward glance to see if the group of rough-looking men on the corner are watching us.

I trip over a curb and she catches me with a laugh, thinking that if I'd hit the ground, I'd break.

I think she is a superhero. I think I am a liability.

Ember fell backwards, clutching her head. "God, stop," she moaned. "Make it stop."

Abby knelt next to her and put her arm around her shoulder. I held out a trembling hand to Ember, but already my vision was swimming again.

I'm standing in the cold, barren kitchen of a cold, barren house. This whole town is cold and barren, devoid of anything but fury, hate, and grief.

Though I can no longer hear the thoughts of my teammates, their inner turmoil is displayed for all to see in every shouted insult, every slammed door, and every bullet fired from their wretched firearms. We're not soldiers. We're not.

I turn and face the man behind me. The sharp wrath in his eyes makes him unrecognizable. He is not my teammate. He is not my friend. And he is certainly not the man who loves me. I don't know who this killer is, and I'm frightened.

I put my head between my knees, the sheer wave of emotion in her memories too much for my stomach. My abdominal muscles clenched, and then I was on all fours and throwing up. My pounding head protested at having two psyches battling for dominance, twisting like snakes inside my skull.

Blood pours down Jillian's face. She is too weak to stem the flow of blood, so I hold my hand to her wounds. The blood drips between my fingers and down my wrist. Her words are faint, and I strain to hear her.

All at once, her worries for my safety are drowned out by images of me strapped down to a metal table and screaming, my back arching as I fight against my bonds. Beau Trent's imagination sucks me under as he fantasizes about how much he'll enjoy torturing me. Through it all, there is the promise of untold wealth for him if he can simply make me use my powers to find the JM-104.

Ember's roiling, choking fear mixed with my own confusion. I collapsed onto my back, my chest heaving. Silver specks floated in my vision.

"I'm sorry," she whimpered. "I have trouble controlling projection when I'm upset."

"The hell was that?" I groaned, sitting up.

Abby was standing knock-kneed in the snow, nibbling on one of her fingers and watching us with trepidation. I couldn't imagine how bizarre the scene had just been to her. Had she been close enough to catch some of Ember's telepathic projections?

"Scary," she whimpered. "Little Reuben scary. Big Trent scary. Yellow hair man scary. Want hide, Trent."

Well, that answered my question. *Poor Abby.*

"Nothing. That was nothing," Ember said. She sniffed and added, "Don't worry about it. Abby, please forget what you saw."

After I'd stood and brushed off my tunic and pants, I took a steadying breath. "I've promised Reid that after this is all over, he and I would talk. How about we have a talk, too?"

Ember was silent for several seconds. "Fine," she said. "I'm sorry for jumping you."

"I forgive you, but that's the first thing we're going to talk about." Namely, just what was going on in her head? "But moving on... any luck finding, uh, people who need help?" I asked, referencing their cover story.

"No," Ember muttered. "For the last time, I'm trying not to scan too much. My presence is easier to detect the more times a person feels it. This whole stupid cover story depends on them believing that we don't know they're here."

A light breeze began to blow, causing the edges of Ember's bobbed hair to flutter below the edge of her winter hat. Abby whipped around. "Sun!" She raised her nose into the air. "Sun and Little Reuben and Artemis. Artemis sleep?"

In the distance, barely visible, two men approached in the middle of the road, leaning on a floating platform. The shorter one limped heavily. Laying on the platform was a still figure.

Abby gasped. "Tiger!" She transformed and bounded away through the snow.

Ember and I exchanged a sad glance and began to walk towards our friends.

We all met in the center of the silent road and halted. Blood poured from a wound on Marco's chest, staining his purple tunic and khaki pants. Rips in his clothes revealed several sets of deep gouges in parallel lines, reminiscent of fingers. Reid's left eye was swollen shut.

Berenice was the worst of all. Her entire uniform was blood-stained and shredded, revealing her fleece winter undergarments and bulletproof vest. Her face, once beautiful, was barely recognizable— smears of blood mixed with ripped skin and shattered bones to create a horrific picture of recent violence.

Abby laid her furry head on the platform while Ember and Reid stared at each other in sad silence. Ember slowly raised her hand to him, but lowered it after a second and turned her attention to Berenice.

"Berenice first," Marco gasped when I reached for his face. I obeyed, and instead laid my hand on Berenice's ruined cheek, cradling it gently without consciously deciding to do so. Sticky blood and torn flesh between my fingers caused my skin to crawl, but I did not remove my hand immediately, as she probably would've wanted me to. Only when her wounds had completely faded did I repeat the gesture on Reid and Marco. They both sighed.

Reid gestured for us to follow him into the mouth of an alleyway. When we were hidden, he directed the platform with the still-unconscious Berenice to the ground, then leaned against the brick wall of the adjacent building, his head bowed. "Well, *that* wasn't easy."

Ember kneeled down and laid Berenice's head in her lap. "I'm going to direct Berenice into consciousness again. I don't think her mind knows she's healed. Abby, lay next to her so she can feel your body heat."

When the women were situated, I turned to Marco and Reid. "Kyle's dead?"

Marco nodded, a massive shudder running through him. "I really thought the fight would be easy because there were three of us." He laughed without humor. "I'm an idiot."

"How'd you lose to a guy made of rock if you had Reid with you?" I asked, my tone accidentally sounding more judgmental than I meant it to.

Instead of lashing out, Marco slid down the wall and huddled like a small child. "Ember, can you show him?"

Ember nodded. "Ben, get ready."

For the second time in thirty minutes, I became someone else.

"THIS IS DUMB," Berenice muttered. "What kinda imbecile would actually believe that we're out here collecting freaking firewood at the freaking witching hour in freaking Baltimore?"

"Lady, do us a favor and shut up," I replied, never pausing in my constant search for Kyle.

The last time I'd seen him, he'd been a rangy teenager with sallow skin and zits who'd chased every available skirt in camp, and quite a few skirts that weren't available. However, if he'd worked his way onto a strike team, I'd have to rid myself of any assumptions. Kyle was a killer.

Eh, but so was I. And there were three of us.

Berenice started muttering inaudibly. I rolled my eyes and scanned the upper windows of an apartment building.

The chapping wind cut through my clothes, prickling my skin uncomfortably. Yet, I wasn't nearly as cold as Reid and Berenice, thanks to my inner battery which kept me at a toasty 109.3 when I was at full power.

Reid had huffily refused my outer jacket a few minutes before, informing me that *he* was from Idaho, and they knew how to handle cold—unlike us Georgia heroes. Obviously the subfreezing temperatures had addled his brains even more than Ember's unceremonious dumping of him had, making him forget that he'd nearly frozen to death right along with us Dixie losers in Wyoming.

"We're taking a break and getting out of the wind," Reid said, clearly trying to keep his teeth from chattering. "Berenice, you need to warm up."

We stepped behind a shuttered taco truck parked in a driveway. A huge shiver ripped down his spine.

Oh, yeah, sure, Berenice is the cold one. I inched closer to him, hoping my natural warmth would radiate off me and warm him up a bit. He wasn't allowed to die until he'd apologized for being such a jerk for the last two weeks.

And neither was Jill. She was going to stay alive until she'd apologized for getting married without inviting us to watch. I had very few sisters left, and like hell was she getting away with that.

As Jill's name passed through my mind, energy began to zero in from around the edges of my eyes. I blinked quickly, pulling it away and back into my core.

Man, my control was pathetic these days—it was like being six again. Six, and at combatives training. I'd been bumped up into a higher class because of my natural proficiency. The older kids had tried to tease me for being roughly two feet tall, but my random bursts of literally-fiery temper had ended *that* on the third day. The one kid who'd persisted had had his front teeth knocked out by eight-year-old Jillian Johnson.

I closed my eyes to stop the energy from seeping in again. She'd make fun of me if she could see how worn thin I was. I needed to hear her tease me again... just once.

We'd rescue her, and she'd shrug off whatever the Trents had done, and she'd throw her arms around me and tell me that I should've been in charge of these yahoos, and that I should've been there to hear this really amazing comeback she'd had for Beau, and that I was her little brother and she'd help me get revenge for my sisters and she really wasn't that hurt anyway and she was going to give up fighting next week and run away with Benjamin and have ten kids and live until she was ninety and I hadn't run away after the tribunal and I hadn't said what I said in Liberty and I hadn't given her such a hard time about everything when she was clearly hurting...

"Dude, what's wrong with your eyes?" Berenice's grating voice cut through the onslaught. "Are you practicing Morse code or something?"

"Let's go," I said. "You're not shivering as much, and Reid's not cold, right?"

He threw me an ugly look, but I just trudged back out into the road without waiting for their answers. My frozen boots weighed a million pounds each. I could no longer lift each foot up over the snow. Instead, I had to push through it with painful lurches, because I didn't dare risk using even an ounce of heat lest Kyle—

I flew into a snowbank, my back slamming against a hidden fire hydrant. I threw my hands up, barely able to block the huge stone hands that flew at my face. I ducked, but then I was hoisted by my collar and thrown several feet.

I hadn't had time to gasp.

There was no fighting him. Kyle was a whirlwind of stone and pain, everywhere at once. As soon as I put up my hand to blast him, he'd moved, and fingers had raked through my clothes and into my skin. In the dark I couldn't even make out his features, statue-like as they were.

Reid's strangled battle yell was cut off as he was picked up and thrown into the side of a car.

Kyle, standing well over six feet tall, marched easily through the snow towards me. How quickly had he attacked us? Only a minute before I'd been in the alley.

He grabbed the side of my head and made a fist. He was going to bash my brains in.

A high, terrifying scream of fury from behind him made him pause and drop me.

Berenice flew out of the darkness and tackled him, her face distorted with rage and effort. She straddled him and unleashed a volley of punches, tiny drops of blood spraying everywhere after each hit. She didn't seem to notice.

"I'll... I'll get him..." I whispered, raising a shaking hand towards the fray. If I emptied all my heat on him, I'd kill him.

But quicker than I could blink, Kyle kicked her off and began his own beat down.

Fury turned to terror as Berenice tried and failed to block two enormous stone fists pounding into her face and torso again and again. Her cries morphed into squeaks with each wet crunch from her ribs.

When she was finally still in the snow, Kyle broke for breath. Over by the car, Reid stirred and looked up.

Thousands of degrees of heat surged out of my arm and through Kyle's, melting his appendage into lava, which dripped on the snow with loud hisses. It was a terrible shot; I'd aimed for his chest.

He grasped his shoulder and fell backwards in silent agony. There was a low, rocky rumble, and then Kyle opened his mouth in a silent scream. He seemingly fell apart at his joints, like a huge invisible child was pulling him to pieces.

Reid was struggling to his knees, his hand extended towards what was left of Kyle. The last of the whiteness faded from his eyes. "We... we need to go..." he said, gasping for breath. "I'll make a stretcher for her."

I SURFACED into my own mind and awareness with a gasp.

Reid and Marco were huddled around Berenice, who had woken up and propped herself on her elbows. Abby was enthusiastically licking the blood off her face. Berenice let her head fall to the side so she could look at me. "Looking pale, Trent," she drawled. "You gonna hurl?"

"Your face was *dented*!" Indeed, if there were anything in my stomach, it would've been in danger of expulsion. Marco's memories had been so vivid.

She touched her cheeks, which were still being licked. "Yes, it was, wasn't it," she said faintly. "I suppose it was upsetting to see." She frowned a little bit, the familiar wrinkle appearing between her eyes. "Thank you for healing me."

"No problem." I couldn't say "you're welcome"—her gratitude freaked me out, though I couldn't say why.

Ember helped Berenice to her feet. When she was stable, she looked down at her ruined uniform and let out a long breath. She reached through a large rip and snapped the waistband of her long underwear. "Well, I guess Baltimore is getting a show tonight."

"They already did," I said quietly. "Daisy attacked Gabriela's house not long after you left. I burned it down and killed her."

"Wow," Marco said. "I wish I could've seen that. I bet... hey, where's Topher?"

Instead of answering him, I met Berenice's gaze and shook my head. "I'm sorry. It was the knives. I couldn't save him in time."

Berenice's eyes widened and filled with tears, but she quickly shook her head. "Was he... did he suffer? No, I don't want to know. She's dead. That's all that matters."

"It was instantaneous. And she's dead, unless she can survive a burning building falling on her. Two down, two to go." I turned to Reid. "What's your call?"

I was eager to move the conversation along, to move forward towards Jillian and away from talk of Topher, lest Berenice dwell too long and decide to blame me for her friend's death.

Reid turned to Ember. "Do you have any idea where Buck is?"

"No," she said with a little sigh. "I'll scan again." She closed her eyes, then jerked them open. "He's really close, just two streets over, but he's not thinking about us. He's heading back to Gabriela's. Daisy was on the phone with him when the house collapsed." She frowned. "Ouch. He's a little messed up about it."

"Let's jump him," Marco growled. "We'll converge from all sides. He'll never know what's coming. It sounds like he's emotionally compromised right now, so he might be easier to kill than Kyle."

"I agree," Reid said. "That's what we'll do. I'll fly us there, making sure to avoid his line of sight, and we'll situate ourselves around the street, covering all points of entry. When we've got eyes-on, we'll attack. Then we'll go find Rube and Lark."

"And then we'll go to Annapolis," I said, barely believing what I was saying. Could it be so simple?

Were we really so close to defeating the team that couldn't be defeated?

ITEM TEN

Translation of coded letter sent by anonymous Mexican spy to revolutionary forces of the Mexican Revolution, January 28, 1911.

To the boss:

I am returning to Sonora following my failure to recruit the Navajo man to our cause. Francisco did not exaggerate his abilities, but contrary to his report, the man, Bidziil, is not sympathetic to the revolution. He would not agree to fight with us, nor even leave the reservation to speak to the other men. When I tried to argue with him, his eyes glowed as the moon does glow and I was chased out of the land by a storm cloud that nearly drowned me twice.

10

The throng of people in front of Gabriela's destroyed home had only grown in the hour since it had collapsed. Two firetrucks had pushed through the snow and parked in front of the smoldering building, which thankfully hadn't spread its flames to the neighbors. Firemen sprayed their long fountains of water through the windows, causing steam to rise up with loud hisses.

Now that I wasn't in fight-or-flight mode, I took a moment to appreciate the enormity of my actions tonight: I'd destroyed Gabriela's home. She was an orphan; likely everything she had to remind her of her parents had gone up in smoke. I'd gotten the impression from Jillian's report of her life that she was a responsible, circumspect businesswoman who would certainly have insurance, but still... I owed her. I'd make it up to Gabriela somehow. Someday. She would not endure penury because of me.

We were all on a rooftop across the street, watching the tragedy unfold from behind the roof access. Nobody on the street would be able to see us from their angle. As it was, the crowd was too interested in the fire to look up and behind them. More helpfully, the emergency flood lights for the firemen between us and them washed us out while illuminating the scene below. If anyone were to look back, all they'd see would be blinding light bulbs.

"Where's Buck?" Reid asked. "There's gotta be a hundred people down there."

"He's in the center of the crowd," Ember said. "But he knows a telepath is nearby and he's ready for us to strike."

"We need to separate him from the civilians," Berenice said, rubbing her chin. "If Emily was willing to stab Jen, then we have to assume that Buck will also resort to similar measures. This could get messy."

"Tiger hunt kill Buck," Abby suggested with a little shrug from behind Berenice. She'd refused to leave her side since Berenice had woken up.

"That still doesn't fix the civilian problem," I said. "You could charge him, but what's stopping him from grabbing a kid?"

I squinted at one of the firemen, who was hurrying out of the front door and back to his truck. Several people oriented their bodies towards him as he moved.

I pointed. "Marco, could you set another fire down the block? Maybe a large tree? The firemen will follow the fire, and the people will follow the firemen. Buck'll probably stay to look for Daisy."

Marco let out a huge sigh. "I have zip heat left from blasting Kyle. Only light. After I use that, I have to wait for the sun to come up."

Two of the firemen emerged from the front door, each carrying a blackened, desiccated corpse in his arms. One corpse was significantly larger than the other. "Baltimore team, look away," I ordered, my throat tight. "You don't need to see this."

Instead of listening to me, Berenice and Abby kneeled and placed their right hands over their hearts. I'd never seen the gesture from my teammates. I turned to ask Reid if it was a camp custom, only to see that Reid, Marco, and Ember had also placed their hands on their hearts, though they remained standing. Reid whispered inaudibly—a prayer, perhaps, or the camp's secular equivalent.

Sometimes I could see little difference between superheroes and warriors in old ballads.

"Metal cover," Abby whimpered. "Metal body naked. Bad honor." Her lip trembled. "Metal cold in snow."

She and Berenice stood up. "We can't right now," Berenice said, patting her shoulder. "Don't worry, girl, the firemen will cover the bodies. Look, they're already laying them down. They'll bring out the white sheets soon." She kissed Abby's forehead, reminiscent of an older sister and her baby sister. "Topher's not cold. Trust me."

I could not bring myself to chastise them for their off-topic discussion. Topher's life had mattered and the feelings of his closest friends mattered still—and I really didn't want to endure a beating from Berenice like the one I'd gotten during Ember's attack. Instead, I watched the crowd, which had moved back a few feet to give the bodies wide berth.

Only one man, tall and muscular, moved forward, pushing and shoving people out of the way in his haste to get to the front of the mob. The people began to jump aside for him, allowing him to pop out into the little clearing just as the firemen were covering the corpses.

Buck McClintock collapsed to his knees and began to sob when he saw Daisy's small, charred body. He pressed his forehead to the ground, his overwhelming grief palpable even at our distance. An old woman in a shawl tried to comfort him, but he refused her efforts, forcibly pushing her arm away. He reached out his hand towards Daisy's remains, then doubled over again, too overcome to do anything but mourn.

Reid and Marco joined me at the edge, flanking either side of me. Reid sighed. "Maybe they were lovers. That would explain his bizarre decision to leave his post."

"Or maybe they weren't, and it's just really upsetting to see the burned body of a teammate," Marco said, an edge in his words. He glared at Reid. "Remember after the tribunal? And honestly, if you called me and said you couldn't get out of a burning building, I'd run over to help you, too. Not every story is a tragic romance."

Reid's reply was lost to me. Something he'd said glued itself into my brain and danced in little patterns: *That would explain his bizarre decision to leave his post.*

Now that I thought about it, why *had* he left his post?

Buck McClintock was the leader of a strike team. Every account I'd heard indicated that the strike teams were the SEALs of the camps. Emily had nearly killed Reid and me. Daisy had certainly been an effective killer and a clever foe. Kyle, from the sound of it, had nearly bested three superheroes in the space of three minutes. They'd tricked, they'd blitzed, and they *should* have won.

In all cases, it was only the presence of my team that had tipped the scales, a presence that Buck's team hadn't counted on or properly prepared for.

I'd saved Reid from Emily, and then he'd saved me. I wasn't supposed to be in the house with Topher. Marco and Reid weren't supposed to be with Berenice. The strike team, as fearsome as they were, had not been designed to take on two superhero teams at once. I wasn't sure, but their training probably mandated some kind of waiting, or surveillance period, or *something*. Common sense dictated pulling back and regrouping.

So why had Buck come out of his hiding place and gone to the one place we were guaranteed to be? He was alone and...

Afraid.

Buck McClintock was no longer operating on orders or good sense. He was operating on fear. The more I thought about it, the more I realized that in all my imaginations of the dreaded strike team, I'd neglected to consider that each and every one of them was a human being—and I knew from the vantage point of an intimate eyewitness what happened when a team leader let fear chip away at his—*her*—ability to command.

He was afraid of losing a battle against impossible odds. He was terrified of losing his teammates and friends. He was terrified of the two rogue teams that, it appeared, had turned their backs on good and embraced evil. His team had walked into a blizzard and discovered that their enemy had doubled in strength and size. He had many reasons to be afraid.

Ember sneezed. I glanced at her uncertain, taught features, the situation crashing down on me.

Buck's fears ran so much deeper than the events of the night. He had fears that were eating at him like worms in moldering corpse—fears of rumors swirling among the camps that the elders were not the paragons of virtue they'd always suspected. Fears of my mother and her cronies attacking in the night and butchering children. Fears of everything he knew and loved being built on a lie.

I would've left my post, too.

"Abby," I said, a plan forming in my mind. "How would you like to go down there and pay your respects?"

I COULD BARELY SEE Abby as she crept through the snow, which had been beaten down by firetrucks and people until it was a hard, icy track. I stood behind the corner of a building half a block away. The others were in strategic positions around the intersection, hidden behind various items.

The plan was the best we could come up with given the circumstances, the most problematic being that Reuben and Lark weren't with us, nor did we know where they were. After that, it was simply the fact that we didn't know what to expect from Buck, grieving and dangerous as he was. We could only set up the trap and hope he took the big, tiger-y bait.

Abby, in all her majestic feline glory, disappeared into the crowd. I had to hand it to Baltimoreans; they'd gotten used to a tiger super-hero, a feat I wouldn't have imagined of them. There were no gunshots or shouts of alarm, just a general cry of surprise as she parted the crowd and lumbered towards Topher's covered body. One small child even tried to jump on her for a ride, but she gently batted him away and shook her head.

If all went as planned, she'd morph back into a human and tell the first responders that it was her teammate that had died. Buck would see her and follow her right into our midst. What happened depended on the skill of the people around me.

Minutes ticked by. I could no longer see Abby in the crowd, which had converged again, concealing the bodies and the two chief mourners. Buck had to have seen her by now, and though I was worried for Abby's safety, I doubted he would strike right there. He'd wait and follow, hopefully too overcome to think clearly.

While I waited for Abby to appear, I recalled Reid's reaction upon seeing a Sentinel carry in the bloodied, still form of Ember after the Westerners had attacked Liberty.

All heads had turned as he'd let out a scream of torment and fallen to his knees, his own injuries forgotten. He'd made a wild grab for someone's sidearm, only to be tackled by Marco. "Later. Later," Marco had soothed, his own eyes bright with sorrow. "Calm down now so you can kill them later."

It had taken me several full minutes to assure Reid that Ember was actually alive. He'd been literally too distraught to comprehend the information, linear as it was: Ember was injured but not dead, I could heal her, she'd be fine.

Not that I could judge him. Immediately following his emotional unraveling, I'd witnessed Dean kiss Jillian in a way that indicated they'd kissed before, so easy and familiar. Her body language—*get away*—had been lost on me. All I'd been able to see was my world, already fractured, crumbling into nothing as my worst nightmare came to life in front of my eyes. In my distress, I'd later lashed out at Jillian and ordered her to stay away from me unless she was dying. I'd forgotten the angry dismissal almost as soon as it had left my mouth.

I was quite sure that that one cruel statement had tipped her over the edge into suicidal ideation, and I would never forgive myself for it.

I closed my eyes and breathed, orienting my thoughts on the present.

Now, hopefully, Buck would join the long line of hot messes and make a very stupid mistake.

Just when I was about to suggest that Ember contact Abby, the crowd parted and let her pass through. Abby's furry head was bowed in sadness, her tail limp behind her as she walked through the snow towards our location. I moved back a little, making sure that I was not immediately visible. She crept forward, her sadness clear to everyone.

Buck broke through the crowd and followed on the sidewalk, many yards behind. He never took his eyes off the tiger ahead of him.

On the other side of the street, Ember made an obvious "what the hell?" gesture. *Idiot. He's not even trying to be stealthy. He wants to kill her, revenge for Daisy, blah blah blah. Not even considering that we're here. He senses me but...he just...doesn't give a crap. Wow.*

Ember's disgusted summation swam around my head. He really *wasn't* thinking clearly. As if to underline the point, Buck walked under the large tree in which Marco was sitting, completely oblivious to the grown man sitting among snow-covered boughs just eight feet above him.

When Abby was in the middle of the intersection, she paused and turned around as if she'd just sensed that she had a follower. Her whole body stiffened, and she growled—a horrifying snarl that made my hair stand on end.

"Calhoun!" Buck shouted, grabbing a knife from his belt.

Abby morphed back into a human with the same sucking sound as before. She stood, a wicked grin stretching her thin face. "McClintock!" she yelled back.

The word was still in the air when she swayed and fell butt-first into the snow, no doubt under Buck's power.

"Wipe that smile off your face," Buck ordered. He marched into the snowy road, trembling with fury. "You know why I'm here, don't you? It was *you*, you disgusting, retarded waste of—"

"Turn around." Marco's voice cut through the crisp night air like a razor.

Buck turned around. I closed my eyes.

My eyelids couldn't fully block Marco's flash. White-yellow illumination leaked through into my eyeballs, causing me to drop to my knees and cover my eyes with my hands.

Buck yelled in alarm and cursed, but unless he had the prescience to also cover his eyes, he was blind until I decided he wasn't going to be—which was never.

"You can come out now," Marco called, again with the unusual cutting tone that made his voice sound like someone else's. "He's down." Wispy tendrils of pure energy evaporated from his eyes and hands, gradually dimming until they winked out of existence. In their absence, Marco seemed smaller, somehow. As soon as the last bit of light faded, he began to shiver.

All of us emerged from our loose hiding places around the intersection: inside alleyways, on the other side of a car, and from behind trash cans. We began to converge around Buck, who was kneeling in the snow with his hands over his eyes.

Abby jumped to her feet and twirled in the snow, her long hair fanning out around her as she did so. She came to a stop a few feet in front of Buck. "Buck Buck eyeball *sizzle*," she sang, adding a ridiculous amount of flair to the last word.

Reid turned his laugh into throat-clearing.

Buck uncovered his eyes. I was close enough to see the damage: unfocused, slightly reddened, and completely useless. Though his eyes darted around as we approached, he could not see us. If he had, he surely would've pulled a knife on me as I approached from behind. *Well, Mom always did say not to stare at the sun.*

Instead, I lunged forward and grabbed his spare knives from their sheaths. He cried out and turned around. "Which one are you?"

"I'm the one who was with Topher when Daisy killed him for *nothing*," I hissed. "I'm the one who trapped her in the house and watched it fall on her." I ripped off my gloves and so I could get a tighter grip on my new knives. "And if I'm the one whose wife is dead because I had to waste time with your punkass team, then I'll do what my mom did in Chattahoochee," I said, lowering my voice to a whisper as I leaned close to him, "and break into your camp and kill everyone."

My empty threat had the desired effect. Buck's mouth fell open as he stared where my voice placed me, but he said nothing, likely too horrified to speak.

Marco, a few feet to my right, mouthed angrily at me. I caught his eye and rolled my own before mouthing, *dude, I'm lying.*

He crossed his arms and leaned against a snow-covered car, his face a furious grimace directed at me instead of Buck. I'd have to apologize for my insensitive threat later.

Reid stepped forward. "It's over, McClintock." He pointed to one of my new knives. "You up for it?"

I stared at the long blade, then looked at Buck on the ground. "Um..."

Berenice, who'd been watching from my left, gestured to an apartment window above us. "Not here. Civilians are watching, and they won't care about the 'why' of killing this piece of garbage."

I couldn't help my weak smile of gratitude to Berenice. She gave me a confused look, her eyebrows pulling together as they so often did when I was in her presence.

"Let's take him to the alley," Ember said, pointing to the opening between two large buildings. "No windows. We can make it quick and painless. I'll put him in a trance so he doesn't have to feel a thing." Typical Ember.

"Oh, please, let him feel some pain," Berenice muttered.

"Listen to you all," Buck said, laughing breathily. "You can murder Peter St. James in the broad daylight, but you don't have the stomach to kill me in the night. You're pathetic."

"Peter burn Gabby," Abby shot back. "Gabby civilian. Gabby innocent. Peter guilty, no Gabby."

I could almost see the question marks appear above Buck's head. "That's... what?"

"Peter attacked a civilian named Gabriela, dumbass," Berenice said. "Lark, Topher, and I tried to stop him, and got our faces burned off for our effort. He was about to kill us for daring to stand up to him when Tiger killed him for, you know, breaking the law and being a public menace."

"You're lying," Buck said quickly. "Eli—I mean, all the elders told me—"

"Oh, I'm sorry, do you mean the elders, who said Mercury was dead, told you we deserved to die?" Berenice retorted. "Mercury, who's standing three feet from you? The same elders who decided that a man should be *flogged and branded* because he got married on his own terms? The same elders who ordered the Saint Catherine team to die even after they'd been formally pardoned for their supposed crimes? Buck, you're nothing more than a trained dog."

Buck straightened, though he was still on his knees and unable to focus on anything. "I'm the son of Elder McClintock, and as such, I'm beyond reproach," he said evenly. "And unlike you, I'm following orders. You're the dogs. You have no right to kill me. Daisy had every right to kill Christopher."

Berenice launched herself at Buck.

There was a puff of air, and Lark appeared, her staff extended. She whacked Berenice in the chest, sending her backwards out of sheer surprise. "Now, Reuben!"

Slowly, mesmerizingly, black smoke appeared around Buck's wrists, forming handcuffs that appeared to be made of strange, almost effervescent obsidian.

I spun around. In the distance, Reuben approached on a smoky walkway above the snow, his path materializing under his feet as he walked. He dragged a beaten, surly Emily alongside him. Black orbs enclosed her hands, effectively preventing her from sickening us or grabbing a weapon.

Were my teammates and enemies not present, I would've shed tears of shock and wonder.

His powers had returned two months before they were supposed to. For the first time in twenty-four hours, I began to believe that Jillian truly had a chance.

ITEM ELEVEN

Excerpt of an article from the *Des Moines Register and Leader*, dated August 8, 1912.

MAN FOUND GUILTY OF DOUBLE MURDER

Prominent local merchant Henry A. Gilchrist was led away after a jury condemned him to death for the brutal slayings of his wife and five-year-old son, whose mutilated bodies were found in the Des Moines River last fall. When asked why he committed the heinous crimes, Mr. Gilchrist said, "They were witches. The woman could speak to rabbits and the boy could turn into a butterfly." Mr. Gilchrist, who did not have legal representation, refused to admit to insanity.

11

R euben shoved Emily to her knees next to Buck. "Cross your ankles. Buck, you too."

To my shock, they complied, though awkwardly.

Reuben turned to me. "Questions later."

I nodded quickly, still trembling from surprise and joy. His powers had fully returned two months before they were supposed to. How? When? Were Jillian's back? Had she already escaped? What was going on?

The urge to cut and run for Annapolis was all-consuming. I had to force myself to recite Berenice's cutting remark again. *No running. Just stay put for a little while longer.*

Once again, Reuben took control of the situation by merely being there. He stood head and shoulders above most of us, shoulders back, jaw squared. After him, Lark stood the most imposing, completely unscathed, grimly confident, and armed with a staff I still feared. She turned her back to our foes, instead surveying the rest of us with steely eyes, practically daring everyone there to attack.

None, not even Berenice and Abby, protested. The former had scrambled backwards on her elbows after being thwacked with the staff. Abby hung around Ember's elbow, her mouth open the whole time.

Reuben and Lark were the mountains. We were all just howling storms.

Reuben took a knee in front of Buck, his face impassive. He glanced around until he caught Ember's eye. Ember nodded once. Reuben turned back to Buck. "Kyle and Daisy are dead, Buck. It's time to call it quits."

Buck grit his teeth. "Raphael will—"

"We both know that my younger brother isn't here," Reuben replied, a hint of humor lacing his words. "And even if he were, he wouldn't fight two of his brothers. He has both enough familial loyalty and common sense to know that would be a foolish decision."

Buck's dead eyes grew round. "Did he tell you we were coming?"

Odd—his ferocity had turned to wounded disbelief. Had he been so sure of Raphael's fidelity that he hadn't *once* considered that the third Fischer brother would forewarn the other two?

"No," Reuben said calmly. "This is all a happy coincidence. Emily here tipped us off that the strike team was in town, so thank you, Emily."

I liked Reuben even more now. He could've crowed that Buck had been betrayed by his teammate, like I would've. Compassion could've been the only root for his choice, since there wasn't any strategic reason for protecting Raphael from Buck's wrath. The strike team commander probably only had a few more minutes to be mad about losing.

Emily bowed her head. "I'm sorry, Buck," she whimpered.

Buck smiled sadly in her direction. "I'm not mad at you anymore. I know you used your best judgement."

Once again, the emotion in his response threw me for a loop. That had been almost decent of him. I was much more comfortable imagining Buck as either a carbon copy of James, his racist younger brother, or another version of Patrick. A sensitive guy who cared for his teammates didn't match either picture, and it bugged me.

Reuben drummed his fingers on his knee. "You've put us in a difficult position."

Buck scowled again. "Just kill us, traitor."

Reuben raised his eyebrows. "The elders are the traitors. They failed to protect Emily's sister from the Westerners. I would've thought that you'd be less willing to work for them since finding that out."

"Don't you dare lecture us!" Emily shouted. "You married a civilian!"

"I married the woman I love," Reuben replied, still level. "Perhaps I broke our rules, but what did Gabriela do to deserve death?"

There was a dark silence.

Finally, Buck said, "It's cruel to draw this out, Fischer. They said you were a decisive combatant. Just...just do it. Please. We're down."

Reuben stood and brushed the snow off his pants, then held out a hand to me. "You're right, this has dragged on too long. Mercury, come here, please. You need to do this."

All eyes waited for me to kill my second and third superheroes.

Ember inserted herself in my brain. *It's going to be okay, Benjamin.* She spoke as though she were coaxing a child into the doctor's office for a vaccine.

Please get out of my head.

Reuben wants—

Out. Please.

Ember retreated, and in the corner of my eye I could see her pout.

My brain commanded my legs to move, but my feet would not obey. Nausea twisted in my stomach. Now that it came to it, why couldn't I hand him the tools of execution? I'd done it so many times before when I'd executed the dying victims of my family. Buck and Emily had preyed on us and hindered our mission. They were dangerous beyond the telling of it. They needed to die so that others could live.

So why couldn't I go to Reuben?

"Mercury," Reuben said, his voice just a hair firmer. "Come here, please. Give me your knives."

I could not disobey this time. I strode towards him and handed him the knives I'd taken from Buck. "Here."

My voice sounded hollow. What was he going to do? What did he want *me* to do? Why could I not make myself comfortable with this? It wasn't like when I was with my family. It wasn't like what the Sentinels did to the Westerners. This was protecting myself and my loved ones from people who would hunt us to the ends of the earth. Kill or be killed.

"You don't look good," Reuben said. "Having second thoughts?"

"No," I murmured.

Everyone else in the clearing moved back, some covering their mouths.

Reuben held up the knives, inspecting them. "These are warrior's blades," he said quietly. "Did you know that if we carry weapons, we have to earn them before going into service? Lark and Jillian had special training before being issued theirs. They had to show that they were responsible and dependable." He turned his peaceful gaze to me. "We're not in the camps, but I still think it's a good idea. I want you to earn these."

"By killing them?"

Reuben took my hand and placed one of the knives in it, then folded my fingers around the hilt. "Show me you know how and when to use them."

His gray eyes met mine, conveying his true meaning.

He was asking the impossible.

I gasped. "What?"

He nodded. "I could order you if you want, but I don't think you need that."

"I... I don't understand," I stammered. "Why—"

"Just do it," Emily said, gazing up at us. Her eyes were large with fear. "Stop drawing it out, for pity's sake."

"You heard her," Reuben said. "Just do it."

"Fine," I spat. "Ladies first."

Emily shuddered and bowed her head, whispering almost inaudibly just as Reid had done earlier.

"Emily," Buck breathed. "I'm sorry."

I gripped the knife and stared down at the woman who'd nearly killed me. She'd stabbed Jen, who'd probably never hurt anyone in her life. She'd stabbed Reid, who'd called her a friend. Emily Begay was lethal, and I didn't want to share the earth with her anymore. She didn't deserve to live in the world that was rising up from the ashes of the camps.

The barest fragrance of coffee, poured weeks before, raised the hair on the back of my neck as invisible lips brushed my ears. *We don't always get what we deserve, my love.*

With a cry of anger, I hurled the knives into the snow and ripped off my gloves. Reuben smiled.

My fingers grazed Emily's battered face, her long hair brushing them as healing energy coursed down my arm into her body. She croaked and inhaled deeply. "What?"

Before I could convince myself not to, I touched Buck's cheek, the same energy flowing into him. The churning heat in my stomach faded as his eyes brightened and focused.

He gazed up at me in shock. "Did... what just happened?"

"I healed you, obviously," I grumbled. I turned on my heel and marched away towards Reid, who was in as much shock as the two captives on the ground.

Reuben, ever pleasant, kneeled down again in front of Buck. If he was afraid of Buck's powers, he didn't show it. Instead, he tutted while he chose his words. "I'm taking the teams with me in a minute," he said, his voice a new deadly quiet. "And your bonds will disappear. Go back to your hole."

He leaned closer to Buck, just inches from his face. "But from this moment forward, if I ever catch so much as your scent on the wind, I will hunt you down and kill you without a shred of guilt. That's a promise. You may have *orders*, McClintock, but I have a wife and child to protect. If you threaten them, a knife to the throat will seem like a pleasant death."

Buck blanched. "We can't go back. They'll kill us for failing."

Reuben narrowed his eyes. "Then I suggest you seriously reconsider your current employment situation." He stood and stared down at Buck with disgust. He sounded more heated than before. "Our lives, as we know them, are changing. The government is closing in. It's only a matter of time before the camps are emptied and shut down. I'm giving you a chance to take control of your future and start a new life. I don't care what the hell you do, as long as it's nowhere near me and mine. Give the message to the other strike teams." He turned around and faced his brother. "Reid, get us in the air. I'll give you the directions when we're airborne."

Reid obliged, his eyes glowing white as large sidewalk slabs emerged from the snow and hovered together in the air near all of us. I helped Ember and Abby hop on, then jumped on myself.

When the rest of us were situated around Reid, we began to drift upwards, the icy wind quickly turning devastating now that we weren't shielded by buildings. The melted snow that had leaked into my undergarments refroze. I hoped we were headed towards someplace warm. Maybe an iron foundry.

"Where—?" I began to ask. Buck and Emily were staring up at us, though I couldn't see their expressions. I couldn't think of a place where we'd be safe from them.

"Jen's apartment," Reuben said, his arms around tiny Abby. She clung to him, her emaciated frame wracked with shivers.

Marco swore, then swayed on his feet. "C-c-can't we walk?" His eyes were dull with fatigue and cold.

Ember pulled him into a hug. "Reuben doesn't want to leave tracks. This is faster."

Dark, snowy Baltimore passed beneath us. Reuben and Berenice guided Reid to an apartment block near Johns Hopkins University. It said much that even when exhausted, starving, and unaided by light, they knew the way. Clearly I was in the presence of rebels; a surge of respect warmed my otherwise frozen chest.

We landed in the deep snow and stumbled off the platform, which Reid neatly deconstructed and guided to a clear spot near the cramped, dingy smoker's station. We silently followed Reuben and Berenice towards a stairwell.

While we tromped through the snow, I could see where two people had walked before us, and I smiled. Gabriela and Jen were warm and safe, and though I'd known them for less than a day, I felt better knowing that at least someone in my circle of acquaintances was out of danger.

Reuben had only knocked twice when the door flew open and a crying Gabriela threw herself at him. We let the married couple reunite in private, trooping past them where they stood in the walkway and collapsing in the living room.

For all the people there, it was nearly silent. Jen came out of the kitchen and helped us out of our snow-crusted outer layers. Someone pressed a steaming mug of coffee into my hand and guided me to the couch. Marco whispered something about needing to sit down. Berenice, Lark, Ember, and Abby disappeared into a far bedroom down the hall without so much as "good night." Reid was standing against the wall—and then he was slumped over on the floor, snoring into his knees. Reuben and Gabriela finally blew inside and walked hand-in-hand into the kitchen.

I sat on the couch with my coffee, too keyed up to sleep. Instead, I sipped the bitter instant coffee and tried to be furious about Reuben forcing me to heal Buck and Emily. *Nobody... can make me... they didn't deserve... stupid strike team... Reuben's a butthole...*

Each nattering thought swirled, then incinerated like flash paper. I just couldn't make myself be angry about it, though I didn't understand why.

Grasping at the rage was mentally painful, similar to how I'd felt while taking my junior year-end tests in high school. I'd stayed up the night before on a job with Beau. The next day, each question on the papers had swam in front of my eyes. Thinking had been beyond me. It was only through my parents' heavy "encouragement" had my teachers allowed me to retake the exams.

As soon as I gave up on fuming, I turned my thoughts to far more important matters.

Jillian. More specifically, her powers.

If my family were to catch wind that their "powerless" captive *wasn't*, they'd put a bullet in her head without a second thought. She was simply too dangerous with her powers. My wife was smart and shrewd, but I didn't know if she understood how essential it was for her to keep her powers secret. How could she? She had no way of knowing that we'd mounted a rescue mission. Beau wouldn't tell her, since nothing wore down a person like the belief that there was no hope of salvation.

I laid back on the couch, dizzy from the fear. She must have been so afraid.

I had to go to her. Clearly, my teammates were exhausted and they needed rest, but I could go. I would go. I had to go.

Now that I had coffee and warmth, everything made so much sense. The blizzard had ended a while ago and the Maryland Department of Transportation would've cleared the freeways and major roads. All I had to do was get the truck from Gabriela's and drive to Annapolis. I'd surprise them all and rescue my wife. It was so easy.

I placed the coffee onto the table—what a cheap mug, spilling all by itself—and searched around for keys, not bothering with winter clothes. They'd slow me down, and Gabriela's baby needed them more.

After several seconds, I remembered that the keys were in my pocket. Laughing to myself, I tiptoed to the door, making sure not to disturb the slumbering people in the room with me. I pushed on the door for a few seconds before remembering to pull.

"*Where* are you going?"

I spun around to see Reuben and Gabriela standing in the kitchen doorway.

I pointed to the door. "To rescue Jillian." *Duh.*

He looked at me strangely, then kissed Gabriela's forehead. "*Querida*, can I have a moment alone with Benjamin, please?"

She nodded and went back into the kitchen. Reuben came up to me and gazed at me, the same odd expression still on his face. "Why are you going by yourself?"

I gestured to Reid and Marco. "Because they're all sleeping and I can't disturb them."

He continued to assess me. "And... you're not tired, right?"

"Well, a little. But her powers could be back. I can't waste any time."

Reuben put his arm around my shoulder and gave it a light squeeze. "I was just talking to Gabby about a great rescue plan I came up with. I'm pretty sure it's solid, but I need your input. Beau is expecting you, but he's not expecting this, I guarantee it. There's going to be at least one explosion. You'll love it."

My heart sped up. This was why Reuben was such a great leader. "Really?"

He smiled warmly at me. "Really. It'll take a few minutes to get the computer up, so in the mean time I want you to lay on the couch and rest. That's an order, brother. Let the coffee kick in. Just between us, you sound a little loopy right now, and you need to be in top form when you fight Beau."

"Hell, yeah." The words slurred. He pushed me towards the couch. I laid down on the cushions, closing my eyes and waiting for the caffeine to fully wake me up.

"Ten minutes?" I said. "We need to go soon."

I cracked open my eyes and saw him gently arranging Reid on the floor, placing a pillow under his head and a blanket over him.

"Tell you what," Reuben said softly without looking up. "How about you count out six hundred seconds?"

I closed my eyes and began to whisper the numbers. "One... two... three..."

I was asleep before I made it to ten.

ITEM TWELVE

Excerpt of letter from Rabbi Avner Cohen, resident of New York City, to his younger brother Mordechai, resident of Los Angeles, dated January 22, 1913.

> ...it is a travesty and shame that Avigail would marry such a young man as the Fischer boy and unite our frum name with that of an apikoros one, but we both know of your daughter's iron will and long for her happiness. It may be the mysterious and unknowable will of Hashem that he should become a worthy Jew with Avigail sitting over him.
>
> As both your brother and a Rabbi I agree that Avigail has been touched by Hashem's blessing and should seek a husband with the same blessing, but—are you _sure_ that Benyamin Fischer is the _only_ Jewish boy with the blessing in all of Los Angeles?
>
> California is not a small state, you know. I have a friend, Daniel Shochet, in San Francisco who says his son Avram is a rare intellect at just six years old. If Avigail is willing to wait just a few more years, she might find that Avram is just as blessed as she...

12

A loud crash made me jerk awake. My pillow, no longer held down by my head, fell to the floor. "What's going on?"

Jen was on the floor, disentangling her legs from the laptop cord. She grimaced. "Sorry," she whispered. "I was just trying to clean up the living room before the others came back. You can go back to sleep."

I sat up and scrubbed at my face, the sleep clearing from my eyes a little bit. My body felt heavy and achy, as though I hadn't moved in hours. Judging from the light streaming in through the small, high windows in the front door, it was around noon, maybe later. Who knew that a couch could provide such complete rest?

I stretched my arms, then slouched. "Where's everyone?"

Jen finally stood up. "Reid, Marco, and Reuben went out about five minutes ago to get some things from your truck, but I don't know what. All the rest of the girls are still sleeping in the bedroom." She shook her head. "Whoever said that women don't snore as badly as men never met that crowd."

I couldn't help a smile. My whole being felt lighter and more peaceful now that I'd had a full night's rest. Of course, I remembered where I was and what was going on, but even pessimistic me couldn't deny that we'd defeated the strike team, in a matter of speaking, and had an extra superpowered combatant with us that we hadn't counted on. The scale's hands had finally swung onto our side.

Still, there was no time to waste. I jumped to my feet. "Can you get the ladies up, please? We need to be out of the door as soon as possible. We'll intercept Reuben and the others and get on our way to Annapolis."

Jen sighed. "You have to eat first." She sounded almost bored.

I hunted around for my boots. "No time for that," I said while peering under the couch, where I only found a mousetrap and a moldy granola bar. "Did you see where Reuben put my boots? And where are my knives?"

"Eat, and then I'll tell you."

I paused and looked over my shoulder at the petite civilian. "Um...what?"

Jen crossed her arms. "I said, 'eat, and then I'll tell you.' Don't make me tell you what Reuben said."

I sat on the arm of the couch and tried not to glower. "What did Reuben say?"

"He said he has five younger brothers and he's never lost a fight with any one of them." She made air quotes. "And then he said, 'eat the damn food, you stubborn idiot, or I'll tell your whole team about how you burned down a bookstore after Lark whooped your ass.'"

Heat creeped up my collar into my ear tips. "That's... well, that's just... *Imperator* burned down the bookstore. I just happened to be there."

Jen pressed a fist to her mouth to quell laughter. "And was it Berenice who actually whooped your ass?"

Oh, screw all of you. "No, it was Lark," I grumbled.

This was more than one man's efforts to keep me from running headfirst into danger—this had to be Reuben's version of a power play. Why else would he steal my boots and knives, dangle my atrocious past in front of me, and force feed me from a distance? I'd never met someone who swung so wildly between competent commander and raging jerk, except maybe Dean Monroe.

Jen snickered and disappeared into the kitchen, reappearing a minute later with a plate loaded with frosted toaster pastries, scrambled eggs, tangerines, and a cup of vanilla yogurt. In the other hand she held a steaming mug of coffee. "Here you go," she said kindly as she put the plate and mug on the coffee table. She pulled a fork out of her pocket and handed it to me. "There's lots more if you want. I figured your powers required an insane metabolism. Is that the case?"

Her question softened me, and I answered, "No, I've never noticed any unusual appetite. I don't know where the healing energy comes from, but I've never reached a limit. I knew a guy once who could instantly grow plants from seeds, and he never said anything about needing extra food or rest. It might be the same thing."

I instantly regretted speaking of Dean. I took a sip of the bitter coffee and hoped Jen wouldn't ask more questions about Dean. If she did, I'd lie and say I didn't know much about him. Besides, my powers were cooler than his. I had *two*, and he'd be dead without my healing powers.

She must not have been impressed by Dean's earth-goddess abilities, because she asked, "What about the running?"

"I've never formally studied it, but I think I can run about as long as any other normal guy." I mulled over my second, less-showy ability. "I get winded if I run for several minutes. It's just that I can run a whole lot farther in that time."

"I sometimes wish I had a power," she said, staring airily into the distance. "I don't know what, though."

I finished the yogurt. "Well, you can make Berenice do what you want, and you pretty much have me whipped, so you're on your way."

She turned red. "I hope you don't think I'm mean. Reuben's a friend of mine, and I respect his judgment. He accurately predicted you'd try to skip town when you woke up, and then he said you'd refuse food." She eyeballed my plate, which was already mostly empty. "You wouldn't have gotten far on an empty stomach."

I blushed and ate the last of my eggs with deliberate slowness. "It's hard to be chided by someone I barely know. And my wife *was* kidnapped," I added, trying not to sound resentful.

Jen studied me while I ate. "You know," she said after a few seconds, "You're not nearly as scary as Berenice makes you sound. I was kind of nervous about being alone with you."

I looked up, shocked. "What? What did she say? Did she accuse me of something?" In all my dealings with the team, I'd never indicated that I was the sort of man you couldn't trust a lady with. A shiver slid down my spine at even accidentally being compared to Beau.

Jen shook her head. "Not exactly. She just always made you out to be… like… a really rough guy, I guess. Maybe someone who left crime because it was convenient, not because of morals. She doesn't have much regard for Jill, either, so it makes sense to her that Jill would fall for a creep. At least, she didn't have any regard until recently, and I'm pretty sure that's only because Jill beat up Peter and brought Reuben home. I doubt she really *likes* Jill. Rube and Gabriela won't let Berenice say one bad word against her, though."

I put down my plate. "I'm not a bad guy. I've done bad things, but I'm learning that the latter doesn't necessarily make the former."

Her eyes shone with a warm emotion. "I really am glad you found your team."

Feeling the heat creep back into my face, I changed the subject. "Can I ask you a question?"

She looked surprised. "Uh, sure. Shoot."

"Who *are* you?"

"I'm assuming you don't mean my name."

"No. You obviously know the Baltimore team quite well. How did you meet them?"

She leaned back into the couch and stared up at the popcorn ceiling. "A couple years ago I was on my way home from a night class at Johns Hopkins. I should've called campus escort services, but me being me, I thought that since I was a big, mature sophomore, I'd be safe."

"Mugger?" I asked, already concerned. Jen was so tiny.

"In the plural," she said dully. "Two guys came out of nowhere and knocked me down. One grabbed my arms while the other went through my purse. When he didn't find anything valuable, he started punching my stomach and demanding to know where my money was." She gazed sidelong at me. "You know, because nineteen-year-old undergrads are known for being so rich."

My insides burned with fury. "And then?"

Tenderness transformed her face. "And then Artemis was there," she said softly. "I never really saw her fight the guys. One second I was crying because I was sure they were going to beat me to death on the sidewalk, and then the next she was holding me and telling me I was going to be okay. She called the police and stayed with me until they came. I'd never felt so safe before." She looked at me again. "There really is a sweet woman underneath the sourness. I hope you get to meet her one day."

"Did you stay in touch after that?" I asked, uncomfortable with the idea of a "sweet" woman inside the sourest person I'd ever met who wasn't a Sentinel.

"No. We reconnected at a party I threw the next year. There's a long story there, but basically she was feeling rebellious as hell that night and ditched patrol. She met my friend Elena, who invited her to my party, and that's when we became friends." She shook her head at some private joke. "I haven't figured out whether that's a good thing or not."

"Meaning...?"

She sat up and leaned on her knees, her mouth pursing with uncertainty. "I became the seventh member of the team. I counseled her to leave every time she showed up here with a new burn, I combed the dark web to figure out where the mural artists around here are getting the team's pictures, I did research for them, and I helped Gab with Reuben's injuries after the tribunal. But the more I learned about their stupid cult, the more I realized that my proximity to their lives placed us all in danger. I mean, look at Reuben, for heaven's sake. Don't tell me you believe that's solely because he got married to her. They want—"

"Total and complete control," I finished. "Yeah, I know." I ran a hand through my hair. "Oh man, do I know—did you say you have access to the dark web?"

Her list of activities had finally registered. The dark web was the subsection of the deep web where illegal activities, such as selling torture videos, took place. If Beau had footage of Jillian, it would be there.

"Uh, yeah. Not for crime, obviously, but for—"

"No, no, I get it," I said quickly, grabbing her laptop. "Can you pull it up? I need to look for something." Upon seeing her suspicious expression, I continued, "I need to see if my brother has put up videos of Jillian. She might be trying to send me a message."

"Ugh, Beau. I've heard about him. Give me the computer. Eat while I get it up."

I swallowed the rest of my breakfast in large bites, not bothering to chew. She was clearly an expert in the deep web; I saw several applications on her desktop that provided various types of anonymity while browsing. She logged on and typed from memory the meaningless string of letters and numbers that led to a website that specialized in video footage of superheroes.

"This is where I go to see if the team's faces are visible in any security footage," she explained. "It's not usually a problem, but other teams are downright lazy about keeping their masks on. The Boston team's house is right next to a house with a security camera, and they take their masks off before getting inside. I guess their neighbors don't like them, because they're always selling the tapes on here. I've thought about writing them a letter and telling them."

"I always thought the mask thing was dumb," I murmured as I perused the listings, which named the city, date, and quality of the videos. "It made more sense in the age before smart phones and mass media."

There were surprisingly few videos of my team; perhaps our constant presence on social media reduced the value of this type of contraband. "This website's empty. Any others?" I'd try Beau's special site after trying hers.

"Yeah, they're dumb, but try telling them that," she said with another shake of her head. She began to type another address, again from memory. "Masks make them feel safe, so they wear them even though websites like *this* exist." There was a dark edge in her words. She turned the computer towards me. "I hope you don't mind images of gore."

Row after row of horrific thumbnails filled the screen, each with large sections of red. The website promised the very best in real life superhero violence. One "sample" picture on the side bar showed two young, unmasked superheroes clinging to each other, each one missing a hand. Their stumps gushed blood onto their uniforms, which were noticeably dated. The men couldn't have been older than twenty.

"The 1984 Miami bombing," Jen said. "They were the only survivors. You can buy the rest of the pictures in the file for the low, low price of $9.99. Of course, it's hard to pick out which limbs and guts belonged to their teammates and which ones belonged to the civilians. You can also buy the files for the 1994 San Diego lynch mob attack and the 2005 Nashville riot. Everything else is just a picture or two from various battles around the country."

I regretted eating my breakfast. "Any other sites?" I asked, breathing in through my mouth and out my nose. My uncle had once tried to blow up the Saint Catherine team, yet I'd never spared a thought to how that battle could've turned out had things gone differently.

"Just one," she said, typing again. "It specializes in guesswork of what superheroes look like without their masks. I'm not sure, but I strongly suspect a couple of the artists are disgruntled police sketch artists."

I put my hand on the keyboard. "What I'm looking for isn't on that site. Let me." She slid the laptop to my knees and I took a breath, then began to type and speak, rushing through my words. "My family tortures people for information. It sounds medieval, but it's amazingly effective. Not all information is in a hard drive, right, so our services are occasionally needed, if you're desperate enough." The familiar website came up, with its simple black background. "I think we both know that the people who buy this kind of stuff don't care that it's footage of illegal activity."

"Oh, God," Jen whispered as she saw my brother's offerings. "This is sick."

Each listing promised bona fide footage of someone's anguished screams while my brother and his best friend Will applied untold horrors to their abused bodies. Beau didn't dare ask to film my parents—now just my mother—as they worked; it wasn't "professional," and it certainly wasn't discreet. But the lure of easy cash was too much for my brother, and he was given access to the victims in the downtime so they couldn't rest.

Videos like these could fetch thousands of dollars, depending on the type of torture method, the attractiveness of the victim, and the length of the video. Beau had once bragged to me that a mere three hours with a pretty young woman named Anya, a witness of a mob hit, had earned him a new sports car.

And my team wondered why I never talked about my brother.

I turned the computer back towards me, trying to shield the good person to my right from the images. "If you give me a minute, I'll see if the video I'm looking for is here," I said. "You don't need to—"

She pointed to the screen. "That one says Battlecry!"

My heart thudded double-time as I forced my eyes to read the information. The panic receded as quickly as it had come as I took in the grainy, black-and-white thumbnail. "That's not it."

"Why does it say 1967?"

"Don't worry about it," I said quickly. "It's not what I'm looking for."

How typical of Beau, to try and milk cash out of our home movies. He couldn't have been more gauche if he'd tried.

As my heart went back to its normal rate, I skimmed the rest of Beau's website. It displayed his usual mundane offerings, mostly taken up with drugs, pornography so deviant that it made me blush, and stolen weapons.

Curiously, he was also hawking an elaborate jeweled necklace that I was sure I'd seen in the Smithsonian only a few years prior.

That type of high-stakes theft wasn't his specialty; he must've had a partner. I had a good idea who that partner was.

"Alysia," I grumbled. I'd almost forgotten about Will's twin sister, a vicious young woman who could walk through solid objects. All Beau would've had to do in order to steal the necklace was use his power to shut down the security systems in the museum for a few minutes while Alysia ran through brick and stone to the exhibit.

The front door's handle turned.

I slammed the laptop shut. As if she read my mind, Jen grabbed it and slid it under the couch, and we both automatically relaxed into feigned nonchalance.

Reuben walked in, bearing my boots and knives. Reid and Marco followed; Marco was also carrying clothes. We all nodded in greeting to each other before Marco squinted at me and said, "You've been into trouble." Before I could protest, he dumped the garments on the living room table. "I got Jill's uniform and knives from the truck. Are you ready for the next phase?"

Something about his question angered Reid, because he let out a growl and marched into the kitchen. Jen followed him.

Reuben shook his head and handed me my boots and knives. "Don't worry about him," he said smoothly. "How was breakfast?"

"I think I hate you."

"You hate me because I'm acting like an older brother, and you've never had a positive experience with one. This is how we're supposed to act. I look after you and make sure you don't get yourself killed."

"I don't need someone to look after me!" I jumped to my feet. "Jillian is—"

"Benjamin."

"What?"

"Explain to me, in detail, how you are going to save Jillian. Tell me right now."

My hands shook. "I... I..."

Reuben caught Marco's eye. Marco nodded, then hurried off down the hall. When he was gone, Reuben looked back at me. "I'm waiting."

"I don't have a plan right now," I said through gritted teeth. "But I don't appreciate you acting like—like—"

Like an older brother. Damn it, he was right. Earlier, at Gabriela's, I'd noticed that he was a "professional older brother." He'd aimed his authority and I-know-better attitude at Reid, so it had been acceptable, even amusing. Now that he'd turned his professionalism on me, I couldn't handle it.

But he wasn't Beau. I needed to get over the hang up I hadn't been aware of until thirty seconds ago.

"Yeah, I know you don't have a plan," Reuben said. "You didn't have one last night, either. And I know you want to storm that house *yesterday*, but we can't go into enemy territory without a rock. Solid. Plan."

He didn't sound mad—something told me I'd yet to see him truly angry—but there was no arguing with that tone.

I pinched the bridge of my nose and squeezed my eyes shut. "Fine. But you didn't have to drug my coffee."

Obviously he'd manipulated the events of the previous night so I'd go to sleep. I'd been so tired that I'd felt intoxicated—which I clearly had been.

Yet, he looked shocked by my question. "Drug you? I'd never drug you. You were so tired that you were swaying on your feet. I wasn't worried about you dying at your house so much as I was worried about you dying on the way to the truck."

"You could've just told me that."

A strange emotion passed behind his eyes as he fought a smile. "I think you're forgetting something."

I sank back on the couch and rested my head in my hand. "What?"

"I didn't meet you yesterday."

What was he carrying on about now? "Um, yeah you did."

Instead of answering, a blackish, smokey mask flickered in front of his face, then disappeared. Obsidian was talking to me now, not Reuben Fischer.

My spine instantly stiffened and my calves tensed, ready for action.

He smiled and leaned against the doorway. "I've fought many people, Benjamin. Only two have outwitted and escaped me time and time again, and both of them have the initials BT. When I say that I pinned you as the smarter one a long time ago, I'm not trying to flatter you. You are cunning, you are clever, and when you need to be, you are ruthless. Yesterday you destroyed my house to kill a woman, and I know better than to think that it was purely self-defense. You were angry that she'd killed Topher, and more importantly, she stood between you and your wife, so she had to go."

I had no idea what to say. Beau had always been the smarter one. Where was all this coming from?

The moment ended when the sound of someone sprinting came from down the hall, quickly followed by a door banging open. Seconds later, the wet sound of vomit splattering against porcelain began.

Reuben turned to go, but I held up a hand, secretly grateful for the change of subject. "Don't worry, it's just Ember. She's been struggling with the stomach flu."

"Actually, it's Gabriela," Ember said, walking into the living room. "I feel fine. My appetite came back last night, and I haven't had any nausea this morning."

Reuben transformed in front of me, his hard warrior exterior replaced by almost childlike concern. "Is she okay? Ben, do you think she needs to go to the hospital? I've been reading about hyperemesis gravidarum on my phone..."

"I'm sure she's fine," I said. "Morning sickness usually isn't that serious. I'll check in on her later and see how she's feeling."

Lark, Marco, and Abby wandered into the living room. Abby had let someone brush her hair, lending her a civilized atmosphere she'd lacked before. "Berenice is with Gabriela," Lark said by way of greeting as she draped herself on the loveseat. "Rube, you wouldn't believe how many times your wife got up to use the bathroom last night. You're in for a long ride after the mission is over."

"Did she get enough sleep?" he asked, alarmed. He spun around and faced me. "Is *that* normal?"

"Aren't you the oldest of a million brothers? Surely you've seen pregnancy symptoms before." Was he going to be like this for the rest of the mission? *Yeesh.*

He rubbed his forehead in frustration. "I was always helping dad out on the border, looking out for Westerners. Reid was the one who helped mom with her chores, and with pregnancies and our baby brothers. That's why he took it so hard when she died."

The Fischers were the most dismal group of men I'd ever met.

"Well, then, yes, this is normal. Pregnancy causes a lot of changes. She'll have morning sickness, have to use the bathroom more, and a host of other symptom. She'll probably have headaches, heartburn, fatigue, and things like that, but every woman is different."

Life is wacky. Two years ago, I'd been one of the worst enemies of most of the people around me. Now here I was, hanging around the living room of the Baltimore team's secret seventh member, explaining pregnancy symptoms to quell their leader's new-dad hysteria, three feet from a woman who was licking her hand, all the while worried about my wife, who'd been kidnapped by my brother. What would the next day bring?

Berenice and Gabriela emerged from the bathroom. Berenice no longer wore her shredded uniform, but a freshly laundered one she'd dug up from who-knew-where. Gabriela leaned on Berenice and wrinkled her nose, then said, "If anyone had to hear that, I'm sorry."

Berenice patted her hand and murmured inaudibly. Gabriela smiled weakly at her.

"Looks like we're all here," Marco said from his spot on the arm of the couch. "That is," he called, raising his voice and cupping his hands around his mouth, "if you count *pouting in the kitchen as being here!*"

Reid stormed out of the kitchen at once. "I was eating breakfast."

"Sure you were," Marco shot back.

"Do you have a problem with me, St. James?" Reid growled.

I blinked in surprise—I'd never heard Reid speak to Marco that way.

"Anyway, the sun will start setting soon, so we need to come up with a plan," Reuben said, his baritone carrying over everything.

Reid backed away, never taking his eyes off Marco.

Marco just snorted and turned towards Reuben, who continued, "There's no way around it: the next part of the mission will be the most dangerous. We lucked out knowing about the strike team beforehand, but now we're going into Trent property. Because this is Benjamin's childhood home, he's going to be our strategist. Ben, the floor's yours."

I took a breath and slid the laptop from under the couch, then pulled up an internet satellite map of my family's address. "My family's land is on a small peninsula that sticks out into the mouth of the South River, in immediate proximity to the Chesapeake Bay. To the east and south east is Cherrytree Cove, and to the west, Duvall Creek. Our first consideration needs to be how we're going to get there. It's about thirty-five miles south of here, so we're looking at an hour by car."

"We can't all fit in the truck's cab," Lark said. "And we'd attract too much attention if some of us sat in the bed."

"That's not safe anyway," Jen said. "But don't worry, I know someone with a larger car who owes me a favor. If you give me a few minutes, I'll get them on the phone and see what I can do."

After we'd all murmured words of thanks, Jen left with her phone in hand.

I pointed to the enormous building in the center of the peninsula. "After we get there, there are still several problems we need to work out. I don't know who, exactly, is in the house. My best guess is that we're going to be dealing with my mother, my brother, and the Rowe twins. However, before we ever encounter them, we have to disable the security systems. Beau has set up sensors and cameras all around the estate. We can't get close without him knowing. Even an aerial approach will be impossible." I pulled up an internet satellite map of my family's land and began to zoom in.

"Is there any way we could do this by subterfuge?" Berenice asked.

I looked up, startled. She'd sounded so... normal.

At my expression, she continued, "What I mean is, could we trick our way into the property by pretending to be a delivery driver, or maybe someone who's lost and needs directions?"

Again, there was no sarcasm or anger. It threw me off, making me stumble through my words. "Uh... um, no, I don't think so. Look," I said, turning the computer around. The teams gathered near me and peered at the screen. "It's a gated property, so we'd need to ring the bell. That would raise the non-emergency alarm and all the cameras would be on us. Beau hasn't posted videos of Jillian on his website to taunt me, but I guarantee you, they are geared up for an attack. They'll be expecting something, so the element of surprise is the best way to go."

"What if I break the gate?" Berenice asked. "Could we storm in that way?"

"No. The front end of the property is the most fortified. There are cameras here and here, plus spikes at these three points." I tapped several locations on the screen.

She pursed his lips and studied the map. "I see."

"What about the back end, then?" Marco asked, pointing towards the waterfront part of my old backyard. "The part that borders the South River? There are some outbuildings we can hide in."

Outbuildings? There hadn't been any outbuildings in that part of the estate when I'd last lived there. I focused on the picture, trying to determine what he meant.

Like I remembered, the extreme far end of my family's estate was about a hundred yards from the house. A thick wall of trees partially obscured the view of the water, to my mother's eternal frustration. However, we hadn't cut down the trees because they hid and muffled the generators, noisy eyesores that provided emergency power for our enormous home.

Now that I'd taken a moment, I could see their faint outlines in the trees. They were large enough to be mistaken for small outbuildings by an untrained eye.

"Those are the generators," I said. "The nearest outbuilding is the boat house, over here." I pointed to a white building adjacent to the docking ramp.

Reuben leaned forward and took control of the keyboard. "Those are huge generators." He zoomed in and squinted. "What do they power?"

"They provide emergency power," I said with a shrug. "You know, in case a blizzard or something knocks out the main lines. They probably went on last night for a few hours until the city got the power back on. That neighborhood is really wealthy, so the city usually gets the power on quickly." The house also had an older, smaller, manual generator in the side yard that wasn't visible on the screen.

"A blizzard... or a superhero," Lark said thoughtfully.

Marco straightened suddenly. "Dude, the doors."

"What doors?" I asked. "What's wrong?"

He slid to his feet. "You said that Jill's cell would be electromagnetically locked. That means—"

"We have to knock out the power lines, and then the generators," I finished for him, mentally caught up. "Yes, you're right."

"What else does the power control in your house?" Reuben said quickly. "Think."

I put my fingers to my temples. "Um, all the appliances, the security systems, everything in the basement, the internet..."

"Can Beau use his powers without access to a computer?" Ember asked. "He's a technopath, right?"

"No, I don't think he can," I said, breathing hard. "Okay, guys, here's our tentative plan. We need to find a substation near my house —that'll be the best place to strike to knock out the city power in a way that can't be easily fixed. It'll give us enough time to get to the house. If we're really lucky, the shoreline will have frozen and we can approach on the ice. If not, I know an avenue of approach in the cove. The trees will hide us, especially if we approach after nightfall."

"Are we going to blow up a substation?" Marco asked, a hilarious gleam in his eye. For a second, he looked just like he did when I met him, all eagerness and verve. "I'd love to see what my heat beam can do to one. I suggest you all bring sunglasses."

"And then we'll hightail it to the estate and destroy the genera-tors," Berenice said with an appreciative tone. "Excellent. I wish I could see that smug bastard's face when his powers become useless."

"I'll be in charge of recon, of course," Ember said with a grin. "Figure out who's there, maybe try my hand at mass confusion, like Daisy. I'll contact Jill early on and—"

"You're not going," Reid said coldly.

The room was silent for a few seconds.

"Yes, I am," Ember said, each word laden with exhaustion. "We're not doing this again. I'm tired of fighting, Reid, and I want to talk to you about this, but right now I need to be with the group. Nobody else can do what I do."

"You're sick," Reid replied, his voice even harder than before.

"Not anymore, I'm not. There is no good reason to keep me behind. I'm as much a part of this team as you are."

"This is my last word."

Ember swallowed. "I want to help save my friend."

"*I said no!*"

We all rocked backwards. Reid's eyes had turned white, and he stepped towards Ember. Abby covered her ears and leaped behind the couch.

The whiteness in his eyes flared, causing Ember to cower away from him. She threw up her arms in front of her face. "Please, don't!"

Marco jumped between them. "Back off, Reid." He held up a shaking hand, his own eyes slowly becoming white-yellow. "I don't want to, but I swore after Patrick I'd never be a bystander again. I just never thought it'd be you."

For all his previous wrath at Reid, I could tell that he didn't want to fight him.

Everyone except myself had backed away from them, confusion and horror written on all faces. Lark had scooped Ember up and hidden her behind her back, her own hand hovering over her staff. Berenice had an arm around Abby, protecting her from the Peter-like individual—or so it appeared.

We held our collective breaths; nobody seemed willing to intervene between the two heavyweights facing each other. Even Reuben was taken off guard, shielding Gabriela.

Uncertainty appeared on Reid's face, then vanished. It was enough for me to make a decision.

"Everyone, I need a minute of privacy with Reid," I said, never taking my eyes off his white ones. "No arguments. Please, just go. Marco, you too."

Almost everyone quickly hurried out, worried glances thrown over a few shoulders. Ember was crying quietly into Lark's shoulder.

But Marco didn't move or lower his arm. "I'm not leaving you alone," he said, an audible lump in his throat. "He's crazy. He's been crazy since Liberty. I see what Ember meant now."

Reid's eyes returned to their normal sad gray appearance. He backed into the wall. "I'm not."

I gently placed my hand on Marco's. "I'll take it from here. Go to Ember. She needs you right now." Jillian had told me how comforting he'd been following her suicide attempt in the snow a few weeks before. If he'd been able to summon sweet pleasantries in that hell-hole, maybe he'd be able to summon such pleasantries now.

But Marco just shot Reid a foul look. "She needs his head on a stick," he spat. "Kick his ass, will you?" With that, he stomped out of the room with one final scowl at Reid.

When he was gone, Reid stared at me with tormented eyes. "So what? You going to punch me until you feel better?"

"No."

"Then what do you want?"

I sat on the arm of the couch and gazed at my broken team-mate. I'd once considered Reid Fischer the quintessential super-hero, all rules and honor and classic masculinity. He loved his team, adored—heck, practically worshiped—his girlfriend, and protected his city without complaint. He was unafraid of toil and danger. More than anything, he was spiritually identical to his element, with rock in his soul. I'd thought him unchanging and unyielding.

Obviously, I'd misjudged him.

I'd told both Ember and Reid that I'd talk to them "later" about their problems. "Later" had come, and this time I could not put it off.

I took a few deep breaths. "Why do you think Ember's mad at you?"

My question shattered his armor.

His face crumpled and slid down the wall, then wrapped his arms around his knees. "I don't know," he said, his voice breaking. He hid his face in his knees and began to shake. After a minute of silent grief, he looked up, his eyes bloodshot. "She won't tell me. I've apologized for what happened in Liberty so many times, but she's still furious with me."

I got off the couch and kneeled next to him. "What have you apologized for?"

Resting his cheek on his knees. "For letting my want of revenge override my vows. We got into a huge screaming match about that when we were there. A few, actually. I talked about it a lot with Jill after we got back. She helped me understand where I'd gone wrong. That's what we were talking about that night, right before…"

He couldn't speak for a few seconds. "I'm sorry for not being able to focus on the mission," he whispered. "I want her back, Ben. Please don't think I don't. I just don't see how this can end well. You always said Beau was evil, but after what he and Will said to me after the battle in the compound, I understood what you really meant. I can't be optimistic. Even eating is a struggle now. Everything is."

I steadied my nerves. "I know you're struggling, and I think that's why you need to step down."

He slowly lifted his head up. "What?"

"I think you need to step down and let me lead."

There was no flash of white, no great show of protest. Instead, he laid his head down again. "I've really lost everything, haven't I?"

I placed a hand on his shoulder, willing my power to fix psychological wounds, though I'd never been able to do that. Nothing happened, and I dropped my hand. "How about this. If you promise me you won't kill me in my sleep one night for taking command, I'll tell you why Ember's mad at you."

He jerked his head up. "She told you?"

"Sort of," I said, wincing at the memory of her unexpected assault after Daisy's demise. The mere memory of her choking terror turned my stomach. "She's afraid. You yourself said she complained of feeling unsafe. For a long time, you were the source of her security. And then, suddenly, you weren't. Everything is spiraling out of control and she's feeling used and unprotected. She's angry at you because she's scared of you. And, uh, after what happened a few minutes ago, she's probably more scared of you. Hate to say it, but you were channeling Patrick a little bit. I think you scared a lot of people."

He swore under his breath. "What are the chances Marco doesn't kill me?"

"Low, unless I talk to him, which I will. But I need you to step down. I don't want to continue the popular trend around here of forcibly removing leaders when they go off the rails."

"I'm a shame to my family," he grumbled. "If it's not Marco who kills me, it'll be Reuben."

"Actually, admitting that you can't do something and asking for help *is* honorable. The fifteenth principle: humility." I grinned at his shocked expression. "Yeah, I memorized them, and I don't think they're all stupid. I simply despise what the cult's twisted them into. Here's another reason for letting me take over. The twenty-fourth principle—"

"Sincerity," he said, the corner of his lips lifting a tiny bit. "I will communicate, in my words and deeds, a genuine love and respect for my city and team."

If he loved his team, he'd realize that he wasn't the best leader right now. Despite everything, Reid was together enough to under-stand my reasoning. What was more, he agreed. Miracles did happen.

I stood and extended my hand to him, which he took. When he was up, I crossed my arms and smiled as warmly as I could. "Let's get this mission underway."

ITEM THIRTEEN

Excerpt of article from the *Richmond Times-Dispatch*, dated June 15, 1917

>*...there was nary a dry eye to be seen as the throngs crowded the train tracks, waving lace handkerchiefs and giving our boys their final kisses good-bye before they shipped off to Europe.*
>
>*One mother, identified as Mrs. Patrick St. James of Richmond, fell into such a state of hysterics after seeing her husband and eldest son, Edward, climb onto the train that a local patrolman had to send for an ambulance for fear that she might jump onto the tracks. Her daughter, Mrs. Nella Daniels of Glen Allen, told the Times-Dispatch that Mrs. St. James is recovering and is planning to start a yarn collection drive to send fresh knitted socks to the troops. Details to come.*

13

"A minivan?"

Jen stood her ground, though pink tinged her cheeks. "This is what Erin had. Do *you* have a better option?"

We stood in the twilight, knee-deep in snow, by the dinged-up maroon paneled minivan that had clearly seen better days. Duct tape covered a crack on the back window, which lacked wipers. The dented bumper bore a peeling sticker advertising a local college bar.

"Fine," I grumbled, massaging the bridge of my nose. My breath rose in little puffs, reminding me that even this monstrosity was better than most of our group sitting in the bed of a truck. "Thank you for getting it."

She shrugged. "I basically passed Econ 210 for Erin. She owed me a favor."

A door slammed nearby, and superheroes began to stream down the steps, each bearing a different item. Marco clutched Jillian's uniform and knives, while Ember had Jen's tablet, on which she was studying the satellite map of my childhood home.

Reid, who was carrying a sack of food, kept a respectful distance from both of them. When I'd told Marco that Reid was going to be better from then on, he'd told me he was going to give Reid a beat-down for scaring Ember. It had taken pleading, followed by a desperate "Jill wouldn't want you to," for him to box my shoulder and retreat to Ember's side, which he hadn't left since.

For the first time that I could recall, my muscles weren't tensed with the physically painful desire to leave—to move forward. Reuben and I had perfected a plan of attack, agreeing on the key detail: every step had to happen under the cover of darkness. We would not leave the parking lot until the sun was behind Baltimore's buildings, ensuring that our exit would be that much harder to track. I *wanted* to leave, but I could no more make the sun set faster than I could teleport into my parents' basement.

Jen smiled as she watched Berenice walk lightly down the steps. Abby hurried behind her, and Berenice turned to greet her teammate. Abby said something that made Berenice laugh.

"Look out for them, won't you?" Jen said, watching them with a sad smile. "Keep them safe."

"I'll keep as close a watch as Berenice will let me," I said, elbowing her playfully. "You could even say I'll keep her in my sights."

"That's messed up," Jen said, struggling to hold back laughter. After a few seconds, her smile faded. She tore her eyes away from Berenice to look at me. "God, this whole situation is messed up. You're all marching off into battle, but most of you guys aren't much better than kids. You know, I was worried about them knowing about how uncool the stupid van is until I realized that none of them know jack squat about cars. You could tell them that flying cars had been invented in the 1950s and were stolen by moon men and they'd believe it, if you said it convincingly enough."

The hint of frustration in her voice brought back memories of my own I'd rather have forgotten. "It's not their fault. They were denied education."

"I remember the first time I talked to her about...sheesh, what was it?" Jen said, giving her head a shake. "Medicine or something. She started spouting off what was basically eugenics, and why medicine makes us weak. I remember thinking, "How can these people be so *dumb*?"

In the corner of my eye, I saw Abby whip around and stare, unblinking, at Jen.

"I think it's time to start packing up," I said. There was no reason to dive into this subject yet again, even if Jillian wasn't around to get offended. When I returned, Jen and I would have a long talk over a pitcher of beer. "Is everyone ready?" I asked, raising my voice.

Marco brushed past me and pulled open the van's sliding door. "You'll have to pull Reuben away from Gabriela. They're making goo-goo eyes at each other by the front door." He hopped in and climbed into the back corner. When Reid followed, Marco pointed wordlessly at the seat farthest from him.

Before Berenice got in, she gathered Jen into a bear hug. Abby hung around the edges, watching with a blank expression. "Thank you so much for everything," Berenice said into Jen's short black hair. "I can't ever repay you."

Jen pulled back and looked at Berenice, hands still on Berenice's elbows, and her eyes practically sparkling. "Just come back, okay? Save the damsel in distress, then get back here. I want to hear about how you defeated Beau and all of them."

Berenice actually blushed. However, before she could reply, Abby stepped up. "Jen say Berenice dumb."

There was an ugly silence.

"I beg your pardon?" Jen managed.

Abby cocked her head, a tight triumph in her eyes. "Jen tell Trent Berenice dumb."

Berenice's head turned back and forth between Jen and me. She broke off contact from Jen. "What? Wh-what is she talking about?"

Abby crossed her arms and appeared to concentrate. "Jen say, how... can... they... be... so... *dumb*?" She let out a long breath from the effort. "Berenice not know medicine," she said smoothly. "Jen tell Trent Berenice dumb."

Jen and Berenice gasped in unison. Berenice stepped back, stricken. "Did you really say that? Just now?"

Jen shot me a pleading expression. "I—I mean, I was talking about stuff that happened in the past—"

Berenice's eyes darkened. "*This* again. Are you *kidding* me? You were telling the medic about big, dumb Berenice's stupid former beliefs about medicine? What, were you warning him that I might not want to get injected with something?"

"No, it wasn't like that!" Jen held up her hands and struggled to keep her breathing steady. "Please, it was a passing comment I shouldn't have made. I don't think your dumb! We've been through this," she said, exhaustion and heartbreak mixing in a horribly familiar way.

Yes, they'd been through this. I was beginning to suspect that every civilian who'd ever secretly befriended a superhero had been through this.

But Berenice straightened and crossed her arms. "If you've got a problem with dumb country girls like me, Jen, why don't you just go back to hanging out with your lovely college friends? I can *say* 'pretentious,' but they can *spell* it, right? And that's what matters in the end, isn't it? Now, if you'll excuse me, I need to get into the van with the other idiots."

Without another word, she jumped into the van and threw herself into the seat next to Marco. Abby all but sashayed past us and daintily hopped into the van, sliding into the third and final seat on the back bench. She laid her head on Berenice's shoulder, grinning from ear to ear.

Jen turned to me, a tear sliding down her face. "I... I..."

I put a hand on her shoulder. "You may not believe me, but I know exactly how you feel." This mission was rapidly turning into a broken hearts club.

Jen just nodded and shuffled away towards her apartment, her head bowed.

The back hatch of the van shut, and Lark walked up behind me. "Someone call the police, because I've just witnessed a homicide. I always knew there was a predator inside Abby, but that was just brutal." She climbed into the middle row next to Reid and turned around, her arm casually on the back of the seat. "Ab, that wasn't necessary."

Abby flipped her off.

Lark waved dismissively and turned around, twirling her collapsed staff. "Ben, tell Reuben I've loaded the rest of the crap into the van and we can go now. That is, if you can disentangle him from Miss Guapa up there."

I sighed and trudged up the icy steps. As Marco and Lark had said, he was locked in an embrace with Gabriela by the apartment door, staring down into her eyes with such adoration that I felt the urge to look away. I was willing to bet that I could've been garbed in a clown costume and they wouldn't have noticed me.

"I hate to leave without making a decision. *Eres mi cielo*," he said quietly. Even I knew his accent was terrible.

Yet, Gabriela sighed with pleasure. "Don't worry, *corazón de batata mameya*, I'll be safe. Jen and I will go to her parents as soon as the roads are clear. We don't think anyone will follow us. We're nobodies."

"You're somebody to me. You're the only person that matters. You, and Peewee," he said, stroking her stomach. "How do you say 'Peewee' in Spanish?"

I cleared my throat with as much respect as I could. They both jumped and jerked their heads in my direction, like teen lovers who'd just been caught by a parent. "Um, it's time to go," I said. "We're all packed up, and it's getting dark fast."

"I'm coming," Reuben said, his face falling. He pecked Gabriela's lips. "It's time." He opened the front door of Jen's apartment—I could see Jen huddled on the couch, wiping her eyes—and watched his wife walk inside. They held hands until the last moment, when she finally let go and slowly shut the door.

"Okay, let's go," he said, suddenly brusque and business-like, still staring at the brass numbers on the door. Without waiting for a response, he hurried down the steps towards the van.

He was already in the passenger seat when I opened the driver's door and climbed in. "Got everything?" I asked the people behind us. Ember passed Reuben the tablet, which still displayed the map of the Trent property.

Marco ignored my question and tilted his head towards Reuben. "What on earth were you guys talking about up there? And what's a gwa-puh?"

Reuben didn't look up from the tablet. "We were discussing contingency plans."

Lark coughed a cough that sounded a lot like "baby names."

Reuben shot her a glare. "We were not—"

Berenice leaned forward. "If it's a girl, you'd better name her Berenice. I was the one who saw the robber in the first place. If it wasn't for me, Gab would be dead and you'd still be chronically single."

"But if it's a boy," Reid said, "name him Ryan."

"Whatever you do, please don't name the baby some stupid trendy nature name," Ember said, making a face. "Give the kid a name people will respect."

Marco's incredulous face was priceless. "Your name's *Ember*."

I twisted around in my seat. "Guys. The mission. Focus."

"Okay, fine, yes, we were talking about baby names," Reuben cut in, his loud baritone filling the van's interior. "As in, what I want my widow to name our child if I don't return from the mission, which is a real possibility. Happy?" He scowled at Reid. "And for Heaven's sake, we're not continuing the R thing."

Everyone had the grace to look embarrassed.

His widow... Guilt slithered in my stomach, though I didn't want to examine it. I wasn't asking anything inappropriate of Reuben. He knew what he was doing by joining the mission. Gabriela knew the risks of marrying such a man. Now that the strike team was gone, she was safe.

But *was* the strike team gone?

Yes, they were gone. They'd been defeated and given a no-questions threat of what would happen if they returned. Even if they wanted to find us, we'd left in such a way that they wouldn't have been able to track us to Jen's apartment. Of course they were gone.

"You need to get on I-97," Reuben said, zooming in on the map.

"I'll tell you when we're near the exit to the substation." All of his recent aggravation was apparently gone, too.

"Gotcha," I said. I started the engine and put the van in drive, then checked the rear view mirror.

Six unhappy people stared off in different directions, all of them doubtlessly wishing they were somewhere else, with someone else, doing anything else. The whoosh of a sent text made my eyes flicker down to Reuben's phone. His final text to Gabriela read simply: *Te amo.*

I shoved the gear stick in park and cranked up the heat. "You know," I said as casually as I could, "We're going to have the heat up in here for a while. With all the people, I bet it'll get hot. Rube, can you run inside and get the flat of water bottles on top of Jen's fridge?"

There was no flat of water bottles on top of Jen's fridge, but if he went inside, there would be one more minute with his wife. I now knew the value of sixty seconds.

"Uh, yeah, sure, good idea," he said, placing his phone on the center console. The text screen was still displayed. "I'll just be a second."

When he shut the door behind him, the vibration caused his phone to slide off the console and into the foot well.

I leaned down and picked it up, unable to help a smile at the wallpaper: a picture of Gabriela on their wedding day. Before I could tell myself not to, I opened up his picture app and scrolled through his photos. Picture after picture of Gabriela filled the screen, including some which I had to hastily flip by.

An amusing sequence, clearly at dinner in her destroyed home, made me grin—in the first picture he held a glass of red wine, in the second he was sipping it, and in the third he was grimacing. The final picture was a selfie of the two of them in which Gabriela held a glass of wine in her hand and was laughing, while he was nearly green.

You shouldn't snoop, Benjamin. Ember's chide cut through my silent laughter. *Is this a bad habit from your information gathering days?*

You're one to talk, telepath.

Um, rude.

I pulled up his phone's internet history. What did a superhero like Reuben do on his phone? Jillian was eternally on her favorite social media app, while Marco watched medical videos, of all things. Ember watched nature documentaries. Reid texted Ember and watched cooking tutorials.

My smile faded as I read Reuben's recent searches.

Legal rights of widows

Baby names meaning "gift"

How early can baby hear my voice

Can a woman miscarry from stress

I turned around in my seat. Reid rested his head against the glass, his eyes heavy with sorrow. In the back seat, Ember and Berenice gazed off into nothing, both clearly thinking of better days. Abby sat between them, obviously confused and hurt by their silence. Marco had spread out Jillian's tunic so he could see the emblazoned BATTLECRY on the back. He was running his fingertips over the lettering. Lark held a small nugget of metal in her hand, turning it over repeatedly in her scarred fingers.

I pocketed the phone and turned off the engine. "I'll be a minute." I wasn't speaking to anyone in particular, but nobody questioned me.

My boots crunched in the snow as I walked towards the apartment. I mentally rehearsed what I was going to say, but as I neared the apartment, the words fell out of my mind like sand from a sieve. Was my decision compassionate or just plain stupid? Was there even a difference in this situation?

When I was at the door, I knocked three times and closed my eyes.

Reuben answered. "Sorry, I'm still looking for the flat. Jen says she hasn't bought water bottles in a while. Are you sure it was on the fridge?"

I put my hands in my pockets. "I, uh, came here to talk about something else."

He rolled his eyes. "What did Reid do now?"

"Nothing." I straightened my spine as much as I could. "I've decided that... that it would be better if you stayed behind." I took the phone from my pocket and held it out. "Your part in the mission is over."

He took the phone and stared quizzically at it. "I don't understand."

"You've got a different mission now." The words had sounded less melodramatic in my head.

Reuben stepped out and shut the door behind him. "I made a promise. You helped me protect Gabby, and now I'm helping you save Jillian. Even if you hadn't helped me, I owe her. You didn't see me after the tribunal. This is more than duty, this is about honor."

I swallowed. "If I were in your place, I'd want you to do this for me. I'm sparing you a choice you don't want to make. Take Gabby and Jen and leave Baltimore. You don't know if the strike team is gone. That's the real honorable option."

"Ben—"

"And on top of that," I added, my tone evening out, "I've got enough lovelorn teammates at the moment. I don't need my co-commander constantly worried about his wife and Peewee." I stepped back. "They need you more than I need you."

I turned and strode towards the stairs. The sun was fully set now, and I needed to leave. *Don't argue, don't argue, don't argue...*

"Ben."

I suppressed the urge to swear aloud and turned around. "Yes?" If I had to whack him with the baton Jen had returned, I would.

He was still standing by the door, phone in hand. "Take care of Reid. He's slipping. And please... take care of my team."

Perhaps the light changed infinitesimally, or maybe the cold subtly altered my senses. But for a fraction of a second, I didn't see Obsidian, fierce leader of the Baltimore superhero team. I didn't see Reuben Fischer, professional older brother and proud son of Couer d'Alene camp. I didn't even see my new friend.

Instead, I saw a guy. Just a guy standing in an apartment complex stairwell, cold and tired and uncertain about what lay ahead for him and his. He could've passed for an older college student as easily as he could a young husband and father. He could've been anything. His ambiguity did not diminish him—it strengthened him. He was the embodiment of potential.

I was looking at the first true ex-superhero.

I nodded once and hurried down the stairs. When I was in driver's seat, I locked the doors and turned over the engine.

"Hey, where's Reuben?" Lark asked.

"He's not coming," I replied. "Ember, I need you to navigate." When she'd switched seats, I handed her the tablet. "You ready?"

I glanced at the faces in the rear view mirror again, and this time I did not see broken hearts and drama. Instead I saw potential, as delicate as gossamer.

It was enough. Now I wasn't saving one person, but many.

ITEM FOURTEEN

Letters received by Christina St. James, April 2, 1918.

Madam,

It is my painful duty to inform you that a report has this day been received by the War Office notifying the death of 1st Lieutenant Patrick St. James on the 13th of January, 1918, and I am to express the sympathy and regret of the Army Council at your loss. The cause of death was influenza.

And:

Madam,

It is my painful duty to inform you that a report has this day been received by the War Office notifying the whereabouts of your son, 2nd Lieutenant Edward St. James, as unknown. His company was engaged against the German Army near Blois, France on the 17th of January, 1918. Following the battle, he was unable to be found among the living or the fallen. The Army Council expresses their deepest condolences and thanks you for your sacrifice.

14

M arco and I came to a stop at the ten-foot tall chain link gate. I gazed up at the spindly, complicated framework of the substation, pretending for a minute that I could smell electricity as my father had been able to.

The various towers and lines laced together above us to form a skeletal complex that, if struck by high heat, would cause an explosion so powerful that Reid had built an in-ground bunker in a nearby hill. The others were waiting there for me to return from our little recon mission.

"Can you hear it?" Marco whispered. "Can you hear the power?"

I closed my eyes. Yes... there it was, a low humming I knew from my father's power. A quarter million volts of electricity coursed through the substation each second, providing half of the Annapolis metropolitan area with light, heat, and much more. The generators on the Trent property would have to kick on once we took out the substation.

Marco and I halted at the chain link gate. A crooked sign hung on the front of it, illuminated clearly by the bright full moon that shone above us.

DANGER

KEEP OUT

EXTREMELY HIGH VOLTAGE

"Danger, keep out, nyah nyah nyah," Marco grumbled in a childish mocking tone. "Whatever. Back up." He raised his hand.

"Whoa!" I pushed his hand down. "If you blow it up now, there won't be anything left of us."

He shoved my hand away. "I'm melting the padlock," he hissed. "I know what I'm doing."

I took a large step back, heat crawling up my collar. Marco had displayed his vicious side before—most often in the last twenty-four hours—but I still couldn't make myself be comfortable with it. I knew what he could do when he was pissed off. How could I forget?

And while he'd apologized to me for killing my father, he'd never once vocalized regret over taking a life—just that the life taken had been a relative of mine. He'd joked at Gabriela's about a final show-down with my mother while Jillian and I had romantic reunion, but his current steely gaze said it all: he fully intended to make me an orphan. This was just a necessary technicality before doing so.

Was I even allowed to be upset about this? And if I was, who'd sympathize with me?

Giving my head a little shake, I crossed my arms as casually as I could. "Sorry, go ahead."

Heat rippled out of his hand and lit up the padlock, which glowed orange, then red, then yellow, then near-white. Metal drops plopped to the gravel, hissing when they landed on the cold rock. Without further ado, he pushed open the gates and marched into the substation.

I jogged to his side. "What are you—?"

"I'm determining where I need to strike," he said, turning his head all around and taking in the structure. "It's going to take an assload of heat to cause an explosion. Since we're attacking your old house before sunrise, I need to conserve as much heat as possible for that battle." He clenched and unclenched his fist, staring down at it. "I just don't know…"

"What's wrong?"

"I'm so tired," he murmured. "I need to throw at least a couple thousand of degrees at this thing, but I don't know if I have the strength to stop it. I could barely keep it together when we fought Kyle."

"Stop it?" I asked, confused. "Why would you want to stop it?"

Marco laid his weary look on me. "I use the term 'battery' to describe my power, but really, I'm more like an atomic bomb, with a ton of energy just swimming around inside me. I use tiny bits of my power when I need to warm you guys up or something, but when I really let my power go—"

"Like when you killed my dad," I said without thinking.

"Yeah, like when I killed your dad," he said dully, "I'm just wrenching back the floodgates. That kind of blast is almost impossible to stop until I'm completely out. I don't know if I'll be able to stop. I might not be able to help… when…" His last few words were tinged with worry, almost heartbreak.

After a silent second, he shook his head and pointed to a transformer. "I'll aim for that. The explosion will trigger other ones there and there," he said, pointing towards large boxes emitting low buzzing.

"What's so wrong if you run out?" I asked with a shrug, undeterred by his abrupt subject change. "It doesn't kill you."

He took a huge, shuddering breath then spun around. "Go. Now. Get back to the bunker. When you're there, I'll send two little flashes of light as a warning, then I'll count to ten. For the love of God, plug your ears. Don't worry about me. I'll be a safe distance away."

He turned and walked out of the gates, leaving me to watch him in confusion and concern. All of us, it seemed, were giving in to mood swings under the stress of the mission. We were being… what was the word…

I laughed quietly. *Mercurial.*

A minute later, I was at the opening of the crude bunker Reid had built. In the dim moonlight I could see Marco on the far end of the long hill, crouching and watching me. His vantage point allowed him the best line-of-sight to the target transformer. My view was blocked by a large oak tree.

A flash of light flickered once in his hand.

I slid halfway into the bunker, which was little more than an earthen room built into the hillside. "Plug your ears," I barked to my friends, who were all sitting against the far wall. "Remember the plan."

"It's not hard to forget 'wait for the big bang then run like hell,' Trent," Berenice said before yawning.

A second flash.

I crouched down and hoped that Marco was crouching, too. Was he counting Mississippi-style? Or just—

"Ears!" Ember shouted.

The force of the explosion slammed into my ribs like a sledgehammer.

I was thrown backwards into the rear wall, my head colliding against the stone with brain-rattling force. Just as quickly, I fell to the ground, becoming entangled with someone's legs.

When I realized I was alive, I inhaled deeply, the musty scent of dirt filling my nostrils—I was face-down. My fingernails scraped the dirt as I pushed myself up, each inch of motion causing my head to pound with every beat of my heart.

When I'd gotten a few of my bearings, I tried to listen to what was happening outside, but a high, rushing whine filled my ears, drowning out all sounds.

At least, I thought it was drowning out the sounds. Around me in the flickering, orange-tinged blackness of the bunker, I could see people jumping to their feet and groping around. But it was so quiet. Their actions implied confused babble and yelled orders, but I couldn't hear anything except the roar in my ears.

Berenice shoved me off her legs and said something, her mouth forming angry words that I could not hear. When I didn't respond, she appeared to repeat what she had said, though her face was less furious, more concerned. Her eyebrows pulled together and she squinted at me. She spoke again, but I couldn't hear her.

We realized the truth at the same time: the explosion had deafened me.

I began to hyperventilate. She reached out a hand to my face, but I turned away and hoisted myself through the bunker's small entrance, desperate for air. As soon as my head broke through to the chilly outside, I froze.

The substation was utterly engulfed in billowing orange flames, their rounded edges capped with oily black. The inferno soared up from the ground—eighty, ninety, one hundred feet, scraping the midnight sky before disappearing. Every few seconds, white flashes in the substation would briefly arc and pop, and then disappear into nothing. The heat seemed to extend invisible claws towards me, prickling my skin and raking its nails across my cheeks.

Yet, the conflagration was completely silent.

Berenice spun me around and shouted something at me, her lips forming an impassioned plea. She appeared almost demonic in the fire's light, her green eyes and blonde hair now a shimmering yellowy orange. She pointed towards the van.

I shook my head. "I don't understand." At least, that's what I thought I said.

She shook me and shouted again.

Another, smaller explosion tossed us backwards into the snow, but I still couldn't grasp the enormity of the moment. I was deaf. I was *deaf*. Was it permanent? Had I sabotaged myself in an effort to sabotage my brother? Was my plan doomed?

My breaths became more ragged. Would I be able to save Jillian? Would she still want me with this kind of disability? Could I even serve anymore? What would happen to me? To my team?

Benjamin Trent, pull yourself together. Ember's stern command cut through my near-hysteria. *Marco is to your right. He's can't hear anything, either. Heal him and get to the van.*

Her lucid orders were what I needed. Ignoring shaking arms, I pushed myself off the ground and lurched towards where I remembered Marco last being. Berenice ran off towards the van. I struggled to stay upright, falling face-first into the melting snow a few times.

Sure enough, Marco was sitting in the snow, rubbing his face and shaking his head. He smiled dazedly at me when I approached and said something, holding out his hand.

I touched it briefly, and he jumped up and began gesturing to the fire with an ain't-it-crazy expression, but I shook my head and pointed to my ear, then shrugged.

He frowned for a second, then signed in the camp sign language: R-Y-O-U-D-E-A-F

I nodded and slumped.

Marco gently grabbed my jaw and tilted my head to the side, inspecting my ear, and then the other. He frowned and held up his hand. N-O-B-L-O-O-D

So my eardrums probably weren't damaged, but I was still deaf. I signed a choice swear word.

Not to interrupt, Ember interrupted, *but a battalion of emergency services are about five minutes away.*

I turned to run towards the car and immediately teetered on my feet. Marco caught me before I fell again. With nothing more than an impish grin, he threw my arm over his shoulder and began to help me to the van.

Ember threw open the door as we approached, then pointed towards the empty seat in the middle next to Reid. *Benjamin, you're going to take it easy for the drive.*

"No, I'm not!" I had no idea how loud I was. What the *hell* was she talking about? Even if I wanted to rest for the final portion of the trip, I couldn't, because I was the only driver. Ember knew that. Maybe the blast had addled her brains.

But Marco shoved me into the van and slammed the door shut, then sprinted around to the driver's seat, where the keys were still in the ignition. I moved to grab the keys—Marco was not killing us all in the middle of the night in suburban Maryland, by *God*—but Berenice grabbed my shoulders while Reid fastened my seat belt. I struggled and probably shouted, but they held fast.

Marco hastily buckled himself in and turned over the engine. All my muscles tensed, prepared for the inevitable impact with one of the enormous power poles around us...

Marco put the van in drive and expertly, if somewhat carefully, maneuvered us out of the gravel lot in which we'd parked. He checked his mirrors and pulled out onto the road, driving as if he'd been doing so for years.

I stopped fighting. *What... on earth...*

Ember touched my cheek, and flashes of memories flitted behind my eyes: Marco's burning envy that I could drive when we were on the way to the tribunal. His agonizing grief over his sisters' deaths that demanded distraction. Watching online driving tutorials in the week following our return home to drown out the pain. His careful attention to my actions while I drove to Baltimore.

Berenice slowly removed her hands from my shoulders. I didn't move.

Marco had taught himself how to drive.

In a *week*.

As if he'd heard me, he turned his head slightly and gave me a sly smile before focusing on driving again. He drove in the perfect center of the lane, like any overcareful brand new driver.

Lark turned and spoke casually to Ember, gesturing towards Marco and laughing.

Lark says to not look so surprised, Ember said, her internal voice laced with laughter. *Please forgive me. I told them all that he taught himself drive before you got to the van. You're the only one that's shocked. He's known in our peer group for being a quick learner.*

"Why?" I said, still too stunned to be annoyed.

Another memory passed through my mind, though this time it was Ember's. It was far more controlled than her earlier flood of pain and fear.

"Hi." Ember extended a shy hand towards one of her new teammates. They were standing on an icy bridge at the edge of the city.

The young woman, white-skinned, dark-haired, and sour-faced, returned the handshake with an iron grip that hinted at super strength. "Jillian Johnson."

Ember could feel her uncertainty in her new role and picked up a fleeting thought, an observation that her new leader, Patrick, didn't seem very friendly. Ember didn't know what to think about this Jillian just yet.

The other teammate, a boy with light brown skin and a charming smile, extended his hand. "I'm Marco St. James," he said, puffing his chest out in a clear attempt to make himself bigger. It didn't work.

"How old are you?" Ember blurted. His voice was still boyishly high.

Marco faltered. "Um, I'm seventeen, but elder says I have to tell civilians that I'm eighteen." The truth flowed easily from his mind, self-conscious reflections that although he'd broken the record of early graduation by finishing his courses two years early, he was still so obviously underage. Would anyone ever respect him?

Ember's memory ended, bringing me back to the crowded, smelly van. I settled back into the seat, slightly awed by my youngest teammate. I'd known that he'd been told to lie about his age, but I'd never once pondered the reason he was sent out so early.

Jillian had said that Marco had been released into service because Marco's uncle wanted them to stay together, but what if that was merely why he'd been released to Saint Catherine instead of another city? He'd "graduated" a whole two years early? Why hadn't he told me? What else didn't I know about Marco St. James?

A niggling thought wormed its way into my head: *maybe Marco should lead.*

Ember leaned forward and took my hand in hers.

Ben, we still need you to lead us. This is your old house, it's your brother, and Jill's your wife. We're a few miles away from the stopping point. You sound normal when you talk, though your voice is a little loud sometimes. Don't worry about it. I'll be here to translate if you need me to.

"Thank you," I said. As soon as the words left my mouth, I sat up. I'd heard myself, faint and distant, but definitely audible. "Hey! My hearing!" I sounded like I was a mile away.

Marco turned slightly again and said something, his voice nothing but a murmur to me. Ember took my hand again. *Marco says your eardrums probably weren't damaged, just the little hairs. Your hearing should return soon.*

"Since when are you a medic?" I said, hoping I sounded more teasing than sarcastic.

His jaw moved, though this time he didn't take his eyes off the icy road. I felt Ember's laugh as she relayed his reply directly into my brain: "I was the medic before you flirted your way onto the team, remember?"

The raucous laughter of six other people was the first thing I truly heard since the explosion. Shock, relief, and adrenaline collided in my system, and I began to laugh, too. Ours was such a weird story.

"Turn onto the road coming up on your left," I directed a minute later, after I'd collected myself. Reid winced and pointed down repeatedly, letting me know to lower my volume.

Marco turned off the main street onto a boulevard that bisected a wealthy neighborhood lined with McMansions, each a squarish million-dollar monstrosity squatting in its own acre of manicured lawn. All but a handful of the enormous houses were dark, a certain sign of their electricity-less state. Even at midnight, homes in this neighborhood would've had security lights and small floodlights to illuminate their house numbers, statues, and front doors.

We were getting close now. The tension seeped back into my muscles, this time from the turbulent mix of anticipation and anxiety. The high of the explosion and horror of deafness had worn off, and now the need to move forward enveloped me again. Jillian was less than two miles away.

An unbidden image of her sitting in a cell seared my mind. Blood dripped down her fingers and onto the freezing cement floor.

Ember touched my cheek, replacing the image with a fantasy of Jillian, slightly scuffed but otherwise unharmed, embracing me and whispering in my ear. *Thank you for rescuing me. I knew you would.*

I cleared my throat and pretended to massage my eyelids out of stress. "There's a right turn coming up that leads to a small rec area. Pull into the playground's parking lot. Everyone, get your things. We're about to go by foot."

Lark stopped twiddling her collapsed staff and sheathed it. In the rear view mirror, I could see Berenice and Abby exchange a meaningful glance. Abby's eyes glinted ominously, momentarily changing from blue-gray to a feline gold. Berenice's biceps seemed to flex visibly beneath her shirt.

Next to me, Reid placed a hand on my shoulder and nodded curtly, his jaw set. For once, he didn't look haunted by his recent tragedies. His lips moved: "I'm with you." He glanced at Ember, his face falling, but then looked away. His face smoothed over.

When Marco had parked the van in a shaded corner of the lot, I opened the van's door and looked around. We were by a playground where I'd played with my childhood best friend Jake countless times. His house was just down the road, though he was currently at MIT. We'd once pretended to be jungle explorers in the nearby woods, and the remarkable discovery we'd made one hot summer day was about to have consequences I couldn't have predicted.

I gestured in a circle above my head, and my team obeyed the order, forming a circle with all eyes on me. I put a finger to my lips and they nodded.

Ember held out her hand, which I took. *I'll relay all orders, if you want.*

I'd never been so grateful to know a telepath. *Yes, please. We're going through the trees to the bridge.*

Ember must have repeated my message, because they all fell into a single file behind me, Reid taking up the rear.

Right before we entered the tree line, the moon slipped behind a heavy cloud bank, robbing us of nearly all light. I slowed, squinting at the snowy path, trying to make out the white ribbon from the ground around it. Jillian wouldn't have had any problems, but the rest of us floundered.

A large tiger crept past me. When she was a few feet ahead, she turned back and stared at me. Apparently all but *one* of us were floundering.

Abby kindly guided us through the woods, lifting her paw periodically and tapping on branches, roots, and anything that would make noise underfoot. True affection stirred in me, and I caught myself thinking that I was glad I'd never faced her in battle before. She deserved better.

The fresh scent of water was the first indication that we were near our destination. If my hearing had been at normal levels, I would have strained to hear the lapping of small waves on the shore, or perhaps a buoy's bell in one of the distant shipping lanes. Maybe even a fog horn that carried over from the nearby Chesapeake Bay.

Instead, in my deafness I relied on the stinging breeze that blew unceasingly from the river, and the briny scent it carried. I didn't feel the cold anymore, just the strange calm before every fight. I'd more than moved forward. I'd moved to the finish line.

Inside me, a dark version of myself grinned, desperate for blood.

The trees thinned and we popped out onto a beach, still in near-complete darkness. The ghostly light from behind the cloud was a little more apparent now that we were under nothing but the sky.

To my surprise, I saw moonlight reflected on the water. We wouldn't be able to cross on ice, and I couldn't see well enough to find a boat at the eleventh hour.

But I'd prepared for this.

I beckoned for my team to follow me along the final step of the journey, and the startling discovery Jake and I had made all those years ago. Straggling trees gave way to scrubby bushes, which petered out into nothing but sand as we approached a splintery wooden bridge. Across the bridge lay a sandbar, only ten feet wide or so. Two huge breakwaters flanked the sandbar, guarding it from the valid threat of hurricanes that occasionally struck Maryland. I'd been so shocked as a child to discover this little finger of land, but more so by what I could see from it.

At the edge of the sandbar, I knelt and stared directly ahead at tiny pinpricks on a far hill. The moon would have to come out some-time, and when it did, the rest of our path would reveal itself. I didn't trust my memories of this vantage point, and no matter how much I wanted to charge ahead, I would not risk ruining everything when we'd come so far.

Ember knelt at my right, Marco at my left. The rest of them lined up, low and tight, on both sides. Ember placed her hand in mine. *Jill is unconscious. There are two more unconscious people in the house, but without knowing them personally, I can't tell who.*

My heart sped up. *Is she sleeping, or...?*

She squeezed my hand. *I don't know, but since it's almost zero one, let's be optimistic and assume she's just sleeping.*

God bless you.

Marco tapped my shoulder, then looked at Ember. Ember nodded. *He wants to know what we're waiting for.*

The breeze answered for me. The full moon slid out from behind a cloud, casting the night into silvery relief. I stood up and let out a long breath, never taking my eyes off the hill across the water. I needed to give myself more credit—it was exactly where I remembered it.

Across the water, the Trent mansion towered over everything like a fortress in a macabre fairy tale. Its white stone and brick reflected the moonlight, making it appear larger than life in the witching hour, which itself was unnaturally dark because of our activities at the substation. The tiny pinpricks I'd seen were outdoor lights, powered by the generators I could not hear.

I'd been so happy to discover that I had a "private beach" so close to my house. The trees lining our property had hidden it from my family.

The rest of the team stood and gaped. I caught Reid's eye and pointed to the breakwaters. He smiled and gestured for the rest of us to lie down on the sandbar. His eyes lit up, as bright as the moon.

Boulder after boulder broke free from the water and gently splashed down in the water, slowly forming a rocky path uniting the sandbar and the far beach. After a minute of directing rocks, he gestured for us to stand up. They looked at me expectantly.

I started to walk.

ITEM FIFTEEN

Partial transcription of an eyewitness account of the events of April 3, 1918, in a Central Powers POW camp located in northern France.

Soldier:

We were all at our jobs in the factory, sewing on patches and things like that. Suddenly there was this...explosion? It was like a meteor hitting the earth.

The guards started yelling about "ein frau," and I could hear a woman screaming, "Edward! Edward! Where's my son?!" And then my friend Ed St. James dropped his work and ran to the window and shouted, "Mama!" I ran to him. I thought he was hallucinating.

Interviewer:

What did you see?

Soldier:

[silence for several seconds] I saw a woman levitating through the air as three machine guns fired at her. The bullets were bouncing off her, and the grenade someone threw just... did nothing.

Interviewer:

And then?

Soldier:

Edward turned around and said, "We just won the war, boys." And then he burst into flames but he didn't burn. He was made of fire.

15

I'd never walked so carefully in my life.

I tested each step as we disappeared into the cover of the trees, gingerly feeling for branches and underbrush that might betray our presence to anyone who would be listening. And why wouldn't they be listening? Whoever was in the house with Jillian had to know that her champions were on the move. They might be asleep, but they'd have some kind of defense mounted.

For the hundredth time, I tried to theorize who the sleeping inhabitants were, and more importantly, *why* they were sleeping. The second question was the stumper, because it wasn't protocol for any of our "guests" to sleep during interrogations. Mom and Dad would question them for an entire working day, and then Beau, Alysia, and Will would have their fun while my parents rested.

Even with Dad's death, I couldn't see why that model would change. Beau and Will preferred the little video business, leaving Alysia to fill in for my father. Mom probably liked that. Alysia and Mom had always been close.

Eleanor, though never in open rebellion against my parents, had always made it clear that she preferred to help my family's business in other ways. Her money-making skills and willingness to commit other crimes prevented my parents from expressing unhap-piness with her as a daughter, but I knew Mom wished her one daughter would help her in the basement. Alysia probably filled a void.

So who was in the house? And why were they sleeping?

If the four were operating in shifts as usual, then it was probably either my mother and Alysia, or Beau and Will. Neither pair was an ideal opponent. My mother could disintegrate heads, Alysia could run through walls and disappear into the night, Beau could crush one's skull with a single punch, and Will could manipulate dead animal flesh. Though I didn't see or smell any dead animals around, I wouldn't put it past him to have a decaying dog or something on hand.

Around me, my teammates slowly crept forward, each lingering behind a tree for a few seconds before advancing to another one. Abby, still in her tiger form, led the way.

When I was flush against a large, spicy-smelling conifer, I became aware of a low sound, a persistent rumble in my ears. I smiled. My hearing was improving steadily if I could hear a sound as unbroken as the generators. We were only yards from them, but they sounded as if they were on the other side of my huge backyard. Still, it was progress. And if they were that loud, then the sound of our presence was surely obscured.

Ember's presence brushed my mind. *Jill is still sleeping. I'm almost positive it's natural sleep. She's dreaming.*

What is she dreaming about? I hoped they were happy dreams.

I somehow felt her smile. *Thanks to me, she's dreaming about dancing in her bedroom to that dumb pop music she likes so much. Ah, now you're there....and I'm getting out of her head. Sheesh, you two. What are you, newlyweds?*

I closed my eyes, a lump in my throat. My wife was there. She was real, almost close enough to hold in my arms. She was safe for the moment, enjoying her reprieve from horror and pain. For all of the effort I'd spent on saving her, I didn't want to disturb her.

The moon went behind a cloud again. Reid dashed over to me

and leaned close to my ear. "Marco is almost out of power. I'm going to destroy them."

I leaned around and waved to Marco. He waved back, then pointed to Ember. Ember nodded and turned to me. *Marco wants you to know that he, and I quote, totally owned the substation blast and was able to save some power. He's going to...* She trailed off for a second. ... *save what he has left for the fight inside.*

Icy pain encrusted my heart. She needn't have been so tactful.

It didn't take a genius to work out that he'd been desperate to save any shred of power he could for the sole purpose of killing my mother with it. He'd been crushed at the substation when he realized that it apparently was a choice between blowing up the substation or personally getting revenge for his sisters. Now that he had a second chance, he was happily giving the rest of the glory to Reid.

I swallowed and focused on the image of Jillian dancing. *Ember, tell everyone to get on their mark and close their eyes so they can adjust to darkness. When Reid destroys the generators, we are going to run as fast as we can into the house. Reid will break down the back door. Attack anyone who isn't Jillian. Take no prisoners.*

Jillian wasn't at risk of friendly fire. She was in the basement and probably would sleep through the storming of the house.

I relished the idea of her waking up to me.

Reid stepped forward and walked towards the generators. They were barely visible now, just huge rectangular boxes beyond some trees. Their gunmetal gray sides melted in with the gloom almost perfectly. When they were offline, the yard would be even darker.

Reid says get down. There's going to be some quaking.

We all hit the ground and covered our heads, but at the last second I risked watching out of curiosity. Would the earth swallow them whole?

In the blink of an eye, the ground trembled and spikes as long as school buses thrust up from the earth beneath the generators, impaling them like bits of food on fork tines. There was no process to take in. One second they were working, and then they were hoisted into the air, dead and—I grinned to realize it—silent.

"Now!" I heard my shout almost like normal and cursed. I could've just given away our presence.

"*No!*"

Ember's scream made me tumble over.

Nobody move!

To hell with Ember. I jumped up and sucked in a breath, ready to sprint.

If we go in now, Jill's dead. Trust me!

The moon had come out, allowing me to see everyone's confused faces. Ember walked toward the house a few paces, then held up a hand. "Just a little bit longer," she pleaded. "You'll see what I mean in a minute."

It occurred to me that she was speaking loud enough for me to hear her, so she must've been raising her voice to near-yelling. Why was she not concerned that we'd be heard?

The entire universe held its breath with me.

After an eternity, she lowered her hand and turned to face me, a beautiful peace overtaking her features. "Now."

I didn't take in my surroundings as I ran, just the back door that was the last true impediment between myself and my wife. It was nearer, nearer...

A large stone flew ahead of me, crashing through the doorknob and unlocking the door.

I bounded up the snowy steps of the back deck two at a time and slammed through the door, shoving it aside with such force that little panes of glass shattered upon impact with the kitchen counter to the right. I heard the crash and gentle tinkling of glass. Whoever was in the house would've heard it, too, no matter how deeply asleep they were.

The rest flooded in behind me, weapons and hands up. Abby leaped over the broken glass and up onto the kitchen table, four-inch fangs bared. Her claws gouged deep marks in the shining wood.

"Find them. Kill them," I ordered, immediately taken aback by my tone. But I didn't wait for a response. I jumped over the island and turned down the long hallway of guest bedrooms that led to the basement access, baton extended. But I wouldn't need it. I could slam someone into a wall so hard that they'd—

I stopped, my eyes on the figure at the end of the hall.

Jillian stood by the basement door, clad in a pink silk bathrobe and staring straight at me.

ITEM SIXTEEN

Headline of the *Richmond Times-Dispatch*, June 1, 1920

MORE PEOPLE SHOWING THEIR POWERS

How many are there? American people amazed and curious!

16

I had no memory of running to her.

One second, I was at the far end of the hall, and then my arms were wrapping around her, my nose in the crook of her neck, my hands stroking her matted hair.

There was no swell of romance that forced us to kiss, no anguished declarations of love. All was silent as the invisible gold dust of my power tumbled out of my fingers and into her flesh, causing her to shake—but from relief or despair, I couldn't tell.

She was there. She was with me. She was *real.*

Jillian broke away from me and stared at my face, her blood-stained fingers grazing my skin. She traced my jaw and lips, her eyes never ceasing to study my features. As her fingers passed under my nose, the lingering smell of blood and something vaguely fishy burned my nostrils, but I didn't stop her. The smell meant she was there.

The last of her bruises were just disappearing, leaving behind bloodstains and minor wear and tear that was visible even in the moonlight shining through the large bay windows lining the hallway. I could even see a fine misted spray of blood on her face.

She clasped my face in both of her hands, still visibly shocked by my presence. "You're... you're here," she said, disbelieving. Her lips trembled, and then fat tears began to roll down her cheeks. "How did you know I was here?" Her eyes widened. "He said he wouldn't show you the tapes until I was dead." Her breaths began to come in quick bursts and she stumbled backwards into the wall. "Oh my God. He lied. You saw them. I... I..."

I couldn't tell whether she was speaking quietly or if my hearing was muting her voice. I gathered her into my arms again. "Graham was still alive when we returned home," I said, stroking her back. "Ember showed us everything. We left right away. We would've come faster but there were some obstacles we couldn't avoid."

There was no need to say the words "strike team" just yet.

"I thought I was going to die here," she moaned. "I thought... I thought..."

"You thought wrong," I whispered.

She began to sob in earnest at the same moment that I noticed movement far to my right.

The rest of the team were all standing quietly at the far end of the hall, their faces colored by various shades of concern. Marco held up a large red fleece blanket from who-knew-where, and I remembered that Jillian was not just barely dressed, but shivering uncontrollably while she cried.

"You guys can come here," I said, grateful for their polite distance.

Marco ran the fastest. When he was at Jillian's side, he pulled her from me and swept her up into a hug, shushing her tears and throwing the blanket around her shoulders. Jillian pulled the blanket tightly around herself and sniffled, failing to really smile.

Her eyes contained more than grief. There was a vacant horror in them that frightened me. I'd seen it in the eyes of the people I'd killed after endless days or weeks of torture. I couldn't blame them; any time they'd seen me before, my touch had meant the whole process starting over.

I moved to the side to let the other emotional reunions begin. Jillian let Ember and Reid gather her into a group hug, shuddering once when Ember touched her face.

"Not now," she moaned. "Later, please. Later." Ember nodded and kissed her cheek.

Reid put his hands on Jillian's shoulders and gave her the kindest smile I'd ever seen from him. "It's all over. And you're on your feet. Damn, you're good. What happened to the other two people who were here?"

"Don't worry about it. They're, uh, incapacitated for the moment," she said, her low voice coming through clearly. She wiped a tear from her eye. "Beau and Alysia are in Virginia. I don't think they'll be back for a least a few days."

Upon hearing that my mother had been "incapacitated," the tension in my chest was immediately replaced by an unnamable feeling. I focused on anything else I could. Jillian was wearing a pink silk bathrobe, identical to the one my mother hung on the back of her door. Why? And where was my mother? Every inch of Jillian's skin was smeared with blood, and she kept flexing her fingers in an odd way. What did it mean?

The Baltimore team hung back, but when Jillian turned to them, Lark and Abby reached out and patted her shoulders.

Abby looked thoughtful. "You fight Peter?"

Jillian was taken off guard. "I... um, yes, that was me. Who are you?"

Abby bounced on her feet. "Tiger. You Miss Stabby. Friends."

"Miss... Stabby?" Jillian echoed, her voice faint. She glanced at Berenice, who was red. "Is that what you call me?"

Berenice hesitated, then cracked into a too-wide grin before playfully punching Jillian's arm. "Busted out of your cell, huh? Badass." She threw her arm around Jillian's shoulders. "You gotta tell me everything."

Jillian shook her head. "I'm not badass," she said softly. "The power went out and the door opened. I woke up and I..." She turned around and looked, stricken, at the guest room door nearest us. "I, uh..." She began to hyperventilate. "I... oh my God..."

"Come with me," Ember said quickly, pulling Jillian away from Berenice, who let her go as if she'd been electrocuted.

"I'm s-sorry," Berenice stammered. "I—I didn't mean—"

"Benjamin, get the generator going," Ember said, cutting Berenice off. "Marco, go with him as a lookout. Before anyone asks, Will and Mrs. Trent won't be a problem, but we don't know when Beau and Alysia will be back." She pulled the blanket tighter around Jillian, who hid her face in Ember's shoulder. "Reid, as soon as the generator's on, get a hot meal going. You three," she said, turning to the Baltimore team, "I've got a job for you."

She inclined her head, a meaningful look passing between them. They nodded quickly and hurried down the hall, then turned towards the stairwell.

When they were gone, Ember gave Jillian a squeeze. "Let's get you cleaned up."

Ember met my eyes. *Don't you dare get mad at me for taking her away from you. You can't hear what I hear. She needs a shower and food. You can have the big reunion later. I'll make sure you get it.*

Ember helped Jillian down the hall and into the guest bathroom, her protective stance so sisterly and tender that it hurt to see. The door swung shut with a final, firm click.

I stood in the hallway with the two remaining men, lost for words. She was gone already.

Marco swallowed. "You know, she did need a shower," he said, obviously aiming for nonchalance, complete with an exaggerated shrug. "I mean, am I the only one who noticed that she smelled like fish? Smelling like, I dunno, soap might help her get it together. And she's nuts about her hair. I bet shampoo and a hairbrush would..."

Marco's voice faded as I wandered down the hall, unable to feel my feet. All of the last two days had led up to this moment, and I still felt so empty.

But what had I expected? I didn't know anymore. Hoping for a happy, healthy Jillian had been delusional. I could see that now. How stupid was I to really believe that she'd be okay? It was a stroke of luck that she was even mobile.

I steadied myself with a hand on the wall, focusing on the flow of breath in and out of my lungs. I just wanted to take Jillian and run.

But where? The Rockies had been beautiful, when I'd taken my head out of my butt long enough to appreciate the scenery. I could steal some money and buy us a house in the mountains near a flower-strewn meadow. We could swim in a mountain creek. We could start a family. We could live in peace. They'd never find us there.

In the foyer, I looked up and saw the three Baltimore women walking around upstairs on the landing. Their murmured words were lost to me, but Berenice held armfuls of clothes.

I could steal a lot of money and buy Jillian a new wardrobe. We'd go to New York City and blow a fortune at designer boutiques. She'd complain that the tiny *haute coutour* outfits were made for Ember-sized individuals, not warrior women with muscles. I'd kiss her nose and offer to buy her an ice cream to make herself feel better. She'd ask for a pretzel instead. Somehow we'd end up with both. We'd have so much fun.

I walked into the kitchen. It was exactly the same as I remembered it, scrubbed to within an inch of its life, yet lush in its own particular way.

The white marble floor had been recently waxed; I could see my reflection staring up at me. Shining copper pots and pans hung from a bar on the ceiling above the enormous range, itself placed in a huge granite-topped island lined with five leather stools. Baskets of fat, ripe fruit were placed here and there around the room. Curtains of Spanish lace softly covered the window above the sink, which looked out over the enormous backyard pool. I'd pushed Beau into the pool once. It had been hilarious.

Maybe I'd take Jillian on a cruise to the Caribbean. I'd reserve the biggest suite, and we'd spend three weeks lounging around poolside decks, sipping on fruity drinks with little umbrellas in them. Jillian would admire the splendor, and I'd admire Jillian in a bikini. In St. Maarten, I'd buy her so many diamonds that she'd clink when she walked.

Nobody had shut the back door, so I walked out onto the deck. The freezing winter wind sucked the air out of my lungs, and I closed my eyes to listen to whatever I could. My hearing was improving—the overhead roar of an airplane headed in to BWI was audible.

"Hey, let's get the generator going," Marco said from behind me.

I didn't even turn around. Instead, I wordlessly led him to the side of the house, where an ugly generator sat next to the air conditioning unit. I'd loved to speak into the blowing air when I was a child to hear my "robot voice."

I pulled the starter cord on the bottom twice and backed up as the machine coughed to life. Immediately, the porch lights above the deck flickered on, and a light upstairs shone through the window. With a dull pang I realized it was my old bedroom's light. Were the Baltimore team in there? Were they going through my things and making fun of my former life?

I walked past Marco and into the kitchen again. Reid was already poking around the fridge, taking out nearly everything and reviewing his options. The pantry door was open, too, and I was pleased to see that it was as stuffed as ever.

Reid looked over his shoulder. "You need to sit down. I've got some coffee going."

My mother had enjoyed cooking in her immense, immaculate kitchen. Every birthday of mine had been marked with a homemade feast of all my favorite foods: fried potatoes and waffles for breakfast, club sandwiches and chips for lunch, and meatball marinara subs for dinner. Her cakes were delicious, especially her secret carrot cake recipe.

She'd be so angry to know that a superhero was standing in her spot, using her utensils, preparing her groceries. She would be *beyond* furious to know that someone had left smeary, bloody footprints as they'd walked from the hallway over to the part of the counter bearing the knife block.

I sat at my old spot on the island. He pushed me a juice box and sat next to me. I sipped the juice, but couldn't taste it.

He folded his hands in front of him. "You don't look good."

I took a deep breath. "I don't feel good."

"I'm a hypocrite for saying this, but you need to talk to me. What are you thinking about right now?"

I stared down at the little box in my hand. "I don't know."

"You don't know?"

I looked up at him. I couldn't feel my fingers anymore. "I don't know what I'm thinking. I have all these memories of my childhood and... and plans with... Jillian... is... not with me..."

"Listen to me," he said firmly, leaning forward. "Listen very carefully to my words. Jill is safe with Ember. Ember is helping her get clean, and then she'll be out here. I'm making her a hot meal. There are no enemies in the house or nearby. She's safe. We're all safe."

I was going to throw up.

A loud, crackling *whoosh* made us both look over at the living room, where Marco had ignited an enormous fire in the hearth. He sat on the bricks and poked at it, apparently at ease now that he was warm.

I turned back to Reid. "Thank you for the juice."

Reid sighed and slid off the stool.

For a few minutes I watched him prepare my family's favorite brand of macaroni and cheese in a large pot, and chicken broth in a smaller pot. Ground beef sizzled in a sauté pan, and when it was browned he added fresh chopped vegetables from the bottom drawer of the fridge.

I didn't let myself wonder why he was chopping carrots with a steak knife instead of the large chef's knife. It was probably in the dishwasher.

Reid lovingly arranged saltines on a ceramic plate he'd found in the china cabinet, then poured steaming broth into a small bowl and placed it on the plate. He took a glass from the glass cabinet and poured some grape juice halfway into it, then filled up the rest with cold water from the pitcher.

Curiosity beat out my melancholy, and I pointed to the glass. "What's that f—"

He smiled again and inclined his head, his eyes on something behind me. I whirled around.

Ember led a scrubbed Jillian by the hand into the kitchen. My wife's long, dark hair was stringy and wet, pulled into a loose ponytail. She wore a set of ill-fitting pink linen pajamas I thought I recognized as Eleanor's from years before. That's what Ember must have set the Baltimore ladies out to find. Over the pajamas, Jillian wore my old black bathrobe. Her feet were clad in my old slippers, which were stylishly monogrammed with my initials, BPT.

Jillian let go of Ember's hand and shuffled towards me. I jumped off my stool and helped her onto it, gently keeping my hand on her back as she got comfortable. Though she didn't smile, she kissed my hand before looking up at Reid and saying, "Thank you for making dinner. What did—"

She broke off, coughing uncontrollably. Her entire body spasmed with each large, wet cough.

Reid grabbed a hand towel and gave it to her. After nearly twenty seconds of coughing, she stopped and stared at the wet spot on the towel with a grimace. She folded the towel and stuck it on her lap. "Sorry," she muttered, embarrassed. "I'm still battling the flu. It's only been, what, four or five days since I was taken?"

There was an awkward silence in the kitchen. "Um, it's been almost exactly forty-eight hours," I said, unable to meet her eyes.

She'd assumed she'd been in captivity for the better part of a week. That wasn't illness or confusion speaking; that had to be a guess based on how long her ordeal had felt. She couldn't even have been formally "interrogated" that long, since Beau and company had had to drive her from Georgia to Maryland.

We never should've stopped in Baltimore, we should've gone straight to Annapolis. I'd been a moron to think that she'd be okay, but if we'd somehow stormed the house twelve or fifteen hours after she'd been captured, the damage would have been significantly less. That was a fact.

And the Baltimore team would've been killed—another fact.

I hid my eyes with my hand, mortified by my own train of thought. As if to make me feel worse, Jillian turned around on her stool. "Hey, y'all."

The remaining members of the Baltimore team came into the kitchen. "We got almost all the cameras you told us about," Lark said, holding up a small handful of SIM cards. "But when we heard your pretty voice, we thought we'd come see you instead."

Jillian zeroed in on the tiny cards, her face paling. "Berenice, please destroy those," she said, her voice constrained.

"Happy to," Berenice said. She scooped up the SIM cards in one hand and reduced them to dust with a twist of her fingers. Glittery bits of plastic and metal fell from her hand, dusting the marble floor and her boots.

Jillian stared at the dusty mess for a long second, then turned back around on her stool. "I'm hungry," she said, taking a deep breath. She broke into another fit of coughing. When she was done, she pointed toward the steaming bowl of broth and crackers. "Is that for me?"

Everyone must have taken that as a cue to sit down for a meal, because there was a sudden scraping of chairs and stools as we all converged around the island, which was more spacious than the kitchen table. Reid ladled out our macaroni and cheese slash veggie slash beef dish, though when he reached Ember he gave her a reserved bowl of the dish without beef.

Ember accepted it with the tiniest of smiles, her hands brushing his. "Thank you," she said softly. "It look delicious."

Reid blushed pink and blinked quickly, then began to pour our waters from the crystal pitcher in the fridge. Each glass had chopped kiwi and fat berries floating in it. He gave Jillian the watered-down juice, which she gratefully accepted.

After dipping a saltine into the broth and nibbling on it, she put down her cracker and gazed at all of us. "I know you all have questions. But first, where are Topher and Reuben? And that jerk, Peter? If they're outside watching for intruders, they don't have to. I sent Beau and Alysia on a snipe hunt. They'll be at least another day. Probably more, because of the storm." She paused to cough again.

The Baltimore team exchanged sad looks.

When Jillian was done coughing, Berenice folded her hands on the island. "Peter died," she said simply. "None of us are upset, so don't waste your energy pretending you are, either. Reuben is with Gabriela. She's pregnant and—" She glanced at me, "—it was agreed that he'd be better off with her instead of being here with us and worrying. Topher..." She stared down into her bowl.

"Topher died in the fight with the strike team," Lark finished. She put her hands on her teammates'. "Peter's death was ruled unwarranted by guess who, so they sent a strike team after us. If your team hadn't showed up when they did, we'd all be dead."

"Which, I guess, we've never really thanked you for," Berenice said, her eyes averted. "So thanks."

Marco, Ember, and Reid murmured little pleasantries, but I was watching Jillian stir her broth in silence. I knew she was searching for some way to blame herself for Topher's death. I didn't know if she'd ever been close to him, or had even met him before her trip to Baltimore after the tribunal, but she was clearly troubled by it.

I patted her thigh before saying, "Let's just focus on the now. How are you feeling?"

She finally took a sip of broth. "My stomach is a little queasy. And my head aches. I had a bad fever last night, so your brother gave me a shot of something and the fever went down. I figured that's what brought my powers back."

Everyone stopped eating at the same time. Lark's fork was halfway to her mouth.

"Your powers are back?" Reid repeated. "Wow, that JM-104 stuff really is crap. Reuben's came back halfway through the fight with the strike team."

I recovered from my shock quickly, having guessed already that her powers might come back if Reuben's had. "If Reuben's power came back without an injection, then Jill's probably did, too. I imagine he probably just gave her a fever reducer."

I mentally tabulated the dates. Reuben had been given a three-month dose that had only lasted about a month. Jillian had been given a three-week dose that had lasted a little over a week. From what I knew of the substance, Bell Enterprises had stopped producing it decades ago, driving up the price. It had probably entered its chemical half-life, thus lowering its effectiveness by two-thirds.

Or maybe Bell had purposely given the elders an ineffective product?

Jill took another sip of broth. "Well, anyway, my powers came back and I knew if I could just get Beau and the rest to leave me alone for a while, I could probably figure out a way to escape. I pretended to cave and made up some bull about where the JM-104 was. They bought it, and left me in my cell while they went to search. I was still coming up with an escape plan when the power went out and my door opened. I sorta just..." she trailed off, her eyes flicking towards me. "I'd like to talk to Benjamin alone, please."

There was a pause, and then everyone slid out of their chairs and grabbed their bowls. I took Jillian's hand in mine and pointed towards the stairs. "If you go upstairs and to the right, the third door on the left is a rec room. Make yourselves at home. The bathroom is right next door." They trooped out.

When we were alone, I led Jillian to the living room, where the fire was crackling merrily and bathing us in warmth. We sat down on the squishy couch and I tossed an afghan over her lap. She stared at the brightly-colored blanket for nearly a minute before whispering, "I'm Miss Stabby."

I wasn't sure if I heard her correctly. "What was that, sweetheart?"

She looked at me, tears sliding down her cheeks again. "That's what Abby called me. I'm Miss Stabby."

I pinched the bridge of my nose. "Berenice called you that in jest back at Gabriela's. It wasn't an insult, I promise. But if you want, I'll ask her to apologize." Actually, I'd ask Ember to ask Berenice to apologize, and make it clear that failure wasn't an option in this case.

But Jillian just shook her head. "No, she's right." The tears came harder. "After my cell opened, I don't know what happened. I don't remember deciding on what I was going to do. I was running and then I was in the kitchen at the knife block... and then I was hunting them down." She looked up, her lip trembling. "I killed Will in his bed. I've never felt like that before. I just kept stabbing him over and over and over. My vision wasn't normal. I wasn't even human for a minute."

It was difficult to care about Will. But the other half of the story was different. With a terrible weight in my stomach, I prompted, "And my mom?"

She hid her face in her hands. "Her body is still in her bed."

ITEM SEVENTEEN

Title of book published by anonymous author, copyright 1924.

A Survey of Casualties Caused by Powered Americans 1900-1922

17

"The last thing I remember after Beau burning me with the kettle is a smelly rag over my nose. I don't remember going in the trunk. I woke up when we got to your house. It wasn't snowing then, but I remember seeing snow from the guest room window a little later."

"We pulled into Baltimore not long after that."

Jillian stroked her ponytail. "Beau dragged me inside and called for your mom. He introduced me as her 'new daughter,' and oh my God, she lost her mind, Benjamin. She slapped me and told your brother and Will to work me over before the questioning began. They took me into one of the guest rooms."

She lowered her gaze. "That was the first beating. I thought they were going to break my spine. They told me afterward that they'd taped everything and were going to send you the tapes after I was dead. I... I wasn't very brave," she whispered. "And I hated that you were going to see me pleading for them to stop."

I caressed her cheek. "I know Beau, so I figured he'd do that. But I checked the deep web and didn't find anything. Thanks to Berenice, nobody will ever see."

She cleared her throat. "After they'd had their fun, they took me downstairs to your mom and Alysia. They asked the questions. That's how it went the whole time. Your mom and Alysia asked about the JM-104, while your brother and Will just took out their anger on me. Back and forth." She paused, and then broke into yet another round of heavy, wet coughs. "Water, please," she croaked between coughs.

I was at the fridge in a second, filling up a glass of fruit-infused water. I walked back to the living room and handed it to her, noticing for the first time how cracked her lips were. She chugged it down.

"What happened last night?" I said as I took the glass and placed it on the coffee table.

"Your mom was questioning me and I passed out, but she must have realized it was from fever, because when I woke up I was in a different cell with a mattress and a blanket. Beau gave me a shot of something, and said I wasn't allowed to die."

She took a shuddering breath, but her face smoothed over and I saw a hint, just a bare glimmer in her eyes, of the courageous woman I'd fallen in love with.

"The fever went down and my powers came back a few hours after that. I could actually feel my muscles strengthening. When that happened, I realized that I had a chance, though I needed to get as many of them away from me as possible. I waited until Beau came in to check on me, and told him that I was tired of torture and was ready to tell confess where the JM-104 was."

I wrapped my arms around my knees. "Where did you say it was?" She started to speak, then broke into heavy coughs again, this time using the edge of my old bathrobe to catch the expectorant. The robe reminded me of the silk bathrobe she'd been wearing earlier. "Actually, skip ahead to when you got out. What happened?"

"I was sleeping. The power went out and the door slid open. It was dark, but I could see just like normal. I ran upstairs and grabbed the biggest knife from the block. I only had my blanket on. I followed your mom's scent and found her in bed. She sat up, and I threw the knife into her forehead. After that, I grabbed the robe from the back of her door and ran downstairs to where Will was sleeping. I don't know how many times I stabbed him, but cleaning it up is going to be gross." She sighed. "I was so angry at him. Your mother simply asked questions. Will was sadistic."

"What did my mom question you about?" I asked quietly.

Though my heart hurt to speak of my mother, I was not angry at Jillian for killing her. I didn't know what I felt. Certainly betrayed by the woman who'd raised me. Sad that we'd never had a chance to speak just one more time after my father's death. Horrified that her cooling corpse was still indecently exposed in her bedroom. Worried that Marco would irrationally take out his unslaked thirst for vengeance another way, possibly against the nearest blood-born Trent: me.

Did such a combination of emotions have a name?

Jillian resumed stroking her hair. "Just the JM-104. That was the hardest part. There were..." she trailed off and rubbed away tears. "...times when I would've told her *anything* else she wanted to know, but if I told her that I didn't know where it was, she'd kill me. Also, I..." Jillian looked up at me. Firelight reflected in the tears pooled in her eyes. "I wanted her to think I was as brave as my grandma."

She broke down.

I pulled Jillian into my arms and held her for several minutes, never speaking, just rubbing her back and staring into the fire.

My wife had spoken often of Battlecry I, the late, great leader of the 1960s Philadelphia team. It was difficult to parse through the various accounts of the martyred heroine and her teammates, since their glorious era had ended so ignobly.

Or had it been glorious? As far as I knew, they'd lived and fought just as every other team had at that time. Perhaps their tragic deaths had cast a certain glow on their tenure for certain modern heroes, and an ugly tarnish in the eyes of others.

Now that I had lived with superheroes, I believed that Jillian St. James and her team had been no more or less than brave, flawed people who'd been in the wrong place at the wrong time. Fifty years wouldn't have changed human nature, nor would any ridiculous list of principles.

But my wife's grandmother had died bravely. Nobody, not even the grandson of her killers, could argue that.

Jillian mumbled something.

"What was that?" I said, giving her a squeeze. "You'll have to forgive me, since my hearing isn't the best right now."

"I said my hands hurt," she repeated, sitting up and laying her hands palms-up on her lap. "I think your healing power doesn't work as well anymore. And my chest and feet hurt, too." She flexed her fingers again. "I need a medic."

"You're in luck," I said as I arranged myself so I was sitting across from her on the couch. I lifted up her right hand in my own. Her skin was dry and warm, but unharmed. Her bones were strong, and the muscle tone firm. "Tell me where it hurts," I said, gently massaging her hand.

She pulled her hand away and cradled it to her chest. "All over. They've hurt since the needles. My feet have hurt since they were burned. My chest has hurt since the first beating."

I took her hands into my own again and kissed her knuckles. "I think you've got psychogenic pain. There's no physical source, but it doesn't make it any less real. When we're back in Saint Catherine, and if you're still hurting, ask your therapist to refer you to a colleague who can prescribe you something for it."

Jillian's therapist, Erica, was going to be seeing a *lot* more of her. Grew up in a cult, suffered from depression, was kidnapped and tortured? Jillian was going to be in therapy for the next thirty years. I had half a mind to root around in the house's medicine cabinets and see if I could find any sedatives. Heck, I'd give Jillian an opioid if better options weren't available.

But right now, I didn't want to leave her to find pills. I wanted to be close to her and feel her body heat. We wouldn't be having sex for a long time, but that didn't mean we couldn't enjoy each other's company for a few minutes right here in the living room. What could we do that would cheer her up?

The answer came immediately. "Hey, guess what I brought."

"What?"

I pulled the small velvet box out of my pocket. The fact that it had survived a fight with Daisy, the confrontation with Buck, the explosion at the substation, and storming the house seemed like a small miracle.

When I opened it, the flickering light from the fireplace made the white gold heart appear all the warm colors of fire. The peridot and blue topaz gemstones threw beautiful sparkles into her eyes.

I lifted it from the box and held it up. "I thought you'd want to wear this."

"Oh, yeah," she breathed, clearly charmed. I hooked it around her neck, and she gently stroked it. "It's so pretty."

Yep, my wife was still there. What else could I do that would cheer her up?

"Mrs. Trent?"

"Mmm."

"Would you like to dance?"

She rubbed under her nose. "What?"

I stood up and walked to the huge speaker system in the corner. I fiddled around with it, hooking it up to my phone, and quickly scrolled through my music until I found the song I wanted. I'd downloaded it last summer.

Frank Sinatra's croon wrapped around us, filling the room with romance. I held out my hands to Jillian, whose mouth had opened slightly in surprise. She let me pull her up, though her face fell. "I think I've forgotten how to dance," she said softly.

I pulled her close. "Don't think about your feet," I said, my lips brushing her forehead. "Just feel the music and let it move you."

She shivered, then laid her head on my shoulder.

We swayed in a slow circle while the song played, our hearts beating in unison. I closed my eyes and reveled in her heat, her soapy smell, her soft skin and damp hair.

My wife was with me.

She was alive, and that meant she'd won. We'd won. The sun would come up before too long and she'd see another day. We were all different people now than we'd been at the start of this mission, but for once in my life, I was at peace with who I was and what I had.

I held her tighter.

The song ended and Jillian stepped back, her lips turned up in a tiny smile. "Just once I'd like to dance with you without having a migraine."

And there goes the moment. Jillian was still sick, and she needed sleep more than dancing and conversation right now. I kissed her forehead again. "Let's get you into bed."

"You'd love that, wouldn't you." The same shimmer of the old Jillian appeared, then disappeared behind a coughing fit.

"Right now, I'd love for you to sleep for twelve hours," I said, tucking the afghan around her shoulders.

She followed me up the wide, curved staircase to the landing, at which I could hear voices and laughter from the rec room. *Laughter?* Shaking my head, I continued to lead her down the hall, though she stopped at a display of family photos.

She pointed to one. "Is that you?"

My face heated up. "Yeah, that's me. That was taken at my tenth birthday party."

In the picture, I was sitting at a large table surrounded by other young boys and a veritable mountain of presents. I'd grinned at the camera, my smile giving my rather large face even more roundness.

"You were so chubby," she said, another small smile lifting her lips. "I want to kiss those round cheeks."

"You sound like my mom." The words came out without thought, and immediately I regretted speaking as pain gripped my heart—and Jillian closed her eyes and hid her face from me in her hands. "Let's get you to bed," I said, pulling her gently through the door at the end of the hall.

My old bedroom was untouched by time or other Trents, though someone had dusted regularly in my absence. Perhaps my mother had truly believed I'd return one day. The vase on the side table next to the couch contained roses that were only a little dry instead of mummified, as they should've been. She'd left up the posters of various female athletes and lady action stars, though I knew she'd preferred I'd decorated some other way.

Saint Catherine was never meant to be our permanent home. We'd moved there merely to facilitate a large contract with the Howards, always intending on returning to the family seat: here. As such, I hadn't even packed. Georgia was a different climate, so I'd bought all new clothes. The few treasures I'd taken with me had fit into a backpack, which itself had fit perfectly underneath the seat on the airplane.

Jillian didn't wait for an invitation to crawl into my plush queen bed. She sighed in contentment when I pulled the down-filled duvet over her, and then mumbled something about "so soft" before rolling over.

All I could do was sit in the edge of the bed and watch her fall asleep while I stroked her hair.

When she was asleep, I got up and followed the giggles and voices coming from the rec room. I opened the door and paused, unable to process the scene before me.

Marco was propped up in a leather easy chair that nearly swallowed him. Reid was sitting cross-legged on the other. Lark, Berenice, Abby, and Ember all easily fit onto the leather couch, and they were passing a huge bowl of popcorn between them, which had been popped in the microwave that sat on the counter in the corner.

Bags of candy were scattered on the floor next to empty dinner bowls. Cans of soda, many more than people there to drink them, littered the carpet. All eyes were fixed on the six-foot curved flat screen television on the wall, itself above a crackling fire.

And—holy crap—they were watching the *Danger* series.

Berenice didn't look away from the cheesy rescue scene as she said, "You *did* tell us to make ourselves at home." She lazily draped her arm on the back of the couch and turned her head in my direction. "I found the DVD set in your closet while I was looking for a bathrobe. Nice poster of Streamline, by the way. I'd never seen a picture of my great-uncle."

"I wonder if there are any posters of us," Lark said. "I bet Reuben would be popular. Ole Tiger here would sell a million copies if she were in her kitty cat form." She gave Abbie a noogie.

Abby grinned and squirmed away. "Where Miss Stabby, Trent?"

I was still taking in the scene. "Don't you think we should, I don't know, watch out for Beau and Alysia?" I was fine with them relaxing, but now? All at once? And they were actually enjoying the schlockiest dreck to ever be put on the small screen?

"I'm listening for them," Ember said calmly. "In the meantime, we're having our first break in forever." She pointed to the screen. "No wonder you wanted to be a superhero. This guy has rescued five people in thirty minutes, and they're all leggy babes."

"I think Cassandra is the bad guy," Marco said while sipping his soda. "The orchestra played the song from the opening theme when Danger rescued the other ladies, but the music got all low and weird when he rescued her."

"Also, who randomly ends up down a well while wearing stilettos and a negligee?" Berenice said with a frown. "I mean, that would make *my* day more interesting, but it is suspicious."

"Stop talking," Reid ordered, leaning forward on his elbows. "That guy in the trench coat and sunglasses is spying on Danger again. I want to know who he's working for."

"Stick out," Abby said, her mouth twisting. "L.A. people wear tiny clothes. Danger not see Trench Coat. Danger dumb."

I shut the door.

If my friends were relaxing, I would not bother them for the next step.

My mother's body needed burial, and though I could not be the son she wanted in life, I would be the son she needed in death. I could give her a respectable burial, though it would be difficult in the frozen ground. Additionally, I wanted to get this task out of the way while Marco was distracted.

I was halfway down the hall towards my mother's room when the rec room door opened and shut. Abby jogged up to my side. "Red say Little Reuben bury bodies. Trent no bury. Sleep next Miss Stabby."

I sighed. *Fine, Ember.* "I'm not tired. Well, not tired enough to sleep. Also, can you please think of a different nickname for Jill? 'Miss Stabby' hurts her feelings. Maybe just 'Jill' or 'Battlecry.'"

Abby appeared to think for several seconds. "Sweetheart," she said with an air of finality. "Trent call wife Sweetheart."

I crossed my arms. "I'm the only one who's going to be calling her that."

Abby lolled her head and crossed her eyes at me. "Sweetheart, Sweetheart, Sweetheart."

"Oh, stop that. You're not dumb. You're doing this just to annoy me."

She straightened, her face smoothing out. "Abby not dumb," she said, suddenly serious. "Peter say Abby dumb for everything. Mom say Abby dumb for want Eddy. Ozark camp say Abby dumb for talk bad. Abby not dumb. Abby..." She trailed off, lost in thought. "Little Trent might think Abby mean." She shook her head. "Artemis *never* say Abby dumb. But Jen say Artemis dumb. Abby make Jen go. Abby not mean. Abby protect Artemis."

I had the feeling she'd been wanting to share this with someone for a while. Why else would she divulge such personal feelings with me? And who was Eddy?

But now wasn't the time or place. There were still chores that needed doing while we had the house to ourselves before the inevitable battle.

Still, I was curious to hear about the inner workings of the Baltimore team, and to find out who this Eddy guy was. "Would you like to talk about it more with me later?" I asked. "I need to go down to the basement and do something. Maybe after that?"

Abby looked surprised. "We get cameras in basement."

"I know," I said, my stomach twisting at the thought of someone like her down there. "How many did you get?"

She held up five fingers.

"Did you open the door at the end of the hall? The one with the padlock?"

"No. Door shut. Bird say probably booby trap."

"What about the guest room by the basement door?"

"Abby smell dead body, we stay away."

"That's fine," I said, relieved. I didn't care what happened to Will's corpse, but I didn't want Jillian's violence on display to people who might judge her for it. "Why don't you go back and enjoy the show?"

Abby looked surprised. "Where Sweetheart?"

This wasn't worth arguing over. "Jillian's sleeping. Please don't wake her up, especially for the *Danger* series."

Abby smiled a smile of unbelievable affection. "Abby guard Sweetheart. Sweetheart sick. Need Tiger. Tiger." With her final word, she leaped and transformed in midair, the tiny woman replaced in a fraction of a second by the majestic tiger I'd come to admire. She landed deftly on the runner and padded down the hallway, her flicking tail the last thing I saw as she disappeared into my room.

Somewhat more at ease now that the world's most effective predator was guarding my sleeping wife, I walked down the stairwell onto the silent first floor. Jillian's story had started in the guest room, so that's where I'd start, too. I hadn't been able to count how many SIM cards Berenice had crushed, but at a glance I could tell that she hadn't found all of them.

The north wing of the house was dedicated to guest rooms, four in total. Two of them were the unofficial permanent bedrooms of the Rowe twins, who traveled from Bel Alton so often that they kept clothes and toiletries here. Will and Beau had always gotten along famously, while Alysia tagged along and either spent time with my mother or harassed me. Eleanor was too old to care for her, and like most people of our ilk, Alysia had probably sensed that Eleanor was not one to bait.

Will's guest room door opened without a sound. I flipped on the light and gasped.

Blood was *everywhere*.

Thick, congealing blood dripped down the sides of the bed, off the sheets, and was even sprayed on the headboard. I had little doubt of whose blood it was. Still laying in bed, his face eternally frozen in wide-eyed shock, lay the mortal remains of William Rowe.

I was no forensic investigator, but his manner of death was simple to deduce from wounds. She'd probably sprinted at him while he was sleeping and stabbed him with—where was it?—the chef's knife that was now laying on the floor. I counted no less than twenty knife wounds in his abdomen.

I stood over his body for a long minute, searching for words. What was there to say about a man who'd lived his life to deprive others of theirs? He hadn't even killed, really. He'd taken pleasure in causing suffering. It had been *funny* to him.

There was nothing to say. Instead, I strode over to the bland portrait of a lighthouse on the far wall and moved it aside, revealing a little alcove in which a small digital camera was hidden. I removed it, popped out the SIM card, then threw the camera at the mirror above the dresser with all my might. My reflection shattered, and I walked out of the room.

Will could rot where he'd died. Maybe a human necromancer would come along and turn him into a puppet for once. Or maybe Beau and Alysia would come home after we'd all left and be greeted to the ripe smell of moldering cadaver wafting from his room. Both possibilities cheered me immensely.

The basement door was still open, since the electromagnetic field that kept it locked had been powered by the shish-kabobed generators. I descended the cement stairwell, taking care to not step on the bloody footprints that marked where Jillian had ascended not two hours before.

The basement was exactly as I remembered it, one long hallway flanked by doors that were now open, pulled back into the wall. The left side of the hallway contained cells, all but one no larger than an average house's bathroom. The sixth cell was larger, since it contained a tiny mattress intended for sick prisoners.

The right side of the hall contained interrogation rooms. Only the door at the end of the hall remained shut and locked. My grandfather had insisted that it remain unchanged by time, as a memorial to my family's finest hour.

Jillian's cell was easy to find. They'd put her in the third cell, and bloody smears still marked the floor. I stepped inside the freezing room and knelt down in the corner, where the bloodstains were the most concentrated. She'd curled up on the floor; I could see where she'd placed her hand after the needles had been applied.

I laid my fingers on the hand print and closed my eyes, hoping that with the gesture, my love for her somehow travel through time and space to that moment.

The Baltimore team had industriously removed every SIM card from the open interrogation rooms, so I didn't linger in each one and imagine what had happened there. Instead, I headed straight for the final door at the end of the hall. I stared at the padlocked handle.

Lark had rightly been suspicious of the one door that required touching to open. In this house, in this basement, it could've been anything. Though I knew what was behind the door, I couldn't help but smile. At one time, I'd been thwarted by the padlock.

I kicked the door open.

But I'd learned some new skills since leaving home.

The large cement room contained just three items: a projector, a wooden chair, and a projector screen. The chair's seat was smeared with fresh blood, and handcuffs hung loosely from one of the rungs. Along the far wall, beneath the projector screen, seven faded brown spots marred the cement floor.

Though she hadn't said as much, Jillian had been brought here before any formal interrogation. I couldn't imagine a better way to break a person's spirit than to play the video reel.

I walked over to the projector, adjusted the reel, and pressed play. While the beginning fuzz played, I sat down in the chair and tried to watch the movie as Jillian would've seen it.

A young man, no older than eighteen, appeared on the screen. His right eye was swollen shut, and blood poured down his temples from wounds beneath his thick, black hair. He was kneeling in front of the cement wall that now bore the screen, and his hands were bound behind his back.

My grandfather's voice came from the speakers on each side of the projector screen. I'd never heard his voice in person, because he'd died shortly after this video had been made. "State your name and codename."

"Alexander Williamson," the young man rasped. "Aquarius."

"Any last words?"

Alexander fought tears, then stared straight at the camera. "I love you, Dad."

A man appeared from off camera with a knife in hand, his face cut off from the camera. Without any further ado, he grabbed Alexander's hair, pulled his head back, and sliced his jugular open.

Anguished cries were audible from elsewhere in the room. Alexander crumpled and fell, his neck pouring out the blood that would eventually cause the faded stain to the far right.

One by one, each of the next five team members were pulled in front of the camera. My grandfather ordered each one to identify themselves and asked if they had any last words.

Ada Dumont, the famous Horizon, stared with tortured longing at one of her teammates, whose low voice told her that he'd be with her soon. I'd never been able to determine which of her male teammates had spoken.

George Yazzie, called Blink, smirked even though he was probably partially blind from eye trauma. "I told you you'd never get me to talk."

Renee Monroe, who'd fought as Aura, was so dazed that one of her teammates identified her, and she had to be held up by someone else as my grandfather killed her. She probably hadn't been aware of what was happening.

Katherine Theodorakis, whose code name had been Lyric, jutted her chin up after identifying herself and told my grandfather that she'd see him in hell.

Alan Harris, Spitfire, looked so much like Ember that I covered my mouth in shock. How had I never noticed? Was he her grandfather? A great-uncle? Once the surprise wore off, I let myself be impressed as always by his final words. He merely stared off screen to the final prisoner and said, "It's been an honor."

The last teammate landed on her knees with a rough thud. She was in early middle age and of middling stature, with the same swarthy features that she'd passed on to her youngest daughter Gemma, who had herself passed them on to my wife. Yet, the elder Jillian's eyes were large and shining, so like her grandson's. Her face shape, more round than long, also hinted at Marco more than my Jillian.

"State your name and code name."

"Jillian St. James, Battlecry." Her voice was hoarse, no doubt from whatever it was they'd done to her to silence her ultrasonic scream. Indeed, she coughed after speaking.

"What is your position on your team?"

"Commander."

"Any final words?"

I leaned forward, studying my favorite part of the reel with renewed interest.

Jillian coughed again, and then surprise flitted across her face, quickly replaced by calculation. She gazed up at my grandfather. "Do I have any final words?" she croaked, a malevolent gleam in her eye. "Yeah. See you soon."

Then she opened up her mouth and let out a diabolical, eardrum-scratching scream.

It seemed that her power had also returned at the eleventh hour.

The footage ended abruptly as the projector fifty years ago had been knocked over. Or maybe the lens had shattered. Dad had never explained the details of what happened afterwards, only that my grandfather had died the next day of massive internal bleeding.

There were seven stains, though, so someone must've finished the job. Now that I thought about it, I wondered if my mother had showed the final portion to my wife. As horrific as the first six deaths were, my wife would've derived amusement from her grandmother's attack. I sure as hell did.

I stood up and turned off the projector. The hidden camera was behind a dummy speaker in the wall, and like before, I removed the SIM card and destroyed the camera.

When I came upstairs, I could see that pre-sunrise light lit up the foyer in long gold-and-scarlet beams through the windows, reminding me that our time here could not go on as it had. Ember was no doubt scanning intently for Beau and Alysia, but they would return eventually, and we had to make a decision. Jillian wasn't in any state to fight.

Where could we go that was safe until she recovered? Jen's parents' house was out of the question, as was Saint Catherine. We needed to get far away, preferably somewhere off the grid. Unfortunately, the only place I could think of was Liberty. Clearly we needed to brainstorm and come up with a better option.

Low voices in the living room caught my attention. I peeked around the corner and saw Ember and Reid sitting close together on the couch in front of the fire, as Jillian and I had done not long before.

I was about to leave when Ember called, "Ben, you can come here."

I dashed to the back of the couch in a second. They were holding hands. "What's up?"

"We've talked," Ember said, smiling prettily up at me. "We both owe you an apology for how we've been acting on the mission. We're very sorry, and hope you can forgive us."

Reid looked away, shamefaced.

A small tension unraveled in my chest. These two had been a pillar on our team, and the world wasn't right when they were apart. "Gladly," I said, placing my hands on their shoulders. "Are you guys going to be okay now?" I didn't care how or why they were back together, just that they were.

"We're getting there," Ember said, turning her smile back to Reid. "We've both gotten some perspective while we've been here."

"That's excellent." I gave both their shoulders a light squeeze. I hurried out of the living room to give them privacy, but the soft, feminine pats of hurrying feet made me stop in the hallway.

Ember caught up to me. "I wanted you to know why," she said, clasping her hands in front of her and chewing on her lips. "It's because of you. Well, you and Jill."

Jillian and I had convinced her to forgive him? I was touched, but also confused. I frowned, hoping she wasn't offended. "How so?"

She winced as she said, "I know you were upset when I sent you away while I helped Jill clean up. But please know, that was by her request. She didn't want you to see evidence of her injuries. She was sparing you that." She bowed her head. "The whole time in the bathroom, all she thought of was you and how frantic you must have been since she was taken."

Another knot of tension unraveled. I *had* been hurt by Ember's insistence that she look after my wife, leaving me in the cold hallway. But now that I knew that Jillian had requested it, I understood. "And that helped you with Reid?"

Ember nodded, a deep red blush appearing in her cheeks. "I realized that if she can still think of someone else's feelings immediately after being tortured for two days, I can think of Reid even if I was scared in Liberty. Jillian loves you, and I love Reid—but I need to start showing it."

She rubbed the back of her head, her eyes unable to meet mine. "I told him about how frightened I am all the time now, with all the uncertainty about superheroes..." She took a deep breath and finally looked up at me. "And the unavoidable fact that I should've been the one in the basement, Ben." She wiped her eyes. "Jill was the backup option. I... I've seen in her head... what... they did..."

I didn't wait for an invitation. I wrapped my arms around my thin teammate while she wept and held her to my chest, her terror and embarrassment over her relief pricking at the edges of my mind.

She feared my judgment, but her fear was groundless. I didn't want to be tortured, either. Who would?

"I'm not like the others," she said after her tears had subsided. "All the other women can kill you with their thumbs, but I'm always relying on someone else to protect me. That gets to you after a while." She stepped back and made a face. "Oh, Ember's so *pretty*. Ember's so *fragile*. Ember's so *obviously* the token damsel in distress."

"I've seen *Ember* order dogs to tear chunks out of people's flesh," I reminded her. There was no way she was repeating the thoughts of any of us. Yeah, she wasn't much of a martial artist, but then again, neither was I. Jillian, Reid, and Marco held the telepath in high esteem and had never once complained about watching out for her.

"I need my powers for that," she said, her tone dark. "And Beau was ready and able to take them away with that poison." Her gaze unfocused for a second and she laughed under her breath. "Though, you know, in other circumstances, I might welcome that," she said, more to herself than me. "Nobody would come after me if I were just another civilian."

"Darling?" Reid turned the corner. "Are you okay?"

She held out her hand to him, her unhappy visage melting into a beautiful smile. "I'm fine. Let's go back to the fire."

Reid's relieved half-grin punctured my heart. Here was a man who'd lost everything and found it again—rather like myself, I supposed.

When they'd wandered hand-in-hand back to the living room, I went upstairs. Berenice's voice made me pause outside Eleanor's room, her tone indicating she was on the phone.

"...everything's fine." There was a long pause, and then she said, "No, I called to apologize. I kinda freaked out back there and I feel bad. I'm really sorry." Another pause. "Aw, Jen, please don't cry. It's a sore spot and I didn't think before I spoke. You know I'm a huge jerk and you shouldn't take anything I say seriously. You've been nothing but super nice to me. To all of us."

Eleanor's mattress squeaked and Berenice sighed. "Creep One and Creep Two aren't here, so we're all relaxing. Lark and Marco are watching this awesome series that we're watching together when I get back." She laughed. "Girl, you should see the size of the television they've got here. Ember and Reid made up, I think. They're probably downstairs making out." There was another long silence. "I think she's with Jill."

There was a brief silence, and then, "No, she's not okay. Neither of them are. I don't know if either of them will recover from this." She breathed a laugh. "Well, no, he's not my *favorite* person, but I can pity someone whose wife was tortured." Yet another pause. "She looked like she'd been hit with a baseball bat a few dozen times. She was still walking around, though. But I could've told you that she could take a beating. Damn woman never stays down. For Heaven's sake, she was tortured for two days and all she has at the end of things is a bad hack."

I tiptoed away, shaking my head. I knew with all my heart that if I asked Berenice how she felt about me, she wouldn't bat an eye as she said that she hated my guts. Jen had been right. There was a, well, not sweet woman underneath the sour exterior, but someone whose bark was slightly worse than her bite. Maybe.

There was only one place I wanted to be for these final few hours before the decision-making had to begin. I knocked softly on my door to alert Abby, then went inside. She was laid out on the carpet by the foot of the bed, her forelegs crossed in recognizable leisure. Her furry head lifted in interest as I walked in, and then the tiger dissolved into the woman.

Abby clambered to her feet and pointed to Jill. "Much water. Need Trent."

"Gotcha," I said, grateful for Abby's attentiveness. Jill would need to drink regularly to replace all the fluids she'd lost, even if my powers could replenish blood cells. I zipped to the rec room and grabbed a bottle of expensive filtered water from the mini fridge—Danger was now embracing the first of many buxom love interests—and was at Jillian's side just as quickly. I could feel the heat radiating from her body through the duvet.

Abby came up to my side, her eyebrows drawn together in concern. "Why bottle? Water," she said, as if she were correcting me. She placed a hand on Jillian's collarbone. "Need no bottle."

I still had no idea what she meant, but I sensed that it was important. "Abby, please explain to me what you mean like I'm the stupidest person you've ever met. Explain it to me like I'm Peter."

I expected her to either laugh or grimace, but instead she bit her lip as her eyes darted back and forth. "I... hear... water," she said, the immense difficulty of speaking normally causing visible strain on her face. "In Sweetheart chest."

My ear was on Jillian's chest in a second, my own chest rising and falling heavily. Jillian had only been gone for two days. There wasn't time for her flu to turn into anything more serious.

At least, that's what I wanted to believe.

I strained to hear the bubbling, crackling sound described in my nursing textbooks...but I could hear nothing, because I was still partially deaf. Mute horror crept over me—Jillian had probably been presenting with the audible symptoms of pneumonia since we found her, but I hadn't been able to hear them. Without a stethoscope, there was only one person I trusted to maybe offer a reliable description of the sound in her lungs.

I was in the rec room an instant later. "Marco, I need you."

He jumped up, alert. "What is it?"

"Listen to Jillian's lungs. Tell me what you hear."

The urgency must've come across, because both Lark and Marco ran past me though Lark ran down the hall towards Eleanor's room.

In my room, Marco slid into place next to Jillian, whose face was damp with a sheen of sweat. He placed his head on her chest. "Rales," he whispered. "Crackling." He put his ear to Jillian's slightly open mouth. "Wet. How did I miss it?" He put a hand to her forehead, then yanked the duvet back and began untying her robe. "Dude, she's burning up. Was she this hot when she went to sleep?"

"No," I said, pulling off her socks with equal haste. She complained of a headache and..." *Oh, no. Oh my God, how did I miss it? Why didn't I think to check?*

"What?" he demanded. "What did she say?"

"Chest pain," I said. "She complained of chest pain. I think she has pneumonia. We need to move her *now*." I moved past Marco and sat on the bed, cradling Jillian. "Sweetheart, you have to wake up," I said loudly. "We're taking you to the doctor." Jillian's eyelids fluttered, but she couldn't be roused. "Wake up," I repeated, shaking her a little. "Jillian, wake up, please. Jillian!"

"She looks like you did when you had Emily's fever."

I jerked my head towards the door. Reid stood next to Ember, both of them holding damp rags. Reid handed me the cloths, which I laid on Jillian's forehead and behind her neck.

"How did they get it down?" I asked, desperately dabbing at her face. The cloths were already warm. Beau had given her a shot of fever reducer, but I had no idea what it was, who made it, or if there was anymore in the house.

"Emergency medicine," Reid said. "I don't know what they did."

"We need to call 911, then," I said, pulling out my phone.

Marco grabbed it from me. "No, we can't. Hospitals aren't safe, as we saw in Baltimore. Beau and Alysia will be looking for us before long. Jill is going to need a long time in whatever hospital we go to." He steeled himself, then looked at Reid. "Call them. This is what they exist for, isn't it?"

What? "Who do you mean? What's going on?"

But Reid was already out the door, dialing his phone. Marco ran out after him, leaving me with Ember.

I held up my hands in a "help me" gesture. "Can someone please explain?"

Ember obviously did some quick thinking. "You know that we can't admit ourselves to civilian hospitals," she said slowly. "Though sometimes civilians like Jen drag us into them, and they're not allowed to deny us medical care. But do you know *why* we can't admit ourselves?"

"No," I said, rubbing my temples. "What does this—"

"Because we're at our greatest disadvantage when we're recuperating," she said, the picture of patience. "A lot of us used to die in hospitals before the laws were changed. Insurance companies were also getting tired of shelling out millions after attacks. Now there's just one hospital we go to, and it's the safest building on the planet. Luckily, it's not very far from here."

I slowly stood up, the pieces falling together. "You're talking about the Super hospital in Leesburg."

Leesburg, Virginia was just an hour and a half west of Annapolis. I'd visited once when my high school's JROTC battalion had competed against Loudoun County High School's in a regional competition.

"Yes," she said, biting her lip. "Reid is on the phone with the police right now. They're going to call in the medevac helicopter. It'll probably be here in ten minutes."

Something about her tone, the way she hesitated when speaking, bothered me. "What's wrong, then? What aren't you telling me?"

"Before I answer, tell me that you understand that it's the only place she can go."

My heart began to beat double time. "Ember, what the hell is going on?" My voice had grown higher.

"Tell me that you understand. I need to hear you say it."

"It's the only place she can go."

"You know how it's so fortified?"

"Yeah..."

Ember's fingers twisted in the hem of her tunic. "Jillian told Beau that the fortifications were secretly for protecting the JM-104. He bought it. That's where Beau and Alysia are now."

ITEM EIGHTEEN

Letters sent between Christina St. James and her daughter Juliana
Harris, dated March 1927.

Juliana,
Perhaps I did not make myself plain enough. I am not
unsympathetic to a widow's pain and desperation—I miss your
Papa every day—but if you insist on whoring around with that
colored man, I will have to take action.
Edward and I have been working with the Richmond city
council to set up an official "team," and we can not have you if you
insist on living with Harold. If you don't care for me anymore,
think of the precious children you had with Arthur and how you'd
shame them. They wouldn't be able to hold their head up in public.
Furthermore, the only reason the country loves us is because we're
moral. Consider the impact if we acted like the rabble.
Love,
Mama

Reply:

Dear Mama,

I'm already pregnant. If it's a girl, I'll call her Christina after you. If it's a boy, he'll be Marco, for grandpa. I want to start new family naming traditions. Don't worry, I won't "shame" my other children by calling my new children Harris—they'll be St. James! Oh—two St. James families, one white and one colored. I can't wait for the heads to spin!

Xoxoxoxo

Juliana

P.S. Take off your white hat, Mama. You can't stop me.

18

I had fifteen minutes to do this.

The snow-covered dirt opened up in front of us, and a six-foot-long, four-foot-deep grave appeared with no fuss. There was only room for one body, since I truly didn't care what happened to Will's remains. He'd polluted my childhood—he wasn't going to permanently pollute my yard. Even at this somber moment, I still liked the thought of Beau discovering Will's remains where they lay.

The morning wind blew in strong gusts from the water, unbroken by the trees. The flap of sheet that covered my mother's dead-eyed stare whipped up, and I found myself looking down into her clouding eyes.

I jostled the heavy corpse in my arms, trying to nudge the sheet back in place, but instead her whole face became exposed. There was a perfect vertical slit between her eyebrows.

"Let me help you," Reid said, holding his arms out to take the heavy corpse from my arms. "I'll be very careful."

I stepped back, my teeth chattering. "No, I need to do it," I insisted. "I'm her son."

I had no idea what I was going to do, though. Placing her manually into a hole that deep would be awkward, and hardly dignified.

"You're shaking," he said quietly. "What if I just make a platform and lower her down?"

Instead of waiting for an answer, his eyes glowed again and loose dirt from around the grave flew up and formed a plank. The platform floated up to me.

My arms *were* about to give out. My entire body had been wracked by shivers since I'd stumbled out of my bedroom and towards my mother's room just minutes before.

I had no time. We had no time. Everything was crashing down at once: Jillian was lethally ill, we were going to the last place on earth we should, and I had mere minutes to lay my mother to rest and make my peace with it.

And I could not do anything about it.

I laid my mother's body on the plank. *She killed a lot of people. It's not a big loss to you or the world.*

Reid put his hand on my shoulder. "Do you want to say anything?" He glanced over my shoulder, then looked back to me, his face infuriatingly calm. Now that he was assured of Ember's love, he was once again the strong, sturdy hero I'd admired. I hated him for it.

I swore, a terrible lump forming in my throat. "What am I supposed to say? 'Thanks for torturing my wife? Sorry your baby couldn't have been mom's little psychopath'?" My voice grew higher and higher. "Just stick her in the ground. Get this over with. The helicopter will be here soon."

I simply tucked the sheet back around my mother's face. *She never really loved you. If she had, she wouldn't have done any of it. It was all fake.*

He nodded, and the shrouded body descended into the cold earth, coming to rest without so much as a rustle at the bottom of the grave. With a wave of his hand, dirt fell on the body, concealing it from me.

When the last of the displaced dirt was back in place, he lowered his hand in the air as if pressing down on something, and the loose grave dirt compacted. "If you want, I'll get some rocks and mark the grave. They'll also prevent animals from digging up the remains."

The image of animals digging up my mother was too much.

I fell to my knees, my forehead touching the ground, and let the wretched, humiliating tears fall. To hell with Reid, who would never understand. I didn't care if he and the entire Baltimore team saw me crying like a baby on a murderer's grave.

She'd been my mother, and she'd *loved* me.

She'd loved my lisp when I was five. She'd loved my rotund belly when I was ten. She'd loved me when I was fifteen and had cried after killing my first victim. She'd loved me when I was a high school senior sulking in my room after my father had ripped up my acceptance letter to Old Dominion University. She'd loved me when I'd had trouble making friends in Saint Catherine.

Through all of that, she'd loved me and looked at me with the fondness only a mother can have for her child.

She'd loved me, but she hadn't loved my choices. And my choices were objectively better than hers. I would have to learn how to reconcile these two thoughts.

Warm hands appeared on my shoulders.

"Go away," I growled. "Give me a damn minute."

"I would—"

I jerked my head up. That wasn't Reid's voice.

"—but Jill's been saying your name. I thought you'd like to be near her." Marco was kneeling next to me. His large, sad eyes conveyed many emotions, all of them kind. "Ember said you were trying to hide this from me, but I can't figure out why."

"Ember should mind her own business! I just want to bury my mom and not—not—have to defend why I'm sad, okay? She's my *mom*." I stood up and immediately marched back towards the house. Ice had encrusted around my eyes.

"Ben, wait," Marco called, running up to my side. "What do you mean, defend why you're sad?"

I furiously wiped my eyes with my sleeve. "You know what I mean."

"I really don't."

"I'm sorry she killed your sisters," I said, pathetic as anything. He flinched, but I plunged on, "I wish I could go back and fight her off myself. I would in a heartbeat. I wish I could've been a better boyfriend so we would've left Liberty sooner and maybe stopped the attack. I wish I'd never met you guys, because then Jillian wouldn't be suffocating to death up there, and Caroline, and Melissa, and Adora would be alive. I wish I'd never been born, or at least been born different, able to be happy here with my family."

The words flowed out of the fear and anger that was destroying me. I'd dragged them all down.

There was a long silence while he stared at me. Finally, he said, "You wish you'd never met us?"

My thoughts stopped. "I... I... well... you'd be safe if I hadn't."

"Ben, we'd be dead."

I shook my head. "No, you wouldn't. Any time I saved you after meeting you was because of—"

"Do you have any idea whatsoever how miserable we all were?" His words lashed out like a whip. "What it was like before you came into our lives? No, of course you don't, because we hate talking about those days. But maybe we should."

He put his hands on his hips, looking comically like Jillian when she was put out with me. "Maybe we should talk about what it's like to hear your teammates screaming in other rooms while your leader beats them for made-up infractions. Maybe we should talk about what it's like to see women you regard as sisters pull their hair out in clumps because of stress. Maybe we should talk about being in pain every single day because of injuries that nobody on the team had the skill to attend to."

"Marco, I—"

"I think we should talk about actually wanting to study and learn medicine but having no idea how! Maybe we should talk about how I've always thought you were cool and kept studying medicine to be more like you! Maybe we should talk about how yeah, sure, we're all uneducated, but nobody ever held your relatives against you! We all think it's great that you wanted to be like us and gave up *everything*! I mean, look at your house, for God's sake! It's a mansion! You have a room just for television! And..."

He stepped back, his hands on his head. "Dude, I saw your senior portrait on the wall up there. You were wearing a school uniform. You went to a fancy private school, didn't you? You could've gone anywhere and done anything with your life, but you chose to be with us. You chose us," he repeated faintly. "And it's made our lives better. So don't stand there and tell me that you wish you'd never met m—us, because you have no idea what you're saying."

I didn't know how to respond, so I dropped my head. "I'm sorry," I whispered.

He stepped back and surveyed me. "And I have never been angry at you because of what your mom did, nor will I ever be. I came out to tell you about Jill, but also to say that I'm sorry you had to do this. I know what it's like to lose family. If you have anything nice to say about your mom, I won't stop you from saying it."

I closed my eyes and recalled the last time I'd seen her alive, half a year before. I'd stood on the roof of the submerged school and pleaded with my parents to leave Jillian and me in peace. Mom had been so convinced of my loyalty to my family that she'd deluded herself into believing that Jillian had somehow forced me to desert.

I'd always remember my mother's desperate, plaintive face as she'd pleaded with me to come home, and then with my father to spare my life. I knew without a doubt that if I had taken her offer, my mother would've immediately forgiven all the pain I'd caused her. She would've embraced me and kissed my cheek—those formerly chubby cheeks that she'd loved so much—and called me her Benny.

Dad was gone. Eleanor was gone. Mom was gone. And now, Jillian was about to be gone, too. The urge to run made my feet itch, though I couldn't think of a location. I just wanted to get *away*.

"My family's disintegrating," I said faintly, staring up at my bedroom window. "I can't stop it. What do I do?" I turned back to him. "I can't heal sickness."

He gestured at the door. "Right now, you can go inside and hold

Jill's hand. You're her husband, and that's what husbands are supposed to do. Just being there for her will be enough for now."

I was at the bedroom door in less than three seconds. Jillian was awake—sort of. Abby was holding her up in bed and offering her the bottle of water I'd fetched, but Jillian was only half conscious.

Abby turned to me. "Helicopter?"

"In a few minutes," I said, sitting on the bed and delicately taking Jillian from Abby. "Go get your team together. We're all going to the hospital."

After Abby had hurried out of the room, I simply leaned Jillian against my chest and stroked her hair. Abby had industriously undressed Jillian to just her linen pajamas, cooling her off a little bit.

"You're going to be okay," I whispered. "This will pass. You're going to be safe at the hospital. Beau and Alysia can't get in. You were very smart to send them there. You'll be fine. You'll be fine."

Jillian began to cough and sputter. Heat poured from her, making sweat bead on her temples and forehead. When she was done, she gave my hand a tiny squeeze. "Drums," she said. She tried to pull back to look at me, but her head swayed to the side.

"Easy," I said, laying her back in the bed. "Don't stress yourself."

"Drums," she repeated, louder. "War drums."

Was she delirious? I grabbed the cloth and poured water from the bottle on it, then mopped her forehead. "What do you mean, sweetheart?"

Her head dropped to the side and she pointed weakly to the window. "I hear them."

I paused, then turned around to face the window. I saw them immediately: two tiny helicopters in the sky, approaching rapidly over the water. The sound of the blades were lost to me at this distance, but to my wife's sensitive ears and fevered imagination... they sounded like the rapid beats of war drums.

A shiver shot down my spine.

ITEM NINETEEN

Excerpt of open letter written by Christina St. James, printed in the *Richmond Times-Dispatch*, November 9, 1931

Some well-meaning Americans have taken to calling my team "super-heroes," hearkening back to those mighty men of legend as well as acknowledging that which differentiates us from them. I embrace this term, because like those men, we aspire to the highest moral highs and abjure all vice.

But I also posit this: our enemies, those vagabonds and brigands who have betrayed you all by turning their powers against you instead of using them as God intended, are not mere criminals but villains—corrupt and devoid of moral fiber. Perhaps even "super-villains," if one prefix deserves another. We solemnly swear and affirm to dedicate our lives to finding and apprehending all such creatures.

19

The downdraft from the blades made Ember's hair dance as she faced me in the front yard. Behind her, Lark, Berenice, Reid, and Abby were situating themselves into the seats that lined both sides of the second red-and-white helicopter. I'd be with Jillian in the main helicopter, of course, and we'd all agreed that she'd probably want Marco there, too.

Ember grasped my hand. *The nurse knows what to do. This isn't the worst thing she's dealt with.*

I turned and watched the flight nurse in my helicopter speak to Jillian as they secured the stretcher to the floor of the helicopter. *How is she?*

Ember sighed. *She's out of it. Try to keep a happy face for her, will you?*

I gave my best smile, but I could feel how pained it was.

Ember grimaced. *Just don't get bogged down with the burial. You've got to keep moving forward. That's your new motto, right?*

"Hey!" Marco yelled from the helicopter door a few feet away. "Stop gabbing and get in your seats!"

I squeezed Ember's hand and leaped into the helicopter, where

Marco had his arms folded over his chest and a glare fixed on his face. *Moving forward,* I reminded myself. *Focus on the here and now.*

The flight nurse slammed the door, shutting us in. Marco and I buckled up in the spare seats, placed there for the predicted team members of whatever hapless superhero was in the bed. At least, that's what I figured. I'd never studied the design of the air ambulances that serviced the Super hospital.

The dim whine of the rotor grew higher, and then we were in the air, the helicopter nosing forward slightly. Marco's glare melted away, replaced by sincere childlike wonder.

I elbowed him. "Never been in a helicopter before?"

He stared all around us, his mouth slightly open. "No," he said, dazed. "Just the plane to Baltimore last month." He twisted around in his seat and pressed his nose against the window. "Whoa. Is that the Chesapeake Bay?" He pointed to the iron-gray body of water to the east.

"Yep. And we're over the South River now."

"How far to the hospital?" he asked, still staring out the window.

The flight nurse, Genele, answered without looking up from Jillian, who'd dozed off. "Half an hour."

We both turned our attention to what she was doing. Genele expertly set up respiratory support, inserting oxygen tubes so Jillian could breathe better. Next, she inserted an IV to keep her hydrated, then a bag of broad-spectrum antibiotics. Finally, she drew a sample of blood and sat at a tiny desk to analyze it. I was tempted to ask her to explain what she was doing, but I knew better than to interrupt an EMS professional at her work.

"What are we flying over now?" Marco asked after several minutes of thoughtful silence.

I gazed out the window at the neighborhood below. "Northern Virginia, I think," I said, taking in the enormous houses and highways. "D.C. is that way," I added, pointing towards the pink-and-orange sunrise, "and Saint Catherine is that way," I finished, pointing south.

"I can see a hospital," he said, squinting. "There's a helicopter pad and the big buildings. It looks just like Saint Catherine General." He turned to Genele. "Is that the Super hospital? It doesn't look anything like how I've been told."

Genele glanced out the window for a fraction of a second before returning to the vial of blood. "We're over Reston. It's viral pneumonia, by the way." She stood up and adjusted Jillian's IV bag. "Ten minutes, guys. I need to go speak to the pilot."

She pulled open a small door that separated us from the cockpit, then shut it with a bang.

"Where am I?"

Jillian's quiet, wheezy voice made us both spin around in our seats and grin.

"Guess," Marco said. "Just guess. I bet you can't."

She made a face at him. "Is this an ambulance? It doesn't sound like one." She coughed again, then rubbed her forehead. "I feel like I was hit by a truck."

We both threw off our belts and leaped to our feet. "We're in a medical helicopter," I explained, brushing away the lock of hair that continually skimmed her face. "You sound better already." And she did, if exhausted. Her eyes were a little clearer, and she was speaking relatively normally. What the heck was in that IV bag?

The sun glinted off the metallic logo on the bag: Bell Enterprises.

Oh. Well, they'd made the Supers. Nothing should surprise me anymore.

Marco leaned on the edge of the stretcher. "So, guess where we're going?" he said, his tone laced with teasing.

Jillian's face cracked into a huge grin and she sat up as much as the straps would allow her. "Home? Are we going home?" She reached for my hand. "I can't wait to sleep in my own bed." She leaned back on her pillow, dreamy satisfaction erasing years from her face. "Maybe I'll get some more reading in. I found an online used bookstore that sells paperback romances for a buck each. Ah, I can't wait."

I couldn't meet her eyes.

Marco shook his head. "Sorry, kiddo. We're going to the Super hospital. You went and got yourself viral pneumonia. You know, like a champ."

Her smile fell off her face. "The *Super* hospital? That's where Beau and Alysia are. Why didn't Ember *tell* you?" Her fingers tore little holes in the sheets. "I—we can't. We have to go somewhere else."

I was with her on this, but I didn't have any idea where "somewhere else" could be, so I elected to kiss her knuckles and hope she didn't see the anxiety I felt.

Yet, Marco actually smirked and said, "If you can make a good argument for how Beau and Alysia will get in, I'll freak out with you."

Jillian scowled at Marco's calm face for several seconds. Finally, she said, "A bomb."

He threw his head back and laughed. "Oh, come on. Like they haven't thought of that. The only bomb that would work is a nuke, and I think we can safely assume that Beau doesn't have one of those."

She rolled her eyes and muttered something. Her words weren't audible to me, but Marco scoffed, "A know-it-all? Please. I just remember what I learned from the final test."

"What final test?" I asked. Conversations like this were a painful reminder that they'd had a completely different life than I had.

Jillian's unhappy countenance softened. "We all had to do a battery of exams to qualify for service. Some were physical, like the obstacle course, and others were mental, like the problem-solving portion." She paused to cough, gesturing for Marco to continue for her.

Marco sat back down in his seat. "There are about fifteen different questions that they recycle among trainees. Mine was to figure out how to break into the Super hospital and stop a supervillain from releasing a deadly virus into the air."

"What did you do?"

"Eh, it was an elaborate scheme that involved me fake-breaking my leg or something. I kinda pulled it out of my butt, but it worked. The important part of this story, though, is that I was told all the defenses." He shook his head. "If I didn't know any better, I'd think that they were guarding the US gold reserve."

"Tell me," I said as I sat down next to him.

Jillian watched us, a sleepy smile back on her face. Though she sometimes moaned about how hard camp life was, deep down I knew she loved the ferocious competition with herself that this life provided, and all the grittier aspects of her training she'd endured. After all, this was the woman who'd returned to Saint Catherine despite everything. She hadn't exposed the camps because she hated superheroes, she'd done so because she hated the system.

Marco folded his hands on his lap and chewed on his lip while he thought. "The hospital complex is in the middle of a huge campus. The perimeter of the campus is surrounded by two walls, both of which are six feet thick. The walls have the usual: razor wire, electric field, all that. Manned guard towers line the wall every... thirty feet, I think? Something like that. They've got machine guns, grenades, the works. Between the walls is a twenty-foot-wide moat, but it ain't filled with water."

"What's in the—"

"They never said," he replied with a significant look, "But I was told that if I ever stepped in the liquid, I'd swiftly regret it."

Ah. "Go on, then."

"The walls themselves are filled with weird layers to stop people like Alysia. Do you know if there's anything she can't go through?"

That was easy. "Water." Alysia avoided all pools and other places of aquatic merriment on principle. She always had to be at the advantage.

He laughed quietly. "Both walls have a bladder of water in the middle. She won't be able to walk through them, and even if she could, she wouldn't want to." He grinned. "Beyond the walls is a half-mile of land mines."

"Land mines."

"Yep, land mines."

"Well... damn."

"They've got some sophisticated monitoring going on, too. Lark told me that she heard from someone that there are weaponized drones on site now, though she's not sure if that's true. But the biggest defense isn't ordnance," he said, gesturing all around us. "It's this, the helicopter system. Nobody can drive in. There isn't even a road. Everyone is vetted out the yin-yang and flown in. The staff lives on campus. When Reid made the call, he had to give our numbers and information. We were run through a computer before the choppers were ever dispatched. But the computers are on a private network, so it's unlikely that Beau would be able to hack in without physically being on the campus."

"There's no computer on earth that's safe from Beau," I said, but my head was spinning. I'd always heard that the hospital was guarded, but I'd assumed that entailed lots of metal detectors, cameras, and maybe an armed patrol. What Marco described was more in line with a military weapons testing facility than a hospital. "Just one more question."

"Shoot."

"Who pays for all this?"

"Bell."

Of course. They'd shown themselves to be knee-deep in every aspect of the Supers, most especially where superheroes were involved. If we opened up the can, how many worms would we find?

Jillian rearranged herself in the stretcher. "He could still get in, you know," she said with a yawn. "Ember said he distracted y'all with a bomb a few nights ago." She began to fiddle with the straps to get comfortable. "He's a scumbag, but he's not stupid."

Marco crossed his arms, his eyebrow quirked in amusement. "Sure, he could toss a bomb. Then he'll have to develop magic bullet-stopping powers, dodge drone strikes, cross that stupid moat—let's assume it's filled with either gators or acid—and then play hopscotch with landmines. Frankly, I'd pay cold, hard cash to watch that."

"Smart ass."

"Wow, you said that without coughing up a lung. I'm impressed."

Marco and Jillian launched into an enthusiastic insult war, punctuated by coughs, that I could only watch in wonder. Jillian was almost her normal self, but where was the angry, let's-murder-them-all Marco I'd seen over the last two days? Where was the guy who'd threatened to kill Ember and Reid if they didn't stop fighting?

Jillian stopped mid-sentence to cough, at one point struggling for breath from the virulence of her effort. Marco tenderly held her hand and spoke in soothing tones while she recovered, eliciting a beaming smile from her. I leaned my head against the window, awareness dawning like the sun behind us.

Angry Bitter Young Man was a mask he wore, and without a reason to wear it, I was now seeing what was underneath.

In that regard, he and I were a lot more similar than I'd first supposed.

The door cutting us off from the cockpit slid open, and Genele stepped back in. She saw Jillian struggling with the straps. "We're almost there. There's no point in trying to jump out now." Her world-weary tone hinted that superheroes busting out of the stretcher and jumping from the helicopter was a regular part of her job.

I looked out the window. We were low, flying over a subdivision of large, boxy houses on the edge of Leesburg. We were so close to the ground that I could see children playing in the snow. Some of them stopped and waved at the helicopter, probably hoping that one of the superheroes would see them. Our shadow slid over a flat, white back-yard and then crossed a road.

Woodland appeared.

And then a wall.

And then another.

I could see the machine guns mounted behind turrets. Between them, liquid shimmered in the moat, the light refracting in such a way that I instinctively knew that I'd never want to drink it.

I turned back to Jillian, whose eyebrows knit together in worry. "What is it?" she asked.

What did my face look like?

"I was wondering... what problem did you have to solve before qualifying for service?"

Jillian paused, then laughed in little wheezes. "I had to save the president's daughter from terrorists. Why are you asking about *that*?" Her laughter was so beautiful that I vowed to record it somehow in the near future.

Little drones darted all over the wide, flat, snowy minefield. We were only twenty feet or so off the ground.

Marco closed his eyes and shook his head, though he was smiling. "What were the two unknown variables they threw at you?"

Jillian's smiled widened. "She was pregnant and couldn't run, and then it turned out that the terrorists had an identical decoy. I was like, okay, I'll just carry her, and I can totally smell which one is the real daughter and which one is the impostor. There is no such thing as an identical decoy when you're me, as *someone* back in Chattahoochee can tell you."

There was an armed patrol. They were lined up around the perimeter of the helipad.

Marco looked out the window, then back to Jillian. "Remember when Davey got to the top of the Jacob's ladder--"

"—on the obstacle course, and he started crying and wouldn't come down?" Jillian finished for him. "And then we all had to take a break while the instructors—"

"—climbed up there and tried to reason with him." They both cracked up. Marco playfully punched her shoulder. "And remember Berenice falling into the creek later and how she kept saying for the rest of the day that a fish had bit her?" Jillian began to laugh so hard that tears streamed down her face.

I sat back down in my seat. Something was so wrong. It was in the air. Marco felt it, too. That's why he was helping me distract her.

The helicopter's nose angled down ever so slightly. Genele stood up and patted Jillian's leg. "We're landing. You ready?"

Jillian looked at me, and I nodded. "I'm not going anywhere."

There was a hard lurch as the helicopter touched earth, and then the doors flew open, revealing a medical team led by a doctor in a starched white coat. He began to shout over the din of the blades, but I couldn't hear him.

The war drums were too loud.

ITEM TWENTY

Excerpt of article from the *New York Times*, dated May 11, 1933

Three schoolgirls were killed in a tragic super-power accident yesterday when a super-powered youngster, identified as Ellen Cannostraci, 11 years, lost control of her youthful temper and set fire to her friends' clothes on the playground. Miss Cannostraci's parents have removed their daughter from school to protect the other children.

This marks the seventh such tragedy in the state since the beginning of the year, and eightieth since the beginning of the decade. The debate of whether to segregate super-powered citizens continues to rage; as the body count grows, it is super-powered people themselves who advocate the loudest for segregation. Mrs. Christina St. James, the well-known mouthpiece of the segregation movement, was unable to be reached for comment.

20

B linding sunlight shone down on us through glass ceiling panels as a six-man medical team wheeled Jillian through silent sliding doors and into the main building. I hadn't had time to take in the exterior of the hospital, so efficient was the group of doctors and nurses.

One nurse consulted with Genele while nearly running alongside the gurney, while the doctor who'd greeted us and unloaded Jillian asked my wife questions about how she was feeling.

Jillian, to her credit, appeared to be almost perfectly comfortable, though I saw the tension around her eyes and jaw. We could never forget that Beau and Alysia were somewhere nearby.

When our large group reached solid wood double doors, Jillian's gurney was pushed through with a sharp bang. One of the nurses turned to us and blocked our passage.

The last I saw of Jillian was her sitting up in her bed, her eyes wide and her hand held out for me.

The nurse's badge read Laura. She looked surprisingly like Jillian, tall and dark and muscular, with a similar face.

Marco let out a low whistle.

Laura raised her eyebrow at him for a second, then said, "Patients only past this point. Josh will show you all to your dorms. I'll come get—" She stopped to consult her notes, then frowned. "My file doesn't have a listed commander."

"*She's* the commander," Marco said, jutting his head at the double doors. He jabbed his thumb at me. "*He's* her husband."

Laura opened her mouth in surprise for a second, then closed it. "Okay, that's fine," she said, a tiny verbal question mark hanging off her words. "The flight nurse says that Jillian's signs are already improving, and from what I could see, she's out of the danger zone. You guys were right to call us, though. We're going to treat the infection and monitor her condition until the doctor says she's okay for discharge. Treatment for pneumonia usually lasts a couple of days, so I'll have my colleague show you around and make sure you're comfortable."

She waved at someone behind us, and we all turned. A young man in the same navy blue uniform approached with a warm smile. "Josh, show them to the dorms, please." She looked back at me. "I'll come get you soon."

She disappeared behind the wooden doors.

Josh took us all in. "Okay, teams, if you'd follow me, please." He beckoned for us to follow him down another glassy, bright hallway. "So do you want the short or long speech?"

"Sh—" Marco began.

"Long," I said. I wanted to know everything about this place.

"Okey-dokey. Bell Enterprises welcomes you to the Josiah Bell National Superservice Medical Center, established 1972. We're the premiere, and only, hospital and trauma center dedicated solely to the care and service of superheroes."

He waved his badge in front of a scanner by another set of wooden doors, then pressed his palm against the glass beneath the small red light. The red light turned green, and the door clicked open. "We have one hundred beds, plus fifty dorm beds for well visitors contained in twenty-five suites." He held out his arm. "The dorm wing."

The dorm wing was another bright, modern hallway, all glass and angles. Through the glass, I could see an indoor courtyard on my left, while to my right lay the outside. Snow-covered trees hid any view of walls and machine guns. Potted plants with waxy leaves lined the hallway between plain, numbered wooden doors. The whole place smelled vaguely of latex and disinfectant.

Josh stopped at the end of the hallway, where a wide bay of windows overlooked another indoor courtyard, this one containing a large koi pond. He pointed to three rooms. "Ladies, you're in rooms one and two. You two gentlemen," he said, indicating Reid and Marco, "are in room three. I believe I overheard that you're the patient's husband?"

"Yes."

"Then I'll set you up in her suite as soon as they call us back. In the meantime, you guys can get comfortable. The cafeteria is down the hall to the left, and the rec rooms are across from the cafeteria. There's a little office at the end of that hall where you can get pajamas in your size, toiletries, that kind of thing. You can go anywhere in the dorm wing." He gestured to a small red light bulb affixed to the ceiling. "If there's an emergency or security breach, red lights will flash and the siren will sound. Security personnel will direct you at that time."

"What about a library?" I asked, thinking back to Jillian's plan to read her beloved romance novels. I wasn't going to relax as long as we were within one hundred miles of this spot, but that didn't mean Jillian couldn't enjoy a good book while she was stuck in bed.

Josh did a double-take. "Uh... wow, um, nobody's ever asked for a library before. I'm sorry, but we don't have one." He brightened. "Although, there are a few volumes of *Leadership and Wisdom* in the rec room. I'm sure our permanent residents would love to have some new faces at the nightly readings. Would you like me to tell them that you're coming tonight?"

Seven unamused pairs of eyes dared him to do it.

The dim thud of helicopter rotors cut through the awkward silence, and then two helicopters flew over the dorm wing, their shadows darkening where we stood for a moment.

Berenice stared up at the glass. "That ceiling doesn't seem very secure."

"Don't worry," Josh replied with a shrug. "It's one-way, shatterproof, all that. Patients and visitors reported feeling confined in the old building. This facility is only fifteen years old or so."

"When can I see my wife?" I asked, a hand on my hip. "If she's awake and stable—"

"You'll be notified right away," Josh said in a practiced, soothing tone, making me wonder how often he answered similar questions. Just then a little black device on his belt beeped, and his eyebrows flew up. "Sorry guys, I gotta go. Busy day around here."

After he'd run down the hall towards the main hallway, the ladies broke off into pairs, Ember and Lark, and Berenice and Abby. I joined Marco and Reid in their dorm room.

The dorm was spacious, though sparsely decorated. Two twin beds with thick gray comforters were pushed into the far corners, with bedside tables next to them. Between the tables was a curtained window, which overlooked the inner courtyard I'd seen on the way.

A desk and chair stood on one side of the room, while a dresser and couch sat opposite. A bathroom off to the side was identical to any normal household bathroom. There were no television or bookshelf.

Marco sat on one of the beds and bounced a little. "At least the mattress is nice. I wonder what the food is like here."

Reid sat on the other, while I fell into the desk chair and closed my eyes. "Let's get serious," I said, rubbing my eyelids. "Beau and Alysia—"

"Dude, chill out," Marco snapped.

My eyes flew open. "What?"

"I said chill out. I wasn't lying in the helicopter. Do you actually think those two are the first people to target this place? Do you have that much confidence in your brother? Because the way I see it, he's really not that big of a threat."

At my expression, he rolled his eyes. "Let's see... he only managed to slice Jill's neck open because she was high as a kite and, oh yeah, had *you* to distract me. He couldn't friggin' kidnap Ember, an unarmed, untrained woman, even though he allied with the Western-ers. He needed three people as backup to grab Jill and *still* lost some-one, and she didn't even have her powers. And, later, he was stupid enough to fall for Jill's really obvious lie. Hell, he couldn't even keep his prisoner under correct surveillance, and he can talk to the cameras. I'm not impressed."

I chose to not address his allusion to the warehouse. Instead, my mind reeled. This was dangerous overconfidence on Marco's part. He knew better. How could he just sit there and act like Beau was noth-ing? He'd kidnapped my wife. He'd *allied with the Westerners*. He was perfectly comfortable killing innocent people.

And yet, Reid fought a smile as he said, "You know, he has a point. We're safe here, Ben. I think you need to relax."

"They're still out there!" I exclaimed, jumping up so fast the chair fell over. "How can you just—"

"We've won," Reid said, scrubbing his face. "That's how I can just sit here and say it."

There was a pregnant pause.

"Excuse me? We've *won*?" I threw my hands up. "You both need to either give up what you're on, or share it with the rest of us."

Reid and Marco exchanged a questioning glance, and then Reid nodded almost imperceptibly. He looked back at me. "Dial it back a few notches and try to hear what I'm saying."

I slowly sat down again, and he continued, "The Westerners are in retreat. The camps are falling. Jill is safe. Beau and Alysia are two renegades rushing around trying to find the JM-104, and that's all. Soon reality will catch up with them, too—probably around the time that the government demands Bell hands over the JM-104. This stupid game between the superheroes, the supervillains, and the government is finally ending. It's time to just... calm down." He stood up and stretched. "Let's go get the ladies and check out the cafeteria."

My mouth was open. "You're serious, aren't you?"

I knew he was serious, but I couldn't believe it. There was no way our mission had ended. It would never be over until the loose ends had been cut off the tapestry of our lives. We would never have any peace until my brother and Alysia were in the ground.

And then there were the rest of the supervillain families, untold hundreds of people working in the darkness of the criminal underground. We'd have to organize with other superheroes, create a coalition, plan, strategize, maybe even get the pretty boy in Colorado on board.

They trooped past me into the hallway, leaving me in the dorm to fume while staring daggers at the door.

We hadn't won anything, dammit.

Marco poked his head back in. "Stop pouting and come get some food with us."

With a disgusted sigh, I joined them in the hallway, arms folded over my chest and jaw tense—until Reid knocked on one of the doors and Berenice opened it. Behind her, Abby was jumping back and forth between the beds, and Berenice herself was wrapped in a thick towel.

"They have bubble bath," she said by way of greeting. "And Abby's a little busy. We'll talk to you guys later." She shut the door without another word.

Lark and Ember didn't answer their door. When Reid cracked it open, I saw that the curtain had been pulled, casting the room into darkness, and each bed bore a woman-shaped lump. Tiny flashes of images—a talking cat, Reid, a helicopter—tickled my brain. Ember was dreaming.

"I guess it's just us men," Reid said as he quietly closed their door.

Marco nearly skipped down the hall while we walked to the cafeteria, so eager was he to see everything there was to see. If a door was cracked open, he pushed it open a little more to peek inside. He studied every map and directory, and introduced himself to every navy-blue-clad nurse we passed.

I was dimly surprised that all of them greeted us with a friendly handshake and smile. Nothing else related to the camps had ever been so warm.

It was mid-morning, so breakfast was still being served. Thirty or so heads turned when we walked in, some of which were topped with gray hair. The men and women at the tables were a range of ages, some fairly young, but others in advanced middle age. In the corner, two men were absorbed in a game of chess, their breakfasts untouched. A woman of perhaps thirty years was idly flipping through a volume of *Leadership and Wisdom*. Two young men were arm wrestling.

All of them were clad in bland shirts and pants of neutral grays and blues. The women wore their hair long, except for one woman whose scalp was so badly burned that the hair no longer grew. Instead, she wore a gray bandanna. Another woman sat in a wheelchair. Quite a few people were missing limbs, though their injuries were healed to the point that they didn't trigger my power. Two men wore eye patches. One of them sat alone at a table, his head in his arms, his good eye staring blankly into space.

"I take it you're only visiting," someone said to our left.

An older man in nondescript blue clothes held out a hand to us. It was the only hand he had. He was middle-aged, with softly graying hair and a kind, lined face. I thought I recognized him from somewhere. "I'm Elijah Nussbaum," he said, the warmth in his voice matching in his eyes. "Welcome to the hospital, though I won't insult you by assuming that you're happy to be here. How's your teammate? Or is it teammates?"

"Our leader has pneumonia. She was just admitted," I said as I shook his hand. His warm grip was comforting.

In fact, something about Elijah was inherently mollifying, like I was talking to an old, trusted friend. Jillian was going to be okay. I could feel it in my bones. The certainty of this fact trickled through me like syrup as soon as his skin touched mine.

"She?" Elijah repeated, his eyes crinkling in amusement. "Well, things have changed, haven't they? What's that like?"

In the back of my mind, I knew I normally would've been annoyed by his response, but I couldn't drag the aggravation to the forefront past the smooth calm. "It's just fine," I said, belatedly surprised by my words. "I'm Mercury, by the way. And this is Helios and Tank."

He held up a hand. "None of that here. We're all just schmoes now. No masks, no codenames."

"In that case, this is Benjamin Corsaro," Reid lied smoothly. "And Marco St. James. I'm Reid Fischer. You're from Idaho, aren't you? Did you ever know Esther Nussbaum? That was my mom's name until she married."

Reid and Elijah chatted about common acquaintances, but my brain struggled to wrap around what they were saying. I wasn't tired, but I felt as though the very air itself contained a soporific.

However, when they walked away towards a quartet of easy chairs in a carpeted corner of the room, the feeling lessened slightly.

Marco leaned against the wall, a sleepy smile plastered on his face. "That guy has one heck of a power. I feel like my bones are made of jelly. I wanna be mad at him, but... who cares?" He yawned. "Breakfast?"

Breakfast sounded *great*.

I practically floated to the food line, which took up an entire wall. Pleasant men and women in white smocks and hats were serving various healthy options: fruit of all sorts, whole-grain breads, lean meats, and juice, milk, and water. Though a small sign on the sneeze guard sternly ordered us to not take more than two slices of ham, the young woman behind the bar slipped me a third with a little wink.

Red-faced, I hurried to an empty table, where Marco joined me. He pulled back the foil on his orange juice and sipped before saying, "Well, if Jill dies, you can choose between her twin Laura or the chick behind the counter... who's still looking at you, by the way." He speared my forbidden third slice of ham and put it on his own plate.

The last of the strange peace evaporated at once, hauling up the furor of worry and frustration I'd felt earlier. I stabbed a piece of honeydew. "She's not going to die."

"No, I suppose not," he said, thoughtfully chewing his ham. "That's not really her style."

The absurdity of his response made me snort in my own juice, and then we were both laughing.

Several people glared at us for disturbing the quiet murmur of the cafeteria, but I couldn't stop. Laughing provided a release for pressure that had built up in me for days—weeks, even. If I wasn't careful, my laughter was going to start leaking out my eyes and I'd have to leave the room.

A furious male voice echoed down the hall and saved me the embarrassment. "*No!* I'm not going to just sit on my ass while my teammates die! Let me through!"

Elijah jumped up from his chair, but nobody else in the room moved, or even acted as if they'd heard the man.

"Sir, if you would just—"

"Let—go—of—me—"

"There's no need to be hostile—"

"I'll kill every one of you—"

Marco and I exchanged a worried look and began to walk towards the hallway, cautious of any sudden outburst of power. As I neared the hallway, the sound of a scuffle and multiple voices made me reach for my baton.

"—let me go, you—"

"Sir, you need to calm down—"

"I will *not*—"

"Your teammates are—"

Reid was in the doorway with us, and then he gasped and shook his head. Squaring his shoulders, he beckoned for us to follow as he disappeared around the corner. "Edward Yazzie!"

When I turned the corner, I saw "Edward Yazzie" and almost couldn't contain a grin.

The man in question was tall and handsome, with thick black hair that was slightly mussed from his altercation with no less than four male nurses. As with Emily Begay, my first impression was that he was Native American.

Unlike Emily, his uniform was clearly designed to stand out: his winter tunic was mostly red, but a star-shaped splash of black covered his right shoulder, stretching from front to back. A sporty pair of black sunglasses topped his head, and he bore several knives, though not as many as Jillian did. One of the nurses was industriously disarming him while he fought against the three nurses holding his hands behind his back.

When Edward saw Reid, he stilled, not even noticing when the nurse removed the last of his weapons. "Reid? What are you doing here?"

Reid crossed his arms and sighed, his expression identical to that of a parent who'd just caught his child sneaking out a window. "I could ask the same of you. This had better be good, Ed, because this is embarrassing to watch."

I felt Elijah before I saw him. Bone-deep contentment seeped into me at the same time the tension melted away from Edward's face.

Elijah held out his hand to Edward. "Another Idaho boy! What brings you here today?"

The nurses backed away, giving Elijah looks of silent thanks.

"My team was attacked," Edward said, almost so calmly that it sounded like an afterthought. "A mob of civilians stormed our house. One of them had a machete, and we almost didn't make it."

"Oh my God," Marco said, his mouth falling open. "That had to be ugly."

Edward dropped his head. "It was. I hated to fight civilians, and I hate that I'm the only one unharmed even more, because I think they came for *me*. I should be with my team."

Elijah put his arm around Edward. "You guys are at the right place. I know you're upset, but you're safe here. Why don't you come and have some breakfast?"

Seeing Elijah in that stance, with his arm around another superhero, dislodged a recent memory. I realized where I'd seen him before: He was one of the young superheroes in the picture from the 1984 bombing, who'd lost all but one teammate in the blast. He must've been at the hospital for more than thirty years, and it rapidly becoming clear why he'd never been released into retirement at the Virginia camp.

However, as Elijah guided Edward into the cafeteria and away from us, his power waned and I was able to muddle through something Edward had said.

"A mob stormed their house?" I repeated to Reid and Marco, running a hand through my hair. "I've never heard of anything like that before."

"Maybe he was like Patrick," Marco suggested with a shrug. "The people turned against him."

"No, I don't think so," Reid said, leaning against the wall. "At least, I'd be surprised. I've known Ed since we were kids. He's okay. He was always serious about being respectable, kind, diligent... you know, the principles. Since Elder Lloyd's only kid died back in the nineties, Ed was chosen to be trained for leadership even though he's not in an elder line." He snorted. "He never let the rest of us guys forget it."

Reid's face softened. "But I hate to think of how scared he must be for his team. A machete, man." He studied the ceiling in exaggerated thoughtfulness. "It's really too bad that our ever-so-useful medic is stuck out here. I bet there are a bunch of injured superheroes and a pneumonia patient who'd love a visit from you."

I was starting to wonder if I really knew Reid Fischer.

Swirling healing energy began to swim in my stomach. "Let's go see what we can see," I suggested, pointing towards the patients-only double doors. The need to heal people pulled me toward them like an invisible piece of yarn. The need to be near Jillian pulled me forward like a freight train.

"We can't," Marco said, grinning. "It's against the rules."

We reached the doors. "And if you find someone around here who cares about the rules, make sure to act natural," I said, my hand on the door. "Start reciting the principles or something."

I pushed the wooden door open and slipped through.

The patients wing was yet another glassy hallway lined with plants, but to my surprise, there were no people. Were they all in operating theaters? No alarm had sounded, but I knew without a doubt that I was under camera surveillance, so I didn't stop to ponder the question. Instead, I dashed to the first room on my right.

Empty.

The second.

Empty.

The third: a woman whose abdomen was being sewn up on a blood-stained table. Four medical professionals in scrubs and masks looked up when I opened the door.

"Excuse me," I said briskly, reaching for her hand. Healing surged from my fingers to hers, and then I was gone—but not before I heard the shouts of surprise from behind me.

It took only another minute and a half to find the rest of the team in the other operating rooms. They were all in various stages of being stitched back together. Each time, the medical team yelled in alarm, but I didn't hang around to explain.

I was flexing old psychological muscles by flouting rules made by *those superheroes*, even though I was in fact saving their lives.

I was fighting the system. Standing up to the giant.

"Causing trouble?"

Jillian's beautiful voice made me spin around. She stood in the doorway of one of the rooms I hadn't checked, barefoot and clad in dark purple scrubs, and holding onto an IV pole as if she were claiming the hallway for Saint Catherine. Her lush hair cascaded down past her shoulders, and some of the color was back in her cheeks.

"Jillian!"

"Benjamin," she said, the corners of her eyes crinkling. "I wondered how long it would before you started healing people." She pulled me inside her room and closed the door. "I heard what they were saying in the operating rooms. Something about 'I'm healed!' and 'Who was that?'"

"It was actually Reid's idea."

"Uh huh."

Being so close to Jillian was intoxicating—even more so than Elijah's false calm. Although I'd just upset the smooth order of the hospital and sneaked into Jillian's room, I couldn't feel the fear and worry that had haunted me.

In fact, as I studied her pink-tinged cheeks and vague smile, the months of fighting and combat flipped backwards like pages in a book. We were in the park again, our wildly different lives as yet unbeknownst to each other, just two young people with the future to look forward to. No battles, no uniforms, no scars visible or invisible. Jillian even looked the same now as she did that day, her head angelically haloed by sunlight from the window, and the red in her hair shimmering every so often.

There was a sharp knock on the door, and then it burst open. Three grinning nurses and a harried, red-faced doctor stormed inside.

"Was that you?" the doctor demanded, pointing to me.

No point in lying. "Yeah."

"This hallway is patients only!" he insisted. Some of his hair was sticking out in different directions.

I nodded. "My apologies. Next time I'll ignore the urge to heal the woman with her intestines hanging out."

The doctor sputtered, but one of the nurses looked at her watch and said, "Tony, you have a meeting with the director in ten minutes. Since you don't have any surgeries for the rest of the morning, you might want to get ready for that."

Doctor Tony swore and threw up his hands, then stomped out, followed by two giggling nurses. The third crossed her arms and looked down her nose at Jillian. "Did he heal your pneumonia?"

Jillian shrank back. "No."

"Then get in bed, lady." She walked out.

After making a face at the door, Jillian led me by the hand to her wide hospital bed and slipped back under the covers, then patted the empty space next to her. I pulled off my boots and joined her, careful to not lay on the tubes and wires that crisscrossed the mattress.

She turned slightly so she could face me. "I think there's something in my IV that's relaxing me. I feel better than I have in a long time."

"It's probably a tranquilizer," I said, taking in her soft expression and airy voice. "Were you upset earlier?"

"I wouldn't stop talking about how I needed to be with my team. One of the nurses changed the IV bag and said I'd feel better soon."

Though Edward's plight wasn't remotely funny, I couldn't help a laugh. "I just met another team leader who needed some outside help to calm down. I bet they're used to that here."

Jillian's eyebrows drew together and she opened her mouth, but before she could inquire about to whom I was referring, a booming knock on the door made us startle.

"Come in," we said.

The door swung open to reveal the funniest-looking group of people I'd seen in a long time.

Two men and two women in bloody, destroyed uniforms filed in without a word until they were fanned out at the foot of the bed. They were all older than anybody on our team, probably in their mid-twenties, and each of them had a scowl on their face. One of the men was missing his left arm below the elbow. From what I could tell of their ripped, bloody uniforms, they all had the same star on their right shoulder, though in different colors.

There was a tense silence until one of the men said, "So... where's Ed?"

I sat up and rested my arms on my knees. "If you mean Edward Yazzie, he's in the cafeteria. He's fine."

They relaxed. The youngest woman, whose long brown hair had been partially shaved to facilitate surgery, narrowed her eyes as she looked back and forth between Jillian and me. "I've seen you two before. You're from that video that's been going around. The one that started all of this." Her accent was identical to that of Topher's, all broad New York vowels. She even looked like him a little bit.

At that, Jillian took a deep breath and climbed out of bed, holding her chin up and surveying the group with cool, distant interest. "I'm Jillian Trent, commander of the Saint Catherine, Georgia team. Since *you* came into *my* room, you'd better start identifying yourselves and telling me what the hell you want."

"Commander?" the other woman said. "Are you k—"

The remaining man held up his hand to his teammate, who

nodded once and stepped back. "We're the Burlington, Vermont team, and we have a really good reason to be mad at you. Your speech last week caused the civilians of our city to turn against us."

"Your *names*," Jillian drawled, though there was an edge to her tone.

"Who the hell do you think you are?" the skeptical woman said.

"I think I'm the leader of two joint teams at the moment, plus a very capable killer in my own right. Now, your names, or you will be meeting said joint teams a lot sooner than you'd probably prefer, and you'll very quickly find out how they defeated a strike team."

Superhero sword-measuring contests never ceased to amaze me.

"Danielle Cannostraci," the woman growled, confirming my suspicion that she was relative of Topher's. If she had to find out that Topher was dead, she wasn't finding out from me.

"Luis de la Cruz," said the man missing half an arm. "I'm SIC." He was obviously southern, but since Jillian didn't know him, I placed him from Occonee instead of Chattahoochee.

"Julia Kettlethorpe," said the other woman. Another New Yorker.

"Bobby Campbell," said the final man. His accent was southern, but not like my Georgia teammates. Ozark, then.

Jillian's eyes narrowed slightly upon hearing Bobby's surname, but she recovered and looked at Luis. "Why are you here?"

"They came for Ed's head, and when we jumped in, they attacked all of us."

"You seem fine to me," Jillian said with a smirk, looking them up and down. "Even your stump is sealed up," she said to Luis. "Should I go congratulate the surgeons?"

Their eyes flickered downward simultaneously. "Uh, that was him," Danielle said.

Jillian rubbed her chin. "So let me get this straight. My team uncovers a decades-long conspiracy and reveals the corruption in our camps, then goes public about it so the perpetrators can be brought to justice. After that, a group of civilians—whom I have never met and have no control over—go berserk and attack you guys. However, it's okay because my teammate actually broke the rules to save your lives."

She tutted her tongue and tapped her foot as if she were thinking extremely hard. "Now, what's the phrase people typically use when they want to show gratitude for someone else's hardships and efforts on their behalf? Civilians are always using it when we save them from muggers and stuff."

"I am not thanking the woman who ruined everything," Danielle snarled. "Do you know how much trouble all the teams are in? Do you know how many protests there have been? Can your tiny mind compr—"

A tiny knock on the door cut through her tirade. Luis opened the door and stepped back.

It was Abby.

She was biting her bottom lip and standing on her tiptoes, craning her neck to look for something or someone. When she didn't find it, she seemed to deflate. "Where Eddy?" she asked the Burlington team. "Abby smell Eddy. Nurse say Burlington team hurt. He live?" She took a step closer, her eyes growing large and wet with worry. "Eddy live?"

Jillian and I exchanged a confused glance, as did the Burlington team. Luis recovered quickly and replied, "He's unharmed. He's out in the main part of the hospital, Miss...?"

"Calhoun," I supplied. "This is Abigail Calhoun, of the Baltimore team."

The reaction was swift. An electric shock ran through the Burlington team, and they almost tripped over themselves to help Abby out the door.

"Here, let's go find him—"

"—want to see you—"

"—he's fine—"

"—heard so much about you—"

The door slammed shut, leaving Jillian and me in silence.

Without missing a beat, Jillian slid back into the bed next to me. "I have no idea what that was about," she said while rearranging the many tubes and cords, "But if it got the Burlington Brigade out of my room, I don't care. Also, I kinda like the idea of Abby being famous." She settled into the bed and turned on her side to face me again. "Now, I think you were telling me something about how pretty I am?"

I had no idea what they'd given my wife, but I needed a large dose of it. I kissed her before saying, "You're exquisite, and I'm glad to see you happy again. You were pretty rough after we found you."

A shadow passed behind her eyes. "Can we talk about that later?"

"Of course. What do you want to talk about instead?"

She closed her eyes and breathed in and out for a few seconds. "What we're going to do when we get home."

I sighed. "Yeah, I've been thinking about that, too. The way I see it, even the combined teams aren't big enough to tackle all the supervillain families. We'll need to get as many city teams as possible on our side, and maybe even the government. I could call Eleanor, too, and arrange a meeting with the Sentinels. Of course, if the feds are already investigating their little militia activities, then—"

"That's not what I meant."

I hesitated, trying to figure out where I'd gone wrong. "What *did* you mean?"

"I don't want to do this anymore," she whispered. "I'm tired."

I pulled the blanket up over her shoulder. Of course she was tired; she was recovering from torture and pneumonia. We didn't need to have strategic conversations now. "You should go back to sleep, sweetheart," I said. "I'll stay right here with you."

Jillian stared at me for an interminable moment, multiple emotions swimming in her eyes. Finally, she said, "What I meant was, I don't want to be a superhero anymore."

ITEM TWENTY-ONE

Excerpt of letter sent from Levi Fischer to his mother, Avigail, dated April 5, 1935

Those bastards. Those damned bastards. I spoke with Calhoun, and you know what he said? He doesn't want "Yids" in the camps. The camps aren't even built yet and we're already being treated like vermin even though the Fischers were the first family in all of California to fight. There's been some rumors that we're being sent to Idaho to freeze to death along with the Indians and the Mormons, but I'll tell you what: no. I'm not going, and neither is Leah or the children. Simon, Reuben, Levi, Morty, and Rebecca are all sticking it out, but I'm not going to be treated like this.

But don't worry, I'm not going to do what Hannah did. Last I heard, she and Eli met up with some other anti-normals and have holed up near the Canadian border...

21

I was too shocked to speak.

Jillian continued, "I almost died at your family's hands, and then I caught pneumonia. The last year of my life has been nothing but almost dying, either by attempted suicide, bombs, Patrick, lions... I'm tired. I'm so tired."

She closed her eyes and breathed deeply. "I just want to go to sleep and wake up tomorrow in another life. I thought I was going to die in my cell, or on the interrogation table, and I realized that I wanted to grow old and die in my bed, surrounded by my grandchildren. I want to make a new life with you."

I didn't know what to say. Jillian had always been my driving force —the driving force of the entire team, even. She was the ball of energy in our engine, pushing us forward to fight crime, be heroes, and keep going even when everything looked impossible.

Now, at the dawn of a new era for superheroes, she was poised to be the engine for an even bigger "team," the team comprising all American superheroes and government agents as they fought the rot of the camps.

But I also wanted that new life for her.

Oh, who was I kidding? I wanted it for us. As soon as she'd said "grandchildren," I'd imagined tiny faces with hazel eyes and black hair.

Before those people could exist, though, there was one more job to do.

"Sweetie, we still need to fight my brother and find the JM-104," I murmured. "You can't quit now."

A hard, calculating expression overtook her face. "We've had this conversation before."

"What? When?"

"A long time ago, over coffee. You told me to quit my job and stick it to Patrick. I said I couldn't quit. You didn't know it, but I was thinking about more than just how scared I was of him. I was also thinking about my vows, plus all the people who relied on me. But I don't think that would've mattered to you, if you'd known. You cared only for me. You saw my bruises and fear. You saw that I was in danger."

Guilt squirmed in my stomach. Not only was she right, but I'd considered advising her to simply quit by not showing up to work. While I'd believed that she was an assistant gym teacher at that time, the heart of the matter remained the same: she needed to get away from her abuser, and quitting was the easiest answer. What was the entire superhero structure if not an abuser?

But... what was Saint Catherine without Battlecry?

"You can't quit now," I repeated, ashamed of myself.

"Yes, I can," she said, her voice low but clear. "A crimefighter's mission doesn't have a natural end. I'm choosing to end mine now. I'm not Battlecry anymore, I'm just Jillian." Her gaze bounced back and forth as she appeared to think over a troubling thought. "Do you still want to be with me if I'm not a superhero?"

I stroked her cheek and tucked the stubborn lock of hair behind her ear, then placed a soft kiss on her lips. "I'm not going anywhere," I whispered. "Unless you're going with me."

She entwined her fingers with mine under the blanket and closed her eyes again, her peaceful smile slowly relaxing into untroubled sleep.

WHEN HER BREATHS had become slow and even, I carefully maneuvered out of the bed, tucking her in and tiptoeing out of her room. When the door had clicked shut behind me, I dashed to the wooden double doors and slipped through them into the main hallway.

Reid and Marco were sparring in the gym, adjacent to the main rec room. Marco looked up as I walked in and released Reid from a choke-hold. Reid collapsed and gasped for breath while Marco jumped to his feet. "What took you so long? You missed the best thing *ever*."

I rocked back on my heels. "Edward's team is fine. Jillian's still recovering, but she's in good spirits, all things considered. Thanks for asking."

Reid clambered to his feet, a goofy grin plastered on his face. "Oh, we know the Burlington team is fine. They came into the cafeteria earlier with Abby in tow—"

Marco cut in, "—and as soon as Edward saw Abigail, he jumped to his feet and said, 'Abigail! Sweet pea!'" Marco clasped his hands in mock delight and fluttered his eyelashes. "And then little miss Sweet Pea literally skipped to Edward, and they just stared at each other for a freaking long time. That guy had heart eyes, man. Flowers were blooming in the air around him."

Reid sat on a bench and began to towel off his forehead. "I asked Edward what was going on. Apparently, he met Abigail on a courting swap to the Ozark camp years ago and asked for her hand, but her father put the kibosh on that really fast. He's the elder, you know, so there was no higher power to appeal to."

"Why'd he say no?" I asked, sitting on another bench.

If Edward was really the upstanding guy Reid had described, I'd have guessed that any father would've approved the match, as long as his daughter agreed, and it sounded like Abby would've enthusiastically agreed. I personally couldn't see any romantic appeal in her—how did they converse?—but if they were in love, then more power to them.

Marco rolled his eyes. "Am I the *only* one who gets it? Y'all keep forgetting why Ozark camp was founded." He began to stack free weights back on the rack with more force than was probably necessary. "But now, after all this, I don't think they care anymore. Heck, maybe they figured out how to escape from the hospital and are on their way to the courthouse right now. I haven't seen them since they ran off."

"Where's his team?" I asked, looking around the otherwise-empty gym.

"Last I heard, they were headed to get some new clothes and then get settled in," Reid said with a shrug. "We'll probably see them at dinner."

Marco finished stacking weights. "Do you think they'll let Jill out for meals if she's feeling better? And if not, do you think we can take our meals in her room? I wanna visit her."

I rubbed the back of my neck. "I doubt they'll let her out as long as she's hooked up to the IV, but I know she'd like some visitors. But before we go see her, there's something we need to talk about. Let's go wake up Ember."

THE SAINT CATHERINE and Baltimore teams were crammed into Jillian's hospital room. When Ember had heard what I'd wanted to talk about, she insisted that the Baltimore team be present, too. Only Abby was absent, since nobody had seen her since she'd absconded with Edward, and Ember refused to reveal their whereabouts, only giving me a knowing smile when I'd asked.

Berenice was whispering animatedly in a corner with Lark. Reid and Ember sat entwined on the small guest bed where I'd spend the night. Marco had scrounged up knitting needles and yarn from who-knew-where and was clicking away, the beginning of some woolly garment already apparent. Jillian and I were on the bed again, holding hands.

She looked at me uncertainly, and I squeezed her hand. "You've got this."

She squeezed my hand in return and took a deep breath, then said, "I'll cut right to the chase, guys. I've decided to retire after I'm discharged. I'm going back down to Saint Catherine to settle all the details with the city, and then...well, I don't know, but I'm not going to be in service anymore."

Marco stopped knitting.

Everyone just stared at her for several seconds, until Berenice said, "You're quitting? Why?"

"Because I've dealt with more than enough crap to last a lifetime," Jillian replied in a hard voice. "And now I'm moving on to other things."

"But what are you going to do?" Marco asked. He seemed so small, now that he was faced with the possibility of not having his longtime friend with him.

"Get a job, maybe," Jillian said, picking at the sheets. "Help the government round up the elders and Westerners. Go to school."

"Have kids?" Reid asked, but he was looking at me. "You're going with her, right?" His tone brooked no argument.

"Of course I am," I said evenly. "We've only just decided this, but whatever we do, we're doing it together. We'd like to start a family someday, but now *is* a bad time," I said, giving Jillian a sidelong smile. "We should probably wait until the furor has died down."

Her eyes sparkled for a second, and then she turned back to the crowd. "What you guys do is up to you. As soon as I leave the hospital, you're no longer under my command in any way."

Marco crossed his arms. "I'm leaving, too."

"What?" Reid gasped. "Just like that?"

"Yeah, just like that," Marco said. "I was sent to Saint Catherine with Jillian, and I'm leaving it with her. I'm young enough that I might try to enroll in high school."

"You'd be the first high school graduate from the camps in generations," Lark said. "That's something."

Ember and Reid looked at each other, their minute facial expressions shifting back and forth as they argued silently.

Suddenly, Ember said, "It's not that I don't trust you, it's that the two of us can't help a city of a quarter million."

"But we have a duty," Reid replied. "And... well, you *did* remind me of that in Liberty. We can't just leave the city on a whim."

Jillian and Marco flinched back as if they expected Ember to detonate.

However, Ember just sighed. "I know, but we can't keep those vows now. A team of two isn't a fighting force, it's an easy target. We'd be doing Saint Catherine a disservice by staying." She tapped her index fingers together as she thought. "What if we formally retire as superheroes and offer our time and abilities to the city in a different capacity? That way we're still in good faith, and if they let us go, it'll be because we were asked to leave."

He hesitated. "Well... okay. But where will we go?"

"I don't know," Ember admitted. "But I'm sure we'll come up with something."

Reid and Ember shared a loving smile for a second, then joined hands and faced us. "We're in," Reid said. "Well, out, I guess."

So our whole team had decided to dismantle. It was a quiet end to a team that had had such a momentous beginning seven months before, in the Saint Catherine Police Department's interrogation room. But it also felt right. We'd come together democratically and by choice. Now we were disbanding the same way.

"What about you guys?" Jillian asked Berenice and Lark. "With Reuben, Topher, and Peter gone, there's not much left of the Baltimore team."

"She's right, you know," Lark said to Berenice. "And I have a feeling that we might be losing Abby soon."

"Abby won't ditch us for some guy," Berenice insisted, but I heard the doubt in her voice. "He wasn't even important enough to her for her to mention him once in all these years."

"She mentioned him to me," I said, casually picking at my nails.

Berenice's shocked face was worth the pounding I'd probably get later.

"I have a feeling that Edward isn't just some guy to her," Lark said, a curiously gentle element in her words. "He was the one that she couldn't be with because of her camp's rules. Maybe she didn't mention him because she felt ashamed for wanting someone her family kept saying she shouldn't. I'm sure, if you try very hard, you can summon some sympathy for her?"

There was much hidden meaning in her words, again making me wish I knew the history of the Baltimore team.

Berenice stared down at her boots. "I hope they're very happy," she finally mumbled.

"So I guess this is it," Marco said. "The two best teams in the country are over."

Ember let go of Reid and stepped forward, her mouth a grim line. "We've got one last battle. I meant to talk about this with you two first," she said to Jillian and me, "But as long as we're all here, I'll do it now. I was half asleep when I overheard Dr. Gibson's meeting with the hospital director, but I heard enough to gather that they're planning on keeping Benjamin here permanently. They're debating retiring the rest of us to the Virginia camp, and I don't think that's up for negotiation."

Marco threw aside his knitting needles. "What the hell? *Why*?"

My skin crawled with unwelcome *deja vu*. It hadn't been a full month since the camps had sold me like chattel to the Westerners because of my power. My team had been similarly maltreated at the same time—and now we were all facing the same situation. Unlike the first time, it would not be so easy for us to escape.

Jillian frowned. "What was their reasoning for retiring us? We're not overage or maimed."

Ember shook her head. "I have no idea. Like I said, I wasn't fully conscious, so it was just snatches of conversation. But the intent was clear: Ben stays, we go."

"Screw that," Berenice snapped. "The only way I'm going to the

Virginia camp is in a body bag. This is obviously punishment for us being us."

"I don't know," Ember said, rubbing her forehead. "I don't hear any hostility in the staff. They live on campus and haven't had a new rotation of staff members in over a month, so they haven't heard about the broadcast. Most of the staff actually like Benjamin, and are grateful for his involvement with the Burlington team. Only one or two of the doctors were annoyed, and that was because they're rule people who don't like superheroes messing up how the hospital runs. It's not personal for anyone."

Lark frowned. "Something's not adding up. I can believe that they'd bend over backwards to keep Benjamin around. Heck, if I ran a hospital, I'd do everything I could to keep you here," she said, pointing at me. "That's logical. But why retire the rest of us? That's just plain suspicious. If it's not personal, if the staff doesn't even really know who we are or care that we've pissed off the elders, then why...make us disappear..."

She trailed off slowly, her gaze darting back and forth. "Where even is the Virginia camp? All the camps are named after the national forests they used to be, but the Virginia camp is just that, 'Virginia.'"

We all looked at one another, and I sensed that we were thinking the same thing: something here wasn't right. Like so much of the camp world, this entire scenario had an odor to it. In fact, the more I thought about it, the more illogical the very idea of the Virginia camp became.

Why was there a retirement camp at all? Why didn't perfectly useful, if aging, former superheroes return home and train the future generation? And if there was such a population crisis in the camps, why weren't younger, injured, still-fertile superheroes encouraged to have children and replenish the pool? What were the retired superheroes *doing* in the Virginia camp?

The answer supplied itself, and the realization made me feel as though I were a child again, crying in my bedroom at night because I was certain that the darkness hid monsters.

I took a deep breath. "Has anyone here ever met someone from the Virginia camp?"

Reid shook his head. "They don't supply anybody."

"Doesn't that seem weird, though? Lots of people go there who are of child-begetting age. Look at us, right? We can't be the first group of young people to be sent there for whatever reason. In fifty years, they'd produce somebody with a combat power. Or if not, wouldn't they at least participate in a courting swap?"

"What are you saying, Trent?" Berenice asked, folding her arms across her chest.

"He's saying they're dead," Ember replied quietly. "That there is no Virginia camp... or that it's a death camp."

"A death camp?" Marco repeated. "That's hard to believe, even in light of the other activities the elders have done."

"Is it really, though?" Lark said, her face thoughtful. "The elders have shown that they value power for power's sake. They'll sell their own into slavery to maintain control over us. They fed us lies for years about the outside world." She made a little circle with her finger in the air. "This group can't be the first in history to figure out that they're lying."

"I see what you mean," Jillian said, her face suddenly more lined than I'd ever seen it. "Knowledge is power. And if people with real knowledge of the civilian world went back to the camps and corrupted the youth, then the elders would lose some of their power. Or all of it." She rubbed her eyelids. "Good God, how far down does the well go? When will it end? It's getting to the point that I want to take a shower every time I even think about the elders."

Berenice studied her fingernails. "Well, then. I guess we're going to have to come up with some daring-do to get out of here. Fun."

Jillian yawned, and I tenderly pushed her back onto her pillow. "How about we come up with that daring-do later, when we have more information. We've still got a pneumonia patient in the group, and I think Abby will want to be on board. Maybe even the Burlington team." They owed me a favor.

"Fine," Marco growled. "But I swear to God, if they shoot you in the neck like the Westerners did..." The terrifying expression on his face was the most reassuring thing I'd seen all day. After all, this was the guy who could put Reid into a choke hold. I had no doubt that he could effortlessly turn that move into a broken neck.

"Pleasant dreams, everyone," Lark said as she stretched.

"I hate our lives," Berenice said matter-of-factly. "Topher was lucky."

With that shocking statement, she opened the door and stormed out. Lark closed her eyes and inhaled deeply, then followed Berenice.

Everyone else wandered out of the room and left Jillian and me in peace. She rolled over again, faint shadows under her eyes. "Don't be scared," she said. "Forewarned is forearmed. It's not going to be like last time."

Her IV hissed and released more fluid into her veins. Now that I knew what I knew, I couldn't appreciate the effect of the tranquilizer. It wasn't pacifying her, it was making her docile and easier to control. Elijah did the same thing for the rest of the hospital. Everything —*every damn thing* about my friend's lives—was designed to keep them under control.

Going back to Liberty didn't sound so bad now. For all his unsavory qualities, Dean Monroe and his army had never tried to hold me against my will. I had half a mind to remove the IV from her, but it also contained her medication. *Soon, but not now.*

"You know what I want to do?" Jillian said, her voice thick with sleep.

"What's that?" I said, still glaring at the IV.

"I want to go to the beach. Saint Catherine is famous for its beaches, but I've never been. When the weather warms up, let's get some swimsuits and go. We'll pack a lunch, bring some beach books, and have fun."

My suspicions about the IV's true purpose deepened. She'd just heard that I was going to be kidnapped, and that the rest of them were slated for euthanasia, but here she was, talking about a beach trip.

Drug-free Jillian would've been half-dressed already, pacing around the room and fuming. Heck, she probably would've had a plan already formed that involved crawling through an air vent and hijacking a helicopter. It was a wonder that we all weren't hooked up to IVs for some made-up reason.

I just kissed her forehead. "Go to sleep now, sweetheart," I whispered. "You need it."

"Benjamin?"

"Mmm?"

"Thank you." She closed her eyes. "For everything you've done for me."

I swallowed the lump in my throat and kissed her forehead again. "You've done more. I was just along for the ride."

"...love you," she breathed.

"I love you, too."

She was already asleep.

I silently got out of her bed and pulled off my tunic and vest, then slipped into the small bed to the side of the room. The events of the past twenty-four hours had caught up with me, and exhaustion crawled through my veins. I laid on my side and watched Jillian's chest rise and fall with her blessedly clear breaths.

I pretended we were safe and closed my eyes.

THE ROAR of multiple helicopters overhead pulled me out of my sleep. At the same time, the gnawing emptiness in my stomach told me that I wouldn't be going back to sleep until I'd eaten. Night had fallen, and the small digital clock next to my bed read 20:42—I had only eighteen minutes if I wanted to get dinner.

I put on my boots and clothes and kissed Jillian's cheek, being careful to not wake her, then left her room and hurried out of the patient wing. Soft bulbs in frosted sconces lit the hallway, illuminating the passage perfectly without being painfully bright.

Raucous laughter echoed down the hallway as I approached the cafeteria. As soon as I walked in, I saw the Burlington team, now dressed in clean gray sweatshirts and khaki pants, sitting at a table in the corner with their dinners. Despite our hostile first meeting, it warmed my heart to see them happy.

However, Edward wasn't with them. Where the heck had he and Abby gone?

I walked past them to the dinner line, searching all the while for my own teammates, but they weren't there. The flirty cafeteria woman from before heaped stir-fried vegetables and baked chicken onto my plate with another hearty wink, and this time I merely thanked her and chose a table far, far away from the line.

When I'd eaten, I set out to find my team. Hospitals were lonely enough without the knowledge that I was being preyed on. I wasn't going to be alone if I didn't have to be.

Berenice and Lark were the easiest to find. I heard them before I saw them, with their loud, furious female voices clashing with faintly desperate voice of a young man in the rec room. I peeked in and had to cover my mouth to hide my laughter.

They were standing, hands balled at their sides, in the center of a circle of chairs. An older man, one of the eye-patched gentlemen I'd seen earlier, was holding a copy of *Leadership and Wisdom* and trying to placate the Baltimoreans. Half a dozen other residents were watching, their faces varying between amusement and shock.

"That is the *stupidest* thing *anyone* has *ever* said to me," Berenice replied, her face red. "If my leader tells me to commit suicide, he's the one who's going to die, thank you very much!"

Lark teleported behind the beleaguered man and snatched the book from his hand. "Seriously, who wrote this?"

"Ladies, please! I'm just tonight's reader," he pleaded, wringing his hands.

The gym was much quieter.

Though there were enough machines for at least half of the hospital to work out at the same time, only one person was in there. Marco was on a treadmill at the far end of the long room, running at a steady pace. I raised my hand and waved to get his attention, but he didn't look over at me.

Instead, a few seconds later, he turned off the treadmill and stepped off of it, sitting on a weightlifting bench and wiping his face and the back of his neck with his shirt. When he was done, he leaned his head back against the wall and stared up at the ceiling.

I left him alone with his thoughts.

If I couldn't be with my friends, then where was I supposed to go? I didn't want to go back to my room, lest I wake Jillian. Also, the hissing IV would just piss me off.

The one last place I hadn't visited was the large indoor courtyard I'd passed earlier.

Reid and Ember's giggles floated out of janitor's closet that I walked past on my way to the courtyard. Shaking my head, I pushed open the glass door and immediately sighed in unwilling contentment.

The courtyard was enormous, designed to mimic a sort-of jungle. Leafy trees and fragrant flowering bushes, planted right into the floor, flourished in the dim, muggy room. Piped sounds of birds and chattering monkeys called overhead, making me smile. A path wound through the growth towards the koi pond I'd seen from another angle hours earlier. As I walked down the shaded path, I heard splashing, and then another noise, something vaguely animal in nature.

I reached the end of the path and almost fell backwards in surprise and instinctual fear.

Two enormous tigers crouched at the edge of the koi pond, their whiskery faces not even an inch from the water. Whenever a colorful fish approached, the smaller of the two tigers batted at it and splashed water into the bigger tiger's face. The bigger tiger would huff and shake its head, then lick the smaller tiger.

I'd found Abby and Edward.

I slowly knelt down. "Hi, Abby," I said softly. Of course they'd go to the "jungle." I knew, in every bone in my body, that they'd flee to the real jungle as soon as they could. I'd help them, if they let me. If ever two people were destined to be together, it was Edward and Abby.

Abby slowly lifted her head and looked at me with her large, green-gold eyes, then sauntered over to my side. She laid her huge, furry head on my shoulder, and I stroked her coarse fur.

Edward padded over and settled primly on his haunches, assessing me. I extended my hand. "I'm Benjamin Corsaro."

Abby pulled her head back and shook it, and I somehow knew what she was saying: *Nuh-uh, none of that.*

"I mean, I'm Benjamin Trent."

Edward extended his salad-plate sized paw and I shook it. "I know you guys are on a date," I said apologetically, "But we've been looking for you. How about you let your teams know where you've been?"

They bumped noses, then silently walked into the shadows of the trees. A few seconds later, I heard a door open and shut. I was alone in the jungle, and though I knew I wasn't safe as long as I was in the hospital, I fell onto a wooden bench near the koi pond and let out a deep sigh of contentment.

A second later, I stretched out on my back, my arms behind my head, and gazed up at the stars that were visible through the glass ceiling.

What a mission we'd had.

Names and faces swirled in my mind, mixing together to form a stew of memories I'd never forget. Had it only been a few days since we'd come back to find Graham dead on the floor? And could it have only been a day or two since I'd torched Gabriela's home and killed Daisy? Had anyone found Will's body? Had I done right by my mother?

It felt as though a lifetime had passed, a lifetime of fear, pain, and uncertainty. Where were Reuben, Gabriela, and Jen? And for that matter, where was the strike team?

Most importantly, where was Beau?

A shooting star winked in and out of existence above me in the space of a breath. "Make a wish, Ben," I murmured. My wish came easily. *I wish my brother would show himself so we can finally move on.*

As much as my team insisted that Beau and Alysia weren't a threat, they were. I'd calmed down enough to admit that they probably weren't hiding behind the trees in the courtyard, so to speak, but they were probably in Leesburg.

And no, Beau wasn't the criminal mastermind I'd played him up to be, but after all, I'd played him up because he'd successfully abducted my wife. There was no getting around that. How could I scoff at him believing a "really obvious lie" when we'd been lured away from our home by a bomb? Any supervillain would tell you that the best plans were also the simplest ones.

However, did we have to fight?

I wanted to, but Jillian didn't, nor did the rest of my friends. They wanted to shed their weapons and uniforms and leave this life behind. It had taken all of two minutes for them to adjust to the prospect. Perhaps that was the true difference between us all; I was the only one who had chosen our life. Leaving it behind was a loss to me and the end of an adventure, whereas the adventure was about to begin for them.

"I *should* fight him," I muttered, the words leaving my mouth without prompting. He deserved it. He deserved to be defeated by the brother he'd wronged. He deserved jail. He deserved humiliation and fear.

But we didn't always get what we deserved.

In a short while, I wouldn't be a superhero anymore, and Beau's fate would be in the hands of other branches of law enforcement.

I groaned and made a face. If I couldn't have that satisfaction, what *did* I have to look forward to? I sensed that my path to the military was closed to me, but what about my old dream of nursing? Not every hospital was like this one—and who said I had to work in a hospital? Home nursing companies, hospices, urgent care centers, schools...all of them needed RNs.

There was something beneath the thoughts, a disquiet that caused discomfort. I closed my eyes and focused on it. *Be honest with yourself. Why are you unhappy?*

I was proud of how quickly I admitted the truth: I didn't want to be a nurse anymore. I just wanted to be with Jillian.

Of course I wanted an occupation, but I didn't want to be away from her for long hours. Perhaps the desire was borne of protectiveness after all that had happened to us. But no matter the reason, unless Jillian was working with me, I just didn't want to do it.

And after all, my Army nursing plans had been part rebellion, part boyish desire to fight, and part desire to help people. I no longer had anyone to rebel against, I'd seen far too much combat, and I'd spent seven months helping people in every capacity imaginable. I'd even helped bring down the camps. In a way, my actions would help people long after my lifetime ended.

So what was I going to do with myself? I had to support myself and my family somehow, and a man without a purpose was no man at all.

One of the doors to the courtyard opened, and the sound of masculine footsteps coming towards me made me sigh. I'd just started to relax.

"It's ten o'clock," said a young man from somewhere down the path. His voice sounded familiar, but I didn't think it was Josh's. Where did I know it from? Before I could sit up and look for a face, he added, "It's after curfew. Please report to your room."

I bolted onto my feet, instantly annoyed. *Curfew?* Josh had mentioned quiet hours, but nobody had said anything about a curfew, and I didn't appreciate being sent to my room like I was a kid. I had a long tirade at the ready for this dipstick, and I didn't care who the hell he was.

I stood my ground, ready for whoever came out of the trees.

A nurse emerged on the other side of the koi pond. He was barely older than me.

For one second, I was transported out of the hospital. I was back in the hallway at my parents' house, staring at the picture my mother had taken at my tenth birthday party. Next to my chubby childhood self, another young boy grinned at the camera. Like all of my guests at that party, he'd been the son of supervillains.

I spoke without thinking. "Brock Snider?"

Brock and I gasped at the same time.

His bullet collided with my Kevlar vest in the same second that a bomb exploded in the hallway.

I flew into the bench, which splintered and collapsed. Another bomb exploded nearby, the shockwave shattering the courtyard's ceiling. I shielded my face just in time—glass shards rained down on us, slicing my hands and wrists.

Though my head spun from the gun's blast, the bombs, and the echoing of emergency alarms, I whipped out my baton and stumbled towards Brock, who'd been knocked into the koi pond.

He looked up at me, a vicious scowl on his face. Immediately, snakes and horribly large spiders began to crawl all over my body... or so it appeared.

"Nice try, dick," I growled, shivering as a "wolf spider" scuttled down my arm and into my sleeve. *It's not real, they're not real, they're just an illusion...*

A third blast, much closer this time, caused me to tumble down onto the tile floor. Trees crashed down around me, covering me with palm branches and large green leaves. Tiny bits of rock and brick littered the ground. Over to my side, Brock splashed around in the koi pond for a second, then clambered to his feet before running awkwardly towards a door.

I groaned and pushed the branches off of me. Nothing was broken, but my head was ringing from the multiple blasts. No... that was alarms. All over the hospital, emergency alarms were blaring, their cacophonous screech echoing up and down the hallways to create an eerie, near-yet-far effect.

I stood on shaking legs and cursed myself for wishing on that shooting star. Beau was here, and if Brock was with him, there was no telling who else I was about to meet. How had they sneaked in? And how had they brought so many bombs with them?

I stumbled through the destroyed jungle and shoved the cracked glass door open. The alarms became a thousand times louder, and the emergency lights lining the walls flooded the hallway with an ominous red hue.

A man stood at the far end of the destroyed hallway, facing away from me. He was still wearing his prison jumpsuit.

"Uncle Mike," I said, knowing full well that he couldn't hear me over the alarms.

Yet, my mother's younger brother turned around, his eyes dark with hatred. In his hands, two glowing orbs of explosive energy took form. His thin face was haggard from months of incarceration, containing all the ill will he'd stored up since he'd fought my friends and lost half a year ago.

I backed up. We were no longer uncle and nephew.

I was Mercury.

He was the Destructor.

And this time, it was personal for him.

ITEM TWENTY-TWO

Headline of the *Richmond Times-Dispatch*, October 29, 1942.

CHRISTINA ST. JAMES DIES
Nation Mourns Its First Super-Hero

22

Almost as soon as Uncle Mike had turned around, half a dozen armed guards flooded into the hallway behind him, their M4s pointed at the both of us. The leader shouted something, but his orders were drowned out by alarms, distant screams, and my own partial deafness.

The man shouted again and pointed to the ground.

Never taking my eyes off my uncle, I slowly knelt and put my hands up. I was fast, but I couldn't outrun bullets.

My uncle's eyes hardened. Jillian had once described to me how his eyes had flashed before he tried to kill her, and I'd been confused —he'd never looked like that when I'd known him. But now I saw what she meant. A crazed hatred lit up his gaze, making him look terrifyingly inhuman.

I dove for cover behind the open door of a supply closet just in time. The explosion rattled the shelves, and various medical supplies and boxes tumbled down on me, though I wasn't hurt. Instead, I stood on unsteady legs, trying to catch my breath. Nobody was shooting.

Sprinklers overhead sputtered to life, and then water began to spray in every direction, even inside the closet. Cursing, I grabbed my baton and ran out of the closet, determined to beat my uncle's face in. I'd finish him off, then find Beau. Or maybe I'd find my team first. I had no plan, since I wasn't sure what to expect.

My uncle was standing by an open door with his hand raised, a glowing orb taking shape. Faint, terrified screams came from inside as he shot the orb into the room. There was a flash and small explosion, and then no more screaming.

"Hey, Mike!" I gripped the baton so hard I expected it to bend in my grasp. There was too much debris in the hallway to run directly at him—bricks, pieces of wall, pieces of the guards—but he couldn't bomb me if I was near him.

I squared my shoulders and began to walk towards him, never blinking. Unless he was on a suicide mission, his bombing was over. For now.

He faced me and raised his hand, though a wisp of uncertainty lingered in his face. Was he debating killing a nephew, or whether the blast would kill him?

I flicked my baton into strike position. His hesitation would be his downfall. I took a breath and—

He gasped. "*What*?"

I couldn't help a gasp, either.

Every droplet of water from the floor and walls levitated up and flew between us with ballet-like grace, converging into a translucent wall of liquid through which I could almost make out his surprised expression. Every drop in the air stopped mid-flight, spiraling like melted sideways snowflakes until they hit the wall, making it bigger.

I dared to turn around for a bare second. Who...?

Elijah stood at the far end of the hallway, his eyes glowing as Reid's did when he was at full power. Unlike Reid's large, muscular movements when he controlled the earth, Elijah manipulated the water as a marionette master would his strings, with delicate finger movements and sweeping arms, though he *was* missing one hand, giving the whole display a grotesquely comical appearance.

A bomb hit the water-wall, but the water didn't even bow from the extra energy. Instead, Elijah just smiled in his own serene way and shook his head. He flicked his hand outward. The wall surged forward into my uncle, sweeping him up with the rest of the carnage and slamming the mess into the glass wall of the far hallway.

The glass broke under the might of the tsunami, shattering and releasing everything into the snow beyond. I caught a hint of motion, but couldn't make out what it was.

Elijah released the water in the sprinklers, and it began to rain on us again. Without taking his eyes off the broken window, he stalked past me with his hand still raised.

I almost fell sideways in my hurry to get out of the hallway. I had to find my team and come up with a plan. Amid the din, screams and shouts punctured the alarms and general sounds of carnage, but I couldn't make anyone out. Where had my friends gone? Where was I in relation to them?

Surrounded by so much chaos, I struggled to recall the layout of the hospital. I turned a corner and squinted at the empty, red-tinted hallway. The only thing more threatening in battle than combatants was an eerie lack of them.

"Ben!" Marco's strained voice came from a door to my right that I'd just passed.

I dove inside and saw that it was a supply closet full of board games and other pastimes. He was huddled between a shelf and the wall, his hand pressed to his side. Blood leaked through his fingers, and his lips were tight with the strain of not showing his pain. He blinked several times. "It was Alysia," he gasped. "They're here. They're all here. She's got a knife."

I offered a hand and he grabbed it, hoisting himself up as his wound healed. "What happened?" I asked in a low voice as I shut the door. "What do you know so far?"

"I was looking for more yarn in here when the bombs started going off," he said quickly. "I ran out to see what was going on when that stupid cow bum-rushed me. I singed her, but not before she got me. I saw Beau at the end of the hall. There are a few others. I don't know where the teams are."

I swore under my breath as another bomb went off, making

plastic bins full of card games topple over on top of us. Either Uncle Mike was still alive or my brother had brought ordnance. Both were entirely possible.

Immediately after the explosion, motion at the door caught my eye. Alysia's long fingers phased through the door, followed by the tip of her nose.

I shoved the door open, slamming her backwards into the hallway. "Marco, go!"

He sprinted down the hall and out of sight.

Alysia had already recovered. She stood up straight, her drenched brown hair hanging in strings around her face. An ugly burn marred her cheek. Like Josh, she was dressed in a nursing uniform. Unlike Josh, her uniform was covered in blood and gore—or so I thought. The omnipresent red light from the alarms made it hard to distinguish the color of her uniform, much less where the stains were.

"Alysia." *Get her talking.*

She twiddled her knife. "Bleeding Heart Benjamin," she spat. "You're still the same little runt as ever, I see. I suppose if you're here, then sweet little Jillian is, too. Or did you fly her carcass here for the autopsy? Wanted a description of my handiwork?" She shook her head to get the water off her face.

Though heat flooded through my cheeks, I ignored her braindead taunts and analyzed what she'd said. She didn't know if Jillian was here or not, which meant that their mission was solely to find the JM-104. And if she didn't know that Jillian was here, that meant she hadn't returned to the house. And *that* meant...

"Have you heard from your brother lately?" I asked, trying not to smirk.

She stopped playing with the knife. "I... what are you talking about?" She shook the water off again, obviously uncomfortable with being wet.

I couldn't help a grin. "I'm talking about how Jillian turned him into Swiss cheese."

"No!" Alysia raised her knife like a psycho.

I slammed into her before she could phase through me. Her head hit the glass wall with bone-cracking force, yet she was able to slash at me, missing my eyes by inches. I moved to throw her into neck-breaking position, but she kicked me in the groin.

I stumbled backwards, falling into a crouch as I figured out how to fight someone with her powers. What was her weakness?

She lurched forward with her knife in hand. No doubt she'd chosen it for intimidation, because I'd never seen her wield a weapon before. In fact, I'd never seen her fight at all. Six months of knowing Jillian allowed me to see that Alysia's handling of the knife was embarrassingly amateur. Alysia was all smash and grab, leaving the ugly bits of life to her brother. In a way, she was like the evil version of Ember.

With that realization, my strategy immediately presented itself.

I slowly stood, contorting my face into the blackest expression I knew how. I rolled up my sleeves, subtly drawing her attention to my muscles, which were far larger than she'd ever seen them before.

Her eyes widened a fraction as she took in "Bleeding Heart Benjamin" before her, water running down my face with no effect.

I flicked my baton. "You know I can kill you with impunity, right? It's a *superhero's* privilege."

She swallowed, her eyes darting up and down as she looked for the "real" me. There was a beat, and then—

I grabbed her just as she'd turned to run through the wall. Yanking her hair, I pulled her back into the hallway. She shrieked and spun around, dropping her knife in alarm and throwing a volley of wild punches at my face, chest, and shoulders. My training kicked in, and I blocked most of her blows, dimly surprised that I could.

My hand found her throat. I threw her against the wall. Not waiting for her response, I banged her head into the wall again, then again. She fell into a heap on the floor and didn't move.

There was no time to celebrate. Bullets from outside shattered the glass wall. I ducked and ran for cover, unable to use super speed because of the pain of Alysia's kick. Beyond the glass, new screams lit up the night. I had to find my team, fast.

I turned another corner and skidded to a halt. Half a dozen

bodies littered the floor, all of them shot in the head. The hallway ended at a shattered window. From the window, freezing wind blew in and raised the hair on the back of my neck. I couldn't see anything beyond the halo of broken glass sticking out of the frame.

A man in a nursing uniform flew out of an open door and crashed into the opposite wall. Marco marched through the door, raised his hand, and shot a narrow, rippling beam of heat directly at the man's forehead. A disgusting burning smell turned my stomach, and I averted my eyes.

Marco squared his shoulders. "This hallway is clear. I'm going through the window."

Nodding, we dashed to the window. I knocked away the sharpest shards of glass with my baton, and we helped each other through into the chilly night. We landed in the soft snow drifts and hurried into the woods.

When we were behind a large tree, I sheathed my baton while Marco let out a long breath and closed his eyes. "I've been trying to contact Ember," he whispered. "But I can't hear a thing."

"Animal telepath?" I suggested, never taking my eyes off the window we'd come through. "They know her weakness." Jillian had told me about how Emma, the daughter of some family friends, had used her locust telepathy to block Ember's powers at the Westerner compound.

"Maybe," Marco said. "But there are a hell of a lot of enemies running around. I hope she's with Reid or Jill or someone."

I picked up on his line of thought. "They're not here for Ember," I said. "They're here for the JM-104 and nothing else. In fact, I bet Brock's telepathic illusions are blocking Ember's powers." It made sense. He himself was quite powerful. Maybe other types of telepathy canceled out Ember's.

"I don't know," Marco said, biting his lip. "She's never had a prob—"

The roars of two tigers drowned out whatever he was saying. We were knocked backwards without so much as a yell as Abby and

Edward pounced from our left. Someone behind us cried out, a strangled, wet shout of terror, and then went silent.

I rolled over in the snow and saw Abby toss a hand away with a jerk of her huge head. Edward gulped something down, low growls emanating from deep within him. He batted snow over the corpse and turned to look at us, dissolving into the form of a man with the same sucking sound as Abby always made. His sunglasses were still on his head.

"Third one I've killed tonight," he said. "He was about to shoot you guys. Next time maybe use some situational awareness, hmm?" He picked up a pistol from the snow and unloaded it, then tossed the bullets into the snow. "If you're looking for your team, they're over there." He pointed to a set of double doors several dozen yards away. Two more bodies lay ripped apart by the entrance. "They were trying to set up a trap, I think, so be careful."

"Thanks," I said as I extended my baton again. It wasn't going back in its sheath until we were a hundred miles from here.

Marco put his hand on Abby's head. "Have you seen Ember? Smelled her? Anything?"

Abby lifted her paw and looked in the opposite direction of the double doors, near the path that led to the helipad.

More shooting and screams interrupted our little club meeting. Edward cursed. "We'll see you around."

He leapt into tiger form and made to go deeper into the woods, but Abby let out a rough, feline kind of sound. Edward stopped to stare at her, and she jerked her head towards the helipad. He shook his head, but Abby nodded. She bit Marco's sleeve and began to pull him towards the helipad.

Edward's sigh sounded quite human to my ears.

"I'll get the team and rendezvous with you guys at the helipad," I said to Marco. He nodded and began to head in that direction, leaving me to go through the double doors without cover or backup.

Keeping low, I ran to the wall of the hospital and hurried along the edge, where the snow wasn't as deep. This part of the wall was brick, not glass, so I was only exposed from one side. As such, I kept an eye on the trees. Several of them had been knocked down by a blast. When I arrived at the double doors, I reached for the knob, straining to hear anything on the other side.

A quiet, masculine groan from my left made me pause. "Reid?" I turned around and searched for my teammate, but didn't see him. "Reid, where are you?"

"Here." The voice came from near the fallen trees. He was lying prone under a tree, pinned by branches as thick as my leg.

"Reid!" I fell to my knees next to him and grabbed his hand.

"Get it off," he gasped. "Can't... can't breathe."

"Yeah, right," I said as I began to pull him out from the branches. Like I could ever get a tree off of someone. I wasn't Jillian. With a grunt of effort, I slid Reid out of the tangle of wood and dead leaves.

He clambered awkwardly to his feet, shivering uncontrollably. "What happened?"

A single gunshot from behind the double doors stopped him from answering. He raised a hand, his eyes instantly aglow, but slowly lowered it. Another gunshot sounded, but nobody was shooting at us. A third gunshot made us look quizzically at each other. These weren't the frenetic pop-pop-pops we'd heard since the beginning of the fray.

Far in the distance, a tiger's roar mixed with Marco's furious shouts.

"Go," I said, pushing him away. "I'll handle the shooter."

Reid stumbled a few steps, then made himself a flying platform and disappeared up and over the roof. I pushed open the door, immediately assaulted by blaring alarms and the hellish red light that muted all colors. It was the operating hallway where Jillian's room was.

A battlefield lay before me. At least twenty people had died here, their bodies limp and bleeding. Two members of the Burlington team, their names forgotten to me, were among the fallen. All the bodies were angled away from the door—they'd died with their faces to the enemy.

Brock Snider stood over a nurse and shot him in the head. He was executing survivors.

After murdering his latest victim, he serenely stretched, as if he were tired, then turned to face me. An infuriating little smile played around his lips as he raised his revolver to my eye level.

I summoned every ounce of strength I had left and prepared to charge him, but a tarantula on my face threw me off for half a second.

I braced for the bullet.

Instead, he swung arm around and shot a woman lying to his side, his eyes full of malicious humor. Then he raised his gun to me again and backed away, never breaking eye contact until he kicked open the door behind him and ran off.

I stepped over bodies as I went from door to door to check for survivors, burying my sadness over the massacre. I'd allow myself to feel it later, when we were out of danger. I'd found Reid and Marco, but where were Ember and Jillian? Ember apparently was near the helipad, but my wife? Who could say where she'd go during an attack?

I put my hand on the neck of the unfortunate man that Brock had shot as I'd watched. Nothing happened. In fact, nothing in the hallway triggered my healing power. I didn't even look at Brock's final victim, the dead woman, as I passed her.

My hand was on the door when I stopped.

I turned around, a lump in my throat that hadn't been there only a few seconds earlier.

The dead woman's long, dark, shoulder-length hair obscured her face, but her tallness was obvious from the length of her legs. Toned arms hinted at an active lifestyle. She wore dark scrubs covered in blood.

I couldn't feel my limbs as I sank to my knees next to the corpse. With shaking hands I tilted the head up and brushed away the hair.

Jillian's dead eyes gazed at nothing.

ITEM TWENTY-THREE

Coded letter sent from Gerald Trent to his brother, Franklin Trent, Jr., dated April 2, 1966.

Gerry,

Don't you dare go blaming me for what happened to Emil. I <u>told</u> him to avoid Battlecry. The doctor says I should thank my lucky stars that her banshee scream didn't shatter my eardrum along with the windshield.

I'm so tired of those white hats. Philadelphia used to be our town. I'm tired of running around in the dark. This isn't how it's supposed to be. Someone should do something.

Frankie

23

Pounding in my ears.

Numbness spreading into my fingers.

Tingling everywhere as my lungs failed me, failing to hold the air I gasped for.

Cold linoleum against my cheek.

Jillian's distant brown eyes staring into mine.

ITEM TWENTY-FOUR

Headline of *The New York Times*, July 23, 1967.

PHILLY HEROES MURDERED
Grisly Film Reel Sent to Studios - Country in Shock

24

I stumbled out into the snow.
Nothing.

There was nothing for me.

Every second that dragged past was an explosion of agony, ripping my skin away from my muscles, my muscles from my bones, each joint separating as I screamed for relief. None ever came, and then the next second would begin.

I dropped to my knees, the pain ripping out of my throat and into the frozen sky.

Nothing.

Somewhere out there, where I ceased to exist and the fragments of other people began, my families were fighting. Streaks of orange and yellow coursed across the sky, fiery hallmarks of battle, all silent beneath the rushing and pounding of blood in my ears.

I lurched to my feet. Stumbled. Fell.

I got up again.

My feet took me into the woods. I crashed down, this time the screams coming out of me until I was hoarse.

They turned into sobs.

She'd been twenty-one years old. Twenty-one, funny, kind, courageous, and so innocent. All Jillian had ever wanted was to save people. Behind the top layer of knife-wielding superhero leader had been a young woman who'd just wanted to *save* people. To help them. To be a hero because someone had to be. She'd deserved the chance to set down her weapons and walk away toward a life of choices.

But people don't always get what they deserve.

I slowly lifted my head, my tears slowing as burning replaced the water in my eyes.

Beau *was* going to get what he deserved. Beau, Brock, all of them. They were going to get what they deserved.

I stood, the sights and sounds of the night newly crisp, yet not a fraction as threatening as before. My racing thoughts pulled me towards just one destination: Beau. He was here, and he was going to die.

But where to start?

I marched through the snow towards the helipad. First things first: disable the getaway vehicles. Maybe get the rest of my team to help. Marco would kill a million men to avenge the death of another sister. Reid and Ember would fall apart, but then again, that wouldn't be anything I hadn't dealt with before. As Marco had demonstrated, threatening to kill them could work wonders.

I flattened myself against the brick wall by the corner before the turn for the helipad.

A bullet whizzed through a window behind me, shattering it and throwing glass everywhere.

Whatever.

All the king's horses and all the king's men had converged on the helipad before I'd entered the hallway where—*no, think about something else*—yet I couldn't hear anything around the corner except...

More explosions. Shots. Alarms.

Damn it, be quiet so I can hear.

A man's strangled yell fought for dominance over a woman's furious shouts. Whose, though?

I turned the corner and stopped at the edge of the wide concrete helipad. Four helicopters were waiting, doors open, for occupants. A fifth's rotors were whirring rapidly, though its door was closed.

Beyond them, Brock was struggling mightily to pull Ember towards the revved-up helicopter. She had a knife in hand; he had several bleeding gashes on his arms and face. She flailed and grabbed a tuft of his hair.

I slammed into Brock. Ember tumbled down onto all fours, while Brock flew into the skids of the helicopter, his head banging hard against it. He dazedly reached for his gun.

I was faster. From then on, I'd always be faster.

I snatched the gun and leveled it at his head, the water returning to my eyes and washing away whatever emotion was on his face.

Ember looked up. "Ben—!"

My finger moved.

There was a sharp silence, underlined only by the roar of the rotors. I wiped bits of Brock off my face, then took a deep breath and scooped up the spare bullets that had tumbled out of his fake nurse scrubs. I methodically loaded the six-round chamber, spinning it when it was done. Without looking away, I said, "Find Beau."

"Ben, you just—"

"He killed Jillian. Find. Beau." I turned to look at her. Brock's blood dripped down my face.

Her eyes almost doubled in size. "No, no, no..." She fell backwards onto her bottom and held her cheeks. "No, that's not possible!"

"*I said find Beau!*"

She shrieked and scrambled away on her elbows. "Please, don't!"

The water overflowed. "Don't what? Shoot you?! I don't want to shoot you! Don't you *get* it? I want to kill the people who murdered my wife! Now get up *and find them!*"

An inferno of hate cascaded through my being, destroying every last shred of mercy or tenderness. If Ember wasn't going to help me, than she was in my way.

And I knew what how to handle superheroines who were in my way.

My breathing slowed, and I lifted my arm again. My vision tunneled, narrowing to just Ember at the business end of my gun. "Do it. Now."

I wasn't sure if it was a threat anymore.

Ember stared at the end of my gun, her face going slack. "You'll really kill me, won't you?"

The gun shook so much that I switched my stance to a more solid double-handed grip. "I'll kill anyone and anything." My chest heaved. "I know J-Jillian wouldn't want me to, but she's not here. Don't bother trying to drop her name. It's not going to work."

She blinked up at me, raw horror on her face. "I can't believe... Even you."

I thumbed back the hammer. "Last chance."

She closed her eyes and breathed. When she opened them, a new darkness clouded her gaze. "Beau's already gone. He found out where the JM-104 really is, and he's on the way there now. If we hurry, we can catch him before he gets it. Get in the helicopter."

I slowly lowered my arm. "Where is it?"

She swallowed. "The chemical lab in Baltimore."

Go figure.

I wrenched open the door to the aircraft. The pilot spun around in his seat. "Hey, you aren't—"

He clutched his head and yelped.

Ember hopped inside and slammed the door. "This is Kevin. He's an employee of Bell Enterprises *and* of the Trent family."

I aimed the gun at Kevin, who was still clutching his head and crying. "What are you doing to him?"

Ember settled into a seat and fastened her seat belt. "Stop waving that stupid thing around. I'm warning him what I can do if he doesn't obey me." She smiled.

Kevin gasped and shivered. "Okay, okay, fine. We're going. Don't do that again, please."

She narrowed her eyes. "Get us in the air in the next five seconds, Kev, and I won't. We're going to Bell's lab in Baltimore. You know the one." There was a pause, and then she rolled her eyes. "Oh, land in the parking lot, for all I care."

His hands flew over the controls, and indeed, just seconds later we were airborne.

A light fog settled on my brain, clouding my thoughts, muddling them. Suddenly dizzy, I sat across from Ember and fastened my own seatbelt, then looked out across the shrinking helipad.

Two tigers were staring up at us. One turned into Abby, and she waved her arms frantically, her mouth moving.

I looked away from the window. "What is she saying?"

Ember snorted. "She's calling for Reid. She thinks we've been kidnapped."

"Do you think he'll chase us?"

"No. He can't go this fast or this high."

"That probably won't stop him from trying, though, right?"

Ember looked out the window for nearly a minute before she spoke. "Yes, he'll try. Like always. And he'll fail, like always."

I leaned forward. "What—?"

"Patrick. The elders. The Westerners. Your brother." Her low voice, laden with the tragedies of a lifetime, carried through clearly across the space. She closed her eyes and touched her delicate fingers to her face. "It's not personal against him...but he couldn't keep me safe from any of those people. Who could?"

Well, yeah, she had a point. "Where was Reid when Brock...?"

"I don't know," she muttered, her eyes still closed. "Something blew up across the campus, and he told me to stay low and out of sight while he went to investigate with the others. I begged him to stay with me." A tear escaped her lashes, and she wiped it with the back of her hand. "I literally begged him. I would've gotten on my knees if he'd stayed long enough."

She shook her head. "Maybe if I'd had the twenty years of training that everyone else had... but no, I didn't." She finally looked at me. "Telepathy isn't like it is in the movies, you know. I can't strike a man dead with my brain. If some psycho is charging at me with a knife, I'd better hope a dog is nearby, or that I can mentally throw something at him that slows him down, like I did with our buddy Kevin over there. Telepaths are a lot of bark, but not much bite."

"I can see what you mean. It's a wonder you weren't on a strike team instead. You're incredibly valuable for recon."

A non-sequitur popped into my brain: *why are we in a helicopter?*

Something terrible had happened, something that I was forgetting. Invisible steel cables tugged at me, pulling me back to the hospital. I needed to get back to the hospital. *Now.* I reached to unbuckle my seatbelt.

Ember glanced at me and squinted.

The mental fog deepened, yet the result was a light sensation spreading through my chest. Relaxation, almost. Soupy and warm, it spread through my veins as a great weight was lifted from my mind and heart. But, still, something *was* missing, the thing that would make the feeling happiness.

I leaned my head against the window. *Of course.* My wife wasn't with me. That was the problem.

Where was she, anyway?

Ember and I were on a mission to stop Beau, but I had no idea where Jillian and the others were. Oh, well. She could handle herself, all trained and strong and stuff. It was part of what made her so incredibly attractive.

I smiled a little. "What were you saying, Em?"

Ember's face darkened. "My abilities are the perfect mix of not powerful enough to be in public service, but obviously way too dangerous to have around the elders' right-hand underlings. Who knows what I would've picked up?"

I shrugged. "State secrets, probably. Or at least camp secrets. They would've had you whacked at some point. That seems to be their MO." I frowned, concern for Ember foremost in my thoughts. We were—

On a mission?

Were we on a mission?

Ugh, why couldn't I remember? All I knew for sure was that Ember had been in danger a minute ago, and she was upset about it. And we were in a helicopter... and I couldn't trust the pilot. I knew that much.

But it was enough. *Protect Ember.*

Ember leaned forward and held out her hands, which I took. I gave them a reassuring little squeeze. "You're going to be okay, Em. I promise."

She kissed my knuckles, her eyes shimmering. "Benjamin Trent."

"Ember Harris," I teased back.

She laughed quietly. "You are one of the most sincere, tender-hearted people I've ever met, did you know that? I've been in a lot of minds, so I want you to understand my full meaning when I say that yours is one of my favorites. You've been such a true friend to me these last few months. At first I was a little hesitant that my best friend was dating a reformed criminal, but now I can say that it's been my sheer honor to serve with you."

My heart swelled, though I was a bit confused. Why was she going all sentimental on me?

She smiled, but there was a bittersweet quality in the crinkles of her eyes. "Because I wanted to see you again. I wanted to see *this* Benjamin, the one who's in love. The newlywed with the world ahead of him."

Disquiet shivered to life. "What are you talking about? What do you—I don't—"

She caressed my cheek. "Shhh. I can see it in your mind that you really do love me, and I'll always cherish that love. But I understand why you did what you did a few minutes ago. There are bigger things at stake, and you had to make a tough choice. You had to be a jackass to get things done. I get it. Maybe, one day, you'll extend the same courtesy to me when you think back to this moment."

I pulled my hands away. *Jackass?* "What are you talking about?"

She leaned back and surveyed me, a new coolness settling on her features. "It's nothing personal, Benjamin. I'm sorry. Like I said, I really just wanted to see my friend again. Not the monster."

"Wh—"

"Jill's dead, Benjamin."

The fog lifted, releasing the tsunami of bloody memories. I collapsed, sobbing anew while Ember idly patted my shoulder.

Nothing.

I had nothing left.

ITEM TWENTY-FIVE

Handwritten letter addressed to Edmund Howard, Jr., CEO of Howard Chemical Engineering, written on HCE letterhead, dated circa 1969.

Mr. Howard,

In the spirit of full disclosure I must tell you about a phone call I received last night from an anonymous gentleman shortly past midnight. He told me he knew about my financial situation following my mother's illness, and he said he was prepared to offer a large sum in exchange for certain information regarding the formula I've been working on these last three years.

But the funny thing is—I don't know how he would know, because I haven't told anyone about the project, not even Sally. But this man knew that I'd just started the 100th version of the formula, that it was for the Super cure, everything.

I think we've got a spy. I'm going to fire my assistants this Friday. I'm sure you'll understand.

My regards,
Dr. J. Macleod

25

I fell out of the helicopter onto the empty, snow-covered parking lot, banging my knee against an object hidden in the thick drifts. I rolled onto my back, shuddering from the unending assault of pain— in my knee, in my heart, in my head.

The dark expanse of the midnight sky stretched over Baltimore, more visible than usual without the light pollution that normally hid all but the brightest stars.

I couldn't even look at the sky anymore without yet more pain. Jillian had loved stars...

Ember roughly pulled me to my feet. "Up. Now." Before I could so much as yelp, she shoved me toward a low, tinted office window. "Break it."

I pointed toward the security shack at the entry gates. "Those guys will—"

"I made them fall asleep. I also made them shut off the security system, so nobody is going to stop us. Shut up and break the window. Or do you not want to stop Beau?"

She'd said the magic words.

I waded through the snow and slammed my revolver against the glass. After a few bangs, a spiderweb of cracks appeared, then grew.

Finally, the window began to shatter and fall away, creating a hole for Ember and me to hop through.

We'd broken into a bland corporate corner office that could've been for anything from HR to accounting. The lone desk, devoid of any personalization, bore just a single closed laptop and a half-empty coffee mug. The shampoo smell of the carpet couldn't quite hide the omnipresent chemical-y smell that permeated the whole building—I remembered from last time. Everything smelled vaguely of bleach, metal, and cold.

Ember scowled. "Okay, the JM-104 is somewhere in this building, and it's hidden. We're looking for a stainless steel canister, about the size of a soda can. That's all I picked up."

There was a short silence.

"And... where's my brother?" I asked, a strange feeling creeping up my neck.

She didn't seem concerned about him, and that alone was odd to the point of being suspicious. Beau was the man who'd almost kidnapped and tortured her just over a week ago. The man who'd nearly murdered her best friend several times, and whose lackey had succeeded in doing so. The guy we were technically pursuing, lest he get the JM-104 first.

And now that I thought about it, the parking lot had been empty, with no hint of anyone else having landed there recently—or at all.

Ember rounded on me. "We beat him here, moron."

I flinched. "I'm sorry, Em, but I can't help but notice—"

She grabbed a fistful of my shirt and pulled me just inches from her face. "Buddy, the last thing your wife told you was that she loved you, remember? Then she fell asleep, believing you would take care of everything and keep her safe." She pushed me backwards into the wall. "And now she's dead because you decided to wander off and *think about* the situation. Well, think about this: she'd probably be alive if you hadn't done that."

I was in the hallway before she could say any more, bending over and hyperventilating with my hands on my knees. Oh God, she was cruel. She was correct, but she was cruel. I did not like this new side of Ember.

Or was this the *true* Ember? I shivered.

She strode out of the office. "Start searching the offices. I'll go downstairs into the storage rooms." She shoved open a double door and walked off, her echoing footsteps quickly fading into nothing.

She hadn't even turned around to face me.

Trembling, I turned the knob of the nearest door and opened it. A gush of cool, stale air greeted me, complete with the office-y smell of paper, cleaner, and toner. I hastily opened all the drawers and cabinets, but there was nothing.

I moved mechanically, searching office after office, all boring and fruitless. Some of them were stuffed with personnel files, others with various financial statements, but none had so much as an aerosol fragrance can, much less JM-104. There were no safes in corners, no promising box tucked in the back of a drawer.

I rounded a corner and paused.

A gold plaque on the lone door teased me. Eliza H. Bell-McCurtis, Chairman and CEO of Bell Enterprises, would almost certainly know all about JM-104. Dean had told me that the substance was so top secret that its location wasn't even on paper.

Who better to hide the stuff than the most important person in the company?

I almost smiled as the pieces clicked together. Why would the Chairman and CEO of Bell Enterprises have her office at a regional lab? This wasn't BE's headquarters—I knew for a fact that Bell's head offices were in Chicago. All supervillains knew that. Maybe this was the *real* headquarters of the company, the place where they kept their most coveted product.

I hastily jiggled the doorknob, breathing hard, but to no avail. I punched the door with growl of frustration.

"C'mon, Trent, think," I muttered, reviewing my options. I backed up and surveyed the door and the surrounding area.

The office had a window that looked out over the hallway. Bingo.

A breath, a sprint—

I grabbed a metal chair from another office and dragged it down the hallway back to Eliza's office. Without any further ado, I swung it with all my might at the glass.

I winced against the shower of glass shards and splinters that flew everywhere, but I didn't stop banging the chair against the remaining glass until it was a safe passage for me. Tossing the chair aside, I climbed through the window, knocked away the battered plastic blinds I'd ruined, and began to thoroughly destroy Eliza Bell-McCurtis's office.

Drawers were yanked open violently, their contents flipped through and then tossed aside. Desk cabinets were cleared in equal measure, then the filing cabinets. I even turned the trashcans upside down.

Then I began to push furniture aside—maybe there was a trap door? Filing cabinets crashed around me. The desk went over. The copying machine was shoved into a corner.

Nothing. Nothing. Nothing.

It had to be here. It *had* to be. It wouldn't be down in the records area, it would be in the heart of the lab, guarded by the most important person. She was probably the only person who knew.

My teeth began to chatter, and I put my hands behind my head, looking all around. Emotion welled in my eyes, and I squeezed them shut. I needed to find the JM-104 for Jillian. She was watching me from Heaven, urging me on. She'd died in Beau's pursuit for it, and now I was making sure that he'd never find it.

She'd died because of the JM-104. In the end, at the closing of her incredible life, she'd been just one more victim of the camps and their Gordian knot of lies. Her life had been cut short in the most senseless and avoidable way, but I could give her death meaning.

A sob tried to crawl out of my chest. After several deep breaths, it retreated in defeat. I let out one last large breath, closed my eyes, then opened them and looked around. Maybe I'd missed something.

A small door in the corner, one that I hadn't seen from the window, caught my eye. What was behind it? Who would put a door inside a private office?

Unless...

My fingers touched the cool metal knob. It was locked—and there was no window to break.

"Damn it! *Damn it!*"

All of my frustration exploded at once.

I hurled a paperweight at the door, then a stapler. A three-hole-punch. The wastepaper basket. A laptop. The chair. Every useless trinket bounced off the sturdy door, laughing at me.

I ran at the door and began banging it with my fists. "Open up! Open up, damn you! *Open up!*"

"Ben?"

I spun around, my revolver in my hand without thought.

Reuben was standing by the shattered window in his old uniform, but no mask. It made the disappointment on his face that much more obvious.

He slowly raised his hands. "Easy there. Let's not make any hasty decisions."

How the hell had he even known to come here?

I swallowed hard. "Are you here to drag me off to jail, *Obsidian*?"

He flinched. "What happened?"

I backed up until I was against the stupid locked door, but I didn't lower my weapon. "What do you mean, what happened?"

"I mean, what happened in the last few days that turned you from a superhero into, well... a guy breaking into Bell's CEO's office with blood all over his face and a gun in his hand? Because there's backsliding, and then there's backsliding."

I did not have time for this.

I motioned with the gun. "This doesn't concern you. We're here for the JM-104, and then we'll go."

"By 'we,' you mean you and Ember, right?"

"Stop trying to distract me! I said leave!"

He didn't move. "Where's Jillian? Does she know you're here?"

We stared at each other for several seconds until I said, "How did you know to come here?"

He lowered his hands inch by inch. "I got a hysterical call from

Reid a little while ago. He said you and Ember had been kidnapped, and they got another pilot to do some kind of fancy search to see where your helicopter was going. I'm, uh, starting to think that you're weren't kidnapped after all. Is Ember okay? Where is she?"

My hands begin to tremble, and once again I switched to a double-handed grip. "She's fine. She's in the basement. That's all? That's all he told you?"

"Was there anything else I need to know?"

My chest heaved again. "You really don't know?" My voice cracked.

Concern flooded his eyes. "Something awful's happened, hasn't it? You look like Reid did when..."

"When what?" I shot back. "When he went haywire and—"

"When they took our baby brother away. And when Stephanie died," Reuben said simply. "And Mom."

Oh, holy God damn, tears were falling down my face. *Not in front of him, please God, make them stop. Not in front of Reuben.*

"Please leave," I whispered. "Please. Just go."

"Where's Jillian? Why isn't she here?"

There was a beat, and I saw the truth in his eyes: he already knew, or at least suspected.

"She's dead," I said, inhaling a shaky breath. "And if I don't destroy the JM-104, it'll be for nothing. Beau is on his way now, and I need... I need to..."

Reuben was speechless for several seconds. "Benjamin. I am *so* sorry."

"Yeah, well, *sorry* can't bring her back," I spat. "But if I find this crap and destroy it, then maybe she can rest in peace. Now leave."

"Ben."

"What?" The word, pushed through gritted teeth, was barely understandable even to me.

"Would Jillian want to see you like this?"

I risked wiping my nose on my sleeve. "Shut up. Just shut up." I squinted at him. "I swore that I'd be whoever and whatever it took to save her. I-I-I can't save her anymore, but I can make it right. I can find the JM-104. Now go. I don't want to shoot you, but I will. Not even you can get in my way."

"I'm not leaving you now," Reuben said quietly. "Put down the gun. We'll get Ember, go back to the apartment, and figure out a better plan."

"Leave!" I brandished the gun. "I'll shoot you! I swear to God, I will! I've already killed tonight, and I'll do it again!"

He didn't even put his hands up. "No, you won't. You won't make Gabriela a widow, you won't rob my child of a father, you won't kill Jillian's friend, and you won't kill Reid's brother. You're going to put down the gun." He held out his hand. "You need to put down the gun, Benjamin."

I took a staggered step closer. "What are you going to do, make me? *Fight* me?"

He looked at me almost pityingly.

Oh, I hated him.

"You want that, don't you?" His voice was soft, filled with the utmost kindness. "You want me to hurt you. Because you've been through so much. You've lost every good and gentle thing in the world and you're desperate for someone to put you out of your misery."

I snorted. "What would you know? You're the team golden boy. I even saw that the last time we met here like this."

Pain flitted across his face. "I wasn't the team golden boy when the elders said I couldn't see my wife anymore, on pain of death."

My fingers were going numb.

Why is he talking so much? Make him stop talking. It's a trick. He's distracting you. Tears dripped off my chin. "You've called the feds already, haven't you? That's why you're stalling." My thumb, slippery with sweat, could not grasp the hammer of the revolver.

He looked me in the eye. "I'm not Beau. *I'm not going to betray you.* Because that's what older brothers do to you, isn't it? They betray you, and attack you when your back is turned."

The gun clattered to the floor. Reuben kneeled next to me while I began sobbing without a sound.

My body shook from the magnitude of everything that had happened in the last few weeks. Wherever I looked, I had lost—my lover, my family, my happy team, my sense of security and self, my promising future.

All I had left was myself. Me, with a gun in my hand and blood on my face.

My memories flitted back to Liberty, to that terrible night when the Westerners had attacked. Reid had seen Ember's supposedly dead body and made a grab for someone's weapon. I'd assumed that he was going to run out of the building and seek violent revenge.

I now knew what he'd meant to do.

Reuben must have followed my line of thinking, because he picked up the revolver and tucked it into his pocket before pulling me to my feet. "Let's go get Ember, and then we'll call Reid and tell him to calm the hell down." He shook his head. "Sometimes I think I've spent half my life telling him to calm down."

He motioned for me to step through the window, but I faltered. "Can you at least help me see what's behind the door? Beau *is* coming for the JM-104. Ember said so."

Reuben simply held up his palm. A black, shadow-like hammer took shape in the air by the door and slammed against the lock, breaking it. The door swung open.

It was a bathroom.

I hung my head while Reuben steered me out of the office.

NEITHER OF US spoke much as we walked down the dark, carpeted hallway towards the double doors Ember had gone through.

Before we passed through them, he pulled out his cell phone and dialed a number from memory, holding up a finger to me.

"Hey, Captain, it's Obsidian. I've just gotten a strong lead about the Bell lab. Call me back as soon as y—"

He frowned and stared at his phone.

"What is it?" I asked.

"My phone just went dead, but I'm sure it was at full power." He tapped the screen a few times and pressed the home button, but it stayed black. He gave his head a little shake. "That's weird. Do you have your phone on you?"

I took out my cell phone and pressed the home button so I could type in my passcode.

My phone was also dead.

The leaden weight of dread took form in my chest opposite the grief there. "I'm positive my phone was at full power, and this thing is built to last."

We both stared at the useless device in my hand until Reuben said, "Do you believe in coincidence?"

I shoved the phone back in my pocket. "Not right now."

A faint, high mechanical whine behind us made me tense, then slowly turn around and look up. A security camera in one corner had swiveled around on its mount and was now looking directly at us.

The camera by the double doors began to turn with the same slow whine, stopping when we were directly in its sights. A third, above a closet door, turned all the way around to face us.

I closed my eyes and swallowed, listening.

Reuben put his hand on my shoulder. "It's him, isn't it?"

I slowed my breathing, focusing on the beat of my heart.

It matched the war drums outside.

———

REUBEN and I almost tumbled over each other in our desperate race to get to the basement. We thudded down the stairs two at a time.

"Ember!" I shouted, flinging a door open. "Where are—"

"Here!" she shouted from a small side room. I sprinted in just as she slammed a filing drawer shut. "Dead end," she said quickly. "I can hear the people in the helicopter." She shot a fearful look at the ceiling. "Oh, God, this is going to be a long night."

"I'm guessing it's not the cavalry up there," Reuben said. He swallowed. "What are we dealing with?"

She gritted her teeth. "Two people are listening to music, probably to keep me away from their thoughts. Someone else is there, too... someone named... Avery, I think."

I swore aloud. "I know him."

Avery Hensey would've been given to the camp allies if he'd been born into a camp family. Instead, he'd been born into the Hensey clan, and they'd made up for his lack of powers by turning him into a firearms aficionado. He'd even trained my siblings and me at one point.

I slipped my shaking hand into my pocket and groped around for extra bullets, but found nothing.

I had six shots in my revolver.

This *was* going to be a long night.

Ember threw back her shoulders. "There's another helicopter on the way. They can see our footsteps in the snow, and they're spoiling for a fight."

Reuben squared his shoulders. "Then let's give them a hell of a fight."

ITEM TWENTY-SIX

A diary entry written circa December 1969 by Miss Lorraine Hotchkiss, aged 12, resident of Chatsworth, Georgia.

Dear Diary,

I wish the men would stop building that wall even on Sundays. The hammering and metal sounds are so loud! The noise echoes around the valley and wakes me up. Mom says nothing good ever happens when a wall like that goes up.

Love,
Lorraine

26

The doors were the first to go.

Wind, far more ferocious than I'd ever seen, ripped the thin metal bay doors off their tracks with a metallic screech and flung them away across the parking lot.

The blast of wind that entered the storeroom brought with it icy cold and... water drops. Moisture clung to my skin and clothes, seeping into my bones. This wasn't just some wind elementalist, but someone who could make storms. I knew too damn well who it might be.

"Aw, come on," I said to myself, my teeth chattering. "It just had to be you, didn't it?"

I dared to peek over the fifty-five-gallon plastic drum to confirm my suspicions, then winced. Yep, it was her. And she'd brought friends.

Wendy Chakrabharti sauntered into the storeroom, headphones on her ears and her usual smirk on her face. Long, wavy black hair tumbled down her shoulders, somehow untouched by the gales she was generating. My brother's ex-girlfriend still artfully lined her eyes with kohl and wore velour designer clothes from head to toe.

She blew a little pink gum bubble and popped it with a perfectly polished fingernail. How very Wendy.

Two men flanked her. As I'd guessed, Avery Hensey was armed to the teeth, bearing two automatic weapons and plenty of smaller handguns. With belts of ammunition looped around his chest, he looked ready to go into battle, and even at the distance I could see the crazed bloodlust in his eyes.

A shorter, slightly chubby guy stood on the other side of her, and he looked as nervous as the other two did confident. Like Wendy, he also had headphones on. The man looked familiar, but I couldn't place him. Perhaps he'd been at a family affair when I was young?

"Terrence Edge," Ember whispered suddenly. "Ben, what's he do?"

I narrowed my eyes. That's how I knew him—he was an Edge, one of the core families in my old world. I elbowed Reuben. "Power mimic. Don't let him touch you. He's probably already gotten a hook on her power and is doubling what she can do."

"What's she doing?" Reuben whispered. He leaned forward. "Ben, can you charge them while I attack?"

Ember held up a hand. "Wait. They want to flex muscles, but not necessarily engage with us. This doesn't have to end with blood. They're waiting for us to do something first."

I nodded in confirmation, and Reuben settled back, though warily. "Remember, these aren't superheroes," I said quickly. "I was taught to run, to hide, and to wait. So were they."

Wendy pulled up the hood of her down jacket and raised her hands, her eyes aglow with whitish-yellow energy. Clouds—actual visible clouds—formed in the high ceiling of the storeroom, their bottoms enveloping the highest level of the shelving as they churned. Dangerous rumbles of thunder rippled, and the wind picked up.

I'd called her Windy Wendy when we were kids. She'd called herself Tempeste.

"Come out with your hands up, Benjamin! Or everyone dies!"

I didn't move. Cartoonish trash talk didn't scare me. I needed her to get cocky and make a mistake—and *then* I would strike.

"You asked for it, you little traitor!" Her eyes flared, and the real tempest began.

Gusts of wind shook the shelves and light fixtures, making everything in the room that wasn't bolted down sway from side to side. Freezing rain began to fall, coating everything with icy water droplets that soaked into my already-damp clothes.

A huge shelf bearing boxes and drums wobbled. Then it fell to the side—right onto another shelf.

Shelves began to fall like dominoes, crashing everywhere. Drums sprang open, spilling God-knew-what over the floor, the oily substances and colored liquids mixing with the water from the rain. Small explosions of sparks and electricity popped in and out of existence as various machines hit the cement floor or power boxes on the wall.

The three of us ran in three different directions to escape the maelstrom of falling shelves. Reuben and I eventually dove behind another row of drums that had survived the shower of barrels and boxes, skidding to a halt on our knees.

After a few seconds, Ember landed on me, clutching her head. "That stupid music is making it so hard to confuse them."

I raised my eyebrows. *Really? You're foiled by music?*

Yes! Now is not the time for this conversation!

Wendy marched sideways toward a stairwell, Terrence following her. Avery moved along with her, his head swiveling as he looked for us.

He caught my eye.

"Rube! Shield!"

His bullets hit Reuben's shield with a terrific clang, flying every which way. Reuben was on his feet immediately, his black eyes menacing and strong, his composure never breaking.

"Get Ember to safety!" Reuben shouted over the roar of the indoor storm.

The wind increased, knocking Ember and me sideways. The rain began to fall harder and colder, slicking the cement floor and making it difficult to steady myself. I reached out for Ember's hand, but she pulled away.

"I can distract him for just a second!" she shouted over the spray of bullets. "Ben, now!" She closed her eyes.

Avery paused, his forehead furrowed in confusion at whatever Ember was doing.

I dashed at him—and lost my purchase a few feet from where he was standing. I slid into his legs at top speed, sending him sprawling into a complicated tangle of shelves, soggy cardboard, and a sticky substance that clung to our clothes.

Fists, skin, teeth, and howls of pain merged together as we fought. I swung for his chin, but missed. He tried to grab a sidearm, but I brought down a random piece of metal shelving onto his hand and crushed it. He screamed.

The wind picked up again, and in the corner of my eye, Wendy and Terrence ran up the rest of the stairs. The swinging lights created a strobe effect.

"Ben, move!" Reuben's shout was barely audible.

I moved—and a large piece of machinery fell right where I'd been, crushing Avery's right leg.

I cut off his agonized scream with a bullet to the forehead.

More bullets rang around me, one even riffling my hair above my ear. Terrence was shooting at me from the overhead walkway. I rolled under a felled piece of metal and kicked a box in front of me, cutting off his line of sight.

The wind finally knocked the power out. The entire storeroom went to black. I let out a sigh of relief; we were safe for now.

The wind died down, though the rain didn't stop. Wendy was probably rethinking the "knock stuff on them" part of her plan, since she'd accidentally killed Avery and cut the power.

"Over here," Reuben hissed from somewhere behind me. I groped around in the inch of icy water, felt nothing, and scooted backwards until I bumped into him.

"What now?" I whispered into the darkness, just audibly enough so he could hear me. "Where's Ember?"

"I don't know. Ember? You there?"

Nothing.

"We'll find her later," I whispered. She had decent survival instincts, so she'd probably run for the basement. I couldn't blame her. "Rube, did you get a good look of where we are in relation to the stairwell?"

"Yeah, why?"

"If you blast everything on the floor with your power, I can run up the stairs at top speed and bum rush them."

"That sounds risky."

"It is, but look at the situation. This isn't a strike team, these are my brother's drinking buddies. They're angry, and I'm willing to bet that they're scared. They may just see me as Bleeding Heart Benjamin, but they see you as an actual bona fide superhero. They're crapping their pants right now. Let's just finish this, grab Ember, and get out of here."

I heard him swallow. "Okay. That's as good of an idea as any." Cold hands groped around for my face, angling it to my ten o'clock. "That way. On my order."

A weird glowing blackness—or rather, two spots of it—became apparent where Reuben's voice was coming from. I stood to a crouch, coiled to spring.

I sensed more than saw his arms spreading wide. The cacophonous sound of metal and water sliding along the wet, grainy cement floor filled the entire storeroom, and then ceased.

"Now!"

I sprinted at normal speed to where I thought the stairwell was, my wet footsteps echoing loudly as I ran unhindered by debris. My hand touched the metal railing and I planted my foot on the bottom step, ready to—

A muzzle flash.

Excruciating, white-hot pain shot up my thigh and into my torso, stunning me as I fell to the ground. Warm wetness leaked out of my leg above the knee, clashing oddly with the freezing water I was lying in.

"Are you dead yet?" Wendy called from the inky darkness above me. "Please tell me you're dead."

That had been a stupid move. They'd heard me run and then stop at the bottom of the stairwell.

That had been a stupid, *stupid* move.

Reuben, at least, had the sense to not shout and ask if I was still alive. Instead, after a few seconds, something grabbed my collar and pulled me along the floor until I was by him again, leaning up against a barrel.

"Shot," I gasped.

"Yeah, I figured that," he whispered. He swore colorfully. "This is the worst fight I've ever been in. Talk about a moronic last st—battle. This is a moronic battle."

He'd stopped himself from saying the truth: a last stand. And if the brave, true captain of the Baltimore team thought so, it was.

Lovely. I was making my last stand in a freezing, dark, wet hole. We barely knew each other, my wife was dead, I didn't know if my other teammates were still alive, I was shot, and Gabriela was probably going to be a widow before the sun came up.

I had the power to fix exactly one of those things.

I swallowed down the pain that was pulsing steadily in my leg. "Rube."

"What?"

"Go home."

"Oh, don't start."

"No, go home. There's a bunch of fire exits down the hall. Make a big noise and it'll disguise your footfalls."

"Trent. Stop talking."

Stupid Fischers and their stupid pride. "Go home to Gabby. Be happy. Die old. Don't—" I bit my hand to stifle a groan of pain. When the worst had passed, I continued, "Don't put her through the nightmare I'm living right now."

There was a long silence, and all I could hear was the steady artificial rainfall, each drop echoing oddly in the semi-flooded room.

The two freaks up on the walkway were waiting for something, a realization that made my stomach fill with heavy dread.

He was coming.

Finally, Reuben spoke, his voice low with an emotion I couldn't place. "You were going to be a soldier. Reid told me so after you took over your team at Jen's apartment. I asked him if you were up to the task, and he said you'd been made the cadet commander of your high school's JROTC program."

I shifted painfully. "Yeah, so? What's this got—"

"I will always place the mission first. I will never accept defeat. I will never quit. What's the next line of the soldier's creed?"

"Why—"

"What is the next line of the solider's creed, Trent? Answer me."

"Screw you. Go home and have a happy life. Consider this repayment for, you know, everything. I really am sorry for shooting Berenice. Please tell her that."

I'd shot her about ten feet from where I was sitting. It was fitting that I'd probably get my comeuppance here.

"If you don't tell me the next line, I'm going to punch your gunshot wound."

"I will never leave a fallen comrade," I hissed. "And if this were a military situation, it would apply. Shut up."

He lightly cuffed my ear. "If a dumbass teenaged supervillain can try to live up to that promise, then I can do one better. The only ways I'm leaving this place are victorious or dead."

"Reid was right," I said through gritted teeth while I held my leg. "You *are* an annoying older brother."

His muffled laughter was drowned by the sound of helicopter rotors. A large helicopter touched down, unseen, in the parking lot.

The fake rain stopped.

"My my, what do we have here?" Wendy called in a tone of mock surprise. "Oh, goodness me, I think it's my friends! Now it's a party!"

Reuben and I said the same four-letter word in unison.

A flashlight's beam cut through the darkness, the bearer hidden by the brightness. "Wendy?" a young woman called. "What's going on?"

Oh, no. I knew that voice. "That's Helen Woods. She can possess people."

"They're somewhere over there, on the far side of the room," Terrence called. "We're staying out their way until the rest of you arrive. Ben's shot, but I don't know how badly."

I instantly slumped and closed my eyes. *Idiots. Reuben, please, please, please figure out what I'm doing. And don't hate me afterward.*

Light crossed my face, and I heard Reuben move. "Okay, you got me. I surrender. Put the gun down, ma'am."

"Is he dead?" Helen asked. Her small, ploppy footsteps came closer.

"Injured and unconscious."

"Good. Beau wants to do it himself." She was right next to us now.

There was a little pop of air as Helen made decent eye contact with Reuben—it was the sound of air filling the vacuum where her body had been a second before. Her clothes and flashlight fell to the floor in a muffled heap. The flashlight shattered and went out, sending us into darkness once more.

A gunshot pierced the silence.

There was a masculine groan, and then Helen's voice sounded again next to me with a shriek. "He shot me!"

The second gunshot was followed by the thud of her body hitting the ground.

I reached out and touched Reuben, healing energy flowing from my fingers into wherever I'd hit him. "My butt," he said, answering my unasked question. "Thanks for that."

Terrence and Wendy screeched curses and various threats at us, but I just laughed breathily, then winced. When the pain had ebbed, I said, "Maybe the rest will be as easy. We'll just pick them off as they come, if that's that case."

I didn't have the heart to say that my strength was failing. I'd lost a lot of blood.

The lights slammed on one by one, the room flooding with brilliant fluorescence and electronic buzzing. After the spots in my vision cleared, I saw that Reuben was kneeling next to me in the corner, and my entire pant leg was soaked with blood. Thankfully, we were shielded from further gunfire from above by a twisted heap of shelving.

Unfortunately, the two people in the doorway could see us just fine.

Robbie and Ashley... yet more members of the old crowd I'd left behind. They were just a few years older than me, and I'd seen them in action.

Yeah, this is how I'm going to die.

Ashley didn't look away from us as she said, "Sic 'em."

Robbie fell forward and landed on his four giant paws, a German Shepherd standing where a man used to be. He sprinted towards us, mouth foaming.

Reuben threw up a shield at the same time that the wind and rain materialized again, knocking me down onto the floor.

Ashley began to walk towards me.

Gunfire rang around us, missing us, hitting the shelving, hitting the walls, ricocheting everywhere. Robbie's diabolical growling and snarling mixed with Reuben's shouts of effort.

I hastily grabbed my gun and tried to aim, though my hands were shaking. If Robbie could just hold still...

Hail began to fall. First pea-sized, then golf ball-sized, it rained down on everything, creating a sharp roar of marbles on concrete and metal. A sharp rap on my forehead was quickly followed by warm blood trickling down my nose.

Reuben was on his back now, trying to toss Robbie off with his powers—but the solid black shadows looked a lot less solid than before.

More war drums beat wildly in the parking lot.

Another golf ball on the forehead. I wiped the blood off my face, but still more flowed down the side of my nose.

Ashley reached down and grasped my hand, her paralyzing touch coursing through my body and causing me to go still, unable to flinch away from the hail or anything else.

"Got you," she said, her lips curling. "Beau will be very happy. Thank you for being a little whelp and not fighting back."

I closed my eyes. *Jillian, I'm coming. I'll be with you soon.*

There was an odd sound—a whoosh, and then a metallic *chuk* followed by Ashley gasping... and my muscles loosening.

I opened my eyes. A steel blade was sticking out of Ashley's chest, directly where her heart was.

I knew that blade. I turned my head, dizzy with a thousand emotions.

I pushed myself up to a sitting position, eyes wide.

Jillian was standing in the middle of the storeroom. Reid and Marco were at her side, eyes aglow and their hands up, powers at the ready.

She unsheathed another knife from her thigh. "Who's next?"

ITEM TWENTY-SEVEN

Article in the *Washington Post*'s Style section, dated March 11, 1979.

Janice L. Lewis Marries Henry B. Trent

Janice L. Lewis of Middleburg, Va. and Henry B. Trent of Annapolis, Md. were married on March 9, at the historic Oatlands Plantation located in Loudoun County, Va. The Reverend Scott Larsen officiated.

Janice, 24, is the daughter of the Dr. and Mrs. John Lewis, also of Middleburg. She is a graduate of Vassar College in Poughkeepsie, N.Y., where she studied Journalism. She is the granddaughter of Mr. Benjamin Lewis, noted D.C. businessman and founder of the Lewis Foundation, and his wife, Leah. She is also the granddaughter of Mr. and Mrs. Andrew Stanhope, of Manassas, Va.

Henry, 28, is the son of the late Mr. Franklin Trent and Mrs. Eleanor Trent, also of Annapolis. He is a graduate of Dartmouth College in Hanover, N.H., where he studied business. Henry is employed in his family's business, Trent Consultants.

Clara Lewis, sister of the bride, served as maid of honor. Bridesmaids were Erin Lewis, sister of the bride, Alexandra Edge, Ashlynn Peery, Danielle Snider, and Amber-Jean Hensey. Flower girl was

Katherine Lewis, cousin of the bride. Michael Lewis, brother of the bride, and Franklin Trent III, twin brother of the groom, were best men. Ring bearer was Adam Rowe, a friend of both families.

Janice wore a custom-designed wedding gown by Chanel, and carried a bouquet of cream and red roses.

The rehearsal dinner and reception, hosted by the groom's parents, was held at their home.

The couple will honeymoon in the UK, France, Switzerland, and Croatia, then reside in Annapolis.

27

A huge tiger streaked past Jillian and the others, bounding up the stairs without slowing.

"No!" Wendy shrieked. She threw herself in front of Terrence. "Stay back!"

Wendy didn't stand a chance. The tiger barreled into her with a deafening roar, slashing at her arms and chest with six-inch claws. More gunshots rang out, but it merely grabbed the gun in its huge jaws and tossed it aside.

In just a few seconds, all that was left of Wendy was the blood that dripped off of the walkway, falling from the edges and through the small holes in the metal.

"I surrender! *I surrender!*" Terrence scrambled backwards across the walkway, making it bounce a little. "Don't kill me, please!" His voice wavered, and then he started sobbing. He fell into a kowtow position, his hands over his head.

The tiger simply sat on him, eliciting a squeaky, muffled sob from Terrence.

Robbie had jumped off of Reuben and backed into the wall, the hair on his back spiky with fear. He growled, tremors coursing through his canine body as he stared back and forth between Jillian and the tiger on the walkway.

Jillian tossed her hair, then looked over her shoulder. "Abby, if you would."

A smaller tiger sprinted from the parking lot through the bay doors. Robbie's growls evaporated into whines, and he leapt over Reuben to escape down the hall. A streak of orange and black collided with him before he could get there.

I closed my eyes, but couldn't stop the sound of Robbie being ripped apart. *Thus always to enemies of Abby.*

Jillian was at my side in an instant, her hands shaking as she moved me into a sitting position against the wall. She didn't bother to hide her tears. "Oh god, you're bleeding really badly. Hold still, please don't move more than you have to. I stopped carrying a tourniquet last year." She laughed without humor. "Why would I need a tourniquet when I had you, right?"

Her fragrant hair, held in place by a ponytail, tumbled down in front of my face, bringing me closer to lucidity. Reuben and Reid were speaking with Marco on the other side of the room, paying us no mind. None of them looked surprised that Jillian was alive.

She ripped off her gloves and stroked my cheeks and eyelids. "We came as soon as we could," she whispered. "I'm so, so sorry. I couldn't figure out where you were when the bombs started going off, and then the battle began and things got so crazy..." She wiped at her eyes. "When I realized you'd been kidnapped again, I..."

I wiped the tears off her chin, but still more came. "You're alive," I said, the words feeling like a prayer of thanks. "How?"

Someone up there liked me. *That* was how. That was the only explanation. A resurrection.

She kissed my hand. "Bombs don't stop Battlecry. Pneumonia might, but not bombs." She giggled, though a little hysterically.

"But you were dead."

Jillian paused and stared at me for a second, then looked over her shoulder and shouted, "Marco! I need you! He's lost a lot of blood!"

Marco hurried over. He was bruised and battered, but otherwise unharmed. "Gotcha." Kneeling next to me, he quickly patted me all over, his face an even mix of angry and concerned. "Ben, can you tell me what they did? Stabbed? Shot? Any kind of needle wounds?"

Needle wounds? Why would he think...

Oh.

Ember had told them that we'd been kidnapped. He assumed I was sporting the injuries of torture.

I swallowed down more pain and shifted my leg, wincing at the fiery flare. "I got shot in the fight, that's all," I said, grunting a little. "I'm bleeding too much."

Jillian whipped out a knife and sliced my pant leg open, then hissed when she saw the bullet wound. It was fairly shallow, and had missed major arteries, but it was still ugly.

"Marco, you know what to do," she said. "Sweetheart, I'm going to give you my sheath to bite on. He's going to cauterize your wound. It won't help the confusion, unfortunately, but since you can't heal yourself..."

She was swaying.

No, I was swaying.

Ugh, *everything* was swaying.

But I didn't need agonizing field surgery. I had enough mental fiber to remember the moron that Edward was sitting on.

I closed my hand around Jillian's and shook my head, then stared up at Marco. "The guy on the walkway. Power mimic."

"On it," Marco said, jumping to his feet. "Hey, Ed! We need the dipstick!"

A laugh escaped my chest, but I wasn't particularly amused. My physical emotions were incongruent with the turbulence in my mind. Jillian was alive—but how? Where was Beau? Was anything real? Was I dying? Was this some kind of supernatural waiting room, with Jillian greeting me with her kind eyes and gentle hands? Had all of my friends, and a few of my enemies, died in the Battle of the Super Hospital?

Jillian leaned down and placed a soft kiss on my lips, then guided my head to the floor. "Rest now."

Terrence shouted in protest in the distance, but was immediately cut off by a terrifying roar. Marco ordered him to keep his hands on his head while he walked down the stairwell.

I was definitely still alive. There was no way Marco and Terrence would've ended up in the same afterlife. Also, the Fischers had disappeared.

"Where's Reid and Reuben? Everyone else?" I mumbled. "Where's Beau?"

"Edward is keeping a lookout up there. Berenice and Lark are cleaning up back at the hospital, working with law enforcement and all that. Abby is patrolling the perimeter. Reid and Reuben are looking for Ember. She contacted Reid from somewhere in the building. I don't know where Beau is, but if he has two brain cells to rub together, he's nowhere near here anymore. We've won, sweetie."

People kept saying that to me. Why didn't they understand? Nobody had won *crap* until my brother was pushing up daisies.

She stood before I could reply, towering above me while she slowly unsheathed a knife from her shoulder. "If you make any sudden moves, Helios will break your legs. Is that clear?"

Terrence pulled a face. "I thought you guys were supposed to all nice and stuff. What's stopping me from turning into a tiger now and eating all of you?"

Terrence was on the ground at once, pinned down by Marco with his arms in a painful submission hold. Marco positioned Terrence's head in such a way that a firm motion to the side would snap his spinal cord.

"You're not very smart, are you?" Marco hissed into his ear.

From up above, Edward shouted, "I call dibs on his pelt if Battlecry kills him!"

Marco visibly suppressed laughter.

Jillian kneeled next to Terrence. "You've been grossly misinformed. I'm not nice. None of us are nice. A few days ago, I slaughtered Janice Trent and William Rowe in their beds. Believe me, buddy, I have no problem ordering a few broken limbs."

"Don't kill me," Terrence squeaked.

"If you do every single thing I say without hesitation, I will let you live. Now, stick out your hand. Marco, let him."

Marco nudged Terrence's right arm out of the hold, and Terrence extended it across the sopping floor.

Jillian carefully moved my arm forward until my fingers were just out of Terrence's reach. If I uncurled them, I would've been able to touch his hand. She aimed a cool expression at Terrence. "You're going to absorb Benjamin's healing factor, then heal him."

She patted my hand, and I closed the small distance between us. My fingertips brushed his. What would my own power feel like? Probably a lot of endorphins.

There was a small pause when nothing happened, and then—

No wonder my family won't let me go.

Warm water coursed through my veins. Heavenly lightness spread its fingers into my muscles, rejuvenating and relaxing as it went, every ache and pain lessening and then petering out into nothing. My whole body seemed to inflate with life itself, making my back arch as I cried out from the shock.

Every single time someone had reached out a bloody, shaking hand for mine... I thought I'd understood. They'd wanted healing, and I could provide it. But now I truly comprehended what my power was like, what it meant to go from brokenness to wholeness.

"How do you f—"

Jillian's question was swallowed by my kiss.

I held her tight, not caring who was watching. The emotions of the last half hour, held back by pain and encroaching hypovolemic shock, were finally free to be felt. They demanded to be acknowledged, but instead of tears, I just kissed Jillian and soaked up her body heat, and her love. I'd lived whole hours believing I'd never bask in her love again, and it had been lifetimes too long.

Brokenness to wholeness—first in my body, and then in my heart.

She broke for air, but I was a greedy man. I pulled her back in for another kiss, and she let me. This really was her. There was no counterfeit in the woman I was holding in my arms.

I knew Jillian, in every sense. I knew her scent, the

sunbaked aroma of the warm southern wind and Georgia mountains. I knew every curve of her perfect body as my hands
rememorized them. I knew the stubborn baby curl at her
temple, always just a shade lighter than the dark brown hair
everywhere else. I knew the long strand of hair on the side of
her face that never stayed put. I knew the little birthmark on
the bridge of her nose, the one shaped like a tiny heart. I knew
the faint scar on her chin from a fight with Berenice years
before.

I knew the way she melted in my embrace, completely given over
to the way she said no man had ever made her feel before.

I knew my wife.

"Benjamin," she whispered, pulling away from me to breathe.
"What did they do to you? You're shaking."

"They didn't do anything to me," I said, sucking in an unsteady
breath. "Ember and I came here because I thought you were dead. I
was coming to get the JM-104 and avenge your murder."

Her mouth opened in surprise. "My murder? Why did you think I
was dead?"

The tears finally came, silent and hot. I kissed her forehead, but
this time so she wouldn't be able to see my face. "I saw Brock Snider
shoot you outside your hospital room. I did. I saw it. I swear I'm not
crazy. I did. I d... I d-did..."

"Nurse Laura was outside your room," Marco said evenly as he
rearranged his hostage in another submission hold. He had the
compassion to study his nails as he continued, "When we were
looking for survivors, I saw her and thought it was Jill for a second.
The red lights made it hard to make out whether she was wearing the
navy scrubs that the nurses wear or the purple scrubs Jill was wearing. Since Jill was standing next to me when I saw her, I'll admit I was
pretty confused. But like I told you over dinner... dying just isn't Jill's
style."

I closed my eyes in shame as I realized Brock's deception. He'd
looked so amused by some private joke when he'd left that hallway,
and now I knew that it had been nothing more than a puerile illusion

to make me think my wife had died. I'd fallen for it, hook, line, and sinker. I'd killed him in cold blood over it.

Oh, *God*. I'd threatened to murder Ember.

I bowed my head. "I need to find Ember and apologize for something. I'll explain later."

Jillian nodded and stepped back. "Actually, we all need to find Ember and come up with a plan. This place will have law enforcement swarming around it in no time."

Terrence looked up from the floor. "No! I can't go to j—"

Marco punched him out cold.

Jillian smiled, and she beckoned for us to follow her down the hall. "Abby, Edward, you can come in with us," she said loudly. "We're regrouping."

Edward raced down the stairwell and met Abby as she hurried into the storeroom. They bumped noses, then walked together past us and down the hall. Marco rolled his eyes and tagged along after them. They all disappeared around a corner, not once looking to see if we were following.

Oh no, that wasn't a sweet effort to give Jillian and me a minute in private. Nope.

Jillian laced her fingers in mine and bumped her nose to mine, too. "I tiger-love you."

I was about to comment on their unexpected cuteness when I stopped and stared at the corner of the storeroom, at a spot behind a bit of twisted shelving. Something had shimmered there, in the air. A mirage in the corner?

I rubbed my eyes.

It was gone.

No, there it was again.

Something was standing in the corner of the storeroom, almost invisible to me. No, some*one* was standing in the corner. I could just make out their shape, which flickered in and out of reality like a glitch in the code of my vision.

I leaned in to Jillian with a small smile, and tucked that one stubborn lock of hair behind her ear, ostensibly to whisper sweet nothings. "There's someone in here with us at your six. Ten meters behind. A possible invisibility power, or some kind of camouflage." I was ready to bet that it wasn't Isabel St. James.

Jillian's long, pale fingers stroked the edge of her knife as she closed her eyes and inhaled, her breath lasting just long enough for me to know that she was searching for the unknown scent.

Her eyelids fluttered, and she turned around. "Ember?"

A whisper of sound passed through my mind: the gauzy breath of telepathy. Ember did not tell me to remain silent, but I could feel her desire that I do so.

Why the hell was Ember skulking around in the storeroom in secret? Where were the others?

Jillian's turned to me, a placid, glazed expression in her eyes. "I'll be in the basement, sweetie. You watch over Terrence."

My cheeks flushed with anger. Jillian had never asked for Terrence's name since arriving. Ember had fed her that line.

Ember had probably been feeding people their lines since Jillian and company had arrived. She was playing a game—I didn't know what type—but now was not the time for her stupidity. Yes, I'd been wrong to threaten her, and I'd apologize. But my patience with Ember and her tantrums had just run out.

Jillian let go of my hand and walked down the hall, humming to herself.

And again, my wife was gone immediately after our reunion. Because of Ember.

I spun around, ready to tear into the infuriating, invisible telepath "What the fu—"

We locked eyes.

She was perfectly visible, weeping, and holding the last can of JM-104.

SHE SWALLOWED. "Please don't me mad. I found it when you were in the CEO's office with Reuben, but I didn't know what to do. I sent the others packing because I need your help. They'll just complicate the process."

"Em, what are you *on*?"

There was only one way to interpret what she'd said: Ember was trying to run off with an invaluable resource that had fueled a human trafficking conspiracy of which I'd been a victim. It was needed for evidence, and then it would be destroyed.

And she was trying to *steal* it.

I began to walk towards her, my hand outstretched. "Give me that can."

She scuttled backwards. "No. You stay right there, mister."

I stopped in my tracks. "Okay, fine. But you're going to be honest with me. What the hell is happening right now? Why are you being secretive? Why did you send the others away, but not me?"

A sob escaped her. "I'm going to use it."

"On who? Me? Knock it off."

"I'm going to use it on myself!"

I flinched as her scream echoed around the wet room.

She brandished the can. "And *you* are going to make sure I don't die, do you hear me? As soon as I figure out how to open this stupid thing, I'm going to slice open a vein and pour it into my bloodstream. You are going to heal me and seal this stuff in." Tears began to flow faster down her face. "You are. You *are* going to do that. You're not going to argue with me, damn it. You're going to let me l-l-live the w-w-way I want to. This has nothing to do with you. *Nothing!*"

The pieces of the situation flew apart, shifting and reorganizing to create a new picture.

People did very stupid things when they were scared, when they were in pain. I knew that better than anyone.

"Ember, put down the can."

"Shut up." She unsheathed her knife. "I'm doing this."

"Don't! Let's talk this through!"

"Screw you! You were going to kill me! You aimed that gun at me and made me use my power! You're just like your brother!"

I gulped. "I'm so, so sorry, Em. I'm *so* sorry. I was suffering, terrified, and crazy. That's what you're going through right now. We can fix this. Put down the knife."

She stared at me with her red eyes, but shoved the knife back in its sheath. "Why do you care so much?"

"Because you're my friend. I've been an awful friend in return these last few hours, but my hand to God, I love you, and I want you to be healthy and safe." I slowly extended my hand towards her. "A teaspoon of it was all it needed for Reuben and Jillian. Less than that, even. The amount of JM-104 in that can will kill you stone dead. Please give it to me. Please."

"No."

"Do you want to go off the radar? Because I can arrange that." If being used for her powers was the problem, then the answer was to make *her* go away, not her powers via poison.

But she just rolled her eyes. "Oh, like you could do that. You couldn't fake your own death for six weeks."

"I can't, but I have friends who can. I know people who will print you fake IDs, everything. I have enough money to bankroll a whole new life for you. And Reid, if you want. You'll never have to worry about being found. I even know people who will do a damn good job of faking your death." I knew a guy who knew a guy who was connected to the mob.

Her face darkened. "No, and Reid isn't coming. He'll just promise me safety again, get me to feel all fuzzy and secure, *sleep* with me, and then run off when the bullets start flying to play hero boy, or militia man, or whatever role he thinks will bring Stephanie back."

Ouch.

I dropped my hand. "Then we're at an impasse, because I'm not going to let you hurt yourself."

"Why? Because you'd have to explain to Jill or Reid that—"

"Because I love you, and if the roles were reversed, I know you'd do the same."

Embarrassment passed over her face, followed by regret. "I... that's not true."

"Yes, it is. You're one of the best friends I've ever had. What about all of our talks every Friday night while I learned my medic skills? When we help each other spar because we're both newbies? When you helped me plan Jillian's birthday party? All the times we picked out vegan recipes together and shopped for them?"

"Ben, I knew Jill was alive the whole time."

What?

No.

No, absolutely not. Nobody could be that low. Especially not my friend. Not *Ember*, of all people. There was no way she'd let me fly to Baltimore in a haze of excruciating mental and emotional pain just to... to what? To have my powers in her back pocket? Just to use me as muscle?

Just to get me away from Jillian. To be mean.

Her phantom hand, a memory but no less powerful for it, grabbed my collar and told me that if I hadn't left my wife alone, she'd still be alive. Even the recollection of that moment had the power to cause pain, and I winced.

She'd told me that as soon as I'd started asking questions.

"That's right," she said, biting her lip. "I was a little angry and crazy, too."

I snorted. "Was?"

Her face darkened. "Watch it."

"Screw *you*. I'm getting Jillian and the others, and then you can tell her your brilliant little plan yourself. And lady, if you go into my mind and mess with me, I'll punch your lights out. Yeah, I said it. What are you going to do about it?" I twirled my finger in the air. "'Oh no, Benjamin just threatened me, he must be a bad man, oh no.'"

I turned on my heel and shoved a large piece of shelving aside, my vision tunneling out of anger. She didn't know how to open the can, so I was fine with leaving her to cry like an idiot. I didn't know what I was going to tell Jillian, but—

"Ben, stop." Her voice was suddenly heavy, like she was holding back an emotion, or trying to communicate something to me.

Whatever. I looked over my shoulder, still walking. "Look at me, not stopping."

"She said stop."

I stopped.

My head slowly turned towards the far corner, a dark area of the storeroom by the bay doors that had been partially obscured by wreckage.

Beau was standing by an electrical panel, his metal hand on the controls.

All the doors slammed shut at once, sealing us in with him.

Beau turned his flat expression onto Ember. "Now that I have your attention, you're going to put down that can, Miss Harris."

ITEM TWENTY-EIGHT

Personnel file record, submitted to the Department of Justice circa late August 1994.

Name: Johnson, Jillian
   Sex: F
   DOB: 21AUG1994
   Camp of birth: Chattahoochee
   Mother: Gemma Johnson (St. James)
   Father: Tobias Johnson
   Siblings:
   1. Johnson, Allison (non-trainee)
   2. Johnson, Mason (non-trainee)
   Notes: Child was delivered by mother's sister Grace St. James (St. James) around midnight. No immediate indications of abilities; mother's reports of unusual kick strength in utero inconclusive.

At moment of birth, Grace was witnessed by three other people to enter a trance-like state (her listed power: low-level prescience) in which she said, "Oh, hello, Heather."

Mrs. St. James has no recollection of this event, and it is unclear at this time whether this event is of importance.

28

I was in front of Ember immediately.

"Stay behind me," I whispered quickly. "Don't talk to him, not matter what he says. I won't let him hurt you."

I thought you hated me. There was an almost childlike confusion in her mental tone.

Lady, for the love of God, learn the difference between "I'm angry at you" and "I hate you."

Beau studied us for a second, then said, "I take it you're not armed. You would've shot me already."

Multiple badass replies flew through my mind, but all of them fell flat on my tongue. My monkey-brain instinct screamed at me to run from the most dangerous predator I'd ever known, but my higher brain told me that not only was that pointless, but that we were beyond fists and threats. There was nothing to be gained by haughtily declaring that he'd never have the JM-104.

Also, I'd dropped my revolver at some point.

"No, I'm not armed. Not with a gun, anyway. Why haven't you shot us, then?"

He drummed his metal fingers on the electrical panel, and the lights flickered in time with him. "The time for fighting is over. I can see that now... the new paradigm. I have new information. I want the JM-104. You want to live. Miss Harris, would you be willing to sell it?"

There were a million creepy aspects about this situation. I didn't know what the worst was: his inhumanly emotionless face, the fact that he'd sneaked up on us so well, or that we were trapped with him.

She gasped. *I can't tell if he's serious. I... Ben, I can't hear his thoughts. Except I can, but they're not... they're not... what the hell is he?*

Beau tapped his temple and smiled ever so slightly. "Are you poking around in here? You won't get far. Now, are you willing to sell it or not? I have money, far more than my brother has squirreled away in that little emergency account he thinks I don't know about."

Arrogant bastard.

"No, I don't want money," Ember squeaked.

"Be quiet," I hissed. "Don't engage with him. Let him talk." My eyes darted all around, looking for any exit, any weapon, any thing that would help us. "Call Jillian."

I've already done that. The whole crowd is coming, but they're a little angry at me. They figured out that I duped them.

Beau appeared to consider her words. "I've met people who don't want money," he said, his tone lacking inflection. "But everyone wants something. What do you want, Ember Harris? Do you want fame? Power? Sex? I can give you anything you want."

Ember clung to my sleeves and pressed her face into the back of my tunic. *I just want this to be over. I want my powers gone and men like him to leave me alone forever.*

I patted her thigh as tenderly as I could, then squared my shoulders. "I don't know what game you're playing, Beau, but talking to Ember is a privilege you lost a long time ago. You deal with me, and me alone."

His flat gaze turned to me, and I saw the difference from before: both of his eyes were mechanical. The pupils kept widening and shifting, no doubt analyzing me—and my weak spots.

He was *too* calm.

That was the creepiest part.

"Beau, what the hell have you done *now*? Were you doing surgery on yourself again? Mom hated..."

I caught myself and almost laughed. Fate had put me in a room with Beau Trent for just five minutes, and I'd already resorted to bringing our mother's displeasure with him into the conversation. Wow.

"I've been calling Mom since yesterday," Beau said. He blinked a few times, then shook his head a little—to clear something out of his digital vision, perhaps. "Why hasn't she picked up?"

I swallowed the lump in my throat. "You know why."

The lights flickered again, and for the first time since I'd laid eyes on him, I saw a hint of life in his expression. "She was our mother. She was your family. She was *our* family. You're a terrible Trent."

"And Jillian is my wife! Don't you dare stand there and pretend you care about family!

My sudden shout echoed oddly around the wet room. Of all the things he could've said that would've gotten under my skin, that wasn't one of them. I'd had weeks to digest Jillian's beautiful vows she'd made in Liberty, and to mull over the meaning of "family."

Jillian, my exquisite wife, was my family by law and by choice. My team was my family by love. The Trents were my family by genes, and nothing more.

Ember squeezed my arms. *Good news! Your 'exquisite wife' is outside, in the hallway. They're all keeping quiet while they figure out a way in. Keep him distracted.*

Beau was nonplussed. "Was it you that killed her? Did you murder your own mother? Is that something your new friends taught you how to do?"

I scoffed. "Oh, settle down. It was your sister-in-law. I wasn't even there."

"And where's Will?"

I grinned. "Still in bed."

"He's not answering his calls."

"Did that new hardware lower your IQ? Pick up on the subtext, dumbass."

Once again, the lights flickered. Beau tapped the heel of his hand to his head, then gave himself a little head-clearing shake.

Though I was playing the role of a cocky adversary, a shudder ran down my back. My revulsion wasn't from his previous actions or anything like that. It ran deeper. He was like a preserved cadaver—he *looked* human, but there was an elusive quality about him that whispered "off."

Again, the calmness was so creepy, but why? He'd always been like this, always...

No, he hadn't. That wasn't true.

He'd been calm, sure. Calculating, definitely. But Beau had been as prone to vengeance, caprice, and foul moods as anyone. He'd never been like this before, and clearly his new update had affected his emotional abilities. All of my insults had merely made the lights flicker.

Wait.

All of my insults had made the lights flicker.

That was the key. He was trying to digitally override his emotions, though I couldn't guess why or how. But the result was incomplete, and his strong feelings were causing little surges. If I could get him riled up, maybe he'd lose control and open the doors.

As plans went, it wasn't the best, but what choice did I have? I didn't know how to handle calm, thoughtful psychos... but I had a growing understanding of hysterical men who were half-mad from their desire to kill and destroy.

Jillian had once fought her own version of Beau with the same tactic. God willing, I'd have the same luck.

And I knew exactly how to needle him. After all, I was his younger brother, and I had younger brother of my own who was very good at this kind of thing. He'd even been so kind as to give me my ammunition.

Ember squeezed the back of my arm. *I hear you.*

I tapped my foot impatiently. "So you're not going to go away, huh?"

"No, Benjamin. I'm not going anywhere until I get the JM-104."

Ember handed me the can, which I tossed to Beau. "Fine, take it."

His eyes began their little in-and-out dance. "You're just going to give it to me?"

I laughed. "Uh, yeah. I wanted to keep it from you on principle, but let's face it, Beau... you're not going to do anything with it. You're a crap supervillain."

He lowered his hand from the panel, and finally a real expression settled on his features: anger. "Excuse me?"

Terrence groaned a few yards from us. We all ignored him.

"Well, let's see," I said, rubbing my chin. "You stood by and watched while Dad got his ass handed to him by my buddy Marco. You couldn't kidnap Ember in the compound. You lost Graham in the fight with Jillian." I laughed for real. "And she was sick that night, Beau! It was two-something in the morning and she was sick, and you still lost someone. I mean, come *on*. Oh, and then you believed the biggest, most obvious lie of all. Damned. Time. You really thought the JM-104 was at the hospital, didn't you?"

He was turning dark red. *That* couldn't have been good for the circuitry.

I shook my head in disappointment. "But you know what the most pathetic part is? You had two full days to break Jillian, and in those two days you had three people helping you, a dedicated torture chamber, years of experience, and a sick and injured victim... but Jillian still walked out of that basement, Beau. She walked out under her own power and killed Mom where she was sleeping."

"Shut up," he whispered.

I smiled. "You think I suck at being a Trent? Sorry, bro, but that's *you*."

Jillian kicked in the door in the same second that Beau whipped out his infamous switchblade—and Terrence lifted his head up, his eyes aglow with Wendy's power.

My hair stood on end as I felt the warning sign of electricity. I knew it far too well, from when my father had been about to blow his stack on one of his disappointing children. *No...*

A massive bolt of lightning struck the earth outside the storeroom, lit up the night, and then plunged us into complete darkness. Sparks flew out of every outlet, dancing across the iridescent puddles on the floor.

It was as if the world stopped turning, and I was in a glass bottle —all the events around me were happening at once, outside of time.

One tiny spark across the room blew from an outlet, and then tumbled a little longer and farther than the others. It gasped to life as a tiny greenish yellow flame in a pool of chemicals.

The flame raced across the floor towards several overturned, leaking barrels.

I raised my hand and shouted, but the words were lost in the roar of the wind that had picked up because of Terrence.

Jillian stopped running towards us, instead looking at the flame. She turned back towards me, her eyes wide, and screamed at the rest of them to smother the fire.

They obeyed—which meant that when the barrels exploded, they were all standing next to them.

A HAND on my collar yanked me upwards from where I'd been lying on the cement floor.

My vision swam with yellow spot and lines, but I could make out Beau's furious face and robot eyes easily enough. He was missing a shirt, and half of the hair on his head had burned away, leaving an ugly reddish patch.

He threw me down on the snow-covered parking lot, next to a man's leg. I recognized the patch on the knee.

It was Reuben's.

Beau's boot came towards my face. I caught it and twisted his leg, pushing him over easily. I pushed myself to my feet.

I didn't even know if I was newly-deafened, or if my brain had broken beyond repair in the explosion. I didn't know where emergency services were. I didn't know what would happen to anyone or anything.

All I knew was that my wife and team had probably just died in an explosion, and I had nothing left to lose.

And I knew how to fight. The training had finally sunk in.

He was saying something. I didn't care. Superheroes didn't care about the lies and pomps of criminals. Of murderers.

He swung towards my face and I ducked, bobbing out of the way and landing a right hook on his jaw. Before he could recover, I raced around and landed a kick on his spine's sweet spot, the place that would send pain into all of his limbs. Reid had taught me how to do it.

Reid had probably been blasted to pieces.

I locked Beau's arms behind his back and slammed him into the side of a helicopter, then pulled him back to do it again. He wriggled loose, but I doubled down on the submission hold, dislocating his shoulder.

Marco had taught me how to dislocate shoulders months ago. We'd clasped hands afterwards, a cool-kid victory gesture he'd once done only with Gregory Johnson.

Marco was probably burned to death while I'd been stunned on the floor.

Beau roared and pushed against me, but I held fast as I whipped out my baton and began to strike his vulnerable spots. Neck, face, knees, injury—all were nothing compared to blunt force. And I had a lot of force I needed to get out.

Jillian had once assigned me to be the bad guy during one of Ember's training sessions. I'd come up behind Ember and grabbed her hair, then pulled her into my grasp like a potential rapist might have. She'd defeated me handily, slamming her elbows, feet, and fist into multiple soft targets on my body. I'd been equally impressed and intimidated.

The last memory of Jillian I had was her face as she realized how it was all going to end.

And Ember...

Wait.

Ember hadn't been near the barrels.

There was a decent chance my sister-in-arms was still alive. I'd been mad at her about something earlier, but that was in the past. Now I needed to find her and save her, even if she was the only one left to save.

I beat Beau over the head with my baton a few more times, then limped back towards the burning building. My body was just overall sore, but I was largely uninjured.

A man's hand stuck out from beneath wreckage and debris that was so complicated and tangled that I couldn't see who it was. Still, I touched the hand, and energy spiraled downwards into him. His fingers twitched.

The fires were blessedly isolated, burning high but in localized spots. This allowed me to maneuver through the huge storeroom relatively unimpeded, though thick smoke made me cough often, sometimes so hard I had to kneel until the fit passed.

I saw Reid first.

He'd been impaled through the spine by a piece of jagged metal, and his mouth was leaking dark blood. He didn't register that I was there, if the glazed stillness in his eyes was any indication. But all the same, my power surged into my hands, and I pulled him off the spike as I healed him.

He cried out and fell into my arms, where he heaved for several seconds and spat out blood. I held him while he recovered from his absurdly-near-death experience.

When he'd calmed himself, he straightened and wiped his eyes. "Are we the only ones who lived?"

I blinked several times, remembering Reuben's leg in the parking lot. "I don't know. I'm looking for the others."

We parted ways and began to comb through the ruins. I started in the corner of the room and mentally mapped out little rows in which I'd search up and down, like a one-man search party.

I found Abby next. Or rather, what was left of her.

Abby had resumed human form before she'd died. Her tiny body had stood no chance against such a blast. Her corpse was remarkably intact, but I could feel the broken bones and mashed-up insides.

I laid her remains next to Edward's body, which was also in human form. Half of him was by the door to the hallway, and the other half was scattered nearby. Putting him back together was a messy job. I arranged them look as if they were sleeping next to each other.

In a way, I was relieved that I wouldn't have to inform Edward that his Sweet Pea had died, or tell Abby that her Eddy was dead. Perhaps I'd be judged for such a sentiment, but it was true.

After I'd closed Edward's eyes, I stood up and stared around, peering through the smoke. Here, at zero hour, it was amazingly easy to not feel anything while I looked around for the bits and pieces of the people I loved most.

My textbooks would've said I was in shock. I probably was.

Yet, my feet moved and I shoved aside item after item, never stopping. The room was growing hotter, but there were still people left to rescue. I was an automaton in the service to my team. Long ago, I would've sneered at the concept of being a brainless fighting machine, but now?

Now I understood.

After a few minutes, telepathy brushed my mind: *Help me.*

I followed the meek call to a pile of smoldering boxes, which I threw aside. Ember was curled up, her skin peeling off, but alive. I knelt down and cradled her in my arms while her skin regrew and —*Lord, have mercy*—swallowed up the bones in her fingers that had been exposed by the burns.

She sobbed as I held her with her head to my chest. I cried with her. There was no more anger in me, no frustration with silly relationship squabbles or questionable choices about getting rid of her powers. All of that had melted away into nothing, leaving just her and me to weep in each other's arms. Ember was my friend, and what a friend she was. She was unbearably precious to me.

A simple picture took form in my head of Reid.

"Let's go find him," I said softly. "He's just fine."

She tried to stand, but her legs were trembling too hard to support her weight.

I sturdied myself, then picked her up and carried her over to Reid. He was holding something in his tunic, something about twelve inches long and bloody at one end.

I stopped in my tracks, not feeling the weight of the person in my arms anymore.

He looked up, his sad gray eyes conveying what his mouth would not: he'd found a part of my wife. And this time, it was really her that had been harmed.

The emotionlessness somehow became more so.

He laid Jillian's limp forearm on the ground, and I carefully passed Ember to him. He sat down with her on his lap, and closed his eyes, his own tears falling. They were together now, and nothing would ever tear them apart again. They probably didn't even remember why they'd broken up.

Marco and Reuben were next to each other near the storeroom door—I'd been in too deep of a brain fog before to see them. Marco was badly burned, but breathing because Reuben had taken the brunt of the blast for him.

Reuben's leg had indeed been blown off an inch above his knee, and though I could heal the most shocking wounds, I now knew from my experience with the Burlington team that I could not regrow limbs. Reuben would be a wounded warrior for the rest of his life.

I touched their foreheads, then looked around, pleading to God that the only reason I hadn't found Jillian was because she was under something, not because she was in a thousand pieces all around me.

Ember raised a shaking finger and pointed out the storeroom door.

My eyes followed, and I finally saw the painfully obvious clue: there was a bloody trail leading out into the parking lot.

At the end lay my wife, alone and face-down in the snow.

I was beside her in the space of a breath, turning her over, healing energy seeping into every cell of her body. Emotion finally flooded into the cavity in my chest, warm and life-giving.

I was amazed.

She'd followed me. Even with her left arm blown off and gushing blood. Even with half of her face essentially gone. Even with burns on every inch of exposed skin that had eaten down to the muscle in some spots. She'd been willing to fight for me even as the life was leaving her body.

I kissed her face over and over and over, brushing aside her wildly-blowing hair, the hair that I had loved from the second I'd first laid eyes on her.

"...Benjamin?" Her tiny voice was as welcome to my ears as a drop of water to a man dying of thirst.

"Jillian," I whispered. "My Jillian. I'm here."

She opened her eyes and stared up at me, her eyes growing large with terror. "Benjamin, we need to get inside." For all of her fear, her words were small.

"It's over, sweetheart. It's all over."

"*Twister!*"

I jerked my head up. Above us, swirling in an all-too-familiar funnel, was the beginnings of an enormous tornado. I whipped around and looked for the obvious culprit.

Terrence had been the first person I'd healed. He was partially pinned under wreckage, his eyes glowing and flickering oddly, and he was staring at us with an inhuman hate in his eyes.

Jillian jumped up, her teeth chattering. "Everyone, get under cover!"

In the corner of my eye, I saw a man limp into the corporate parking garage. His metal hands glinted in the glow of the fires.

"Let's go," I said, pulling Jillian towards the garage.

We hurried into the solid concrete structure, where the snow had only blown in six feet across the floor before petering out into nothing. It was windy in the garage, but not terribly so.

Jillian leaned heavily against a support pillar. "I feel so weird," she said, gasping. "I know my arm's gone, but my brain doesn't know, does that make sense? It keeps telling me that something's wrong with my arm, but there is no arm. My arm's gone, Benjamin!"

I pulled her into a fierce hug, but my eyes searched endlessly for Beau. He was here, and he was hiding. Jillian was maimed. The tigers were dead. The world was ending. And if I didn't find my brother and get back the JM-104 that I'd literally given him myself, this cycle would keep going.

Forever.

The tornado touched down.

It was as if a freight train were barreling down through the industrial zone of Baltimore, Maryland. Roofs were ripped off, flinging shingles and plywood everywhere, even into the interior of the garage. Bits of furniture and household items from a local neighborhood crashed against the concrete.

Siding began to strip off the Bell lab. I hoped the survivors had gone into the basement. There was nothing we could do now.

The helicopters in the parking lot began to tumble. One somersaulted into the side of the parking garage, just feet from us.

Jillian regained control of her breathing and led me into an alcove designated for Eliza McCurtis-Bell's car. We huddled in the corner, our teeth chattering—but we were perfectly safe in the tucked-away stone structure. I could hear the wind, but only a light, sucking breeze touched us there.

She stared at her stump, a tear slipping down her cheek. "My arm. My *arm* is gone. I'll never fight again."

"As soon as we get the JM-104 away from Beau, we're getting out of here. We can get you a prosthetic. We'll do something. Your life isn't over. And now nobody will ever give you trouble about leaving service."

Jillian waved her stump back and forth, then bit her lip. "Beau has it? You're sure?"

"Yeah. I gave it to him. It's a long story."

"Okay. I hear him above us. Let's surprise him, jump him, and destroy the can. He's injured, right? I smelled his blood in the snow by the helicopter."

"Up the stairwell," I said, pointing to our only avenue of approach, since I doubted the elevator was in operation.

Jillian and I dashed across the floor, dodging bits of detritus in the air, and ran up the steps. I didn't bother trying to disguise my footfalls; they were utterly drowned out by the roar of the artificial storm. The tornado was already much farther away than before, but the wind was still raging.

We crouched low on the second flight of stairs, and Jillian slowly peeked up, her hand on her knife, then came back down. "He's on the far end of the garage, facing away. You're going to have to charge him. I'll be there as fast as I can, and then we'll take him out together."

Her lips brushed mine. I kissed her, caressing her cheek, then nodded. "See you there."

And then I'd shoved Beau up against the concrete wall. His freaky eyes were large with shock, and his mouth was open.

Holy smokes, I'd actually surprised him. That was a first.

"Round two," I growled. I tossed him to the ground and threw myself on him. "Where's the JM-104, Beau?" I shouted, grabbing a fistful of his hair. "Give it to me!"

Jillian sprinted up to us and took over.

She lifted Beau up by his neck. He gurgled, but couldn't break her grip. She didn't look away from Beau as she said, "Benjamin, I see the can in his pocket."

Can, out. Switchblade, taken. I handed them to Jillian. With those necessities out of the way, I backed up a few steps to watch whatever was going to happen next.

She tossed him to the ground. "I can hear the sirens," she said loudly, now that we were closer to the wind. "And you've got a choice, Beau. Are you going to go quietly, or do I have to kick your ass again? The choice is yours."

Beau spat at her feet and scrambled backwards on his toes. "There's nothing you can do to me, you redneck whore. No matter where I go, I'll get out. I have friends everywhere. I can slip by any security system, hack any computer, break through any firewall. The world is digital, and I run it."

"That's not an answer." She sounded bored.

"Fine. I'm going to fight you, and everyone like you, until the day I die. I'm going to make that little redhead beg for death. I'm going to make her boyfriend watch. Your pipsqueak buddy is going to join his little sisters in hell, and then I'm going to make you regret ever looking at my brother and—"

Jillian flipped open the switchblade, kicked him backwards so his neck was exposed, and sliced his throat open.

Then she flicked the blade closed and handed it to me.

SOON AFTER JILLIAN had dispatched my brother, the storm had all but evaporated, clearing up as soon as suddenly as it had come on. We quickly found out why: Terrence was dead. His head was simply gone, and the space on the floor where it had been was black and smoldering, as if a giant with a serious grudge against the guy had aimed a humongous magnifying glass at him.

When I'd pointed to the scorch mark with a quizzical quirk of my eyebrows, Marco had shrugged and given me a wide-eyed little, "I dunno."

He'd craned his neck and peered around us into the parking lot. "Where's Beau?"

I shrugged and smiled. "I dunno."

As I'd hoped, the others had hidden in the basement during the worst of the tornado, and they were safe and sound when we arrived back, if subdued to the point of catatonia.

Reid and Ember were sitting together on a broken generator. They were holding hands, and she was resting her head on his shoulder. They made no sign that they could hear the sirens in the distance. Instead, they both stared out at nothing, rarely blinking.

Reuben was kneeling next to the remains of Edward and Abby, pulling a tarp over them. He'd already crafted himself a fake leg from his power. As I watched, he crossed himself and began to pray quietly.

I left him alone to pay his last respects to his beloved teammate and her star-crossed lover. The poor man would have to go home to his wife as an amputee, and then would have to inform Lark and Berenice of Abby's passing. I did not envy him.

Jillian and I joined Reid, Ember, and Marco, who was now sitting on the floor by the generator with his arms around his knees. He was slightly more animated than Reid and Ember; he, at least, greeted us with a half-hearted wave.

She pulled out the JM-104 and held it up. "This is it, everyone. This is what it's all been about. Dean assured me that this can is the last bit of the stuff in existence. What's our move?"

"Destroy it," Marco said dully. He clambered to his feet. "I can do it."

"No," Ember said. "Since this is my last chance, I'll say it now: I want to use it on myself. *All* of it. I'm tired of being a target because of my powers."

Everyone but Reid and me looked shocked.

"But... but why?" Jillian said.

"Jill, when have I ever liked being a telepath?" She heaved a sigh. "I mean, really, think about it. As long as you've known me, it's just been a long trail of Patricks and Beaus. My powers have become a ball and chain. I want to be cut loose."

"But your animals," Marco said, sounding almost hurt. "They need you. You're the animal woman. It would be weird if you couldn't talk to them."

Ember nodded. "I'll miss them. But I do think this is the best course of action, and not just for *me*. Let's face it, we can't trust that anyone will actually destroy it. At least, not after analyzing it and reverse-engineering the formula. If I inject it, my body will metabolize it, and that'll be that. No more powers, no more JM-104. Two birds."

Jillian stared down at the can. "Em, I hate to deny you anything, but... but this could kill you. I can't, in good conscience, let you have this. You're talking about injecting the entire can into yourself, even though a fraction of an ounce could've been the end of Reuben or me. It lowered our immune systems. It hurts like hell. I don't think you understand how much this crap hurts." She shuddered.

"I know. I'm willing to take the risk. The way I live now is so bad, I'm willing to risk death. It'll be the first time that I'm fully taking control of my life and living the way I want to. Think about that before you tell me no. Please."

"Let me see that, please," Reid said. Jillian handed it to him, and he held it up to the light. "I can see the pins," he murmured. "They're recessed. Let me see if I can..."

He fiddled with the can, and suddenly the four pins popped out with a little *cht*. We all took a huge step back—even Ember.

At my smirk, she glared at me. *Instinctual reaction, smartass. Wipe that smile off your face.*

Frankly, I couldn't *wait* for her to not be able to talk to me telepathically anymore.

Reid studied the can for a second, then looked up at Ember. "I can destroy it right now. That'll be the end of it. You don't have to risk your life. I'm leaving service today, with you, and I'll make sure you are never hurt again. No militias, no superheroes, nothing. I'll marry you, with a ribbon, or with a justice of the peace, whatever you want. Everything I will ever have will be yours. I just... please don't do this. You've demonstrated that you can live without me, Em. But I can't live without you."

Ember and he stared at each other for an eternity, until Ember said softly, "You *can't* protect me, because nobody can."

He gulped. "Yes, I can."

And then he jammed the pins into his leg.

Ember's high scream smothered any sound of clicks or hissing. Reid probably didn't make any noise—he just collapsed, his eyes flashing white like a dying flashlight, and then fading as they rolled back.

Emergency personal and law enforcement finally arrived, flooding into the storeroom just as Reuben and Ember began frantic CPR. Paramedics pushed them aside and took over, but Jillian had to restrain Ember from jumping on Reid. She was still screaming. Not words, not cries of anger or fear. Just screaming as the love of her life began to have seizures and foam at the mouth.

Someone bumped into me, and I fell.

The world blurred at the edges, becoming a stew of screaming, flashing lights, shouted orders, and general chaos. Smoke still lingered everywhere, and tiny bits of burning material floated by whenever someone moved too quickly by a smoldering pile of debris.

When blood began to pour out of Reid's mouth and nose, I pushed through the crowd of legs and touched his hand. Nothing happened. I was bumped and jolted backwards, behind everyone, and I lost sight of my friend.

I was adrift in the ocean.

Jillian came over to me and helped me to my feet, then laid her head on my shoulder, enveloping me in her embrace. "I'm here," she whispered. "I've got you. I've got you. I've got you."

She still felt as whole as ever, and like a life preserver, I clung to her.

ITEM TWENTY-NINE

Words carved into a large evergreen oak tree in the former Oconee Superhero Camp, central Georgia. Date unknown, but believed to be recent.

BYE-BYE HOME

EPILOGUE

The days are long, but the years fly by.

Reuben's sage words, spoken with a paternal chuckle over the phone just the week before, had seemed appallingly sentimental when he'd said them. I'd hung up the phone and commented to Benjamin that parenthood makes people sappy.

But now, as I walked down the overgrown path towards my childhood home, I recognized the ring of truth in his words. With each step, all the days of the past ten years seemed to turn back like the pages of a book, stirring up memories and emotions long forgotten—or suppressed. For example, I'd determinedly not thought about the event that had brought me here last time. Who'd want to think about the tribunal?

Those terrible days, those dark weeks following the tribunal, had indeed been long. The longest of my life, even. But the years had flown by. Where had they gone?

"Hey, are you okay?" Brandon asked. "You look sad."

I patted him on the shoulder and grinned, shaking off my mood swing. "Don't mind me. Ever get all nostalgic when you go home for winter break? That's all this is. I grew up here, you know. Well, I grew up at the end of the path. Same difference."

The trees thinned, and before long we were standing at the trench where a huge wall used to be. It had been hastily filled in, and never packed down, so now it was a sunken scar in the forest floor, a reminder for future generations of what had happened for so long in the cleared land beyond.

The others were already there. In the distance, in the main clearing, children were laughing and calling to each other. I recognized every sweet voice.

"Hello?" I called.

"Aunt Jill! It's Aunt Jill! Everybody, look!"

Nora Fischer's high little shout made me smile. At nearly ten years old, the gangly brunette was the undisputed leader of her pack. And what a pack it was; hot on her heels were her next youngest sister Mary Rose, the gray-eyed twins Laura and Mateo, and even squishy baby Paul, still in diapers. He waddled after his siblings with a sippy cup in his chubby hand.

I kneeled down and threw my arms wide. "Gimme some hugs!"

Five noisy children flung themselves at me—and immediately began begging for me to do my "arm trick."

I gave Brandon a knowing smile. "I told you they were going to ask that."

"Please! Please please *please*!" Mary Rose begged. "Just once!"

I gave an exaggerated sigh. "Well…"

"Please! Just once!"

"Please, Aunt Jill!"

"Daddy said you would!"

I could barely contain my own giggles as I smoothed over my face. They suddenly hushed, already enraptured. I raised my left arm, and their eyes grew as round as basketballs. "I'm not fully human," I stage-whispered. "I have… *abilities*. Strange and alien abilities. Nobody can explain them."

"What can you do?" Nora asked, playing along to her favorite game.

"I can move this," I whispered. My prosthetic fingers slowly clenched. "But how? What is moving the fingers?"

They gasped. "It's magic," Mary Rose, ever the imaginative one, said with undisguised awe.

"It's better than magic," I said. "It's science. But I suppose if science can make Supers, then there's not much difference, is there?"

There wasn't anything remotely magical about my prosthetic arm, of course. Two years before, I'd been the recipient of a cutting-edge procedure that had combined the latest prosthetic engineering with neurological mapping.

A dozen world-class scientists and surgeons had cracked open my body and tinkered with my nerves for endless hours. They'd studied the advanced cybernetic hardware inside a corpse that had been anonymously donated to science. I'd read about it in Time Magazine. As a result, I had a somewhat-functional hand, and my honorary nieces and nephews had a party trick to look forward to.

Benjamin had nearly gone crazy during the months afterward in which he hadn't been allowed to touch me, lest he accidentally "heal" the work done to my nervous system and my body reject the prosthetic. But through it all he shared in my joy and optimism, and now we were a normal married couple again. Well, as normal two people with our history could be.

I let each child lovingly stroke my magical arm, then gave them all a kiss on their cheeks. I stood and gestured for Brandon to follow me. "It's not far, now."

As we walked, surrounded by jubilant children, I let myself be happy to be back. The late-June sun beat down on Chattahoochee, filling it with light, heat, and so much life. The thick, waving grass rippled in the breeze like an emerald sea, ridden by moths and butterflies. The fragrant scent of aster and borage perfumed the air, kindling old memories of long-lost childhood games. I promised myself to make flower crowns for the kids before I left.

We walked into the largest clearing, and the kids took off at top speed towards the small throng of adults gathered there. I gestured for Brandon to go with them; I'd seen two people off to the side, beneath a shady tree, whom I wanted to greet.

"Marco? Bells?"

"Jill? *Jill!*" Marco began to sprint towards me, followed by Isabel.

I grinned from ear to ear. He was still the same. Year after year, Marco was my Marco.

They ran up to me, and he laughed as he pulled me into a bear hug. "Hey, you!"

I kissed him all over, and then grabbed Isabel and subjected her to the same. It had only been a few weeks since I'd last seen Marco, but it had been years since I'd seen Isabel. Eight, in fact. She'd waved sadly to me as I'd taken my seat in the witness stand in federal court on that somber day. My testimony had been instrumental in sending the elders to the Super prison, but it had been cold comfort for their victims.

She'd been thin and haggard then, stressed from the detainment and relocation all the Sentinels had undergone. Heaven's own prosecution team had worked out deals for Dean's militia and the people in Liberty. In return for total candor about their activities and every shred of information they had on the Westerners, they were given immunity and put into the Federal Witness Protection Program.

Berenice, of all people, had joined the United States Marshal Service to help out. "It's the least I can do," she'd told me before shipping off to training. "I couldn't go with you when you went after Isabel and Benjamin, but nothing's stopping me now."

We'd clasped hands and bowed our foreheads together. "You take care, you nut job," I'd said.

She'd cuffed my ear. "Don't bring down the government or anything, you hear? They're my new bosses now, and I need a paycheck."

But Isabel and Berenice were both here today, and Isabel looked fabulous. She'd surpassed her brother's height, topping out at about 5'8, and she'd straightened her long hair and put a little wave in it. She'd gained weight and...

Wow.

"Yes!" she exclaimed, following my line of sight. "Two carats! Can you believe it? Alex surprised me on my birthday!" She waved the enormous rock beneath my nose. "Mom and Dad love him, Marco loves him, I love him, and it's going to be such a beautiful wedding! We're going to Hawaii for the honeymoon. He's a Navy nuclear electrician, and he's won three achievement medals, and he's been deployed a bunch of times, and oh my gosh, he's the hottest, sweetest, funniest guy I've ever—"

Marco elbowed her. "Take a breath, motormouth. There's plenty of time to do this later." Marco gave me another, calmer hug, then pulled away. "I'm so glad to see you, Jill. You look great. Just great." He peered around my shoulders. "Who's the beanpole who came with you?" He squinted, then gasped. "Oh! I remember now. Is that the kid you were telling me about?"

"You'll see." I put my arms around their shoulders, and we began to walk towards the others. "Any other shocking developments I should know? And did you dig that hole like I asked?"

Isabel pointed ahead. "Gabby and Rube just found out that they're having another boy, and they're naming him Ryan. Gabby insisted."

A strange throb permeated my chest. How auspicious.

Marco patted my hand. "That's the only surprise. And yeah, we dug the hole."

Everyone stopped talking amongst themselves as we came up. Benjamin kissed me, and I spent a few minutes hugging people and sharing a few words with each of them. To my surprise, there were three faces I didn't recognize, across the clearing and under a tree. Someone else must've invited them. Perhaps Dean?

It hadn't been so long since I'd seen Dean, much to Benjamin's annoyance. In fact, we saw him quite often. Dean and Eleanor had eloped in Las Vegas during the wild and turbulent months following the end of the camps.

We'd been invited to the formal reception a few weeks later, but none of us were comfortable leaving Ember behind, and Ember hadn't been willing to leave the hospital, much less fly across the country.

"He could wake up any day now," she'd said to me when I'd asked. "I'm making improvement. He can hear me sometimes. We talk."

We'd both gazed sadly at Reid then, small and fragile in the hospital bed where he'd lain for so long, hooked up to a complicated mess of monitors and tubing. Wilted flowers had graced every available surface that wasn't covered in Ember's personal effects.

It was hard to heal damage caused by a chemical unknown to medical science.

But heal he did.

Now in his thirties, a married man, a father, and an acclaimed vegan chef, Reid Fischer was the essence of good health. He'd never recovered his powers, but it hadn't stopped him at all. Following the wedding we'd all thrown for the two, they'd moved to rural Georgia and opened up a refuge for abandoned and abused animals of all kinds: horses, cows, dogs, cats, everything.

Ember ministered to the animals, coaxing them out of trauma and into happiness, and Reid cooked special meals for their dietary needs. He'd even gone to cooking school, and now rich businesspeople were offering him opportunities to attach his name to various vegan and eco-friendly food labels. It was all very exciting.

But to their sons, Ezra and Shepherd, he'd always be just "Dad." Ezra, the little strawberry blond six-year-old, was sound asleep in his father's arms, unimpressed by the once-in-a-lifetime event unfolding around him. Shepherd, the four-month-old, was sleeping in a baby carrier on his mother's back.

Instead of a hug, Ember took my hands in hers and beamed at me. I could feel her in my head, and she raised an eyebrow. *You're just full of secrets today, aren't you?*

I winked. *What's the point of living if you can't have a juicy secret or two?*

She finally pulled me into her embrace. "Seeing you once a month isn't enough. Come live with us on the farm. It's four hundred acres. Have Benjamin buy you another house. They're cheap for you guys, right?"

Ah, yes. More twitting about the house situation. *Give away one waterfront mansion to Gabriela to make up for Benjamin burning her*

house to the ground, and suddenly everyone thinks we eat money for
breakfast.

We'd never heard the end of it, especially after Gabriela and
Reuben had sold the Trent estate for a stupidly large amount of cash
and used it to invest in Gabriela's business. Her name was now on
upscale salons in every major city in the America.

Meanwhile, Benjamin and I had moved into a small home nestled
in the verdant hills outside of Saint Catherine. It was nice out there.
Quiet. I could hear myself think, but still be able to see Erica for our
appointments, and meet with reporters and lawyers. I'd been able to
visit Marco at UGSC's nursing school, and then later at the Catholic
school next to our old headquarters. The headquarters was a
museum now. Marco was the school's nurse, a fact that filled
Benjamin with a weird pride.

Dean and Eleanor's charming eight year old, Georgiana, gave me
a brief hug around the middle before going back to her lawn chair,
and her novel. It was one of many she'd brought for the day. Eleanor
and Dean waved at me before going back to their own thick books.

Dean, curiously, had turned into quite the scholar after the
Sentinels disbanded. He was even doing deep research into the
history of the Supers and the camps with the intention of writing an
authoritative book. He'd already collected a few dozen priceless
documents and contemporary sources, and was piecing together the
true picture of our past. He'd even recovered my birth file from
the DOJ.

I greeted Reuben last, and gladly accepted his hug. "Hello, fellow
robot," he said, giving me a second squeeze. "I hope the squad didn't
maul you back there."

"It's fine," I said, warm-faced. "How's the leg?"

He rapped his prosthetic leg with his aluminum water bottle.
"The usual. The doctors were talking about prescribing me some
pretty strong drugs for the phantom limb pain, but I'm holding out
on that for the moment while I explore other options. How's
the arm?"

My lips twisted as I tapped it. "No pain recently, but it itches from time to time. Sometimes it gets so bad that I'm shouting at it to stop. You know how it goes."

"Do I ever. Have you had the sensation of twitching yet? That was a lovely surprise a few weeks ago."

I clasped my hands behind me and rocked back on my heels, trying to keep the smirk off my face. "No, but speaking of surprises, did you meet the man with me? Brandon?"

"I shook his hand, but he just said he was your friend. Who is he? He looks... I don't know, familiar, I guess."

"Come over here," I said, inclining my head as I led him into a small patch of trees. "Reid, Brandon, over here!"

The others didn't follow us, or even question. They'd been briefed.

Reid placed Ezra in a folding chair next to Georgiana's—she didn't even look up—and jogged over to us with Brandon at his side. "What's up?"

I blinked, the emotion of the moment already rising up in my throat and eyes. "Brandon, this is Reuben and Reid Fischer. They're two of several brothers from Idaho. The others couldn't come today, unfortunately."

Raphael had sent a single letter nine years ago saying that he was alive and well, and asked us to leave him alone to mourn his fallen teammates. Robert and Richard had quiet lives with their families, and had opted out of today's meeting. Mr. Fischer, sadly, had passed away a few years after the camps were shut down.

They all shook hands again, and I continued, "Brandon is a journalism major at UGSC, in his senior year. He contacted me last year about the work I do with the former residents of the camps. He wanted to do a big freelance profile on me, my team, our histories, all of that. He'd like to work for the *New York Times* one day."

Reuben blinked in surprise. "Oh? Would you like to interview me? Is that what this is about?" He glanced at me. "If you vouch for him, I'm fine with that."

"No," I said quietly. "That's not what this is about. Brandon, tell them."

Brandon swallowed. "We got to talking, Jill and me, and I told her that I was adopted when I was four years old. My family used to be camp allies. They said that when they got me, they were told to change my name. My name's Brandon Callahan now, but when I was born, my name was Ryan. Ryan Fischer."

The littlest Fischer boy had finally come home.

I stepped back as the three suddenly-crying men embraced each other and thumped each other's backs in that natural, brotherly way I knew they would. They tumbled over each other to compare physical similarities. Ryan had their beautiful gray eyes, but not their mother's pronounced jaw. He had slightly darker blond hair than the others, but the same lean build.

He was a Fischer, through and through.

That reminds me... "Tell them how you're paying for college," I said when they'd all calmed down.

Brandon laughed. "During my tour of the campus when I looking at colleges, I saved the school president from getting hit by a student security van. I got a full scholarship for my troubles."

Reid and Reuben whooped and hollered like idiots about their brother being a part of "the family business."

Brandon rolled up his sleeve and showed off his new tattoo, a list of names: Simon and Esther, and beneath them, their six sons. Ryan had etched his place in his family into his very flesh. Whether he liked it or not, he shared his brother Reid's flair for theatrical displays.

When Reid and Reuben started jabbering about getting matching tattoos, I snorted and walked back to the main group. I wiped away a tear, though. *Goodness, I'm sappy today.*

While we waited for Reid, Reuben, and Brandon to finish their reunion, I tapped Ember on the shoulder. "Who are the new people? Are they ex-Sentinels?"

I couldn't recall ever seeing the middle-aged couple who were lingering in the shadows of a nearby willow tree, friendly but definitely reserved. The woman was short and white, with long blonde hair and a good-natured face. The man bore a cursory resemblance to Gabriela, with light brown skin and wavy black hair, and an overall look that made me think his genetics were from Latin America.

However, the extensive, fading tattoos on his forearms were too old and blurred for him to have been a Sentinel. The ink had to have been at least twenty years old. So who was he?

The younger man was beautiful in a masculine way, and at least ten years younger than me. He was fairly short, but possessed elegant bone structure and inky, combed black hair. His eyes were dark brown and very friendly. He caught my eye and waved excitedly.

Ember took my hand and turned me away from them. "I was worried you'd be angry when I first met her," she said softly. "She contacted me years ago, not long after the big trial."

"Who is she? A former slave?" I craned my neck again and startled. She was studying me with the exact same air of questioning.

"Jill... That's Heather Harris. That's my auntie. She was on the San Diego team thirty years ago. You know, the one that was supposedly murdered by that gang?"

I knew the name. We all knew the name, and the names of her teammates. A little girl bearing the famous, honored name had died in this very camp. The San Diego team had fought and died like heroes—or so I'd been told.

Apparently I'd been lied to. Again.

I gulped down the anger to which I'd become so accustomed to swallowing, and took a deep breath. "Was it the elders? What did they do now?"

"For once, nothing. Heather was going to be sent back and flogged for a stupid, made-up infraction, so the team ran. They were mentally out of the cult already, so they just dropped it all and bolted for the border. Their leader actually died in an unrelated incident, and it was his corpse that was found in the house. They'd never reported his death. That was before regular DNA test..."

Her voiced faded into the background as my vision tunneled.

They'd run. They'd escaped from the cult and run.

Thirty years ago.

And they'd *never* come back to help us.

Ember put her hand on my cheek, her breath picking up. "Jill. *Jill.* Look at me. See that man? That's Miguel. That's her husband. They fell in love when they were nineteen. They have children. Those children are getting married now and are ready to have children of their own. That young man? He's the son of one of the men who got them out. They're us, Jill. They're just like us. They fell in love and wanted to live a life free of the cult. There's no dishonor in that. They just wanted to live. Please don't hate them. Please don't hold this against them."

I squeezed my eyes shut, then nodded. I'd be speaking to Erica about this—and assaulting my punching bag for three uninterrupted hours at some point—but I could be polite and welcoming for Ember's sake.

God, I hated people who didn't do anything with their power. The surge of anger returned, but I stamped it down.

My emotions today! *Sheesh*.

I walked up to them, my hand held out. "Jillian Trent. Ember just told me that you're her Aunt Heather?"

Heather shook my hand. "Yes. I fought as Excalibur. May I introduce my husband, Miguel? And this is Jesse Cipriano. He's the son of the superheroine you may know as Frenzy. Courtney and her husband declined to come today, but I'll let them know that you're well."

Something of my true thoughts must've been communicated in my grip, because she cleared her throat and stepped back. "We'll be over here."

Jesse, however, gave me a hearty handshake that nearly dislocated my shoulder. "I know you don't know me, but I came to tell you that I'm one of your biggest fans."

"Oh," I said, taken aback. "Are you a fan of my time in service, or of the other stuff?"

"Stuff" meant the work Benjamin and I did. There wasn't a word that fully encapsulated "deprogramming camp people, helping them integrate with society, sometimes reuniting families, consulting with law enforcement, and being called in as a subject matter expert on the superhero cult for trials."

"Both! I came to tell you that, but also to say that I've decided to enlist in the National Superhero Corps, and ask if I can be Battlecry II. It would be such an honor." He rubbed the back of his head. "I know you don't even know me, but I've dreamed of being the next Battlecry for years." He cursed. "I probably sound stupid. I'm sorry. I'm just so excited to finally meet you."

Heather and Miguel were watching us, as was Ember. They'd known this was coming. They'd known Jesse would drop this bomb.

But they couldn't have known the significance to me. They couldn't have known the pain in my heart when I'd cried in my room the day a man named Patrick had branded me Battlecry to make fun of me, to mock me for saying that I'd been named after Jillian St. James. To put me down. To remind me of how utterly worthless I was.

And now someone had told me that being Battlecry would be his honor.

Jesse plunged on, "The people at the Corps office said I needed your permission because you're still alive. You see, I find people. That's my power. I was able to get us all here without a GPS or anything just by concentrating on your picture in my head. I'm going to be the superhero who finds everyone. If you want, I thought I could work with you to help locate the missing kids that were given to the camp allies, or maybe we can start on the National Registry for Missing and Exploited Children, or maybe the..."

He quieted and stilled as I leaned in and softly pressed my lips to his forehead. "You have my blessing, Battlecry." Tears finally escaped down my cheeks, but I laughed through them. "And you'll be Battlecry III, by the way. The first one, Jillian St. James, was my grandma, and she was an amazing, brave woman. You're officially in a line of heroes. You've got a lot to live up to, Battlecry."

"Thank you! Thank you so much!" He all but swallowed me in his eager embrace. "Hey, everyone! I'm the new Battlecry!"

The main group of people clapped and whistled. I slung my arm over his shoulder, all anger at Heather and her crew forgotten. They'd produced Battlecry III, after all. I'd invite them to the fancy dinner

Benjamin and I were hosting at our home later. I had a special announcement that I wanted them to hear.

We went back to the main gathering. I hadn't realized I needed it, but the unexpected pleasure of meeting Jesse had prepared me for what was going to happen next.

"Berenice, if I could talk to you and Lark for a second," I said, waving to get Lark's attention. Since I'd arrived, she'd been on her phone with her partners at the brokerage firm she and Jen had opened, absorbed in a conversation that was apparently going to net her half a million dollars by tomorrow morning.

And yet people gave Benjamin and me trouble for selling the house in which I'd been tortured nearly to death. Talk about unfair.

She ended the call and teleported over. "Sorry. I was on the phone with London. Time difference means phone calls at odd hours."

"No problem. Did you two bring what I asked?"

"Got it," Berenice said. She dug around in her roomy pocket. She was wearing her black U.S. Marshals t-shirt tucked neatly into her cargo pants, which themselves were tucked into solid work boots. Today, and today only, I wouldn't tease her about choosing a law enforcement agency that dressed her up like Artemis again.

She handed me a small bronze tiger, and Lark produced a bronze compass. I slipped them into my pocket. "Thank you so much, you guys."

Berenice sighed. "I've got some bad news... I can't stay for the dinner tonight. I just got a call from my supervisor. One of the other deputy marshals, Cash, punched someone. I gotta fly back to Cheyenne and put out a few fires. I'm usually the only one who can knock some sense into that guy." She rolled her eyes, but there was an indulgent air to it.

"Punched someone? A fugitive?" I gasped. "Oh my gosh, was it one of the Westerner hold-outs? Please tell me it was a Westerner."

She grinned sheepishly. "It was actually one of the other deputy marshals. Cash says it was all a misunderstanding, but if you know him the way I do, that's a highly suspect claim."

I choked on my own spit. "You went from one team of rogues to another, didn't you?"

She boxed my shoulder, and then we pounded fists. She really was a cool person, and a good friend.

Lark gave me a hug. "Thank you for doing this, Jill. I think we all need it."

I pecked her on the cheek. "How's the firm?"

"Very well, since we just hit our stock price goal for the quarter. I'll tell you all about it over dinner tonight."

We all exchanged a few more pleasantries, and then we went back to the group.

I was finally ready.

I'd thought long and hard about this day. For the longest time I hadn't known what the specific date would be, but when I found out that the camp's land was going to be turned back into a national forest, I knew my time had come. I'd chosen today, specifically, because it was the tenth anniversary of the day Reid had woken up from his coma.

Well, the upcoming conversion to a national forest was just one of the reasons I'd arranged this meeting. There were two.

I gathered everyone around me and took in their faces. They were handsome or beautiful, lined with age and experience, and friendly. All the faces I'd come to cherish so deeply over the years. Faces of naked hope and realized dreams. Faces of heroes. Faces of children who could be anything they wanted to be because of the sacrifices of the adults around them, and a few adults who weren't.

My chest ached. There were so many faces that *weren't* there.

Gregory had stopped taking my calls six years ago. Dean had lost contact with him following the relocations into Witness Protection, and even Isabel hadn't heard from him. I hoped he was well, and had found the peace that had escaped him for so long.

Topher, almost-world traveller, should've been there. He should've stood head and shoulders above the rest of us, gushing about his adventures in the great, wide unknown. He should've found a life partner to travel with and whisper his secrets to, as I'd found in

Benjamin. He should've toasted us, and roasted Benjamin, at our formal wedding reception we'd held after Reid had woken up.

Abby and Edward should've lived in each other's embrace, free to be who and what they really were. They'd been denied each other for years, shamed for wanting someone of a different race. In the darkest hours of my worst nights, when my nightmares kept me from sleep and the pain of my missing arm made me scream for an end to the agony, I thought of them as I'd last seen them: hand-in-hand, smiling, and ready for a new life.

All gone because of a single spark.

More faces flipped through my mind, people I'd encountered in my new job. I'd met with families I'd known growing up who didn't understand what was happening. Children who'd been wrenched from their screaming mother's arms and given to new parents because they'd lacked powers. The shaking, traumatized victims of the Westerners. Superheroes who just wanted to fight as they always had, but were too illiterate to read the Corps enrollment forms.

I closed my eyes and breathed in, then let my anger leave me in a long exhale. Erica would've been proud. I only had to meet with her once a month now. We'd talked extensively about what I had planned for today, and why I needed to do it.

Ember stepped forward. "Jill, we're all ready."

"Thank you."

We were all standing around the large hole in the ground that Marco had dug at my request. The shovel was sticking out of a nearby pile of dirt.

Without further ado, I pulled out the bronze tiger and compass and held them in my palms. Now that the moment for my words had come, I was dimly surprised that I still remembered them. Perhaps all of my public speaking had finally sunk in; the broadcast, so long ago, had been the first of countless speeches.

"We've all lost loved ones in these camps. For the last ten years, we've constantly looked back. Back at what could've been, what should've been. The people and chances that were taken from us. The childhoods we should've had." I placed the tiger and compass into the hole. "Now that Chattahoochee is being reverted to a park, I'm placing these here to represent the people who never got to leave. Abby and Topher, and so many others…"

A sudden lump in my throat made me stop, and Benjamin put his comforting hand on my shoulder. I gestured for him to continue, as we'd agreed that morning. I knew I was likely to get choked up at least once.

"Let's take a minute of silence for the heroes at the Virginia camp, whose silence is the loudest of all," Benjamin said. Everyone bowed their heads.

The tears came for a second time, but there was no laughing now.

I'd been so proud to be in the convoy of government cars that had been sent to break down the wall of the Virginia camp, tucked deep in the Shenandoah Valley. I'd pushed open the rusting gate myself.

That was the first hint: the rust. It was falling apart from decades of neglect.

After that, we'd expected anything behind the wall. Legions of angry, old superheroes who were spoiling for one more fight. Sad, aging men and women who just wanted peace. Maybe a death factory where superheroes were ground up and turned into food for the camps. *Something.*

But there'd been nothing. Nothing at all.

And then I'd smelled the mass graves.

My memory stopped at that point. Erica said I'd blacked out because of the violence of the emotions. She'd prompted me a few times to explore that day and deal with the trauma in a healthy way, but I'd always refused.

I'd never worked with the people who'd excavated the graves. I'd never spoken publicly about it, though I'd been asked to by the media. I could not be all things to all people, and facing what had happened to the best and bravest of my peers—the people who'd risked their lives every day for their cities—was simply too much.

After the minute was up, and I'd regained control, I cleared my throat. "I also asked some of you to bring mementos of the people who were taken from the camps against their will, so that a piece of them may always occupy this ground."

At that, Marco and Isabel pulled items from their pockets. Marco held a miniature telescope, to represent Gregory, and three bronzed daises. Isabel held up a tiny vial of blood. "For me," she said simply. "My childhood ended that day."

When they'd laid the items in the hole, I removed the last item from my pocket: a letter in an unsealed envelope. The others removed their letters, too. Even Heather. Sneaky Ember.

"I asked you all to write down what you want to say to the elders and the cult, the nasty stuff that you don't dare let yourself say in public. The things that weigh on your heart. The things that hurt you most. You don't have to read them out loud, but I'd like to share mine. I've been in therapy for a long, long time. I've learned that talking helps me. Just so you know, what I have to say will probably upset some of you."

Dean gave me an encouraging smile. "Let it all out, Jill. It's time."

Sweet Dean. I was glad I was still in touch with him.

With shaking hands, I removed the small piece of notebook paper I'd agonized over for weeks. I'd sat at the kitchen table night after night, sobbing until I had a migraine, the tip of my pen on the paper, but unable to write the words I knew I had to. How could I write those three words?

As the weeks had worn on, I'd come to the dismal conclusion that I'd never be able to do this. I was only human.

And then I'd taken a pregnancy test last night.

Seeing the little plus sign had been the final push I'd needed to move the pen across the paper, forming the hardest words I'd ever say. But my child needed me to say them.

I opened the paper and took a deep breath.

"I forgive you."

The crumpled paper fell into the hole.

I fell to my knees and began to sob anew. Forgiveness... the ulti-mate act of compassion, both for the people who'd hurt me, and for *myself*. Benjamin and I had created a child in love, and in love that child would be raised. Not anger. Not hate. Not looking backwards and cursing fate. Our child would be free from the shackles of vengeance and bitterness. Our child would look forward, eyes to the future, with us at their side.

I would be free from those same shackles. I deserved it far more than the elders deserved my forgiveness. In fact, they didn't deserve it at all. But that wasn't what forgiveness was about. We didn't always get what we deserved.

I'd thought that Benjamin might scoff at my desire to forgive the elders, but he hadn't. Instead, he'd told me about Buck and Emily, and Reuben's impossible command. We'd held each other in bed that night, after the long conversation about the nature of forgiveness and the impossible depths of the human heart. It was possible that our child had been conceived that night, too. I wasn't sure, since we'd given up trying to conceive a few years ago, figuring that the JM-104 had permanently harmed my body in a way that it hadn't Reuben's or Reid's.

Benjamin helped me to my feet, and I accepted a tissue from Berenice. I already felt lighter. So much lighter. Worlds lighter. Erica had said that forgiveness was a process, a decision I'd make every day for the rest of my life. But I already felt better. I was ready for the next part of my life.

I was ready to turn a new page. To be at peace. To lift my glass of juice that night and announce to my beloved friends and family that I was finally pregnant, and that our child would never know the pain I had known for so long.

Ember inclined her head towards me. *Look at you, all sappy now that you're a parent. Funny how that happens. Or is this just the first trimester hormones?*

I gave her a watery smile.

I wiped at my eyes as Dean and Lark read their statements, each completely different, but equally tragic.

Dean spoke of how he missed his mother every day, and sometimes woke up in the night to the phantom sound of her calling for help. As he read, I remembered him as I'd first known him, and suddenly the brash confidence of Dean Monroe appeared to me as the thin coat of paint it actually was.

Lark had been Topher's best friend, and I'd had no idea. She confessed to the absent elders that she'd hated the cult the minute she'd first seen women her age having fun on JHU's campus, and she'd hated how she'd been made to feel guilty for it. She'd found a true friend in Topher, and only he had ever really understood her. She'd given him his first compass, a gag gift after he'd gotten lost on patrol one night.

She wiped her eyes and looked at us. "And I don't want any of you to think we were in love, because it wasn't like that. He was my friend, and my brother, and that's enough. That's beautiful all by itself." She removed a thin chain from around her neck, on which hung a tiny nugget of metal. "This is titanium. He gave this to me once, in case he ever lost his own. I'm not going to put it in the ground, because it's my piece of him."

Berenice wrapped her in a hug, and Lark began to sob.

When Lark was finished, they dropped their papers into the hole, and the others followed suit, though without reading theirs aloud. Each one of us took a turn shoveling dirt into the hole, passing the shovel around the circle until it was finished.

And that was that. We'd said what we'd had to say.

I watched Reid as he tamped down the dirt with the shovel, and I wondered if he missed his powers for such tasks.

Not really, Ember answered. *Not anymore.*

As the children ran around and we all settled down for picnic lunches in the summer sun, I laid back on a blanket and stared up at the cerulean sky. My tunic had once been that color. Would Jesse take up my old style, or design his own?

I sat up and looked around for him to ask, but he was absorbed in conversation with Ryan several yards away.

I laid back down and closed my eyes. My codename was in good hands. Perhaps Jesse would grow old and pass it on to my child. Or not. I was fine with either possibility.

I was fine with whomever wanted to bear my codename, as long as they were ready to take on the responsibilities associated with it. It was a big name, hinting at epic wars waged against the insatiable lions of injustice.

Battlecry. It promised bombs and knives. Blood and grit. Staring down the barrel of the gun and never flinching.

I opened my eyes, the warm sunshine streaming down on my face. I was comfortable with someone else having the name, because I was finally happy to just be Jillian.

My battle was won.

THE END

—————

THANK you so much for reading *Mercury*, the final installment of the Battlecry series! If you enjoyed the adventure, please consider leaving me a review on Mercury's Amazon page. Reviews are how I determine what my readers want more of, so they're very valuable to me.

I've included a sneak preview of *Sea of Lost Souls*, the first installment in my next series! Keep reading to check it out.

ACKNOWLEDGMENTS

I never would've gotten this far without a village of people to carry me. Thanks are in order.

First and foremost, I am grateful to our Lord Jesus Christ for blessing me and guiding me throughout this entire process. When I was stuck, I prayed. When I was discourage, I prayed. This is His series more than anyone's.

Similarly, I must thank all the people who prayed for me, with special shout-outs to the women of the Young & Wild Catholic Mamas Facebook group. You're all amazing, smart, and funny, and I'm honored to be among your number.

I must thank Alexander Dodge, husband extraordinaire, for standing by my side every step of the way. There really aren't words to do you justice, sweetie. I hope I've made you proud.

The women of Enclave need a tip of the hat, too! Where would I be without Monika Holabird, Katie Beuche, Ryann Muree, Emily Gorman, and Nicole Andrews? Up a creek without a paddle, that's where.

To Sarah Gonzales, what can I say? You've been the biggest non-Alex supporter of them all. I hope you liked your book. :)

Special thanks goes out to Ken Welch, my father, who gave me his expert advice on the gun terminology and federal organization knowledge. Thanks, Dad!

And finally, a million thanks go out to my readers and fans.

ABOUT THE AUTHOR

Emerald Dodge lives with her husband Alex and their two sons. Emerald and Alex enjoy playing with their children, date nights, hosting dinner parties for their friends, and watching movies. They are a Navy family and look forward to traveling around the nation and meeting new people. When she's not writing, Emerald likes to cook, bake, go to Mass, pray the rosary, and FaceTime with her relatives.

Her favorite social media platform for interacting with fans is Tumblr. Message her on her Tumblr page!

ABOUT SEA OF LOST SOULS

F reedom lies on the open sea. Danger lies within it.

Rachel Goldstein dreams of the vast oceans, and her job in the Navy seems to offer her everything she'd ever hoped for. Her heart seeks adventure, but her mind is still ashore, where the last time she saw her parents, they had a fight that left everyone in tears. She wants reconciliation... which becomes impossible when she dies in a tragic aviation accident aboard her aircraft carrier.

When she wakes up aboard a ghost ship, her new shipmates offer Rachel her only chance to seize adventure again, and she knows what she must do. Aboard this impressive and fearsome vessel is her opportunity to find new freedom — if she can survive it. The ghostly high seas are fraught with danger, from devious officers to murderous pirates. And lurking underneath it all is Scylla, the mythological monster set to destroy anyone who encroaches on her aquatic territory.

Normally ready for anything, Rachel will have to find out if she's stronger than her enemies and the beasts that lie below the waves. And at the end of it all, can she pierce the veil of death and reach through to the world of the living, and to her parents?

Fans of K.F. Breene's paranormal fantasy, Greek mythology, and

Jessica Jones will love the action-packed nautical fantasy of Emerald Dodge's Sea of Lost Souls! Pick up your copy and join the crew today!

SEA OF
LOST SOULS

SHE DIED... AND THEN
HER LIFE BEGAN.

OCEANUS SERIES – BOOK 1

EMERALD DODGE

SEA OF LOST SOULS - PREVIEW

"Man overboard! Man overboard! Starboard side!"

The alert came over the ship's intercom system, echoing down the USS *Taft's* passageways and making my ears ring as the sound bounced around the steel.

I tore my eyes away from the white-red fire of the F-18 that had just landed on the flight deck, and began to sprint into the hanger bay, leaving behind the exciting maelstrom to muster for the third man-overboard alert in six hours. The roar of the jet, the howling of the storm, the crashing waves, and angry shouts from other sailors all mixed with a new sound: the alert klaxon.

I thudded down the stairs and dashed into the reactor office, where I was supposed to be manning the phone during my time on watch. I'd only taken a few seconds during an errand to admire the jets, but there was every chance I'd be written up for not being at my station at the beginning of the man-overboard.

I grabbed the juicy superhero novel I'd been reading and tried to look engrossed. It had already been ten seconds, and I couldn't hear my favorite person cracking skulls.

"Up! Move! Move! Make a hole! Hurry up!"

There he was.

The tired yells came from beyond the open door, mixing with the klaxon. The yeller, Chief Swanson, sounded like he'd just woken up. Considering that it was half past midnight, he probably had.

His concern was all for show. After the first two false alarms, I was positive that nobody cared about the man-overboard. Now, if they found the chucklehead who kept throwing emergency chem lights in the water... yeah, there was going to be an actual man-overboard situation, and every sailor on the carrier was going to cheer.

Chief Swanson stumbled into the reactor office, bleary and half-dressed. I tossed him the clipboard. "Petty Officer Second Class Goldstein comma Rachel present, in body if not in spirit. My spirit is back in my rack getting some sleep."

"Shut up, Goldstein," he said without looking up from the clipboard. "Where's Bickley?"

A booming voice over the intercom interrupted us. "Time plus one!"

It had been a minute since the man-overboard. If all five thousand hands on the ship hadn't mustered by time plus twelve, they'd launch the helicopters and search teams. Considering that I'd seen thirty-foot waves just a few minutes ago, I did not envy anybody who had to search for a single person in that ocean.

I flipped my book open to where I'd stopped. "I took over for him. He's probably on his way here from his rack."

The ship rolled slightly, and a pen fell off the desk with a clatter. Huh. Maybe someone *had* fallen off the ship. The storm was getting worse.

There was the sound of a train passing over head, followed by a vibration that resounded in my chest. It wasn't a train, of course—it was an F-18 landing on the flight deck. I'd overheard an airman say that four planes had been called back to the ship as the freak storm had overtaken us. I'd watched the first one return. Two down, two to go.

Groans and mumbles carried down the passageway as the rest of my muster group wandered into the office. In my opinion, we were the best possible muster group, comprising three good-looking nuclear electricians. Not that our appearances were remotely important, of course. It was just that our good looks made it funnier when people found out that we were nukes, since most sailors thought that nukes were pasty, squishy sewer monsters. *I* thought I was rather pretty, with my fair, lightly-freckled skin, and soft brown curls that stuck out every which way.

Bickley, the oldest of us, led the pack. Pillow marks lined the brown skin of his face, and his white tank top allowed us to see his impressive nautical-themed tattoos that he'd gotten during each of his four deployments. "'Sup," he said through a yawn. When he'd finished, he gestured toward the clipboard. "Petty Officer First Class Jack Bickley, ready for duty or whatever."

"Thank you, Petty Officer," Chief said. "Your eagerness to serve is much appreciated."

I hid my smile. Bickley's military bearing always went up in smoke after midnight.

My best friend, Torres, moved like a zombie down the hallway. She still had a crusty spit trail on her cheek and was blinking rapidly as though she were confused by what was going on. Her pixie cut stuck out oddly on one side, and her feet were clad in actual bunny slippers. Her intricate collarbone tattoo—I'd egged her on into getting it in Marseilles—was on clear display underneath her tank top.

Chief ticked off her name. "Petty Officer Second Class Marisol Torres, check, and nice slippers, by the way. Where's Rollins?"

"He's definitely on watch," I said. He'd complained about it for an hour before I'd kicked him out of the reactor office and told him to go whine to the generators instead. It was a forgivable offense, though; he wasn't normally so prone to complain, but it was the middle of the night in the sixth month of a deployment. We were all getting a little fatigued.

The carrier leaned to the side suddenly, tossing my colleagues to the floor. My rolling office chair merely scooted across the small office like a lame theme park ride. A familiar wave of nausea hit me, and I began to mentally calculate the physics of the motion to take my mind off of it. It was unfortunate that I got motion sickness so easily. I loved the *idea* of going fast and wild. My stomach did not.

"Time plus two!"

Bickley put the wastepaper basket back in its spot. His movie-star good looks, all symmetry and deep brown eyes, were muddled by his lack of sleep.

"Is this a hurricane?" I asked, casting a glance toward the ceiling. "I would've thought we sailed around those. I like some excitement, but this..."

Torres shook her head and patted my shoulder. "Nope, they'll sail right through. Don't worry, though. We sailed through Hurricane Ben during my first deployment, and we were just fine. Not much can sink a carrier."

As if to underline her point, the ship pitched again, and this time they all braced themselves for support. I just rolled back to my desk, little calculations and figures flitting across my mind. *Please don't barf. Please don't barf.*

Another jet landed, the same train-like cacophony rumbling above us. Three were now home safe.

Bickley sat down on the desk, and we bumped fists. I turned to the Chief. "Since you're here, I'll say that there's nothing to report. But I did pass the reactor classroom on the way here, and there was definitely signs of"—I coughed to hide my laugh—"the reactor ghost. Someone had pulled out all the chairs."

Bickley waggled his fingers. "Oooh, the reactor ghost is back."

"Goldstein and I were talking earlier about who it might be," Torres said. "We think it's the ghost of Admiral Rickover."

I couldn't help but crack up to hear my own theory again. The Father of the Nuclear Navy *would* haunt a reactor classroom. Maybe he'd come back to wreak his terrible vengeance on the guy who kept throwing chem lights overboard and tricking the lookout teams.

"Time plus three!" The ship leaned hard to the starboard side, and we all fell to the deck.

Or maybe he'd come to shuttle us all into the afterlife when the ship capsized.

Chief got to his feet with a huff and pointed down the passageway. "Goldstein, go find Rollins. Drag him up here by his ear if you have to."

It was on.

I sprinted down the passageway to the heavy gray door that led to the main part of the reactor department, along the way calculating the most efficient route. I heaved it open, wincing against the blast of air that was hotter than the sun, then all but leapt onto the stairs and slid down the rails. There wasn't even time to blow on my hands—I simply went down another flight and hoped I didn't have blisters later.

Small groups of sailors were huddled here and there for their musters, all waiting for the announcement that they'd either rescued the poor guy who'd fallen overboard or keelhauled the idiot who'd called a false alarm. They couldn't go back to sleep or work until I'd found Rollins.

Where *was* that big lug? *If he's somewhere with his girlfriend, I'm going to kill him.*

"Time plus four!"

I hurried into the reactor control room, a relatively cold room compared to the rest of the reactor spaces. I glanced at the watch bill —yep, Rollins was supposed to be on watch now. I hadn't seen him on the flight deck, so he wasn't the man overboard.

Lieutenant Murphy looked up from her work at her desk. "Goldstein, aren't you supposed to be at muster?" The watch officer didn't leave her desk for anything, as far as I knew.

"Rollins is missing. Do you know where he is?"

"He stepped out to get a log reading in the engine room."

"Thanks, ma'am!" I called over my shoulder as I ran out, heading toward the engine room.

Another heavy metal door, and—

I covered my ears against the deafening blend of engines, generators, various high-tech machinery, and a few things that ran on diesel. Generators the size of school busses roared on many sides, causing my chest to vibrate. There was no point yelling for Rollins, and if he'd been in here when the man-overboard had been announced, it was plausible that he hadn't heard it.

The ship pitched again, and I almost lost my footing right next to an exposed metal pipe.

I hurried through the narrow walkways around and between machines, squinting for my colleague, a relative newbie to the ship along with myself. Rollins and I had gone to nuke school together, though I didn't know him well.

Somewhere, far above the never-ending blast of noise, the intercom called time plus six, setting my teeth on edge. I had six minutes to find Rollins and get him upstairs.

The ship swung again, slamming me into a railing that knocked the breath out of me. When I'd caught my breath, I noticed that a pen had slid out from behind a generator, where I hadn't looked yet.

And it had left a bloody trail as it went.

I dashed around the generator and gasped. Rollins was sitting up against the bulkhead, unconscious and bleeding profusely from a large laceration on his forehead. Blood had poured down his front and onto the engine log, seeping into his green camouflage uniform and all over the metal floor. I'd never seen so much blood from a wound that wasn't in a war movie. Blood dripped off of a jagged piece of metal that stuck off the generator—he must've fallen and banged his head. All things considered, Chief *probably* wouldn't get angry at him for being late to muster.

I steadied myself and slipped my arms under his, wrapping them around his barrel-like chest, and began to pull him toward the door. There was no time to worry about a broken neck; I had to get him to Lieutenant Murphy, who could call the medical team.

I back-stepped, slowly but surely, toward the door, making sure to not catch my uniform on anything and praying that the ship didn't dance in the waves again. Rollins' blood dripped down my arm and onto my hand, making my grasp slippery.

I ignored the tiny voice in the back of my mind that noted how utterly still Rollins was.

"Time plus eight!"

The announcement sounded just as I'd stepped through the door to the passageway. I repositioned my arms, then took a breath. "Lieutenant Murphy! I need you! Now!"

The petite redhead poked her head out, then shrieked. "Get him in here! I'll call the medical team!"

I slowly walked the final few yards into the reactor control room, then laid Rollins down on the steel floor. Lieutenant Murphy, who was on the phone, tossed me her uniform's blouse and gestured for me to put it under his head as she wrenched the intercom speaker from its cradle. "Medical emergency! Medical emergency in the reactor control room!"

Her voice echoed throughout the entire ship, immediately followed by, "Time plus nine!"

I didn't wait for her to dismiss me. I ran at top speed back down the shadowy steel passageway, underneath the endless line of pipes and wires, past the same groups of sailors. They pointed this time. "Hey, yo, where'd the blood come from?" one asked.

I took the stairs three at a time. "Chief! I found Rollins!"

"Time plus ten!"

The hasty thuds of Chief's boots disappearing many decks above me, and the descending boots of the medical team, let me know that all was going to be well—sort of. Rollins was obviously in a grave state, but we wouldn't catch hell from the officers for not reporting during a man-overboard. The helicopters and search teams wouldn't have to be deployed in a near-hurricane...for Rollins, at least. Maybe someone on the flight deck really had been blown off, and if that was the case, I hoped they were found soon.

I finished my journey to the sound of claps that immediately ceased as soon as they saw me: disheveled and covered in blood.

Torres put a hand over her mouth. "Sweet mother Mary. What happened?"

I fell back into my office chair. "From what I could tell, he hit his head. I don't know if he'll be okay, since that was a nasty cut."

"Time plus eleven!"

Chief needed to hurry up and submit that muster report.

Bickley sat on the desk. "I wouldn't worry too much. Head wounds bleed a lot, but they're usually not that bad." He clapped me on the shoulder. "You did good. At breakfast, everyone is going to know about the heroic nuke who saved the day during the man-overboard. Maybe you'll even get a medal. Your parents will have to admit that a medal for valor is pretty cool."

I picked up the book I'd been reading. "And yet, I'm still on phone watch."

Such was life in the Navy. And besides, my parents wouldn't care if I'd gotten a medal for rescuing the Admiral from a great white shark. The last conversation I'd had with them had hammered home their disapproval in my career choice.

My colleagues snickered, and they settled in chairs around me while we waited for Chief to return and let us go back to bed, or watch.

Torres picked up a squeeze toy shaped like a football and tossed it to Bickley. "So, who do you guys really think is the reactor ghost?"

"My money's on Diaz," Bickley said. "That dipstick is a big-time practical joker. I can see him moving our stuff around."

The captain's nasally voice came on the intercom. "Time plus twelve. All hands accounted for. The aft lookout team spotted a chem light in the water." He sounded equally exhausted and annoyed.

We all sagged with relief. Now we just had to wait for Chief to come down and dismiss us.

"It's not just moving stuff around, though," Torres said. "Remember that drawing?"

There was a pregnant pause as we recalled the unexplainable incident the week before. We'd all exited the reactor classroom at the end of a training session, chatting amongst ourselves and heading up to lunch. Torres had doubled back to get her notebook, then shouted for us to "come see."

I nodded thoughtfully. "Okay, yeah, that was weird. But a giant drawing on the whiteboard isn't... isn't... it's not paranormal by itself."

"A drawing of an F-18 suddenly appearing on the board ten seconds after we left the room is just plain fre... what was that?" She slid to her feet, her hand held up.

We hushed, looking at her for an explanation. She strode out the door, turning her head back and forth. "Hello?"

"What is it?" I asked.

"I swear to God, I just heard Rollins. But like... he was far away, but also just on the other side of the wall. Didn't you hear him?" She studied the bulkhead, as if the chart-covered space would suddenly produce Rollins.

"What did you hear?" Bickley asked. "I didn't hear anything."

Torres rubbed her forehead. "I don't even know. Just... just an impression of his voice, I guess." She gave her head a little shake. "I'm probably hearing things because I'm so tired."

"I hear the reactor phone ring sometimes, if I'm using the head on watch," I said. "You're just worried about him." I tossed the squeeze ball to her. "You might as well stay up with me. Your watch slot begins in twenty minutes."

"Ugh. Thanks for reminding me." She raised her hand to throw the ball back to me, but then lowered it, her eyes narrowing as she looked toward the door. "I just heard him again. I'm positive I did."

I sighed. "He's probably getting stitches right now. I didn't hear anything. It's just the late hour, Tor."

"What did he say?" Bickley asked.

Torres closed her eyes. "He said... he's *saying*... 'I'm standing right here, guys.'"

Bickley suppressed a smile. "You've been reading paranormal stuff again, haven't you? I'm telling you, quit hitting the library in your downtime and start playing dominoes, like a normal sailor."

"I *like* ghost stories," Torres said, affronted. "I'm psychic, you know."

I pinched the bridge of my nose. Not this crap again. It was one thing to say you were connected to the "beyond," but it was just tacky to joke about Rollins. "Being able to guess that the galley is going to run out of food on any given day does not make you psychic. It means you have a good grasp of statistics."

Bickley grinned. "Yeah, the hungrier you are, combined with the variable of whether or not you're luckless enough to be a nuke, determines—"

"Shut up, you guys!" Torres said. "I thought you were on my side. You're just as much into the ghost stuff as I am." She smacked my shoulder.

I smacked her back. "Not to the point that I'm joking about saying you hear Rollins's ghost or something."

"I wasn't joking! I really did!"

"Hands to yourselves, you two," Bickley said. "It's way too late at night for me to break up a catfight. "He held out an arm between us. "I know something that'll make you both happy: there's never any line at the pay phones this time of night. Since you're awake, why don't you both call your parents? Tell them you're calling live from a hurricane. It always impresses the civilians. Goldstein, it's only bedtime in Virginia, right? And Torres, you're from around Chicago, right? I bet your dad's up."

Torres lightened up. "Oh, good idea!"

Our resident Navy brat was the daughter of a retired Master Chief, and she was the most complete daddy's girl I'd ever met. Even more than me. Before this deployment, she'd cut her hair like his when he was in the service, accidentally making her look like a little boy from afar. Still, she was proud that he was proud, so we didn't give her grief about it. Much.

Torres began to idly flip through one of the nuclear manuals from the bookshelf, but I turned away and swallowed the new lump in my throat. Before I could resume pretending to read my book, Bickley asked, "You going to call anyone tonight?" His tone carried his real meaning.

I glanced up at him, then away. "I don't think that's a good idea."

His warm hand on my shoulder made me look up again, and he had the expression on his face that underlined why he'd been promoted so quickly through the nuke ranks: stern, yet understanding. "Call home, Rachel."

I gulped and nodded. I needed to, but damn, I didn't want to. What was there to say to the people who'd called me a selfish for joining the Navy? Hashem knew, I loved my parents more than life itself, but the wound was too deep, too raw for a mere phone call.

And I knew how the call would go. Once again, they'd recite the list of things they'd given their only child: the best schools, a private *shul* tutor, the most elaborate bat mitzvah Virginia Beach, Virginia had ever seen, shopping trips to New York, all of it.

"But I want *adventure*," I'd hissed at them, that turbulent day on the pier, minutes before walking onto the USS *Taft*. "I want to see the world, serve my country, and grow *up*. I'm not a little girl anymore. Can't you just be happy for me?"

And that's when my father had spat the worst thing he'd ever said to me. The words had wrapped around me like a curse, sinking into my insides. Even there, in the reactor room, I could still feel the sting of them.

"I'm not selfish," I whispered, the words of my novel blurring together. "I'm not."

Bickley checked his watch. "And I know you're not. As for me, I'll be calling my kids, if Chief ever gets back down here. I wonder if the officers gave him trouble about being so late?"

I let out a long breath, then blinked and smiled up at Bickley. "I doubt it. More likely, he's biting his nails up with the guys on the bridge. There's still a jet out there. I've been counting them. The flight deck guys said four jets were out when the storm came up. I've only heard three land."

Torres snapped the manual shut. "You couldn't pay me enough to try to land a jet on the carrier in a storm like this. They'd be safer flying straight back to Oceana Naval Air Station. We're in the middle of the Atlantic, right? It's not that far."

The sound of boots descending the stairs made us all turn toward the door. Torres poked her head out, then turned back with a relieved smile. "It's Chief."

Finally. "Well, good night, everyone," I said, turning back to my desk to pick up my book. "Enjoy your phone calls. After everything, maybe we all should go vis—"

My vision was snuffed out like a candle.

END OF PREVIEW

THANK you for reading this exclusive sneak preview of Sea of Lost Souls! Sea of Lost Souls is available on Amazon!

CPSIA information can be obtained
at www.ICGtesting.com
Printed in the USA
LVHW011739180219
607899LV00004B/990/P